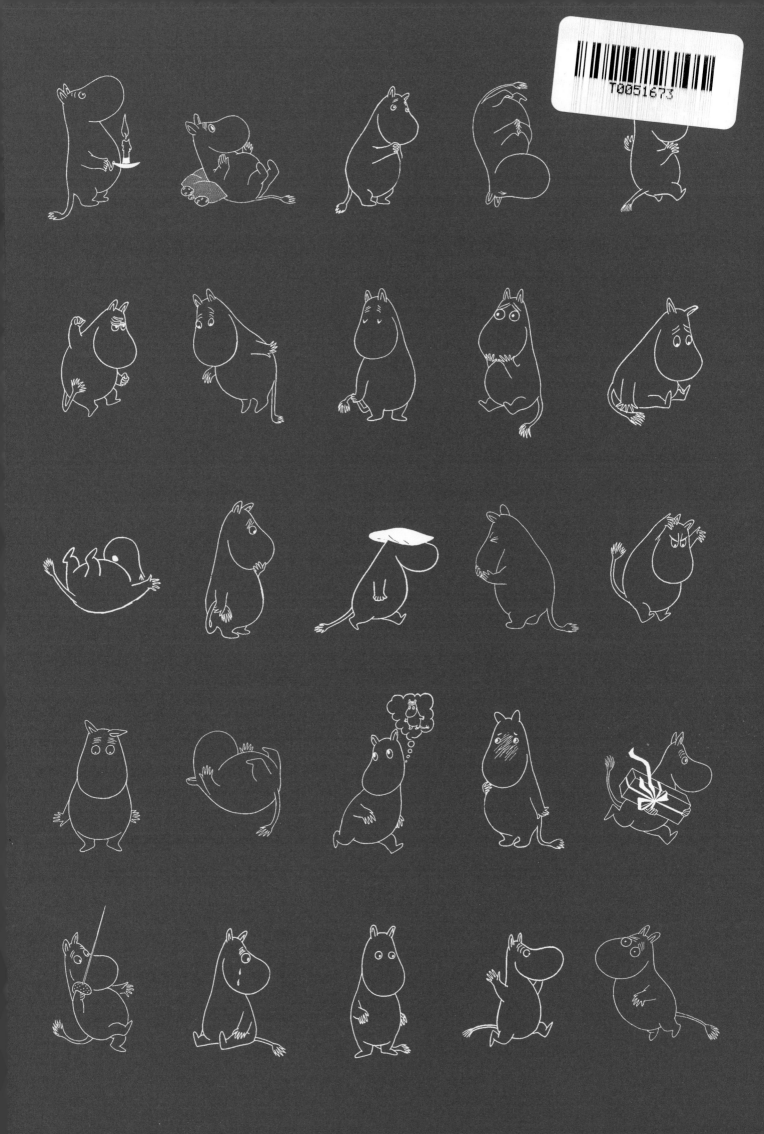

THE COMPLETE TOVE JANSSON

MOOMIN

COMIC STRIP

Drawn & Quarterly

MONTRÉAL

Moomin Book Five: The Complete Tove Jansson Comic Strip by Tove Jansson
The three chapters in this book were written by Lars Jansson and drawn by Tove Jansson.
ISBN 978-1-89729-994-4

First Printing: July 2010
Second Printing: May 2014
10 9 8 7 6 5 4 3 2

Printed in China

Library and Archives Canada Cataloguing in Publication
Jansson, Tove; Moomin : the complete Tove Jansson comic strip / Tove Jansson.
Originally published in the Evening news, London, 1953-1959. Cover title.
ISBN 1-894937-80-5 (bk. 1).--ISBN 978-1-897299-19-7 (bk. 2).--ISBN 978-1-897299-55-5 (bk. 3).--ISBN 978-1-897299-78-4 (bk. 4).--
ISBN 978-1-897299-94-4 (bk. 5) I. Title. II. Title: Complete Tove Jansson comic strip : Moomin.
PN6738.M66J35 2006   741.5'94897   C2006-902218-6

Also available from the Moomin hardcover series:
Moomin Book One (ISBN 978-1894937-80-1)
Moomin Book Two (ISBN 978-1-89729-919-7)
Moomin Book Three (ISBN 978-1-89729-955-5)
Moomin Book Four (ISBN 978-1-89729-978-4)
Moomin Book Six (ISBN 978-1-77046-042-3)
Moomin Book Seven (ISBN 978-1-77046-062-1)
Moomin Book Eight (ISBN 978-1-77046-121-5)
Moomin Book Nine (ISBN 978-177046-157-4)

Available from the Moomin picture book series:
The Book About Moomin, Mymble and Little My (ISBN 978-1-897299-95-1)
Who Will Comfort Toffle? (ISBN 978-1-770460-17-1)

Available from the colour Moomin series:
Moomin's Winter Follies (ISBN 978-1-77046-098-0)
Moominvalley Turns Jungle (ISBN 978-1-77046-097-3)
Moomin Falls in Love (ISBN 978-1-77046-107-9)
Moomin Builds a House (ISBN 978-1-77046-108-6)
Moomin and the Comet (ISBN 978-1-77046-122-2)
Moomin and the Sea (ISBN 978-1-77046-123-9)
Moomin's Desert Island (ISBN 978-177046-134-5)
Moomin's Golden Tail (ISBN 978-177046-133-8)

Published in the USA by Drawn & Quarterly,
a client publisher of
Farrar, Straus & Giroux
Orders: 888.330.8477

Published in Canada by Drawn & Quarterly,
a client publisher of
Raincoast Books
Orders: 800.663.5714

Published in the United Kingdom by Drawn & Quarterly,
a client publisher of
Publishers Group UK
Orders: info@pguk.co.uk

MOOMIN

VOLUME FIVE

19. Moomin Winter

1
MOOMIN
WINTER
IT WON'T BUDGE!
HOW COLD IT IS TODAY... CAN'T YOU GET UP THE CARROTS?
NO. AND LOOK AT THE STALKS!
I THINK GARDENERS SHOULD GET MEDALS. **CARROTS**, I ASK YOU!

2
WELL, **THIS** SPADE CAN'T BE CALLED A SPADE ANY MORE
I **TOLD** YOU ONE SHOULDN'T FERTILISE THE SOIL WITH ALL THAT IRON AND STUFF
IT'S FROZEN!
OH DEAR WELL, NOBODY LIKES CARROTS, ANYWAY.

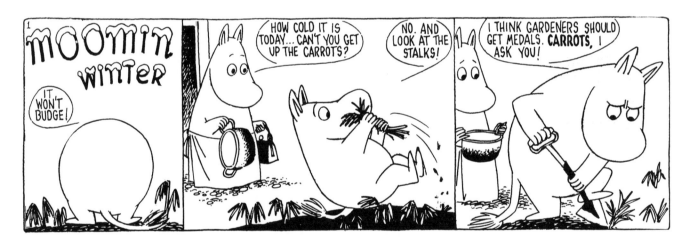

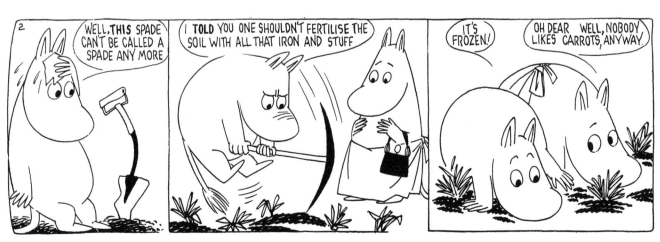

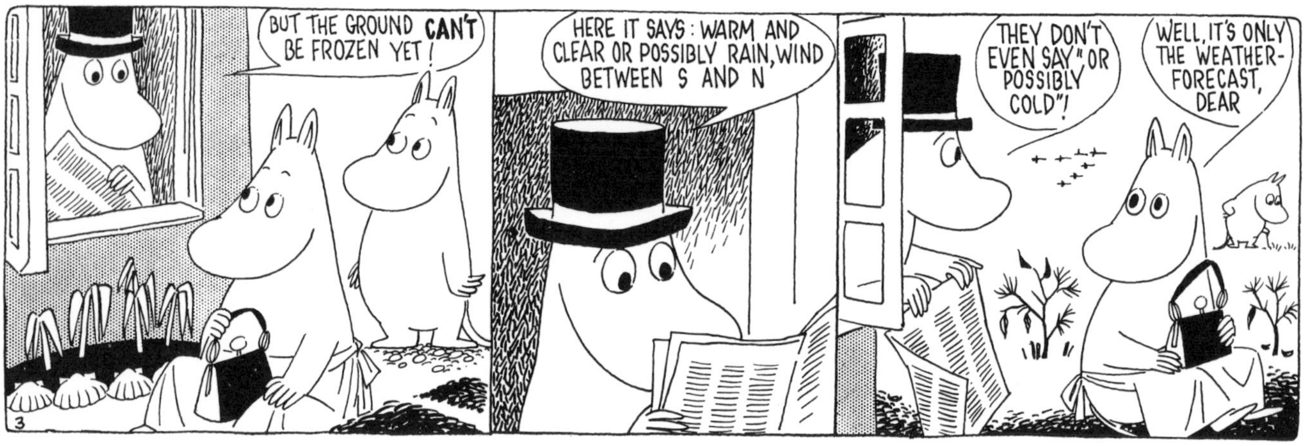
3
BUT THE GROUND **CAN'T** BE FROZEN YET!
HERE IT SAYS: WARM AND CLEAR OR POSSIBLY RAIN, WIND BETWEEN S AND N
THEY DON'T EVEN SAY "OR POSSIBLY COLD"!
WELL, IT'S ONLY THE WEATHER-FORECAST, DEAR

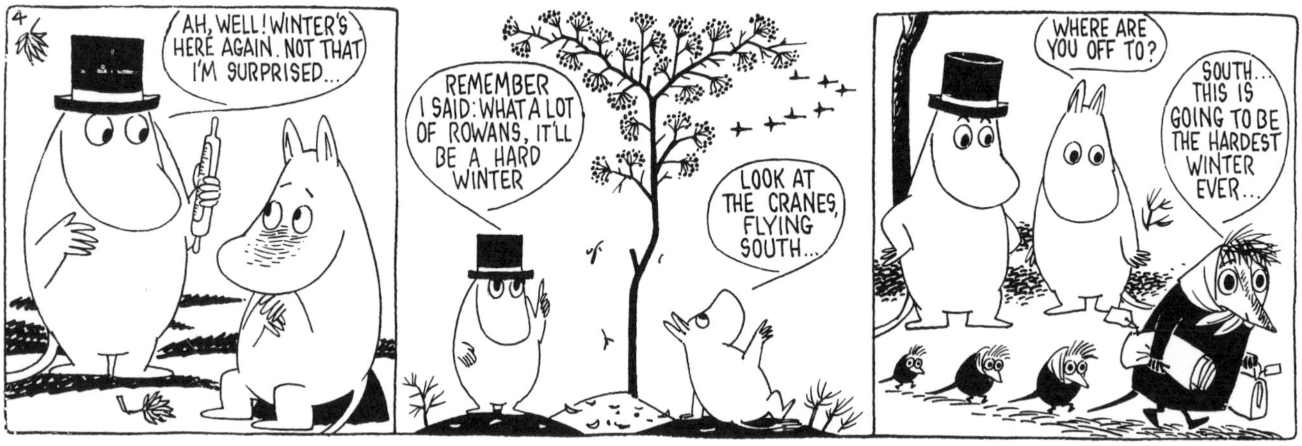
4
AH, WELL! WINTER'S HERE AGAIN. NOT THAT I'M SURPRISED...
REMEMBER I SAID: WHAT A LOT OF ROWANS, IT'LL BE A HARD WINTER
LOOK AT THE CRANES, FLYING SOUTH...
WHERE ARE YOU OFF TO?
SOUTH... THIS IS GOING TO BE THE HARDEST WINTER EVER...

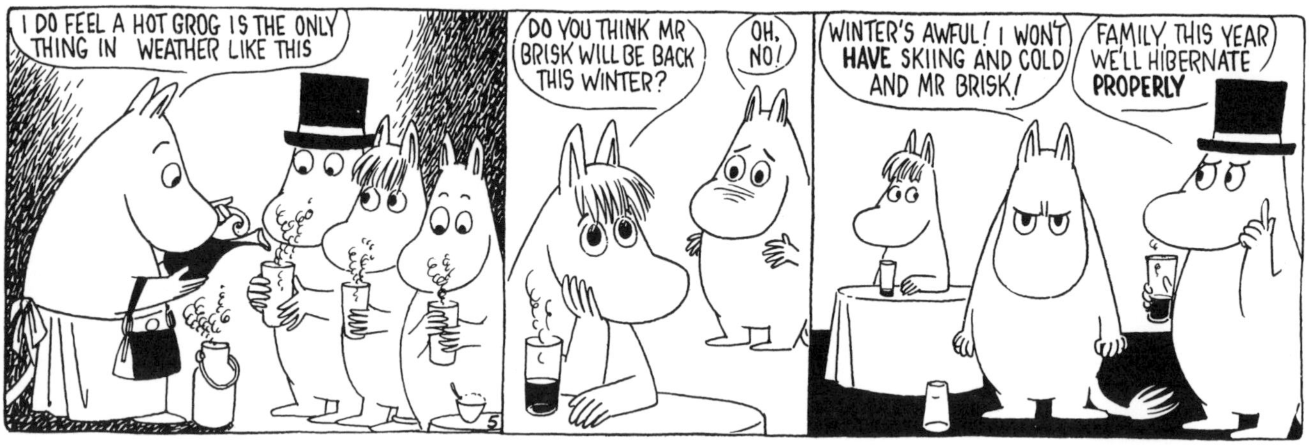
I DO FEEL A HOT GROG IS THE ONLY THING IN WEATHER LIKE THIS
5
DO YOU THINK MR BRISK WILL BE BACK THIS WINTER?
OH, NO!
WINTER'S AWFUL! I WON'T **HAVE** SKIING AND COLD AND MR BRISK!
FAMILY, THIS YEAR WE'LL HIBERNATE **PROPERLY**

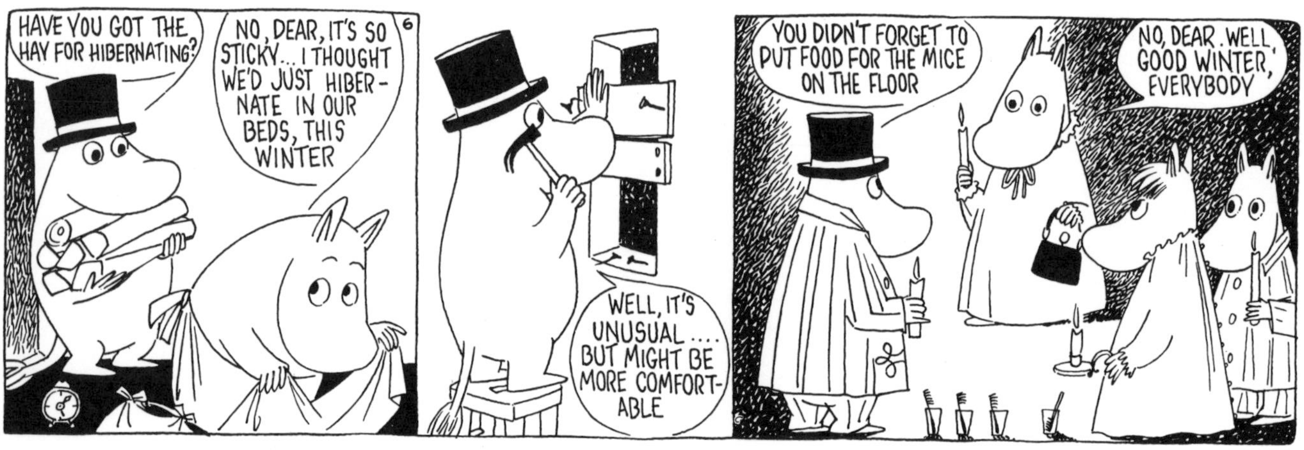
HAVE YOU GOT THE HAY FOR HIBERNATING?
6
NO, DEAR, IT'S SO STICKY... I THOUGHT WE'D JUST HIBER-NATE IN OUR BEDS, THIS WINTER
WELL, IT'S UNUSUAL.... BUT MIGHT BE MORE COMFORT-ABLE
YOU DIDN'T FORGET TO PUT FOOD FOR THE MICE ON THE FLOOR
NO, DEAR. WELL, GOOD WINTER, EVERYBODY

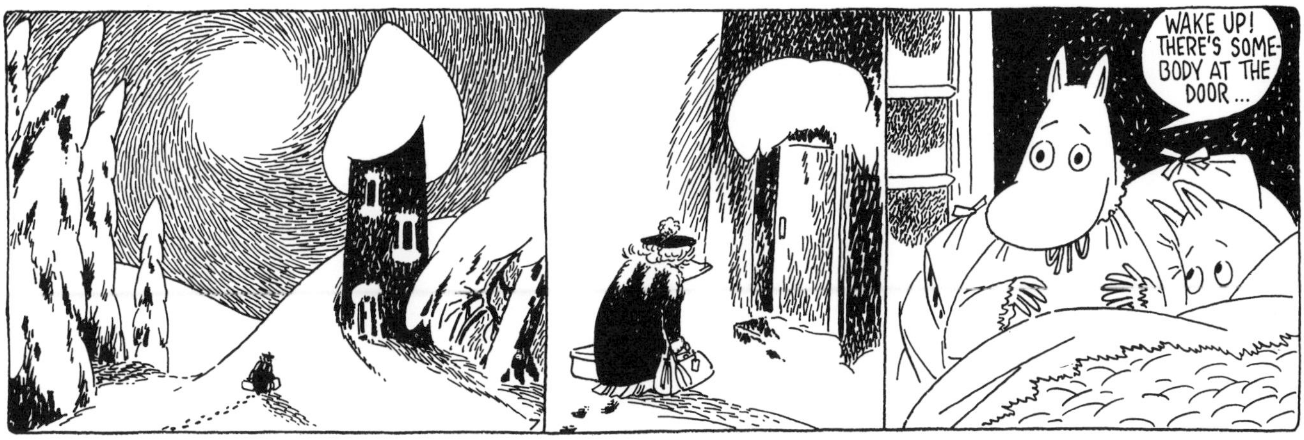
WAKE UP! THERE'S SOME-BODY AT THE DOOR ...

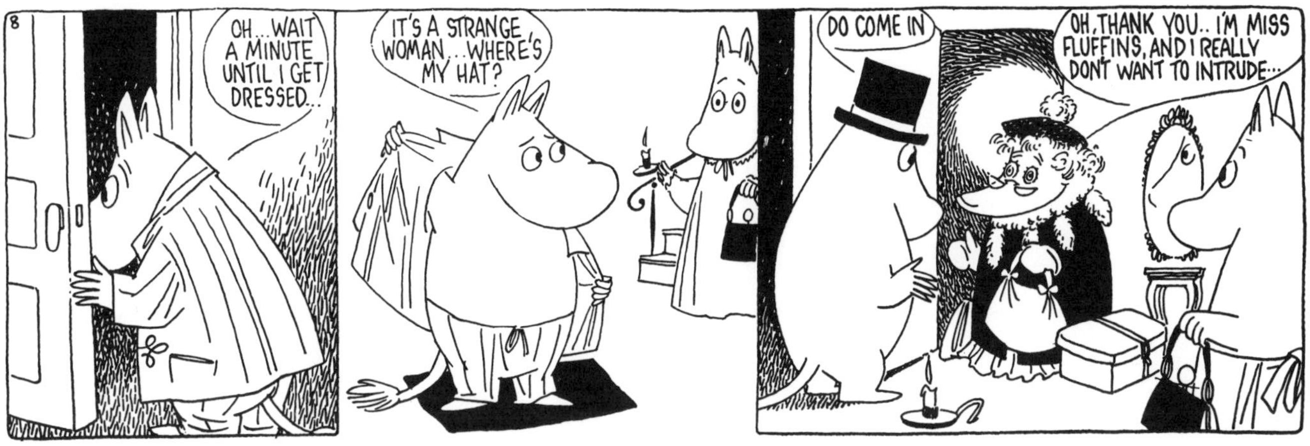
OH... WAIT A MINUTE UNTIL I GET DRESSED...
IT'S A STRANGE WOMAN... WHERE'S MY HAT?
DO COME IN
OH, THANK YOU.. I'M MISS FLUFFINS, AND I REALLY DON'T WANT TO INTRUDE...

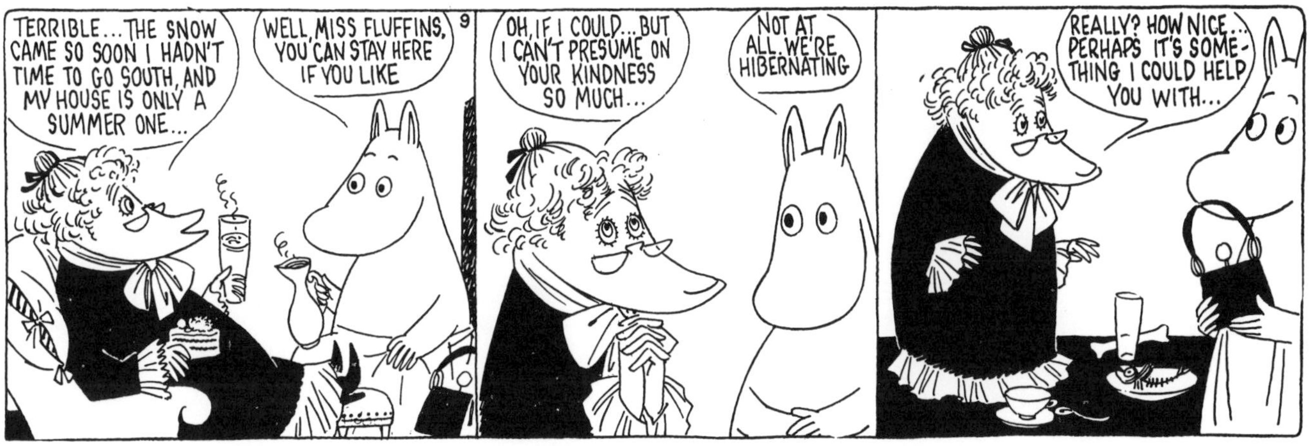
TERRIBLE... THE SNOW CAME SO SOON I HADN'T TIME TO GO SOUTH, AND MY HOUSE IS ONLY A SUMMER ONE...
WELL, MISS FLUFFINS, YOU CAN STAY HERE IF YOU LIKE
OH, IF I COULD... BUT I CAN'T PRESUME ON YOUR KINDNESS SO MUCH...
NOT AT ALL. WE'RE HIBERNATING
REALLY? HOW NICE... PERHAPS IT'S SOME-THING I COULD HELP YOU WITH...

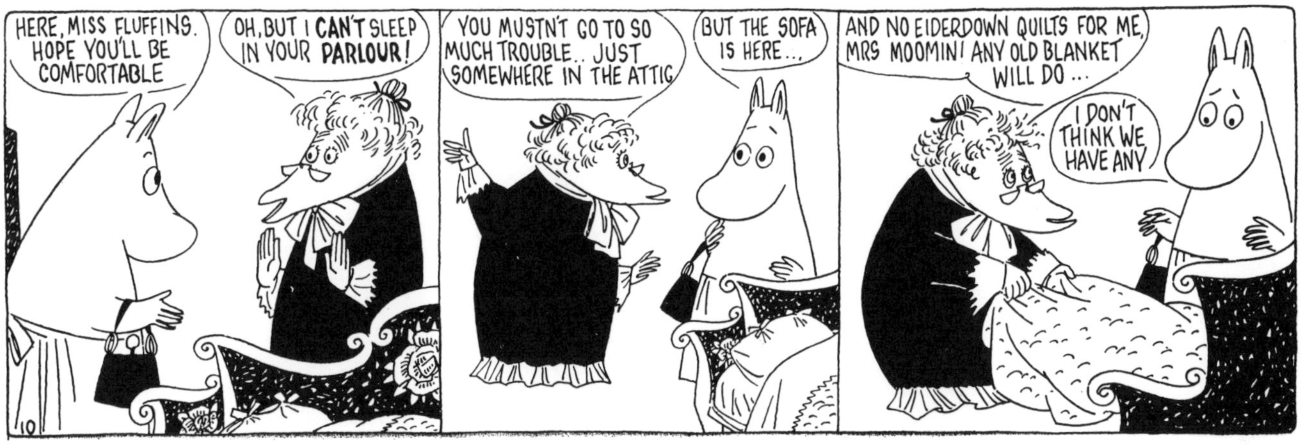
HERE, MISS FLUFFINS. HOPE YOU'LL BE COMFORTABLE
OH, BUT I **CAN'T** SLEEP IN YOUR **PARLOUR**!
YOU MUSTN'T GO TO SO MUCH TROUBLE.. JUST SOMEWHERE IN THE ATTIC
BUT THE SOFA IS HERE...
AND NO EIDERDOWN QUILTS FOR ME, MRS MOOMIN! ANY OLD BLANKET WILL DO ...
I DON'T THINK WE HAVE ANY

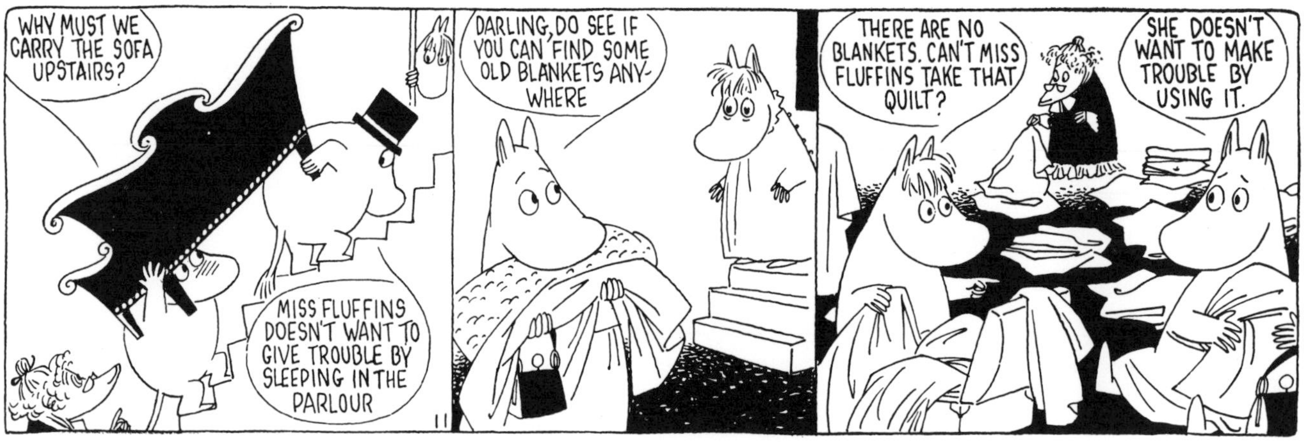
WHY MUST WE CARRY THE SOFA UPSTAIRS?
MISS FLUFFINS DOESN'T WANT TO GIVE TROUBLE BY SLEEPING IN THE PARLOUR
11
DARLING, DO SEE IF YOU CAN FIND SOME OLD BLANKETS ANYWHERE
THERE ARE NO BLANKETS. CAN'T MISS FLUFFINS TAKE THAT QUILT?
SHE DOESN'T WANT TO MAKE TROUBLE BY USING IT.

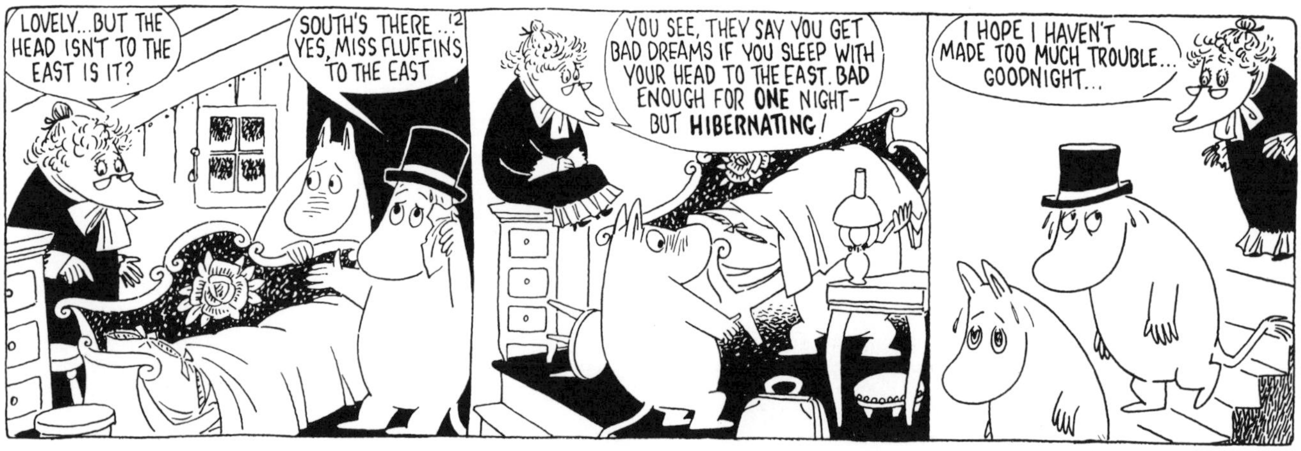
LOVELY... BUT THE HEAD ISN'T TO THE EAST IS IT?
SOUTH'S THERE... YES, MISS FLUFFINS, TO THE EAST
12
YOU SEE, THEY SAY YOU GET BAD DREAMS IF YOU SLEEP WITH YOUR HEAD TO THE EAST. BAD ENOUGH FOR **ONE** NIGHT- BUT **HIBERNATING**!
I HOPE I HAVEN'T MADE TOO MUCH TROUBLE... GOODNIGHT...

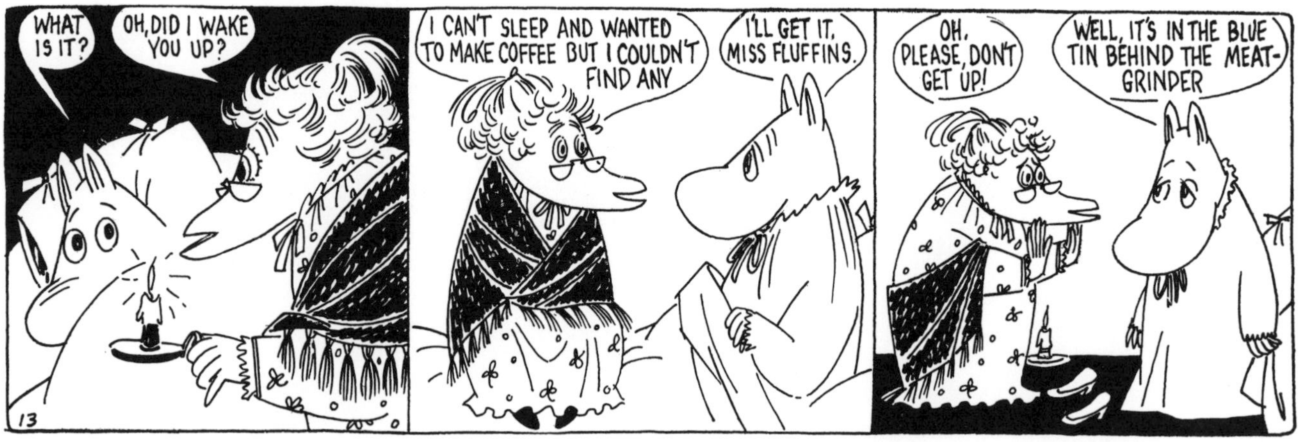
WHAT IS IT?
OH, DID I WAKE YOU UP?
13
I CAN'T SLEEP AND WANTED TO MAKE COFFEE BUT I COULDN'T FIND ANY
I'LL GET IT, MISS FLUFFINS.
OH, PLEASE, DON'T GET UP!
WELL, IT'S IN THE BLUE TIN BEHIND THE MEAT-GRINDER

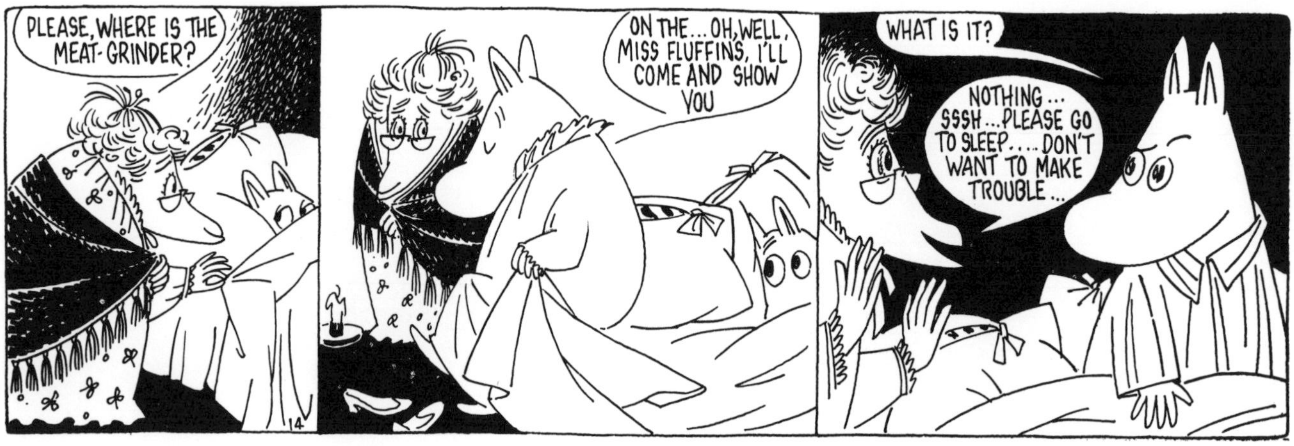
PLEASE, WHERE IS THE MEAT-GRINDER?
14
ON THE... OH, WELL, MISS FLUFFINS, I'LL COME AND SHOW YOU
WHAT IS IT?
NOTHING... SSSH... PLEASE GO TO SLEEP.... DON'T WANT TO MAKE TROUBLE...

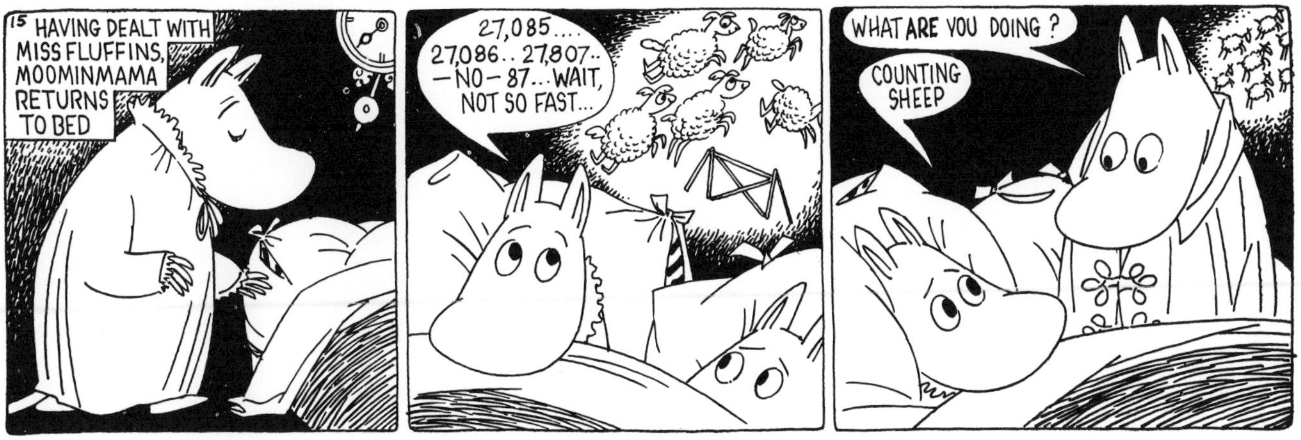
15
HAVING DEALT WITH MISS FLUFFINS, MOOMINMAMA RETURNS TO BED
27,085.... 27,086.. 27,807.. —NO—87... WAIT, NOT SO FAST...
WHAT ARE YOU DOING ?
COUNTING SHEEP

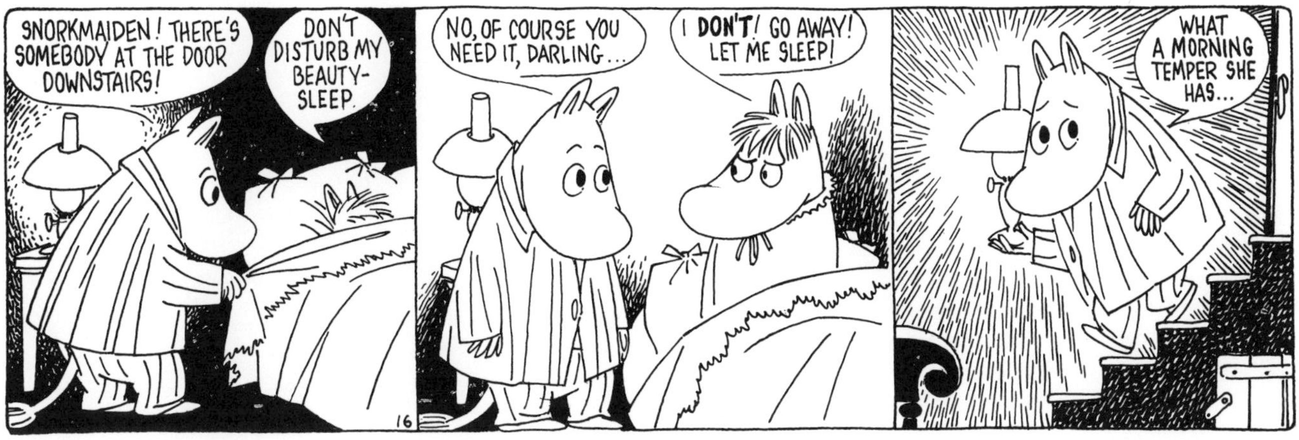
SNORKMAIDEN! THERE'S SOMEBODY AT THE DOOR DOWNSTAIRS!
DON'T DISTURB MY BEAUTY-SLEEP.
16
NO, OF COURSE YOU NEED IT, DARLING...
I DON'T! GO AWAY! LET ME SLEEP!
WHAT A MORNING TEMPER SHE HAS...

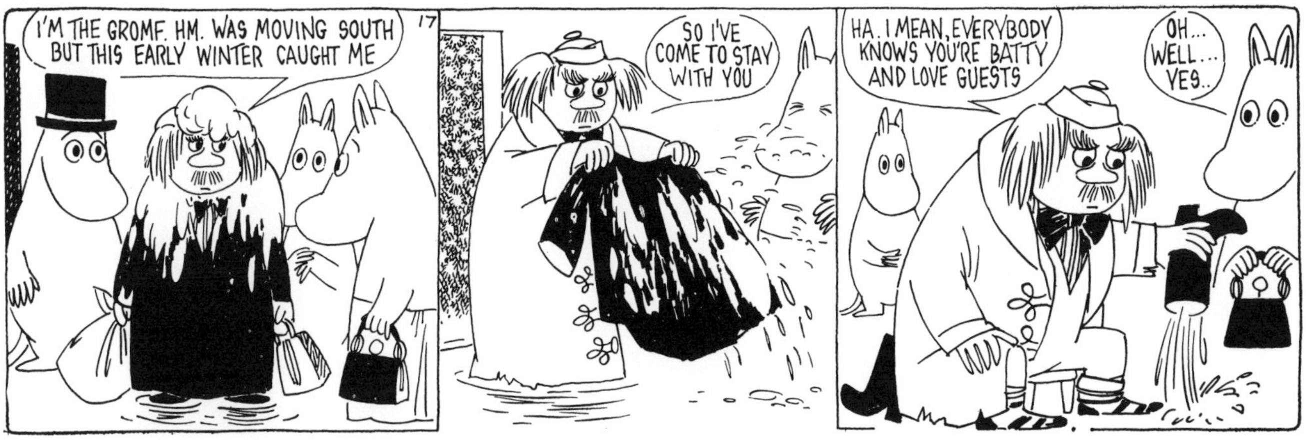
I'M THE GROMF. HM. WAS MOVING SOUTH BUT THIS EARLY WINTER CAUGHT ME
17
SO I'VE COME TO STAY WITH YOU
HA. I MEAN, EVERYBODY KNOWS YOU'RE BATTY AND LOVE GUESTS
OH... WELL... YES..

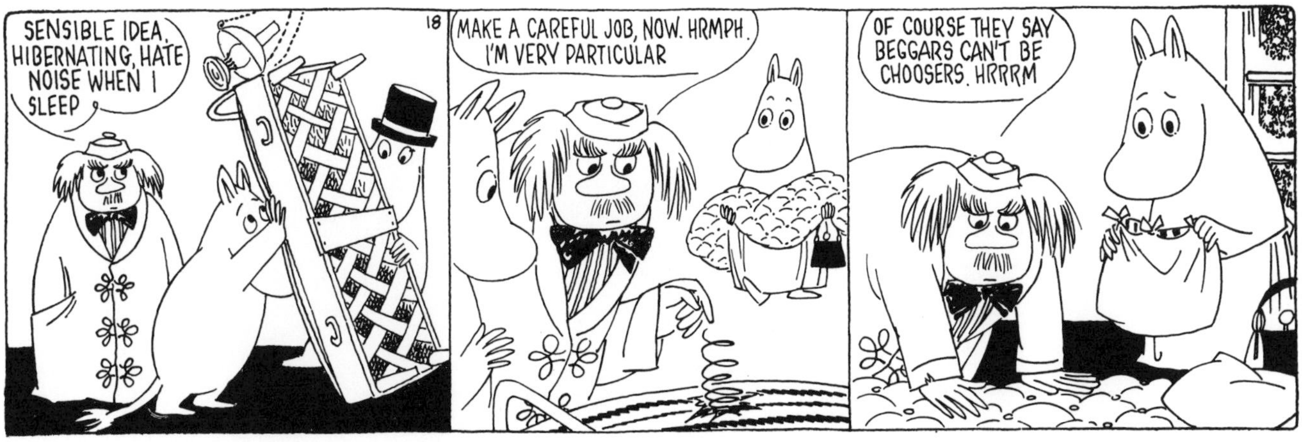
SENSIBLE IDEA, HIBERNATING, HATE NOISE WHEN I SLEEP
18
MAKE A CAREFUL JOB, NOW. HRMPH. I'M VERY PARTICULAR
OF COURSE THEY SAY BEGGARS CAN'T BE CHOOSERS. HRRRM

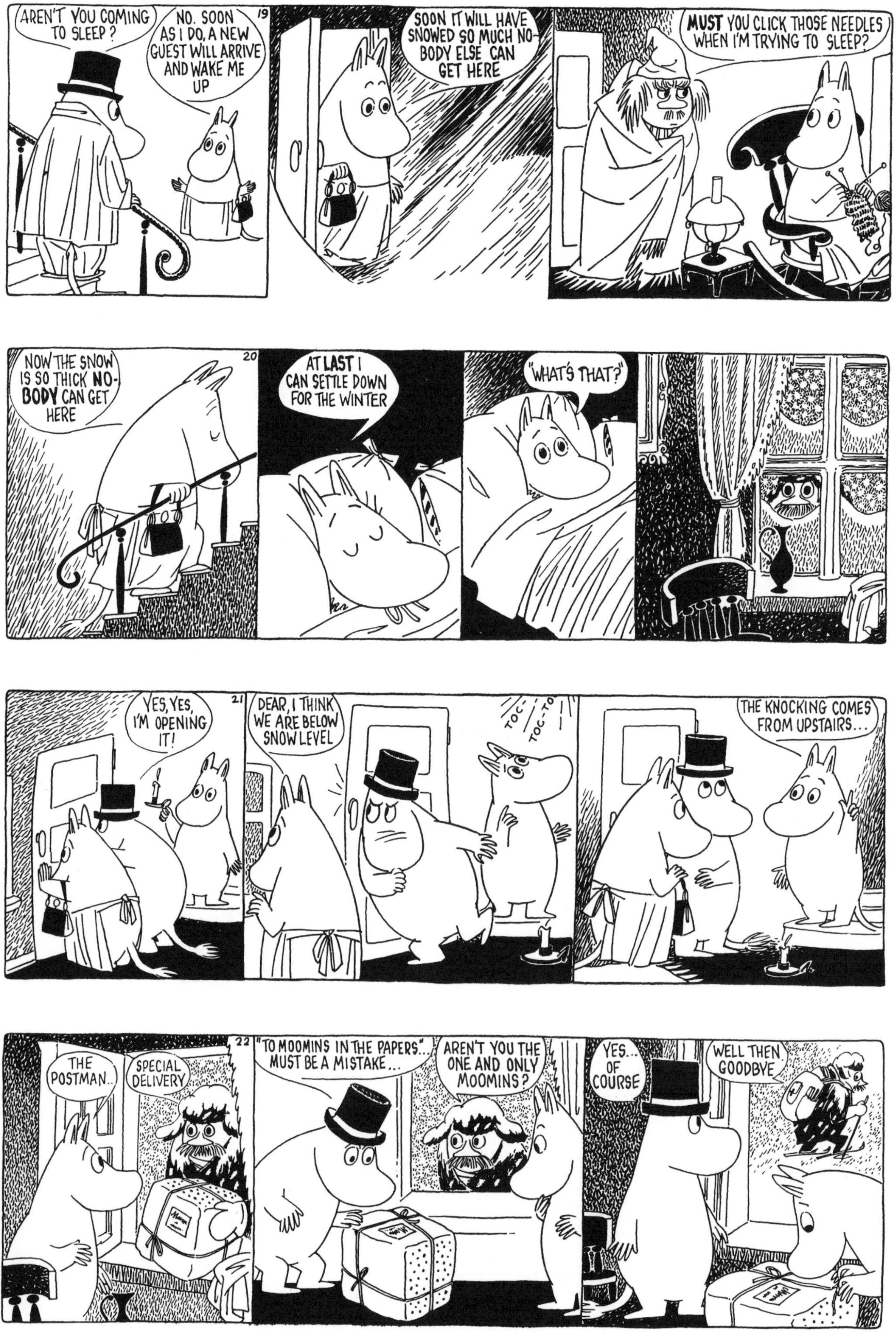
19
AREN'T YOU COMING TO SLEEP?
NO. SOON AS I DO, A NEW GUEST WILL ARRIVE AND WAKE ME UP
SOON IT WILL HAVE SNOWED SO MUCH NOBODY ELSE CAN GET HERE
MUST YOU CLICK THOSE NEEDLES WHEN I'M TRYING TO SLEEP?
20
NOW THE SNOW IS SO THICK NOBODY CAN GET HERE
AT LAST I CAN SETTLE DOWN FOR THE WINTER
"WHAT'S THAT?"
21
YES, YES, I'M OPENING IT!
DEAR, I THINK WE ARE BELOW SNOW LEVEL
TOC-TOC-TOC
THE KNOCKING COMES FROM UPSTAIRS...
22
THE POSTMAN...
SPECIAL DELIVERY
"TO MOOMINS IN THE PAPERS"... MUST BE A MISTAKE...
AREN'T YOU THE ONE AND ONLY MOOMINS?
YES... OF COURSE
WELL THEN GOODBYE

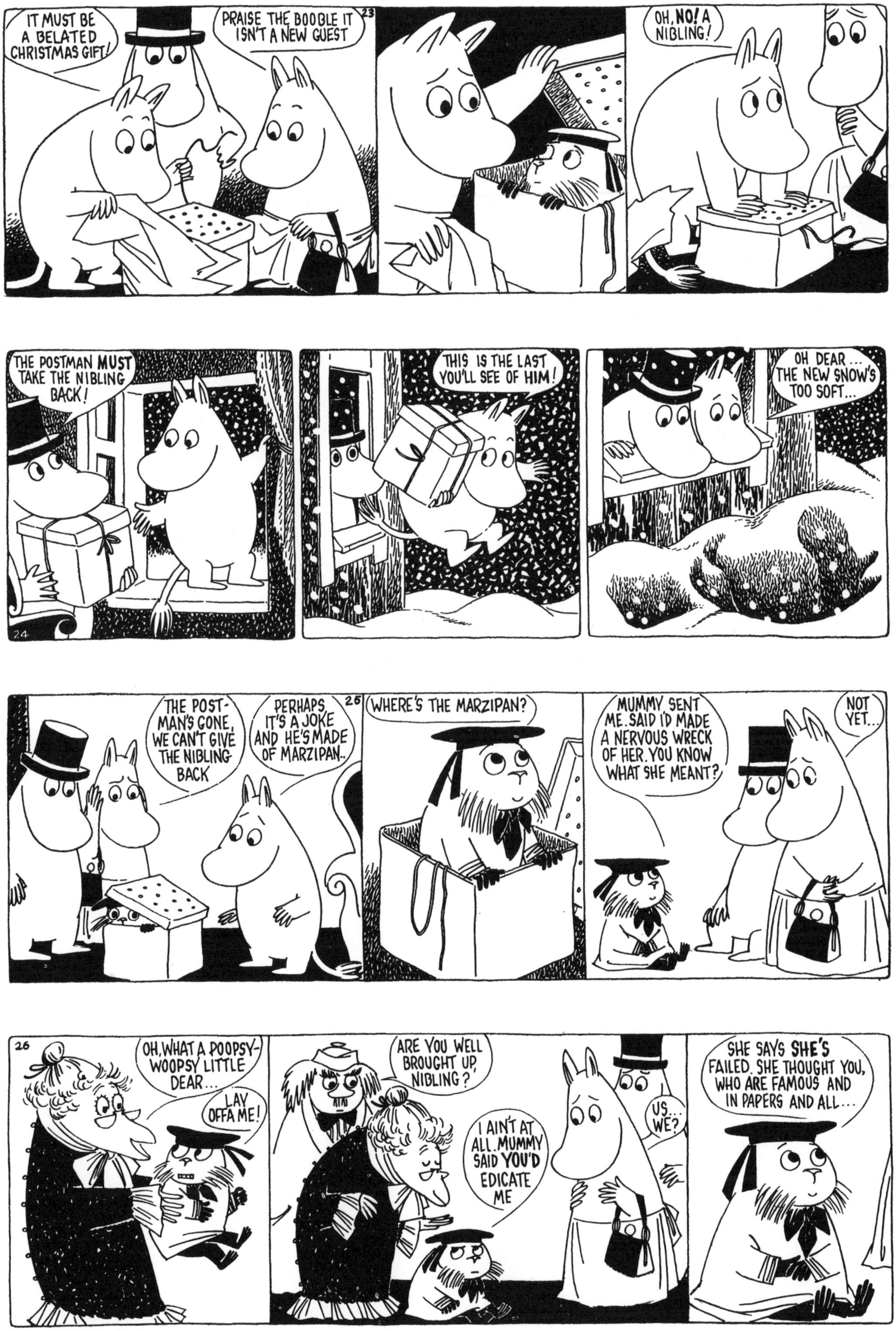
23
IT MUST BE A BELATED CHRISTMAS GIFT!
PRAISE THE BOOBLE IT ISN'T A NEW GUEST
OH, **NO!** A NIBLING!
24
THE POSTMAN **MUST** TAKE THE NIBLING BACK!
THIS IS THE LAST YOU'LL SEE OF **HIM**!
OH DEAR... THE NEW SNOW'S TOO SOFT...
25
THE POSTMAN'S GONE, WE CAN'T GIVE THE NIBLING BACK
PERHAPS IT'S A JOKE AND HE'S MADE OF MARZIPAN..
WHERE'S THE MARZIPAN?
MUMMY SENT ME. SAID I'D MADE A NERVOUS WRECK OF HER. YOU KNOW WHAT SHE MEANT?
NOT YET...
26
OH, WHAT A POOPSY-WOOPSY LITTLE DEAR...
LAY OFFA ME!
ARE YOU WELL BROUGHT UP, NIBLING?
I AIN'T AT ALL. MUMMY SAID **YOU'D** EDICATE ME
US... WE?
SHE SAYS **SHE'S** FAILED. SHE THOUGHT YOU, WHO ARE FAMOUS AND IN PAPERS AND ALL...

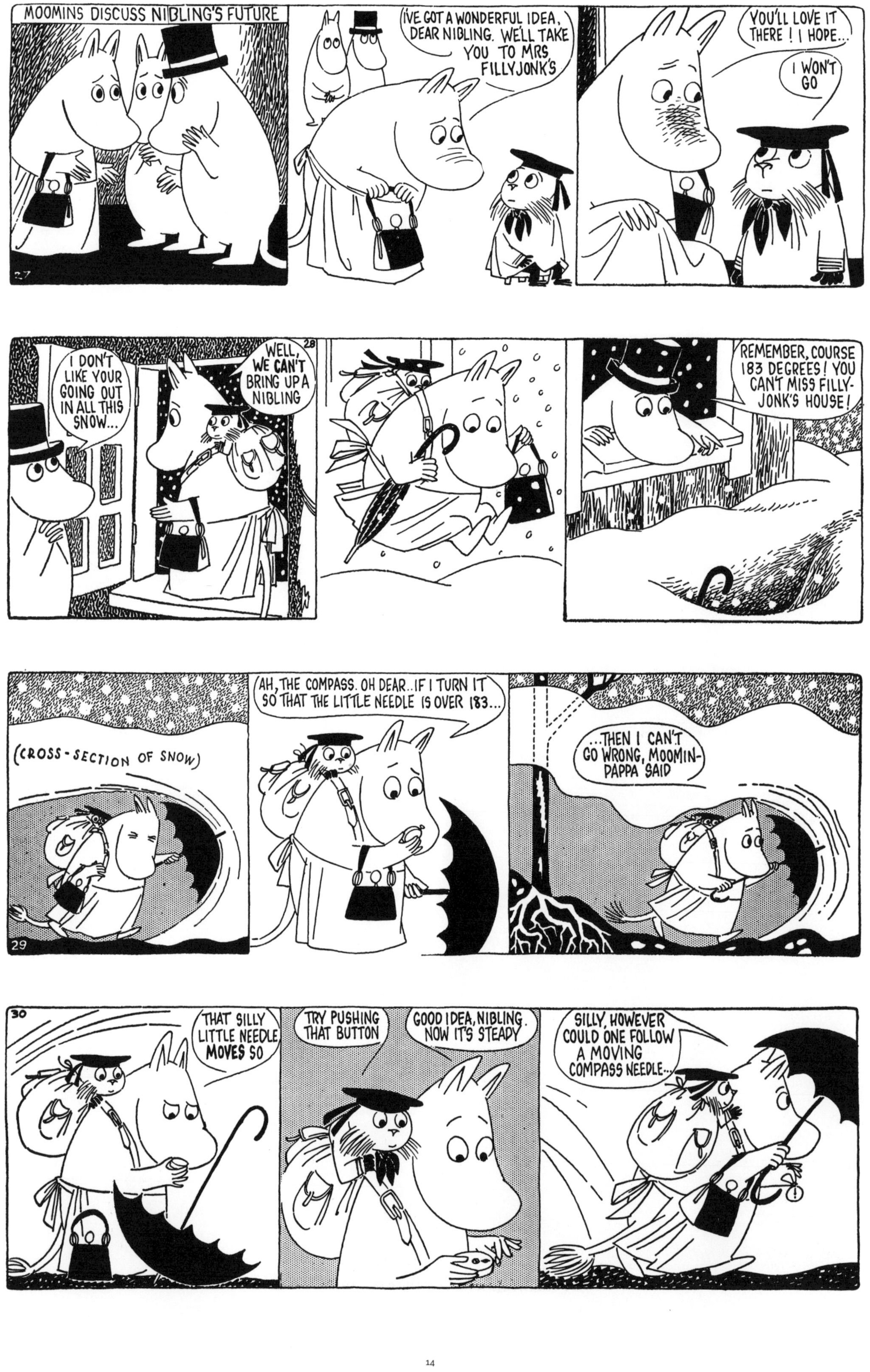
MOOMINS DISCUSS NIBLING'S FUTURE
27
I'VE GOT A WONDERFUL IDEA, DEAR NIBLING. WE'LL TAKE YOU TO MRS FILLYJONK'S
YOU'LL LOVE IT THERE ! I HOPE...
I WON'T GO
I DON'T LIKE YOUR GOING OUT IN ALL THIS SNOW...
WELL, WE CAN'T BRING UP A NIBLING
28
REMEMBER, COURSE 183 DEGREES ! YOU CAN'T MISS FILLY-JONK'S HOUSE !
(CROSS-SECTION OF SNOW)
29
AH, THE COMPASS. OH DEAR..IF I TURN IT SO THAT THE LITTLE NEEDLE IS OVER 183...
...THEN I CAN'T GO WRONG, MOOMIN-PAPPA SAID
30
THAT SILLY LITTLE NEEDLE MOVES SO
TRY PUSHING THAT BUTTON
GOOD IDEA, NIBLING. NOW IT'S STEADY
SILLY, HOWEVER COULD ONE FOLLOW A MOVING COMPASS NEEDLE...

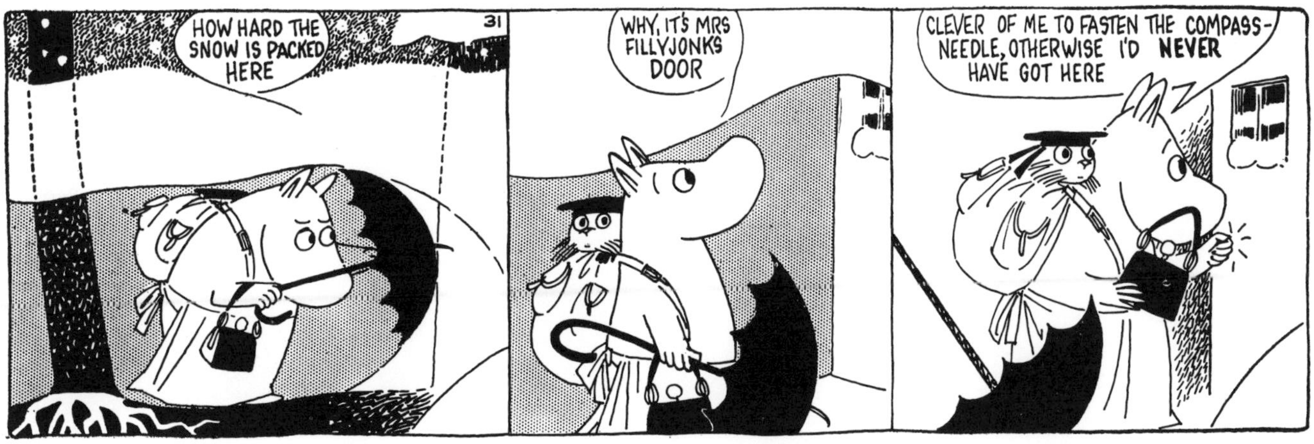
31
HOW HARD THE SNOW IS PACKED HERE
WHY, IT'S MRS FILLYJONK'S DOOR
CLEVER OF ME TO FASTEN THE COMPASS-NEEDLE, OTHERWISE I'D NEVER HAVE GOT HERE

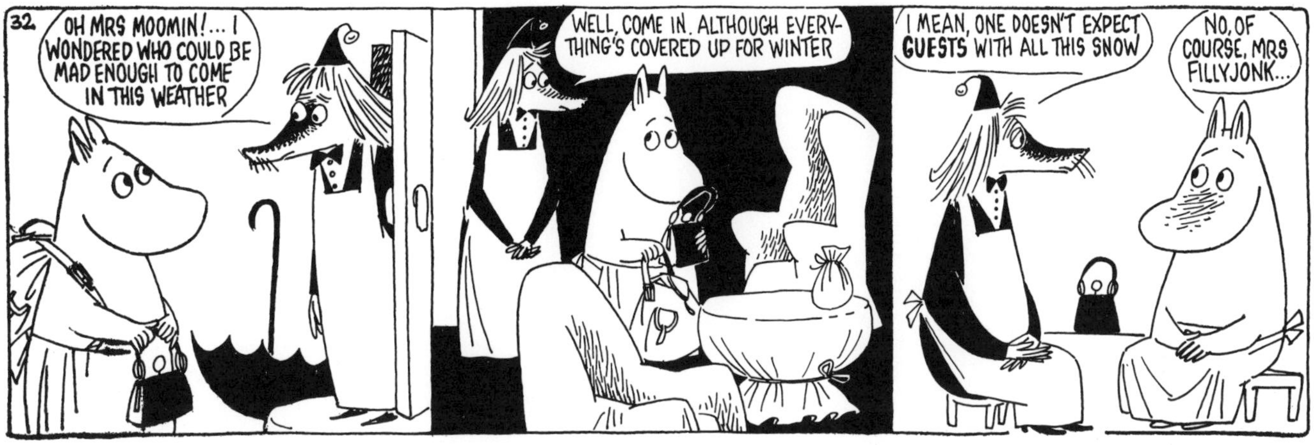
32
OH MRS MOOMIN!... I WONDERED WHO COULD BE MAD ENOUGH TO COME IN THIS WEATHER
WELL, COME IN. ALTHOUGH EVERYTHING'S COVERED UP FOR WINTER
I MEAN, ONE DOESN'T EXPECT GUESTS WITH ALL THIS SNOW
NO, OF COURSE, MRS FILLYJONK...

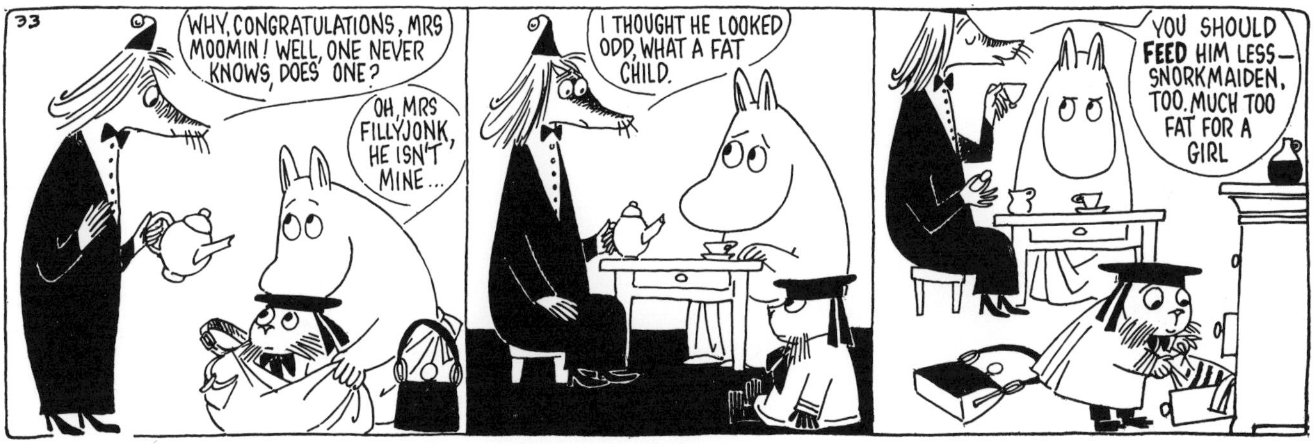
33
WHY, CONGRATULATIONS, MRS MOOMIN! WELL, ONE NEVER KNOWS, DOES ONE?
OH, MRS FILLYJONK, HE ISN'T MINE...
I THOUGHT HE LOOKED ODD, WHAT A FAT CHILD.
YOU SHOULD FEED HIM LESS— SNORKMAIDEN, TOO. MUCH TOO FAT FOR A GIRL

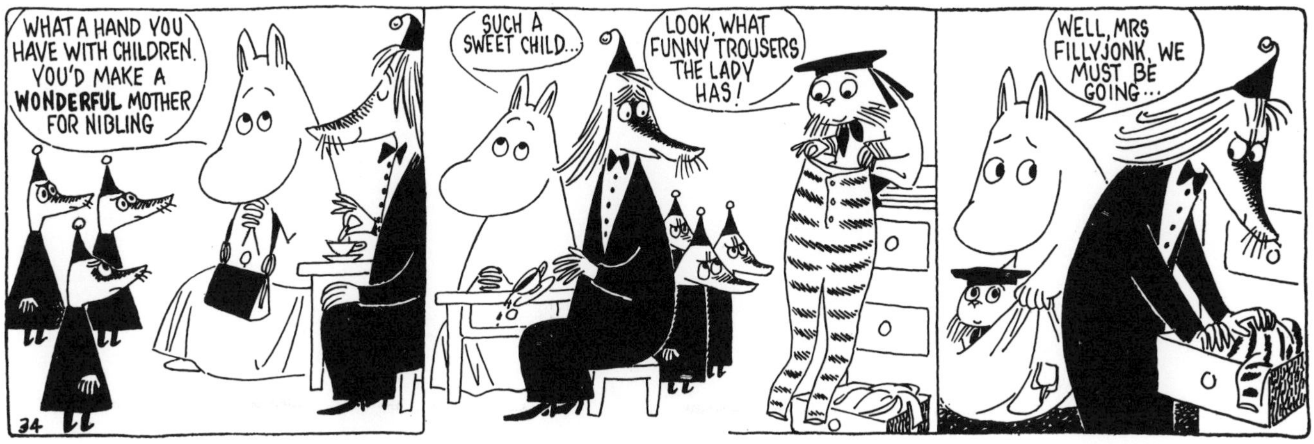
WHAT A HAND YOU HAVE WITH CHILDREN. YOU'D MAKE A WONDERFUL MOTHER FOR NIBLING
34
SUCH A SWEET CHILD...
LOOK, WHAT FUNNY TROUSERS THE LADY HAS!
WELL, MRS FILLYJONK, WE MUST BE GOING...

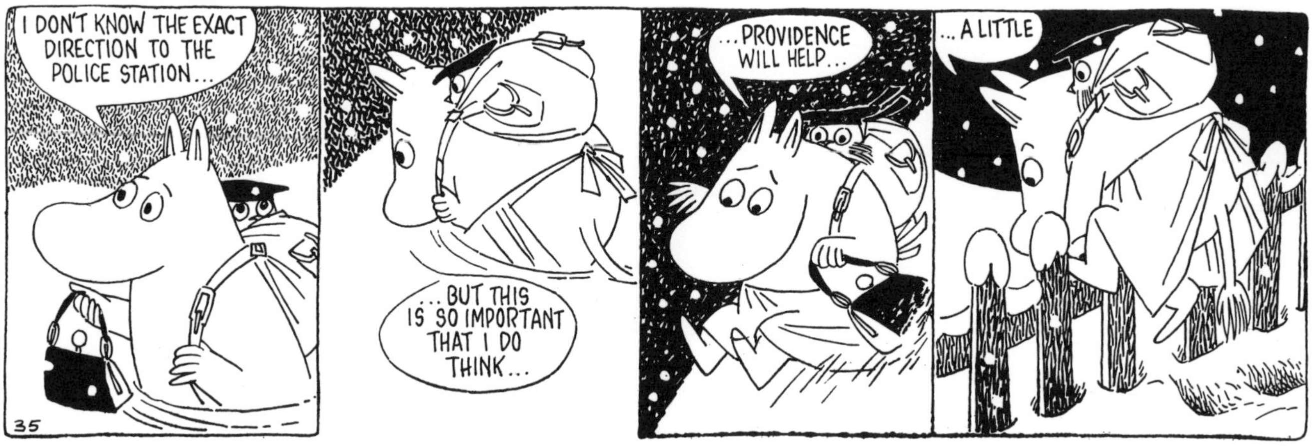
I DON'T KNOW THE EXACT DIRECTION TO THE POLICE STATION...
...BUT THIS IS SO IMPORTANT THAT I DO THINK...
...PROVIDENCE WILL HELP...
...A LITTLE
35

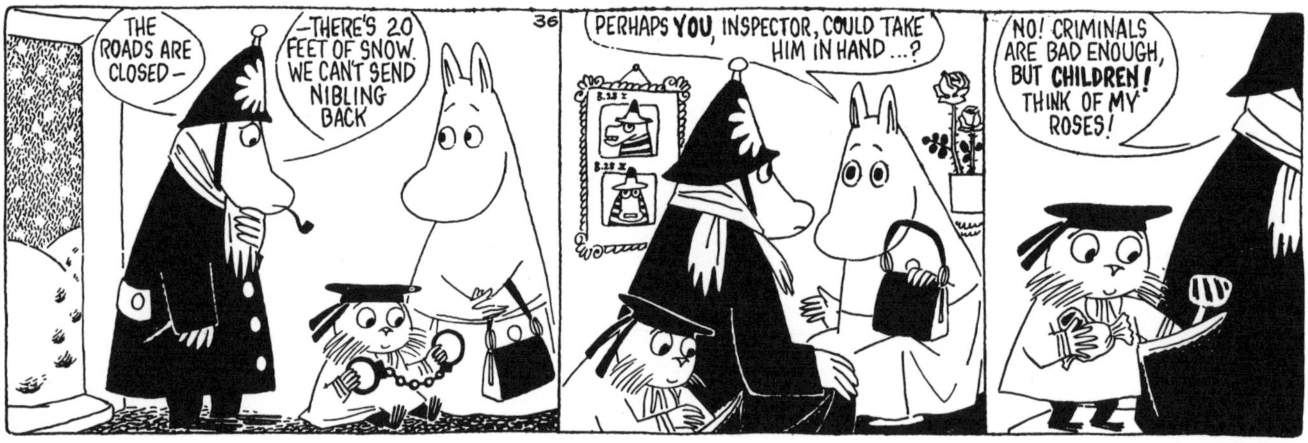
THE ROADS ARE CLOSED –
–THERE'S 20 FEET OF SNOW. WE CAN'T SEND NIBLING BACK
36
PERHAPS **YOU**, INSPECTOR, COULD TAKE HIM IN HAND...?
NO! CRIMINALS ARE BAD ENOUGH, BUT **CHILDREN!** THINK OF MY ROSES!

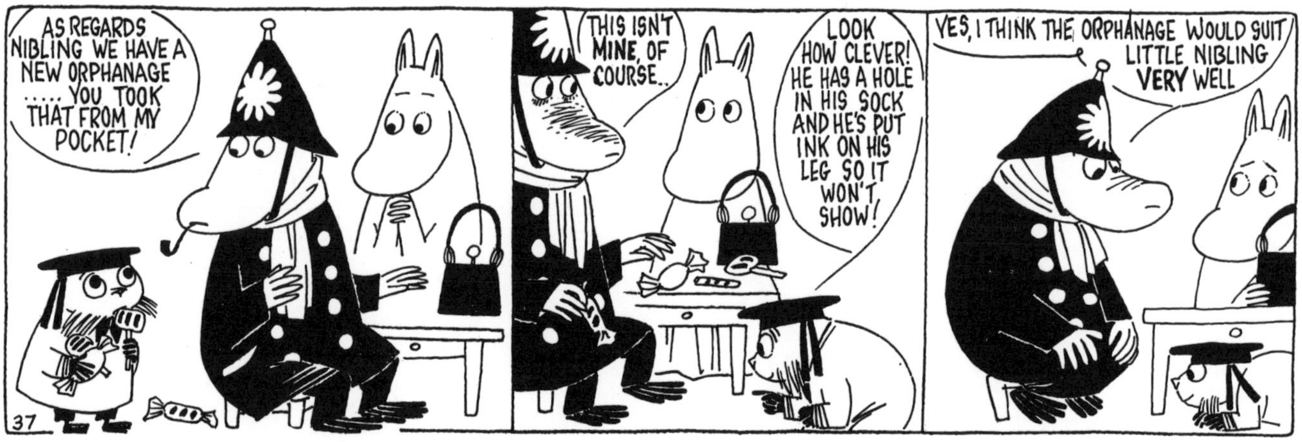
AS REGARDS NIBLING WE HAVE A NEW ORPHANAGE ..... YOU TOOK THAT FROM MY POCKET!
37
THIS ISN'T **MINE**, OF COURSE..
LOOK HOW CLEVER! HE HAS A HOLE IN HIS SOCK AND HE'S PUT INK ON HIS LEG SO IT WON'T SHOW!
YES, I THINK THE ORPHANAGE WOULD SUIT LITTLE NIBLING **VERY** WELL

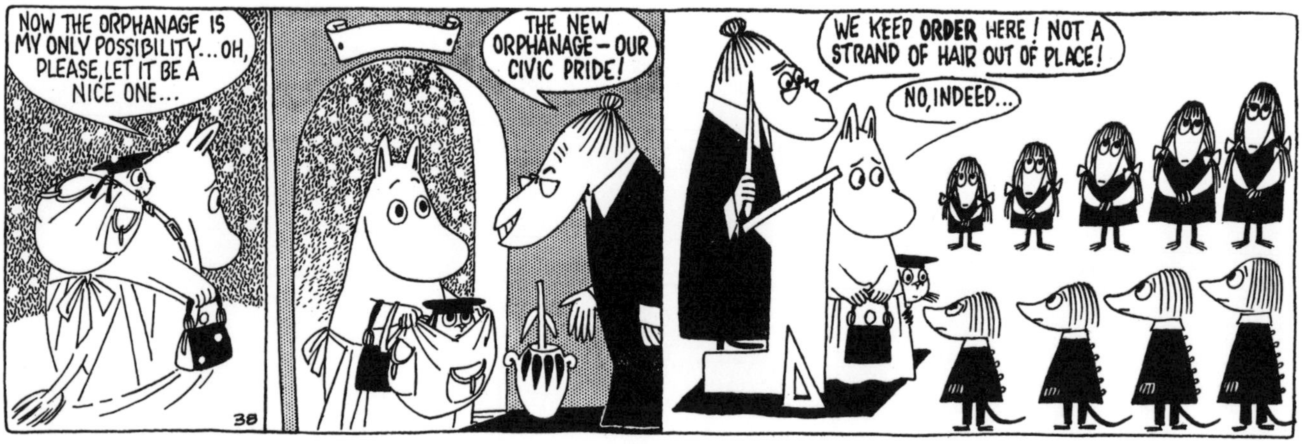
NOW THE ORPHANAGE IS MY ONLY POSSIBILITY...OH, PLEASE, LET IT BE A NICE ONE...
38
THE NEW ORPHANAGE – OUR CIVIC PRIDE!
WE KEEP **ORDER** HERE! NOT A STRAND OF HAIR OUT OF PLACE!
NO, INDEED...

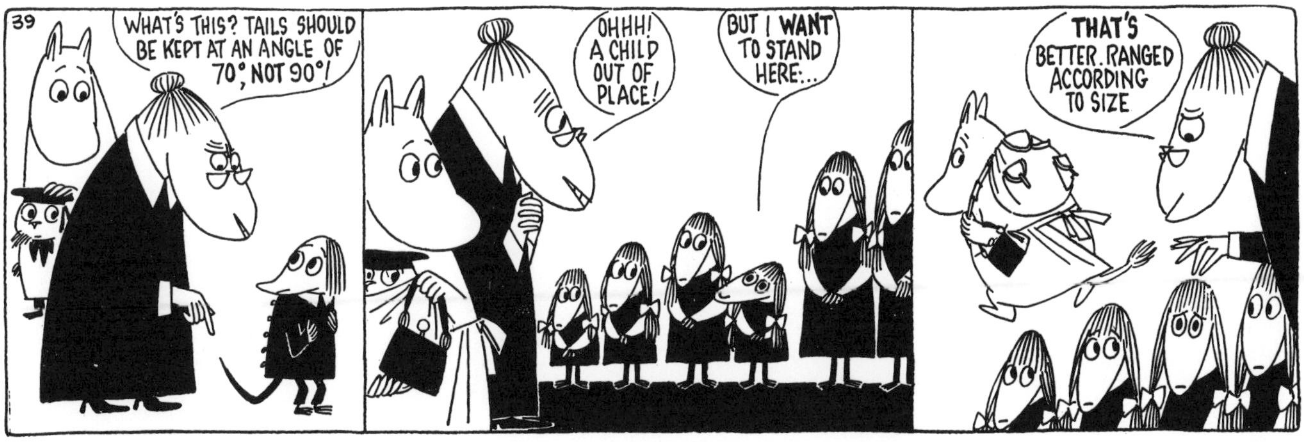
39
WHAT'S THIS? TAILS SHOULD BE KEPT AT AN ANGLE OF 70°, NOT 90°!
OHHH! A CHILD OUT OF PLACE!
BUT I WANT TO STAND HERE...
THAT'S BETTER. RANGED ACCORDING TO SIZE

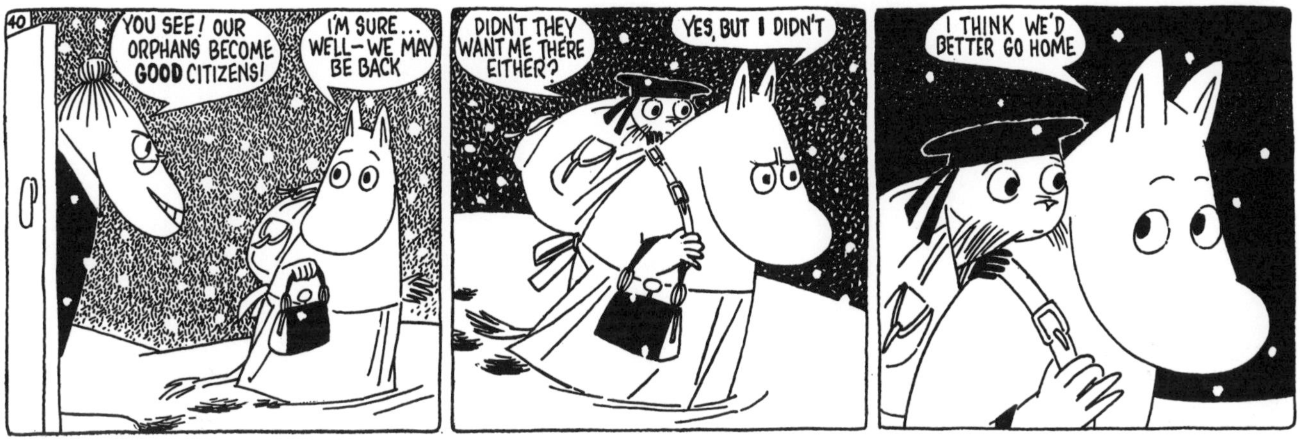
40
YOU SEE! OUR ORPHANS BECOME GOOD CITIZENS!
I'M SURE... WELL– WE MAY BE BACK
DIDN'T THEY WANT ME THERE EITHER?
YES, BUT I DIDN'T
I THINK WE'D BETTER GO HOME

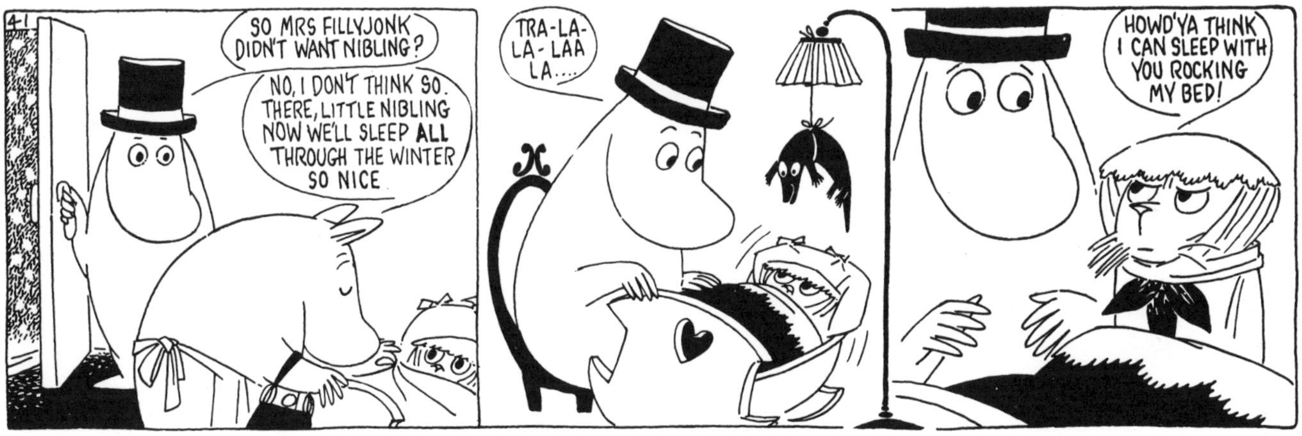
41
SO MRS FILLYJONK DIDN'T WANT NIBLING?
NO, I DON'T THINK SO. THERE, LITTLE NIBLING NOW WE'LL SLEEP ALL THROUGH THE WINTER SO NICE
TRA-LA-LA-LAA LA....
HOWD'YA THINK I CAN SLEEP WITH YOU ROCKING MY BED!

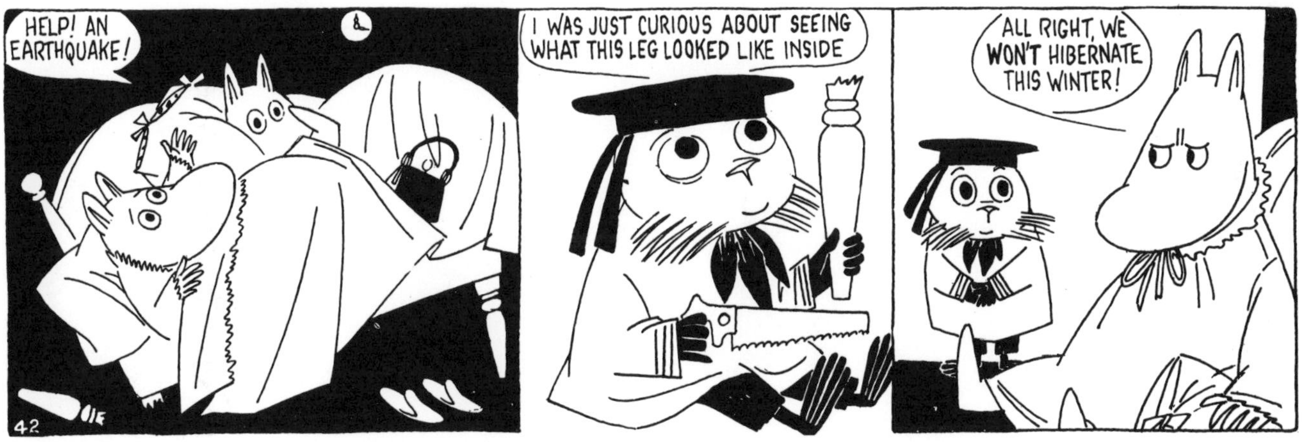
HELP! AN EARTHQUAKE!
42
I WAS JUST CURIOUS ABOUT SEEING WHAT THIS LEG LOOKED LIKE INSIDE
ALL RIGHT, WE WON'T HIBERNATE THIS WINTER!

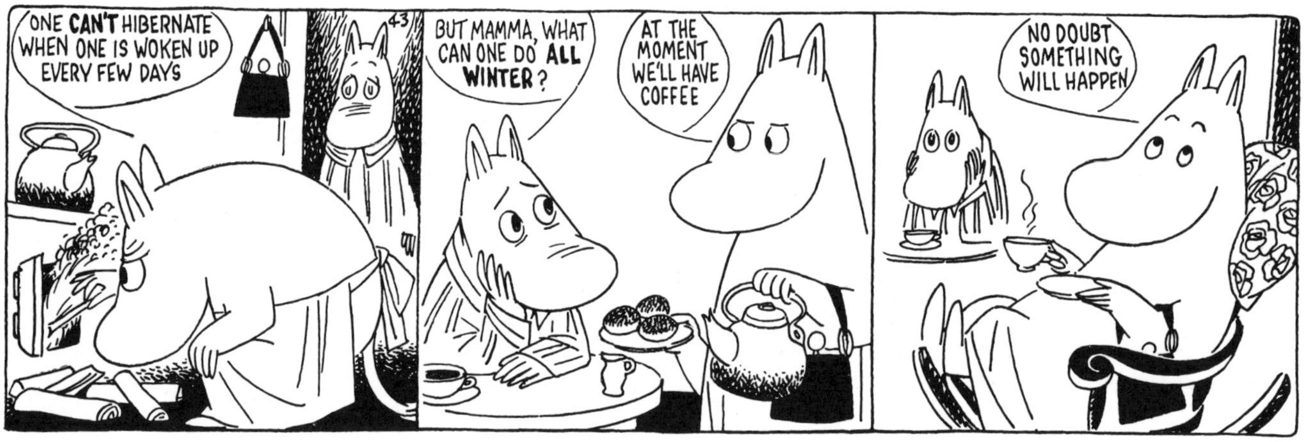
43
ONE **CAN'T** HIBERNATE WHEN ONE IS WOKEN UP EVERY FEW DAYS
BUT MAMMA, WHAT CAN ONE DO **ALL WINTER**?
AT THE MOMENT WE'LL HAVE COFFEE
NO DOUBT SOMETHING WILL HAPPEN

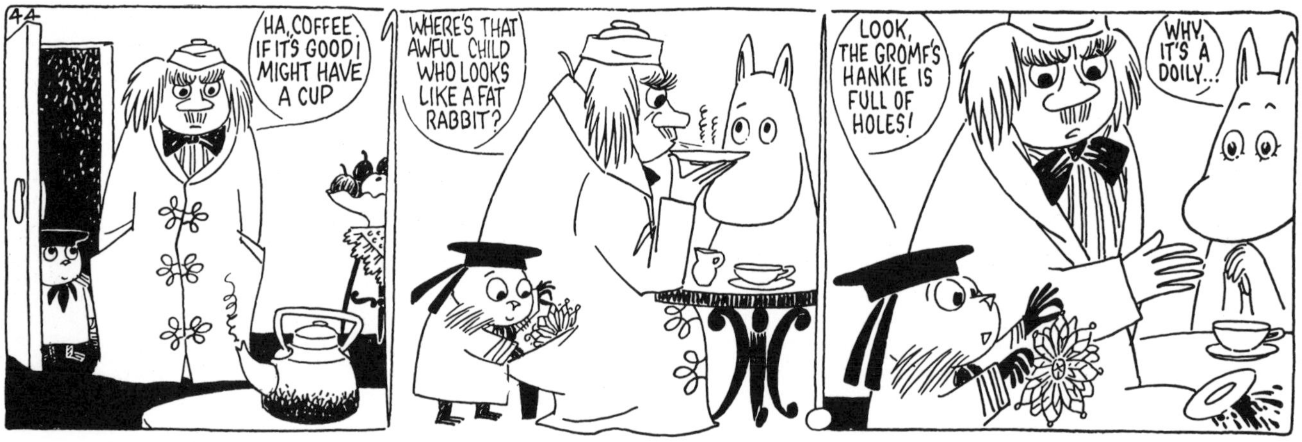
44
HA, COFFEE IF IT'S GOOD I MIGHT HAVE A CUP
WHERE'S THAT AWFUL CHILD WHO LOOKS LIKE A FAT RABBIT?
LOOK, THE GROMF'S HANKIE IS FULL OF HOLES!
WHY, IT'S A DOILY...

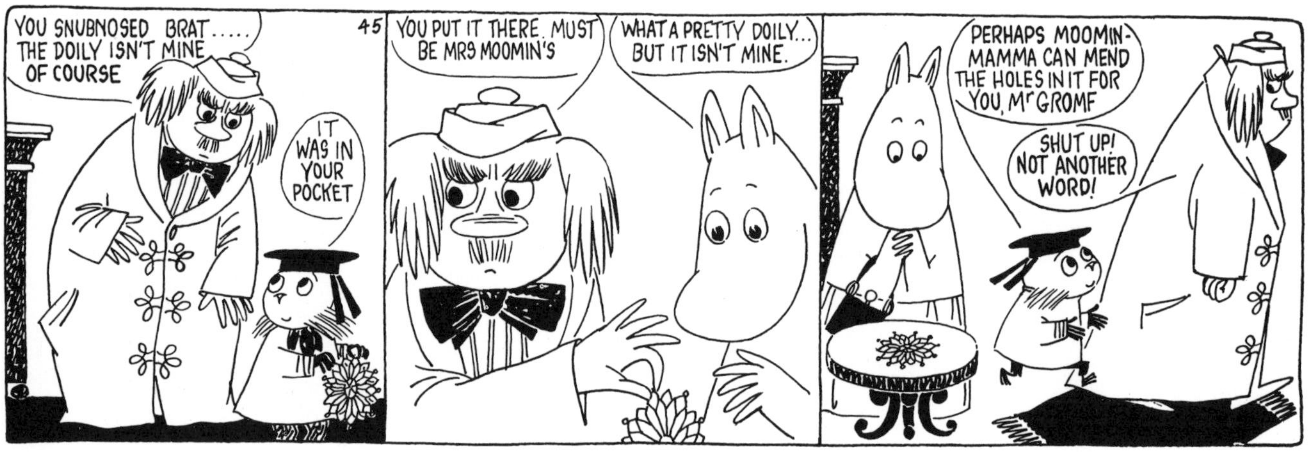
45
YOU SNUBNOSED BRAT..... THE DOILY ISN'T MINE OF COURSE
IT WAS IN YOUR POCKET
YOU PUT IT THERE. MUST BE MRS MOOMIN'S
WHAT A PRETTY DOILY... BUT IT ISN'T MINE.
PERHAPS MOOMINMAMMA CAN MEND THE HOLES IN IT FOR YOU, Mr GROMF
SHUT UP! NOT ANOTHER WORD!

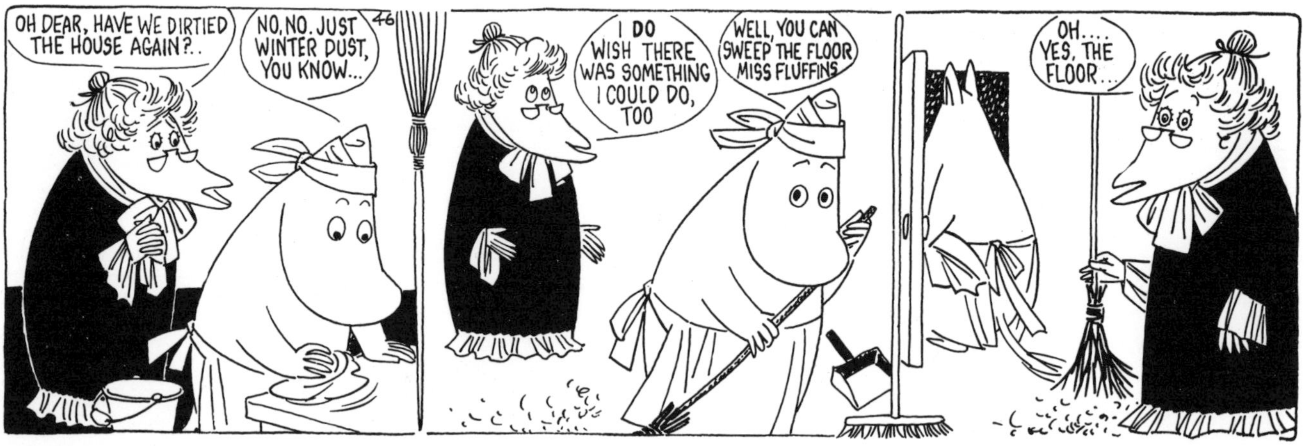
46
OH DEAR, HAVE WE DIRTIED THE HOUSE AGAIN?..
NO, NO. JUST WINTER DUST, YOU KNOW...
I **DO** WISH THERE WAS SOMETHING I COULD DO, TOO
WELL, YOU CAN SWEEP THE FLOOR MISS FLUFFINS
OH.... YES, THE FLOOR...

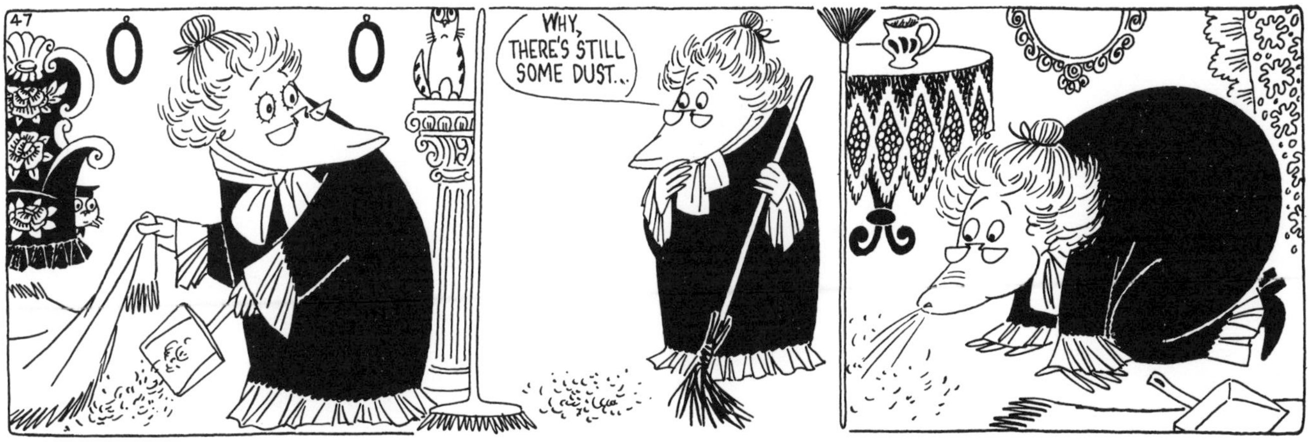
47
WHY, THERE'S STILL SOME DUST...

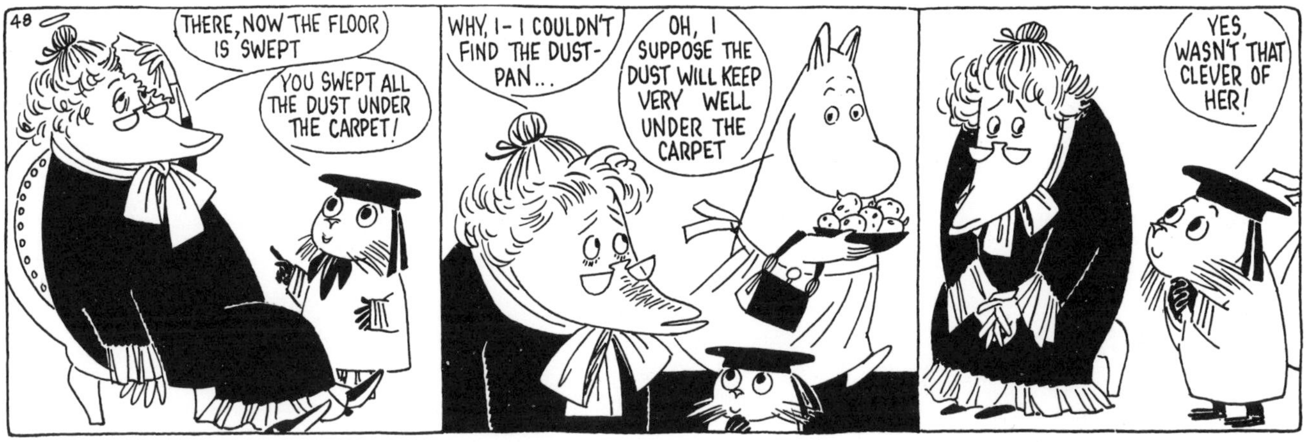
48
THERE, NOW THE FLOOR IS SWEPT
YOU SWEPT ALL THE DUST UNDER THE CARPET!
WHY, I– I COULDN'T FIND THE DUST-PAN...
OH, I SUPPOSE THE DUST WILL KEEP VERY WELL UNDER THE CARPET
YES, WASN'T THAT CLEVER OF HER!

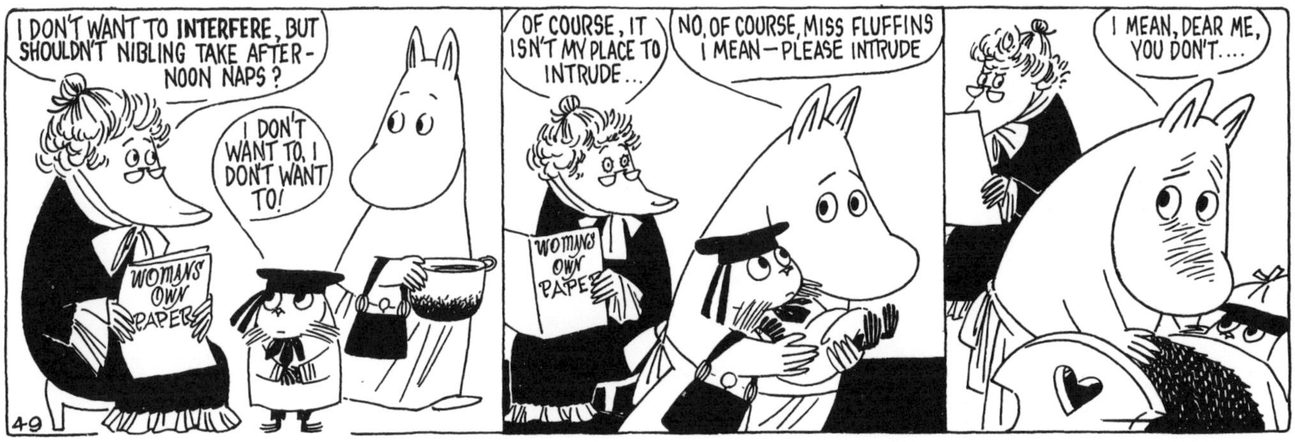
I DON'T WANT TO **INTERFERE**, BUT SHOULDN'T NIBLING TAKE AFTER-NOON NAPS?
I DON'T WANT TO, I DON'T WANT TO!
WOMANS OWN PAPER
49
OF COURSE, IT ISN'T MY PLACE TO INTRUDE...
NO, OF COURSE, MISS FLUFFINS I MEAN—PLEASE INTRUDE
WOMANS OWN PAPER
I MEAN, DEAR ME, YOU DON'T....

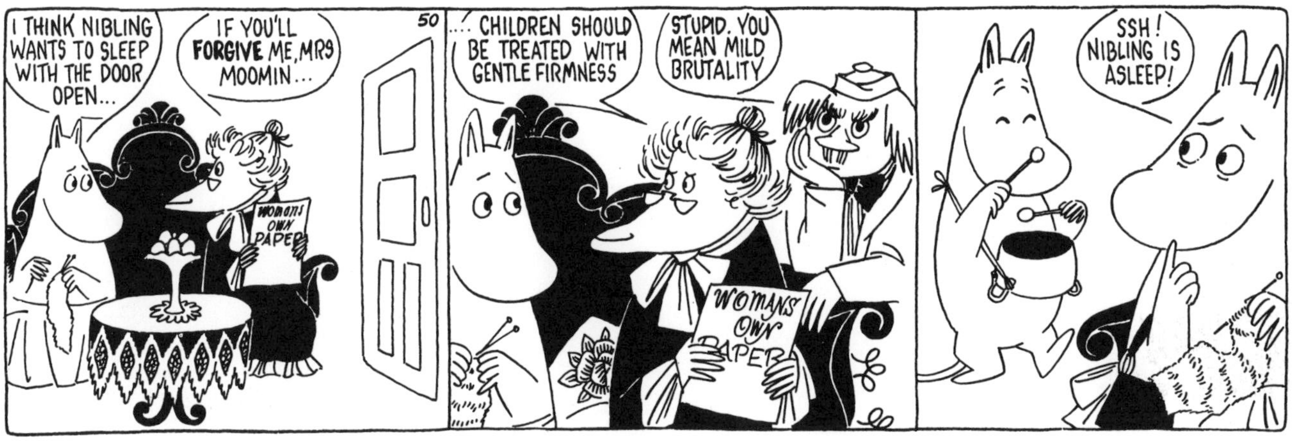
I THINK NIBLING WANTS TO SLEEP WITH THE DOOR OPEN...
IF YOU'LL **FORGIVE** ME, MRS MOOMIN...
WOMANS OWN PAPER
50
... CHILDREN SHOULD BE TREATED WITH GENTLE FIRMNESS
STUPID. YOU MEAN MILD BRUTALITY
WOMANS OWN PAPER
SSH! NIBLING IS ASLEEP!

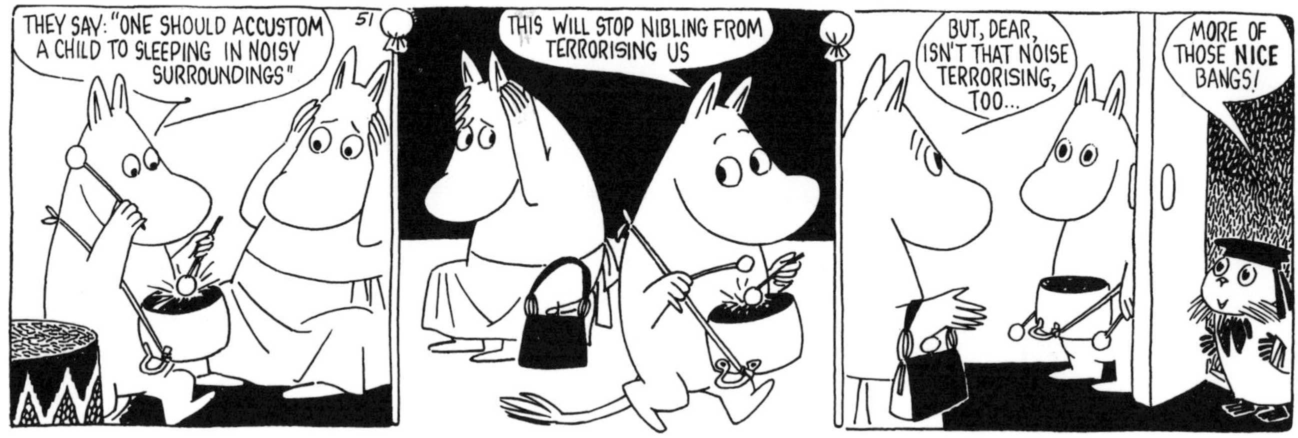
51
THEY SAY: "ONE SHOULD ACCUSTOM A CHILD TO SLEEPING IN NOISY SURROUNDINGS"
THIS WILL STOP NIBLING FROM TERRORISING US
BUT, DEAR, ISN'T THAT NOISE TERRORISING, TOO...
MORE OF THOSE **NICE** BANGS!

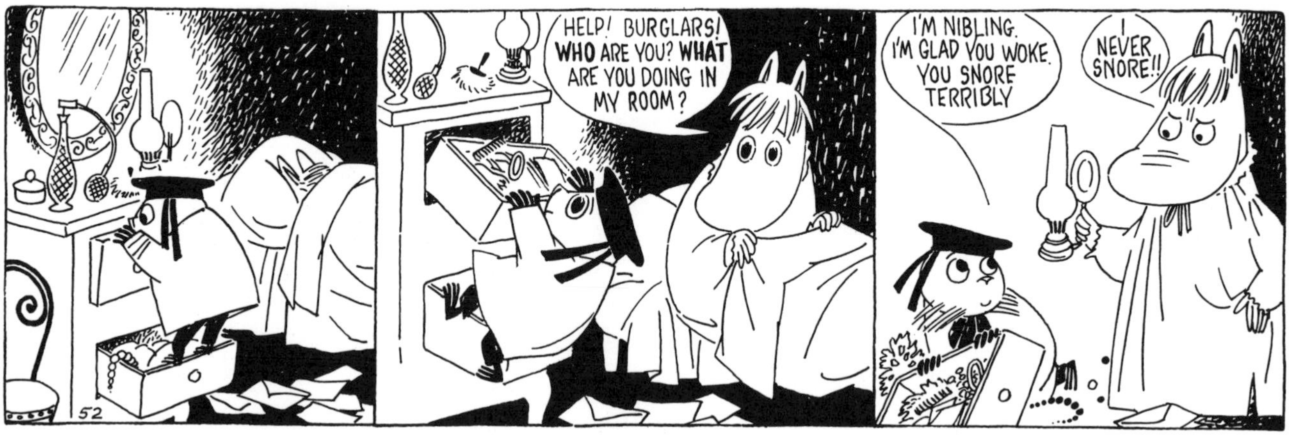
52
HELP! BURGLARS! **WHO** ARE YOU? **WHAT** ARE YOU DOING IN MY ROOM?
I'M NIBLING. I'M GLAD YOU WOKE. YOU SNORE TERRIBLY
I NEVER SNORE!!

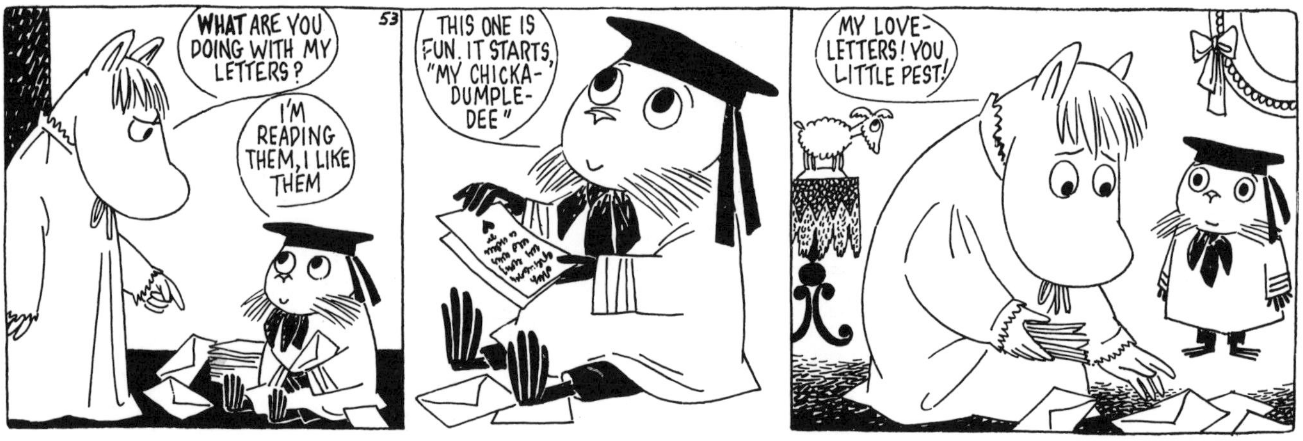
53
WHAT ARE YOU DOING WITH MY LETTERS?
I'M READING THEM, I LIKE THEM
THIS ONE IS FUN. IT STARTS, "MY CHICKA-DUMPLE-DEE"
MY LOVE-LETTERS! YOU LITTLE PEST!

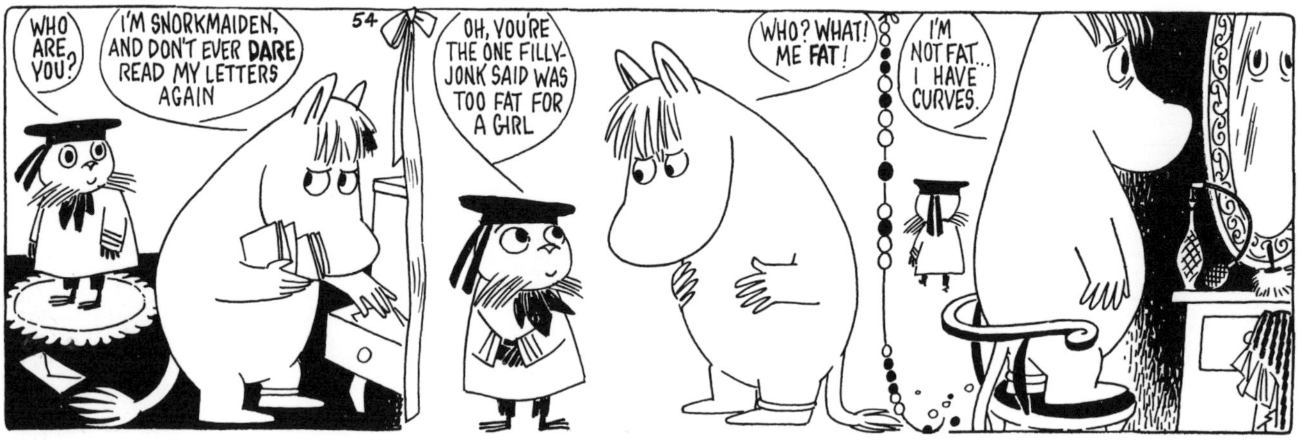
54
WHO ARE YOU?
I'M SNORKMAIDEN, AND DON'T EVER **DARE** READ MY LETTERS AGAIN
OH, YOU'RE THE ONE FILLY-JONK SAID WAS TOO FAT FOR A GIRL
WHO? WHAT! ME **FAT**!
I'M NOT FAT... I HAVE CURVES.

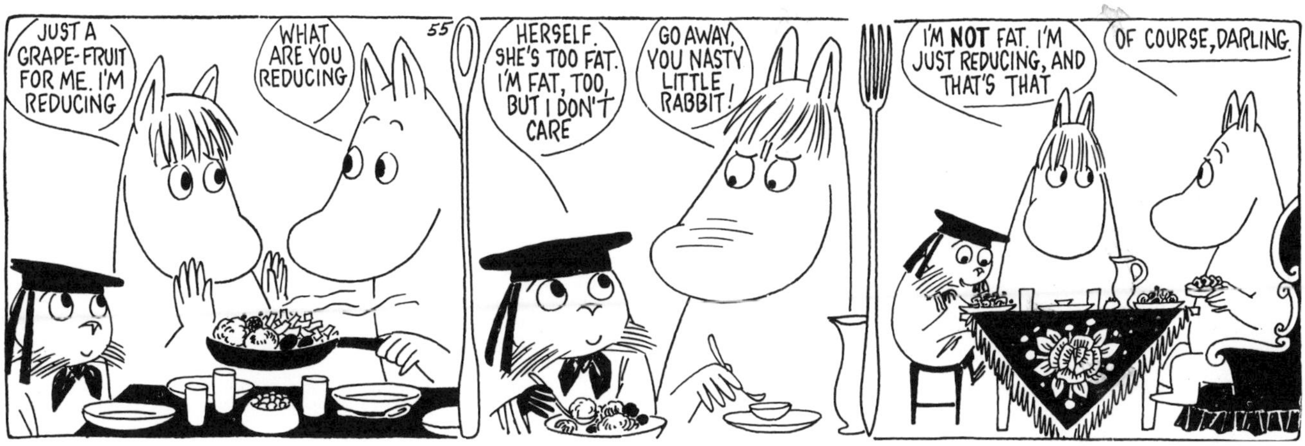
55
JUST A GRAPE-FRUIT FOR ME. I'M REDUCING
WHAT ARE YOU REDUCING
HERSELF. SHE'S TOO FAT. I'M FAT, TOO, BUT I DON'T CARE
GO AWAY, YOU NASTY LITTLE RABBIT!
I'M **NOT** FAT. I'M JUST REDUCING, AND THAT'S THAT
OF COURSE, DARLING.

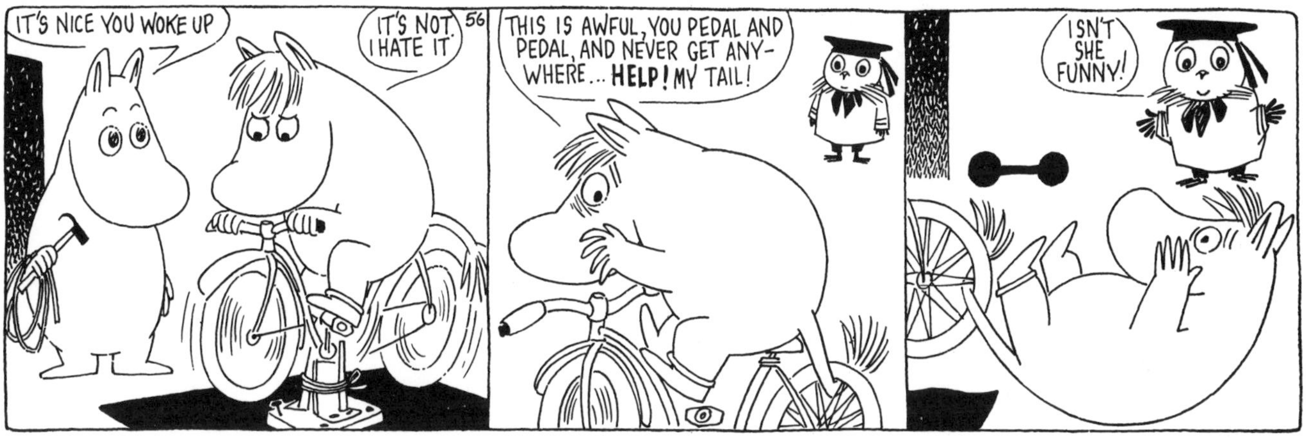
56
IT'S NICE YOU WOKE UP
IT'S NOT. I HATE IT
THIS IS AWFUL, YOU PEDAL AND PEDAL, AND NEVER GET ANYWHERE... **HELP!** MY TAIL!
ISN'T SHE FUNNY!

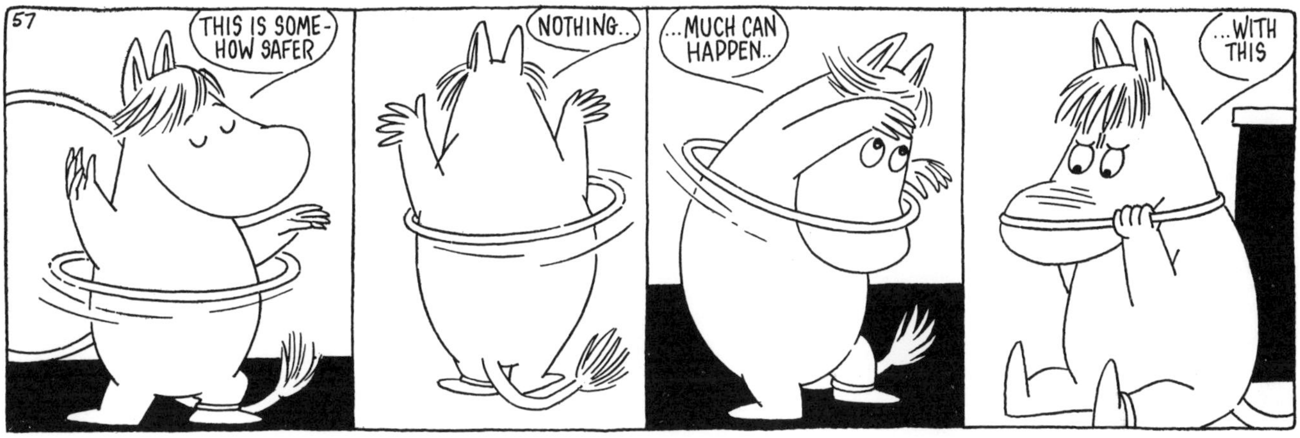
57
THIS IS SOMEHOW SAFER
NOTHING...
...MUCH CAN HAPPEN..
...WITH THIS

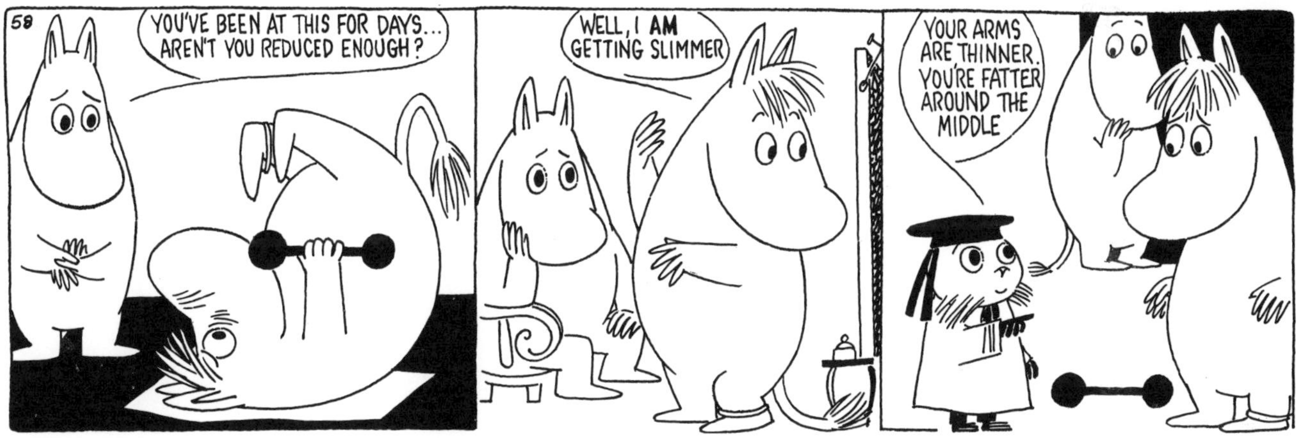
58
YOU'VE BEEN AT THIS FOR DAYS... AREN'T YOU REDUCED ENOUGH?
WELL, I **AM** GETTING SLIMMER
YOUR ARMS ARE THINNER. YOU'RE FATTER AROUND THE MIDDLE

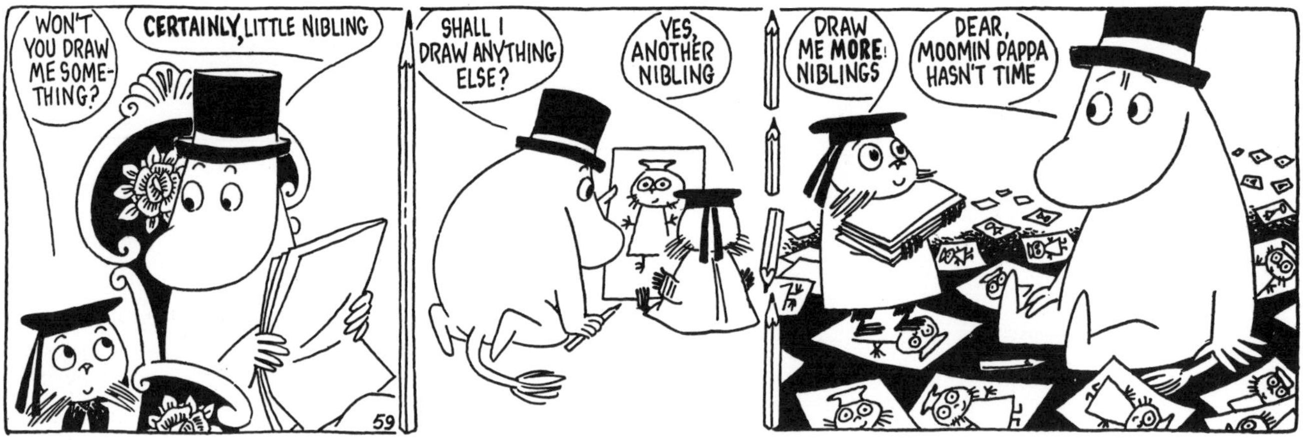
WON'T YOU DRAW ME SOME-THING?
CERTAINLY, LITTLE NIBLING
59
SHALL I DRAW ANYTHING ELSE?
YES, ANOTHER NIBLING
DRAW ME **MORE** NIBLINGS!
DEAR, MOOMIN PAPPA HASN'T TIME

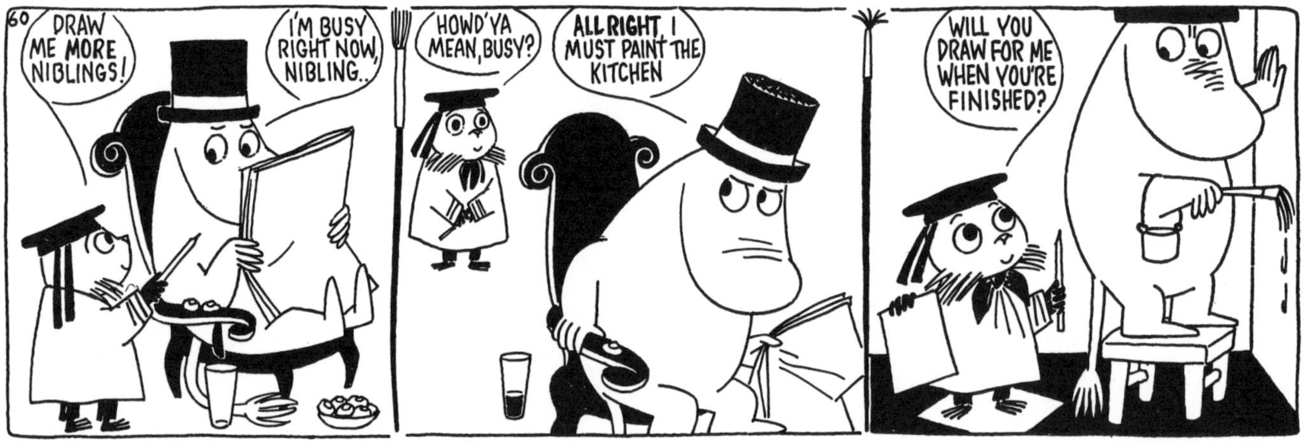
60
DRAW ME **MORE** NIBLINGS!
I'M BUSY RIGHT NOW, NIBLING..
HOWD'YA MEAN, BUSY?
ALL RIGHT, I MUST PAINT THE KITCHEN
WILL YOU DRAW FOR ME WHEN YOU'RE FINISHED?

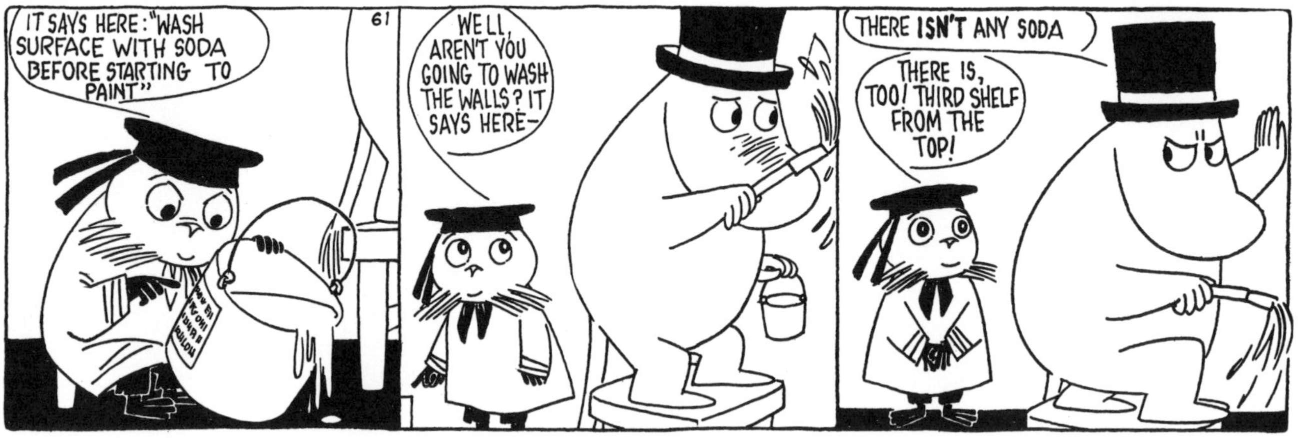
IT SAYS HERE: "WASH SURFACE WITH SODA BEFORE STARTING TO PAINT"
61
WELL, AREN'T YOU GOING TO WASH THE WALLS? IT SAYS HERE–
THERE **ISN'T** ANY SODA
THERE IS, TOO! THIRD SHELF FROM THE TOP!

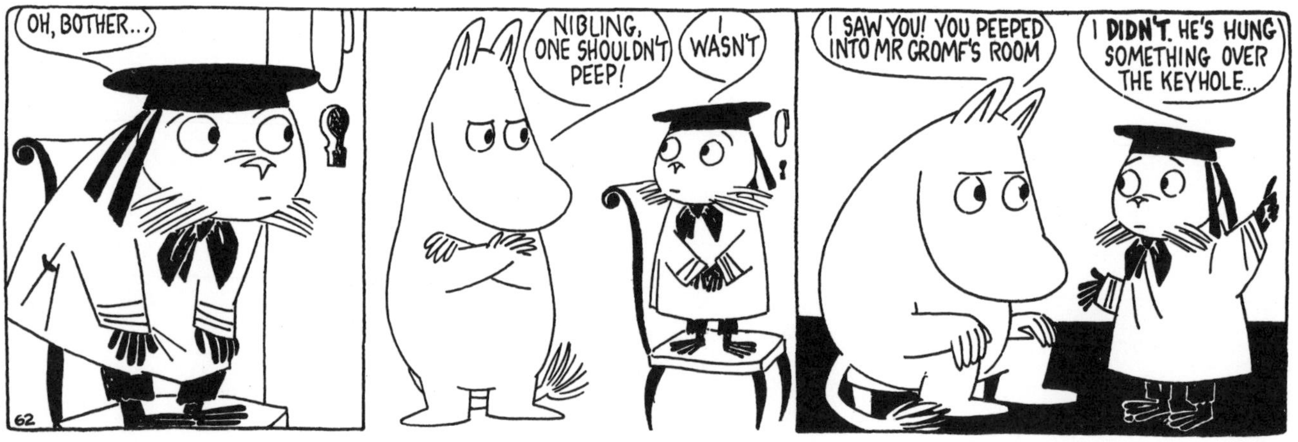
OH, BOTHER...
62
NIBLING, ONE SHOULDN'T PEEP!
I WASN'T
I SAW YOU! YOU PEEPED INTO MR GROMF'S ROOM
I **DIDN'T**. HE'S HUNG SOMETHING OVER THE KEYHOLE...

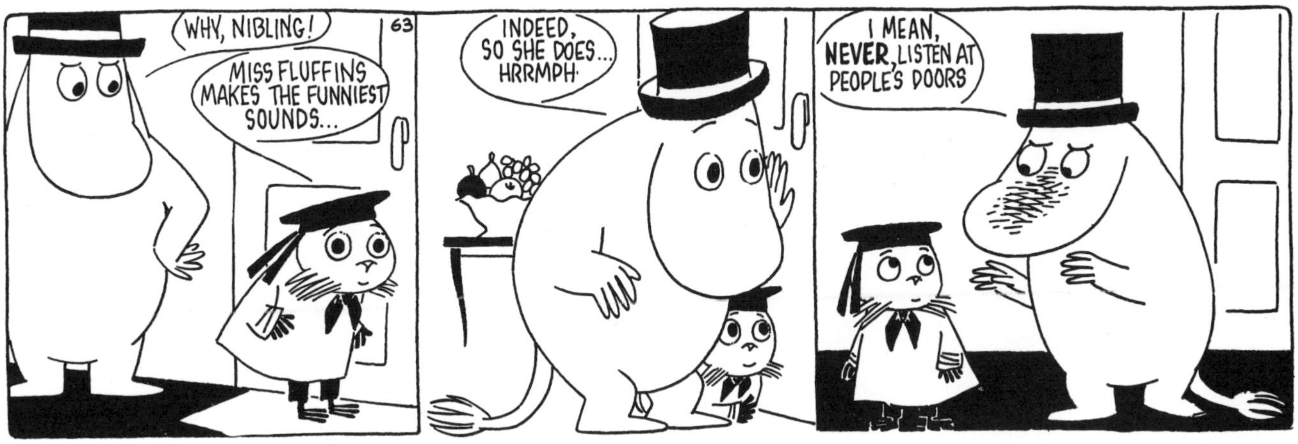
63
WHY, NIBLING!
MISS FLUFFINS MAKES THE FUNNIEST SOUNDS...
INDEED, SO SHE DOES... HRRMPH.
I MEAN, **NEVER**, LISTEN AT PEOPLE'S DOORS

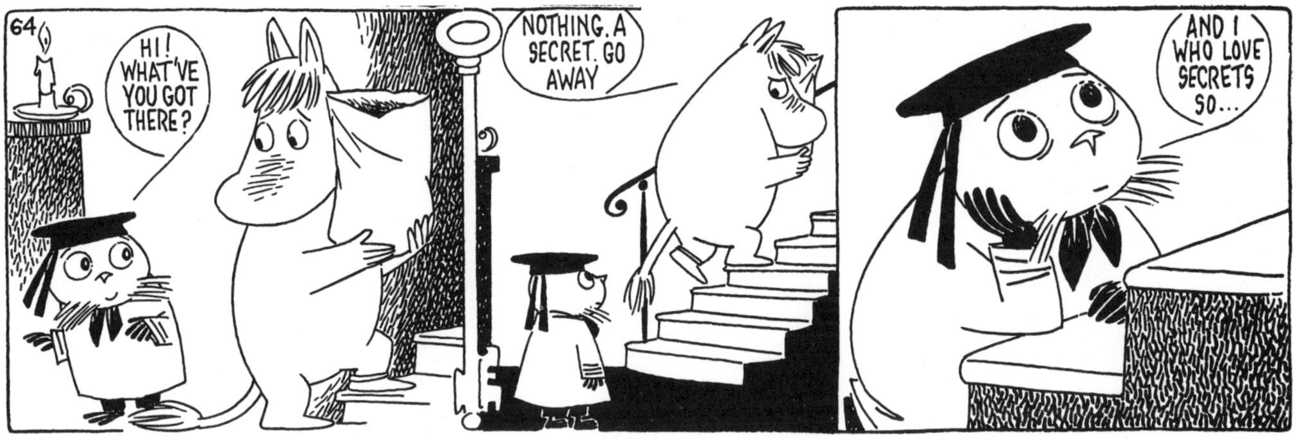
64
HI! WHAT'VE YOU GOT THERE?
NOTHING. A SECRET. GO AWAY
AND I WHO LOVE SECRETS SO...

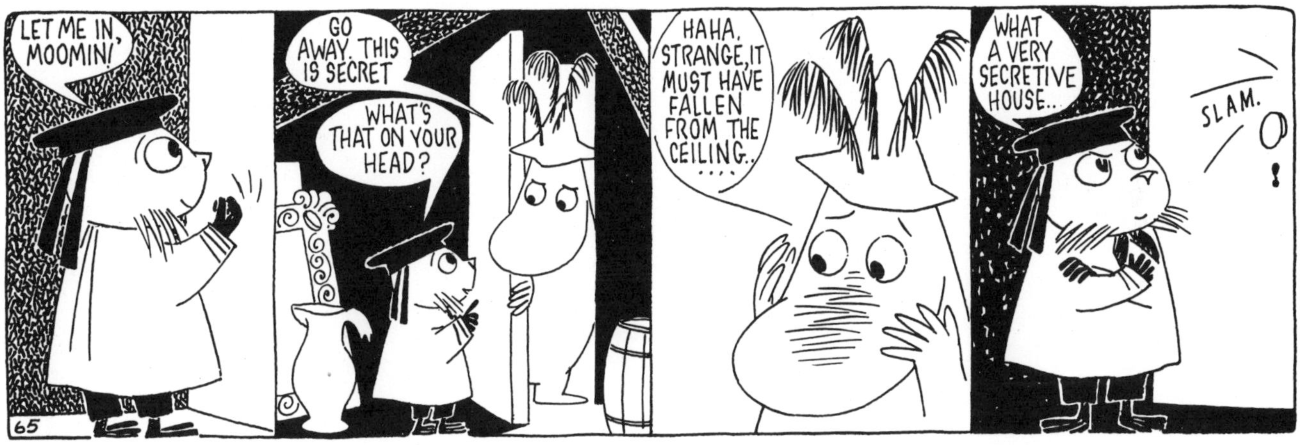
LET ME IN, MOOMIN!
65
GO AWAY. THIS IS SECRET
WHAT'S THAT ON YOUR HEAD?
HAHA. STRANGE, IT MUST HAVE FALLEN FROM THE CEILING....
WHAT A VERY SECRETIVE HOUSE..
SLAM.

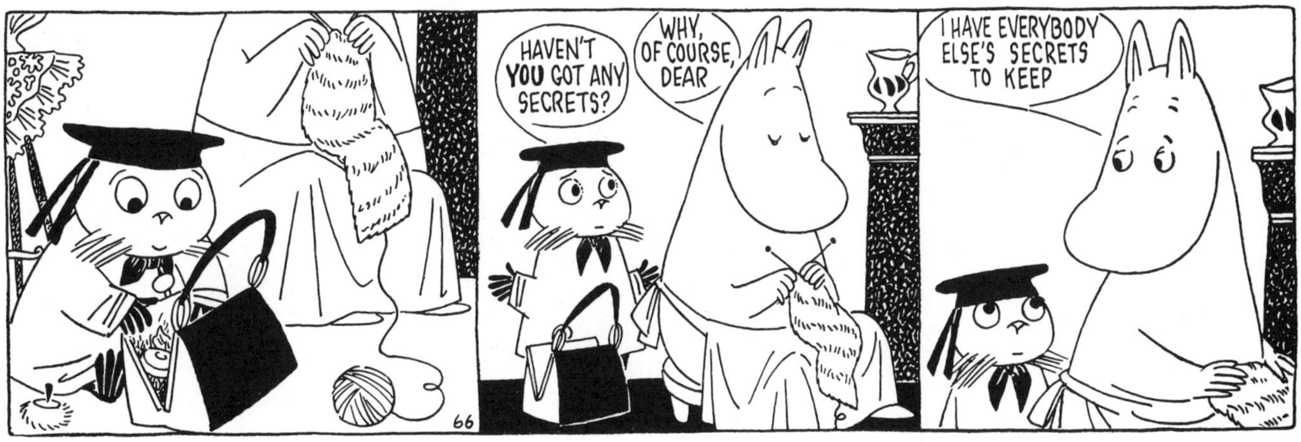
66
HAVEN'T **YOU** GOT ANY SECRETS?
WHY, OF COURSE, DEAR
I HAVE EVERYBODY ELSE'S SECRETS TO KEEP

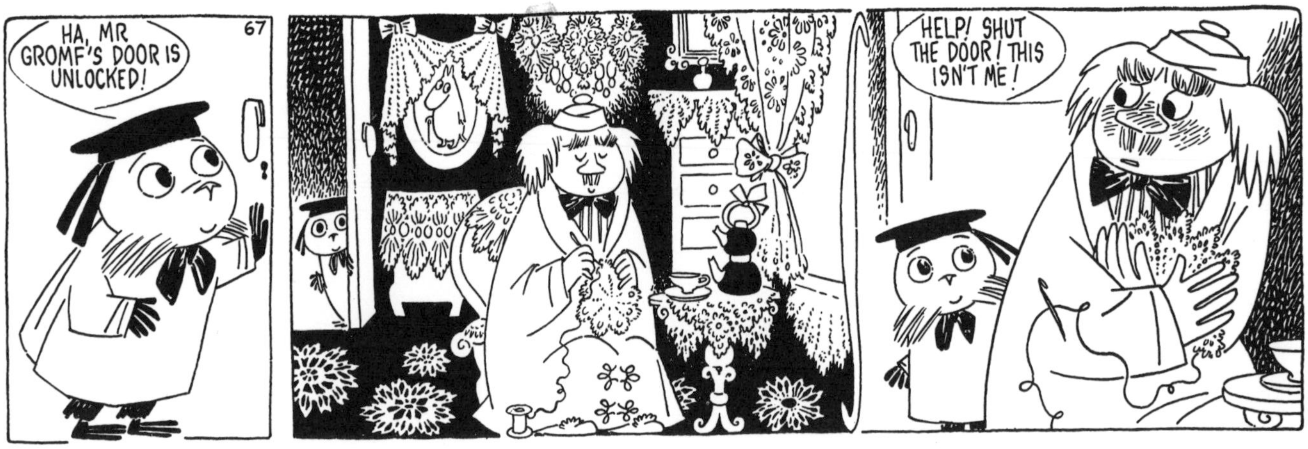
67
HA, MR GROMF'S DOOR IS UNLOCKED!
HELP! SHUT THE DOOR! THIS ISN'T ME!

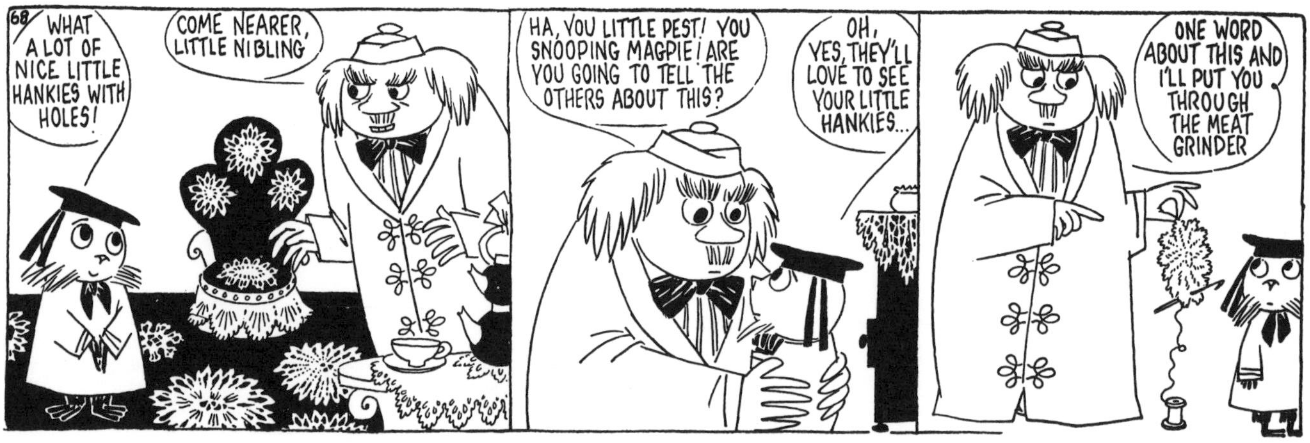
68
WHAT A LOT OF NICE LITTLE HANKIES WITH HOLES!
COME NEARER, LITTLE NIBLING
HA, YOU LITTLE PEST! YOU SNOOPING MAGPIE! ARE YOU GOING TO TELL THE OTHERS ABOUT THIS?
OH, YES, THEY'LL LOVE TO SEE YOUR LITTLE HANKIES...
ONE WORD ABOUT THIS AND I'LL PUT YOU THROUGH THE MEAT GRINDER

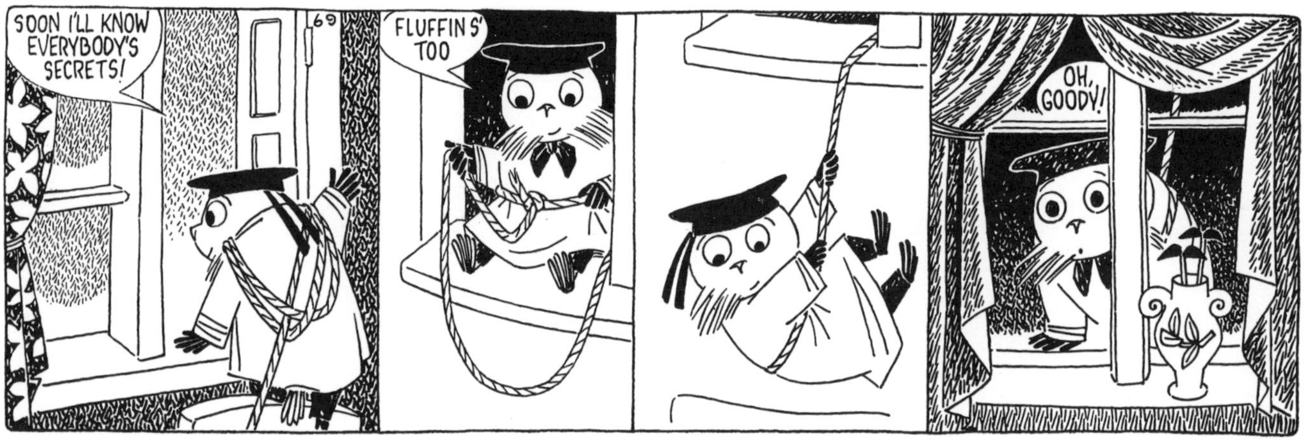
69
SOON I'LL KNOW EVERYBODY'S SECRETS!
FLUFFIN S' TOO
OH, GOODY!

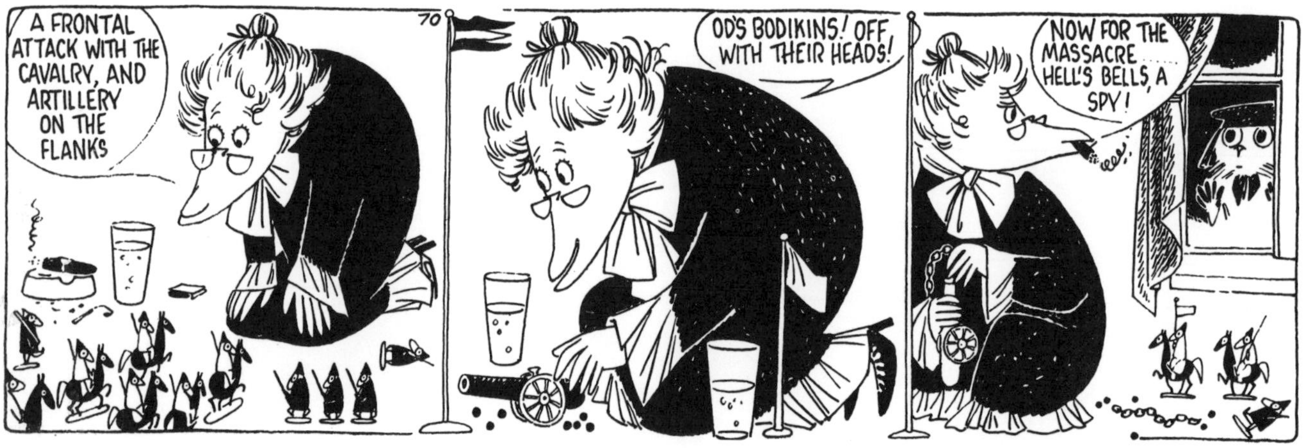
70
A FRONTAL ATTACK WITH THE CAVALRY, AND ARTILLERY ON THE FLANKS
OD'S BODIKINS! OFF WITH THEIR HEADS!
NOW FOR THE MASSACRE ... HELL'S BELLS, A SPY!

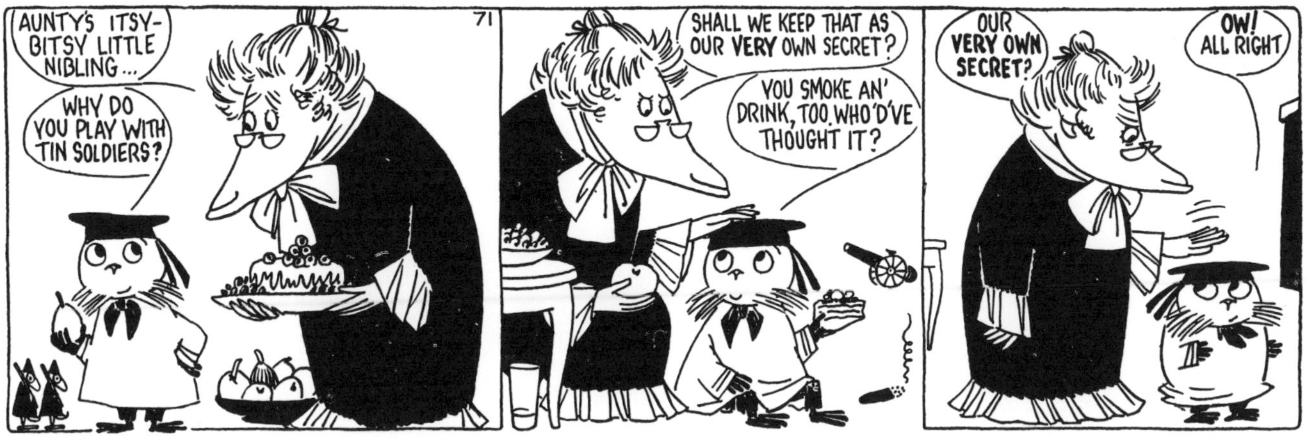
71
AUNTY'S ITSY-BITSY LITTLE NIBLING...
WHY DO YOU PLAY WITH TIN SOLDIERS?
SHALL WE KEEP THAT AS OUR **VERY** OWN SECRET?
YOU SMOKE AN' DRINK, TOO. WHO'D'VE THOUGHT IT?
OUR **VERY OWN SECRET?**
OW! ALL RIGHT

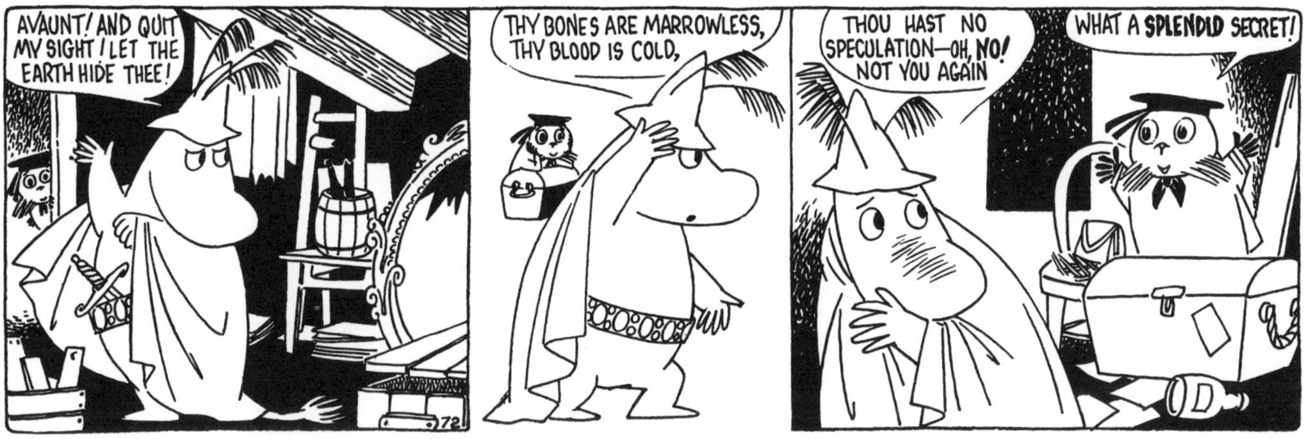
AVAUNT! AND QUIT MY SIGHT! LET THE EARTH HIDE THEE!
72
THY BONES ARE MARROWLESS, THY BLOOD IS COLD,
THOU HAST NO SPECULATION—OH, **NO!** NOT YOU AGAIN
WHAT A **SPLENDID** SECRET!

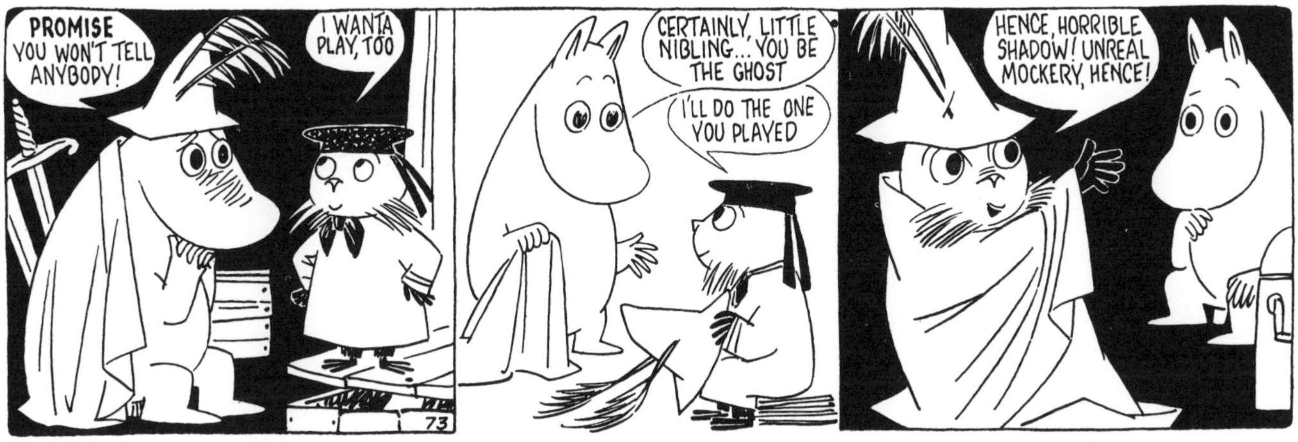
PROMISE YOU WON'T TELL ANYBODY!
I WANTA PLAY, TOO
73
CERTAINLY, LITTLE NIBLING... YOU BE THE GHOST
I'LL DO THE ONE YOU PLAYED
HENCE, HORRIBLE SHADOW! UNREAL MOCKERY, HENCE!

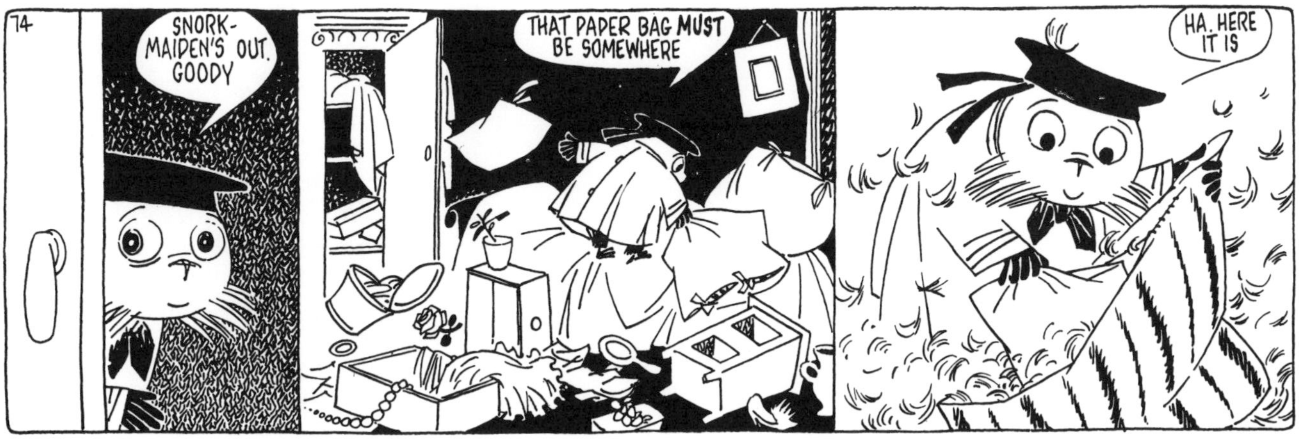
74
SNORK-MAIDEN'S OUT. GOODY
THAT PAPER BAG **MUST** BE SOMEWHERE
HA. HERE IT IS

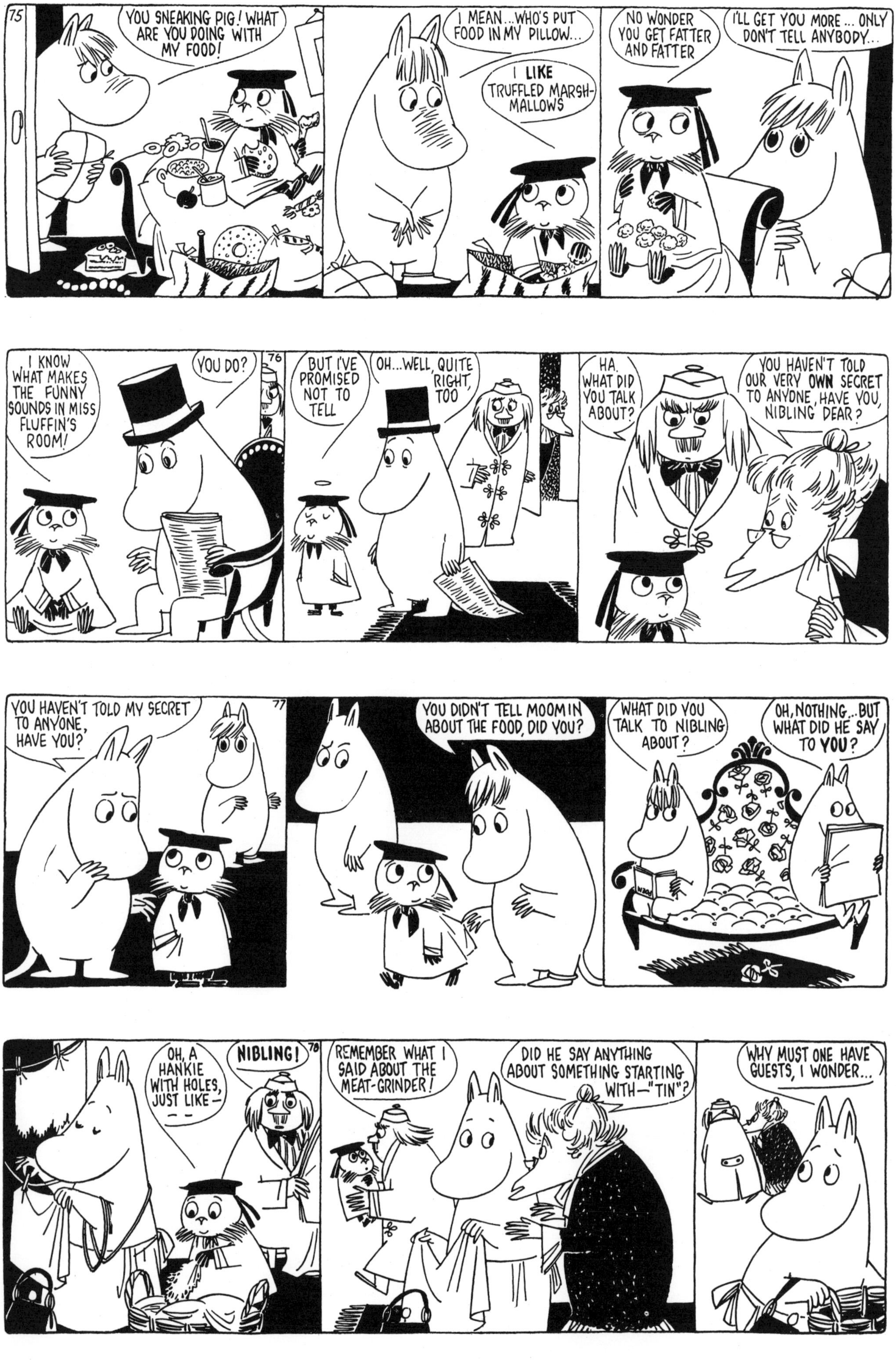
75
YOU SNEAKING PIG! WHAT ARE YOU DOING WITH MY FOOD!
I MEAN...WHO'S PUT FOOD IN MY PILLOW...
I LIKE TRUFFLED MARSH-MALLOWS
NO WONDER YOU GET FATTER AND FATTER
I'LL GET YOU MORE ... ONLY DON'T TELL ANYBODY...
I KNOW WHAT MAKES THE FUNNY SOUNDS IN MISS FLUFFIN'S ROOM!
YOU DO?
76
BUT I'VE PROMISED NOT TO TELL
OH...WELL, QUITE RIGHT, TOO
HA. WHAT DID YOU TALK ABOUT?
YOU HAVEN'T TOLD OUR VERY OWN SECRET TO ANYONE, HAVE YOU, NIBLING DEAR?
YOU HAVEN'T TOLD MY SECRET TO ANYONE, HAVE YOU?
77
YOU DIDN'T TELL MOOMIN ABOUT THE FOOD, DID YOU?
WHAT DID YOU TALK TO NIBLING ABOUT?
OH, NOTHING...BUT WHAT DID HE SAY TO YOU?
OH, A HANKIE WITH HOLES, JUST LIKE— — —
NIBLING!
78
REMEMBER WHAT I SAID ABOUT THE MEAT-GRINDER!
DID HE SAY ANYTHING ABOUT SOMETHING STARTING WITH—"TIN"?
WHY MUST ONE HAVE GUESTS, I WONDER...

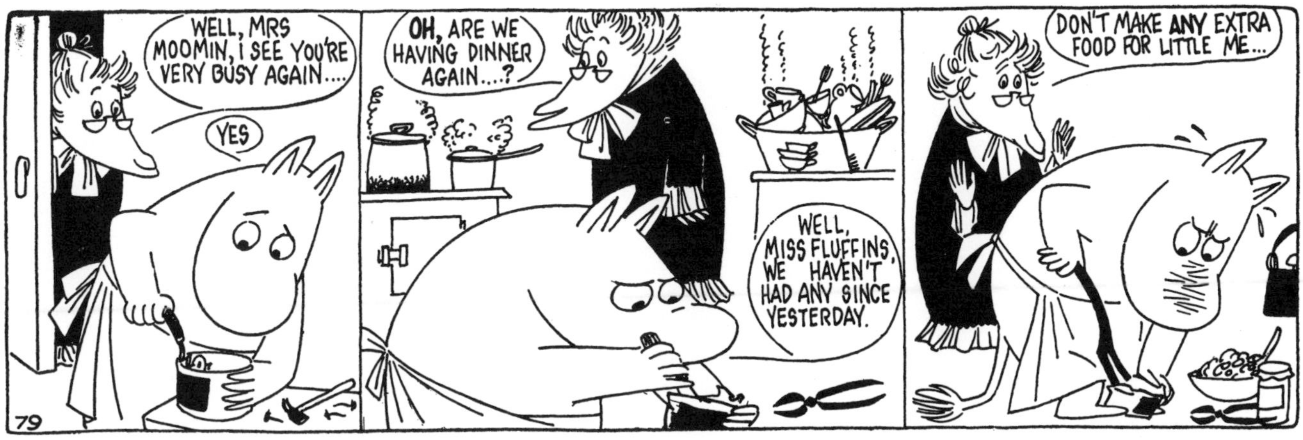
WELL, MRS MOOMIN, I SEE YOU'RE VERY BUSY AGAIN....
YES
79
OH, ARE WE HAVING DINNER AGAIN....?
WELL, MISS FLUFFINS, WE HAVEN'T HAD ANY SINCE YESTERDAY.
DON'T MAKE ANY EXTRA FOOD FOR LITTLE ME...

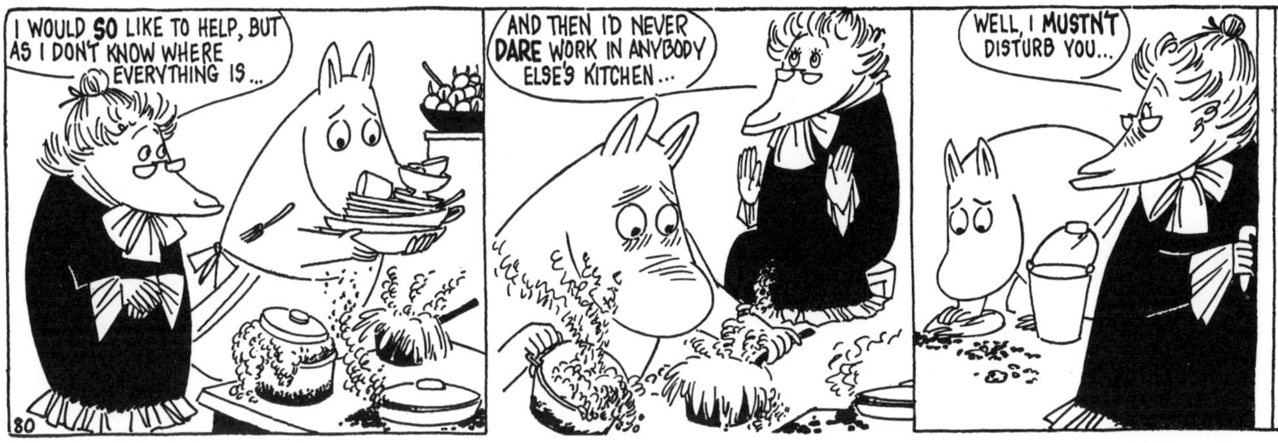
I WOULD SO LIKE TO HELP, BUT AS I DON'T KNOW WHERE EVERYTHING IS ...
80
AND THEN I'D NEVER DARE WORK IN ANYBODY ELSE'S KITCHEN ...
WELL, I MUSTN'T DISTURB YOU...

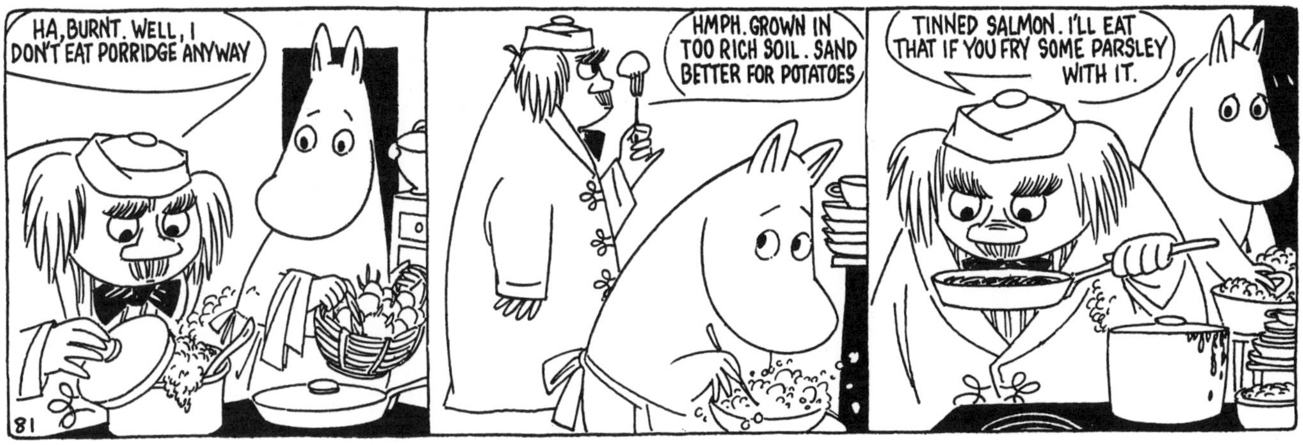
HA, BURNT. WELL, I DON'T EAT PORRIDGE ANYWAY
81
HMPH. GROWN IN TOO RICH SOIL. SAND BETTER FOR POTATOES
TINNED SALMON. I'LL EAT THAT IF YOU FRY SOME PARSLEY WITH IT.

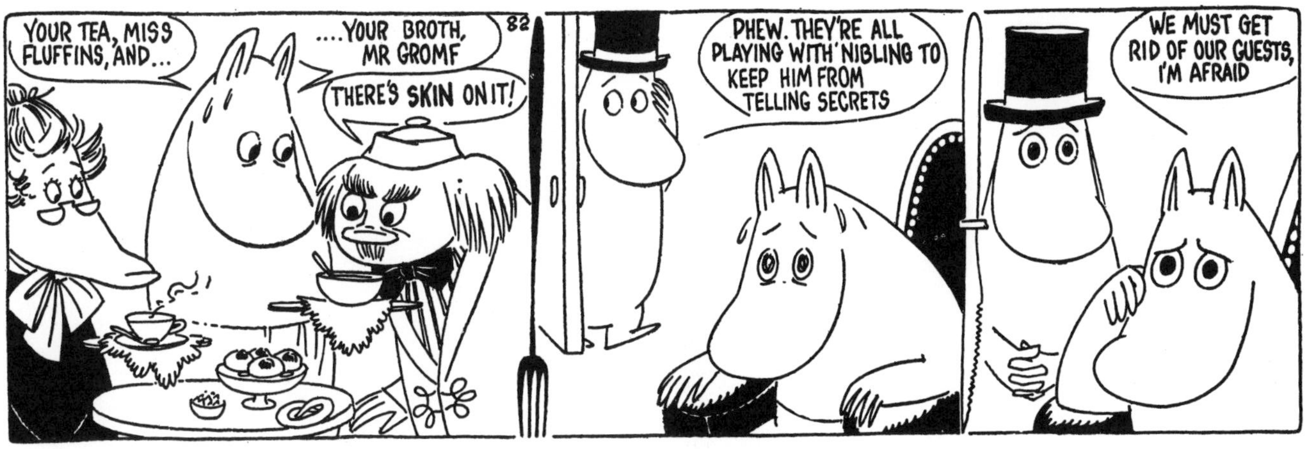
YOUR TEA, MISS FLUFFINS, AND...
....YOUR BROTH, MR GROMF
82
THERE'S SKIN ON IT!
PHEW. THEY'RE ALL PLAYING WITH NIBLING TO KEEP HIM FROM TELLING SECRETS
WE MUST GET RID OF OUR GUESTS, I'M AFRAID

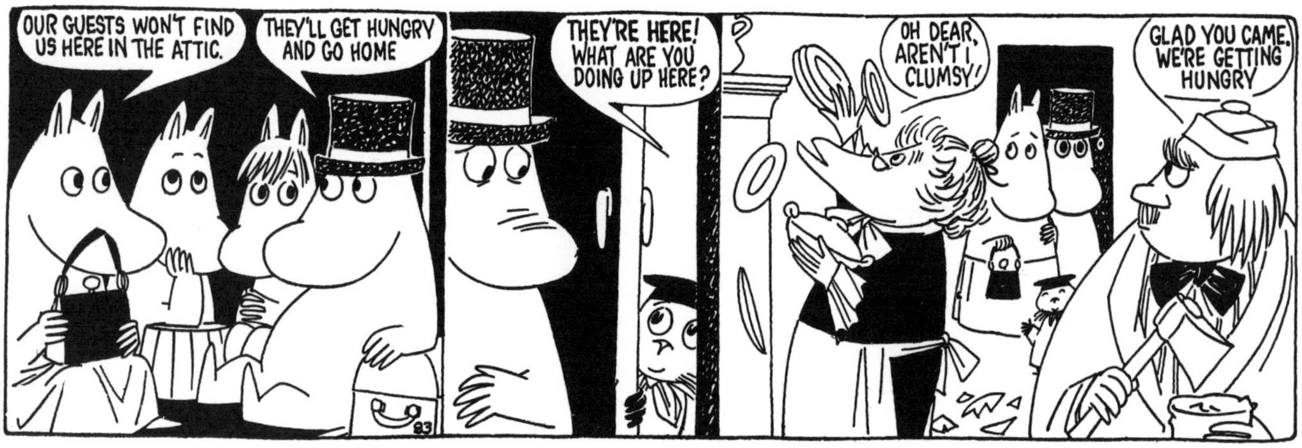
OUR GUESTS WON'T FIND US HERE IN THE ATTIC.
THEY'LL GET HUNGRY AND GO HOME
83
THEY'RE HERE! WHAT ARE YOU DOING UP HERE?
OH DEAR, AREN'T I CLUMSY!
GLAD YOU CAME. WE'RE GETTING HUNGRY

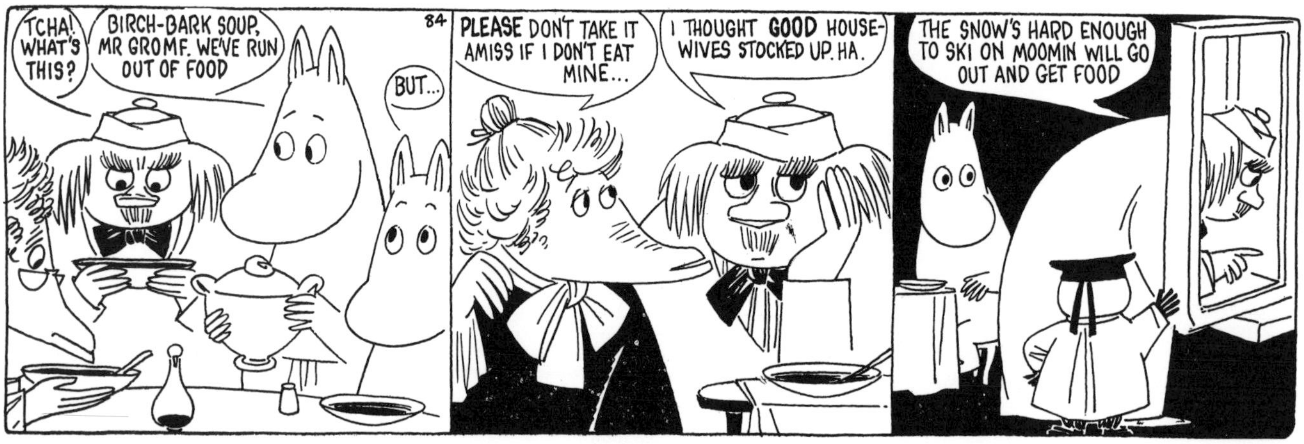
TCHA! WHAT'S THIS?
BIRCH-BARK SOUP, MR GROMF. WE'VE RUN OUT OF FOOD
84
BUT...
PLEASE DON'T TAKE IT AMISS IF I DON'T EAT MINE...
I THOUGHT GOOD HOUSE-WIVES STOCKED UP. HA.
THE SNOW'S HARD ENOUGH TO SKI ON MOOMIN WILL GO OUT AND GET FOOD

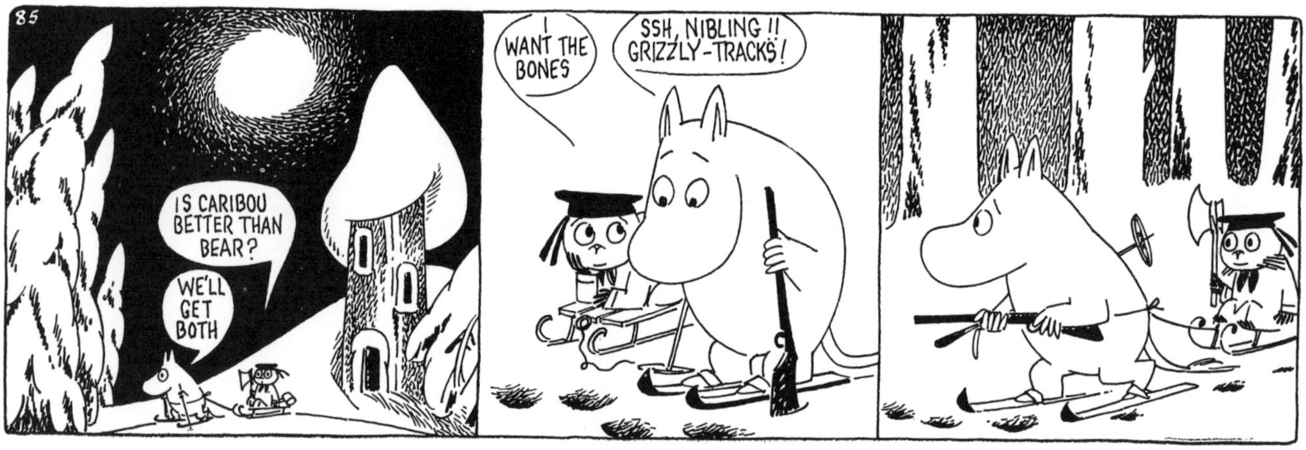
85
IS CARIBOU BETTER THAN BEAR?
WE'LL GET BOTH
I WANT THE BONES
SSH, NIBLING!! GRIZZLY-TRACKS!

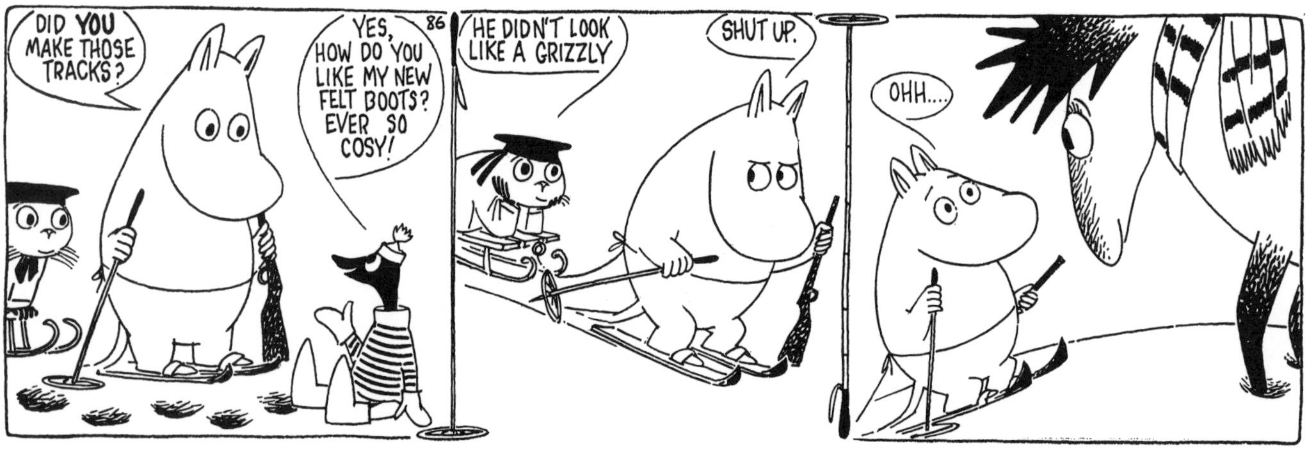
DID YOU MAKE THOSE TRACKS?
86
YES, HOW DO YOU LIKE MY NEW FELT BOOTS? EVER SO COSY!
HE DIDN'T LOOK LIKE A GRIZZLY
SHUT UP.
OHH....

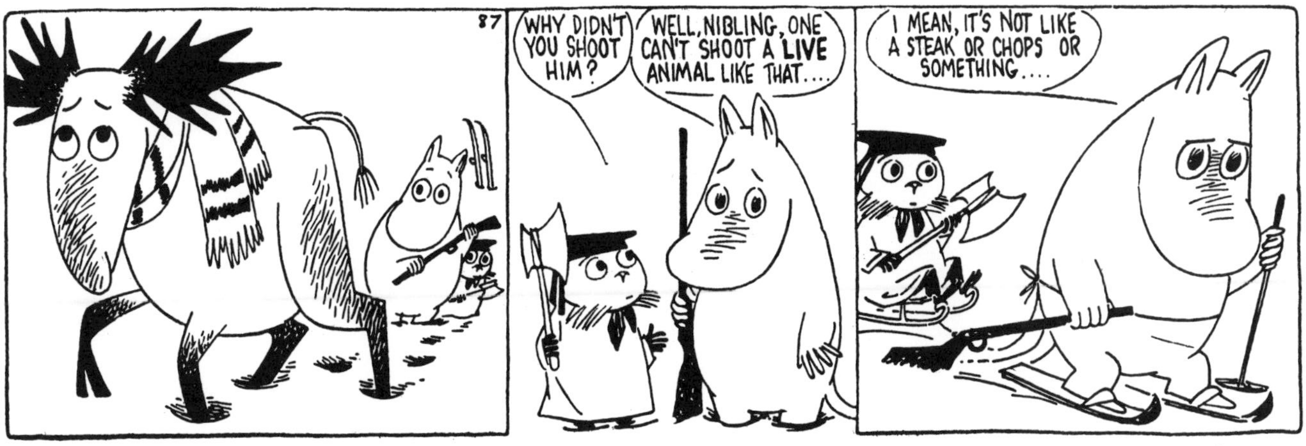
87
WHY DIDN'T YOU SHOOT HIM?
WELL, NIBLING, ONE CAN'T SHOOT A **LIVE** ANIMAL LIKE THAT....
I MEAN, IT'S NOT LIKE A STEAK OR CHOPS OR SOMETHING....

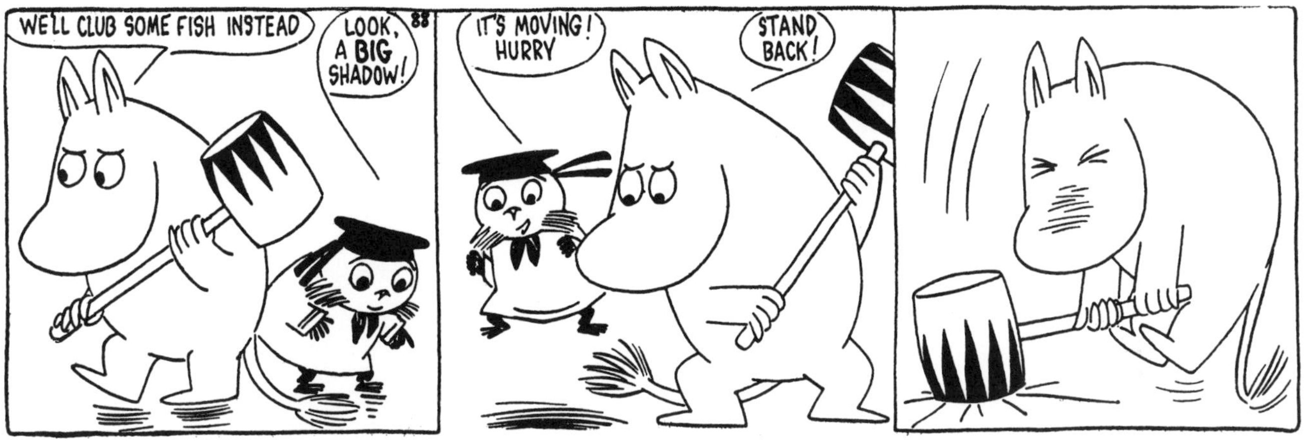
WE'LL CLUB SOME FISH INSTEAD
LOOK, A **BIG** SHADOW!
88
IT'S MOVING! HURRY
STAND BACK!

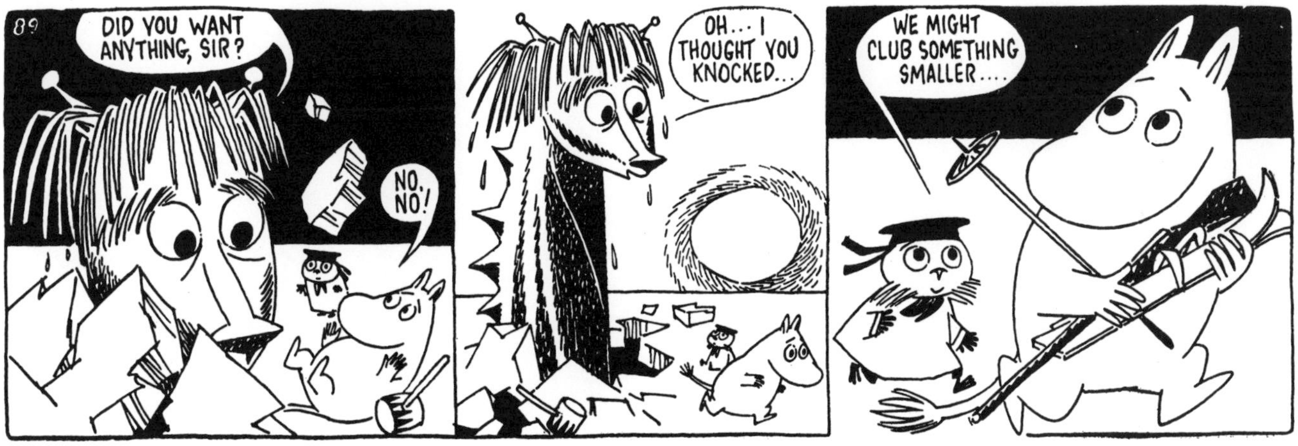
89
DID YOU WANT ANYTHING, SIR?
NO, NO!
OH... I THOUGHT YOU KNOCKED...
WE MIGHT CLUB SOMETHING SMALLER....

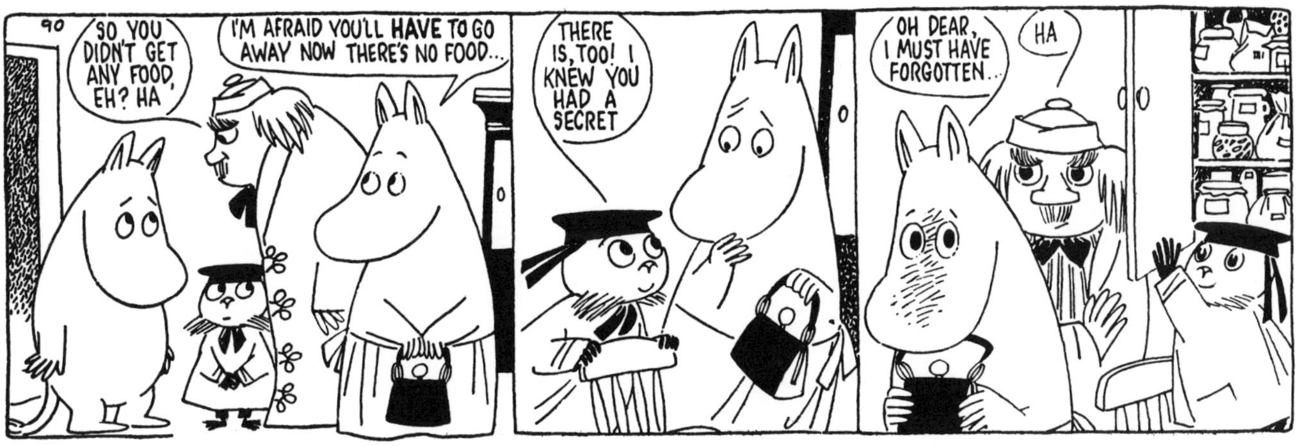
90
SO YOU DIDN'T GET ANY FOOD, EH? HA
I'M AFRAID YOU'LL **HAVE** TO GO AWAY NOW THERE'S NO FOOD...
THERE IS, TOO! I KNEW YOU HAD A SECRET
OH DEAR, I MUST HAVE FORGOTTEN...
HA

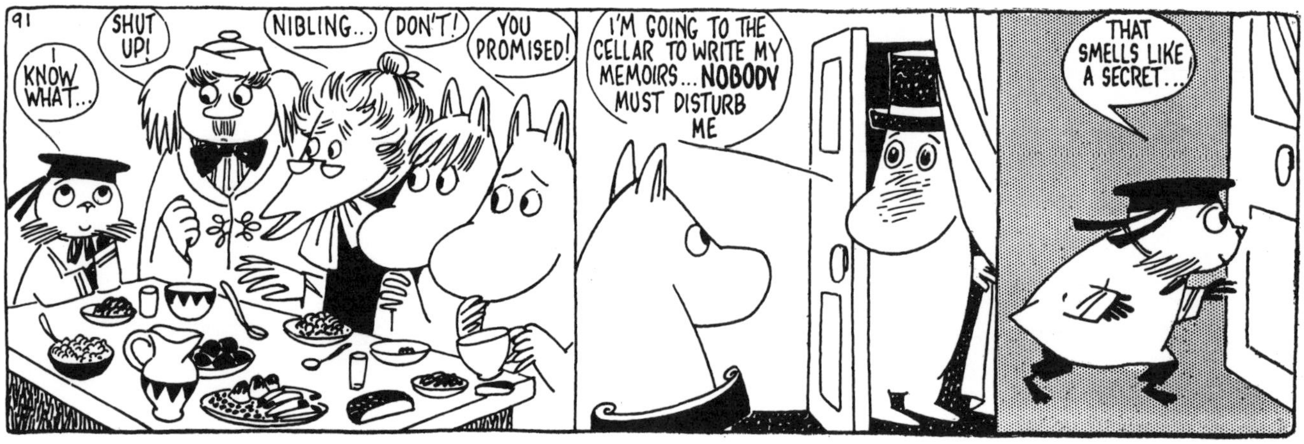
91
I KNOW WHAT...
SHUT UP!
NIBLING...
DON'T!
YOU PROMISED!
I'M GOING TO THE CELLAR TO WRITE MY MEMOIRS... NOBODY MUST DISTURB ME
THAT SMELLS LIKE A SECRET...

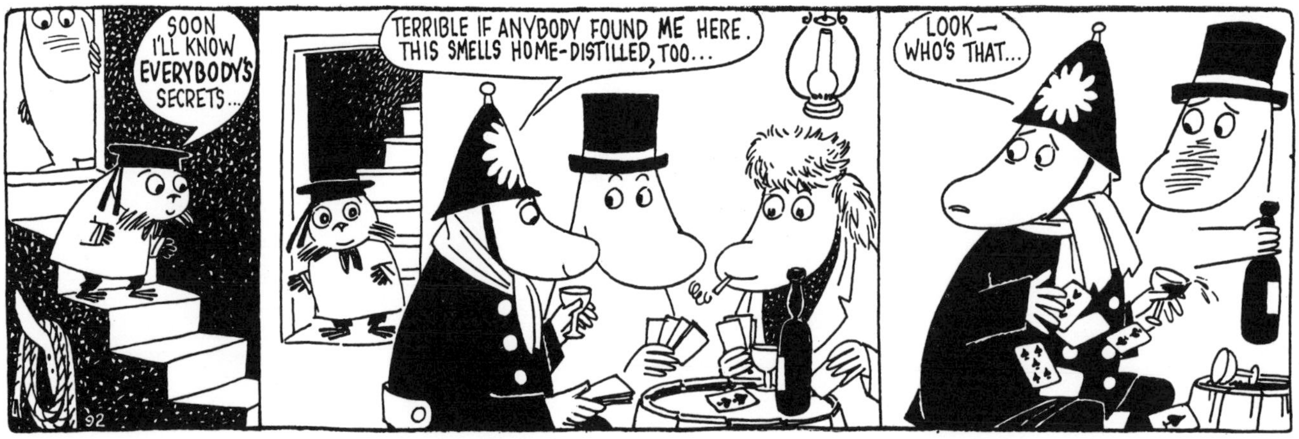
SOON I'LL KNOW EVERYBODY'S SECRETS...
92
TERRIBLE IF ANYBODY FOUND ME HERE. THIS SMELLS HOME-DISTILLED, TOO...
LOOK— WHO'S THAT...

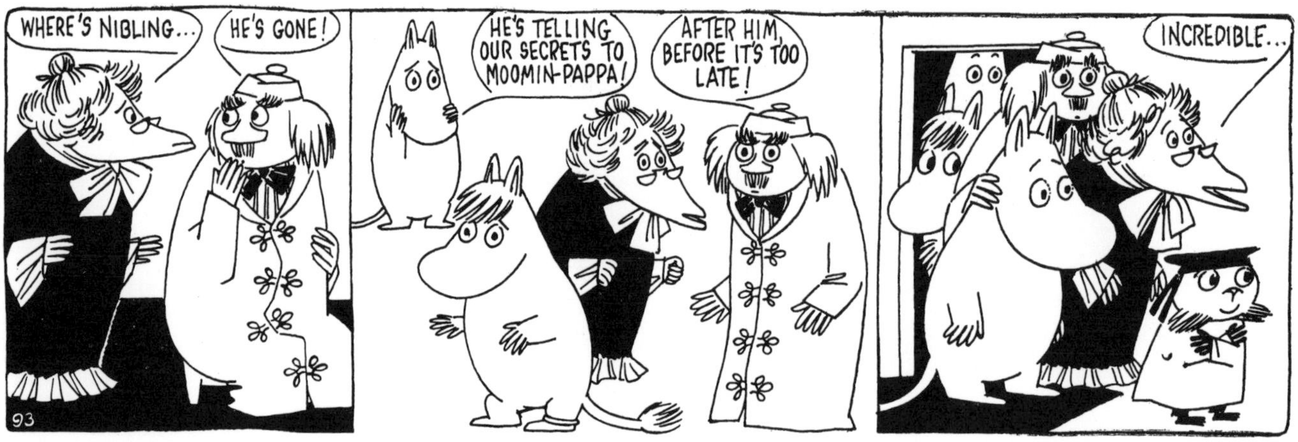
WHERE'S NIBLING...
HE'S GONE!
93
HE'S TELLING OUR SECRETS TO MOOMIN-PAPPA!
AFTER HIM, BEFORE IT'S TOO LATE!
INCREDIBLE...

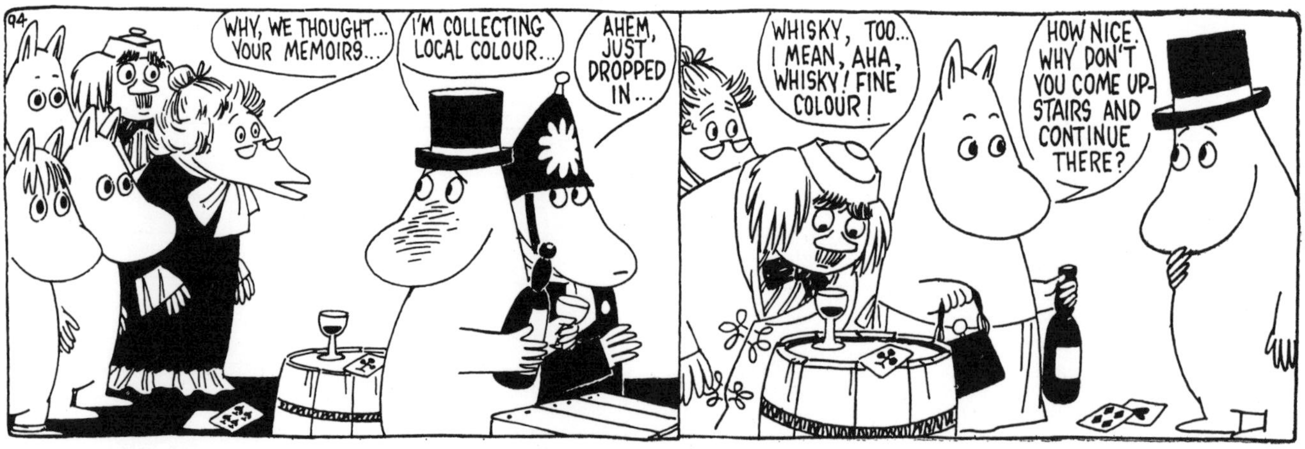
94
WHY, WE THOUGHT... YOUR MEMOIRS...
I'M COLLECTING LOCAL COLOUR...
AHEM, JUST DROPPED IN...
WHISKY, TOO... I MEAN, AHA, WHISKY! FINE COLOUR!
HOW NICE. WHY DON'T YOU COME UP-STAIRS AND CONTINUE THERE?

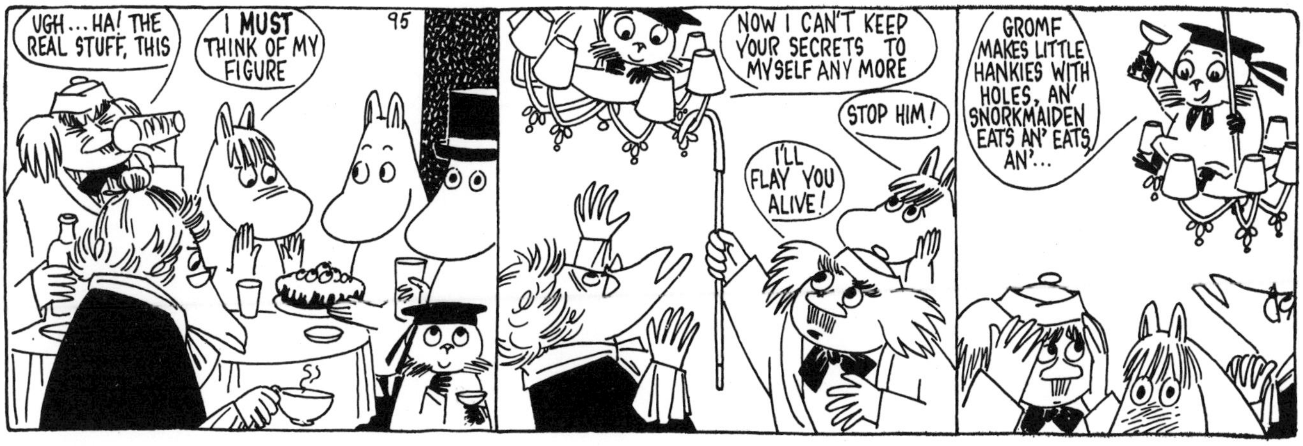
UGH... HA! THE REAL STUFF, THIS
I **MUST** THINK OF MY FIGURE
NOW I CAN'T KEEP YOUR SECRETS TO MYSELF ANY MORE
STOP HIM!
I'LL FLAY YOU ALIVE!
GROMF MAKES LITTLE HANKIES WITH HOLES, AN' SNORKMAIDEN EATS AN' EATS AN'...

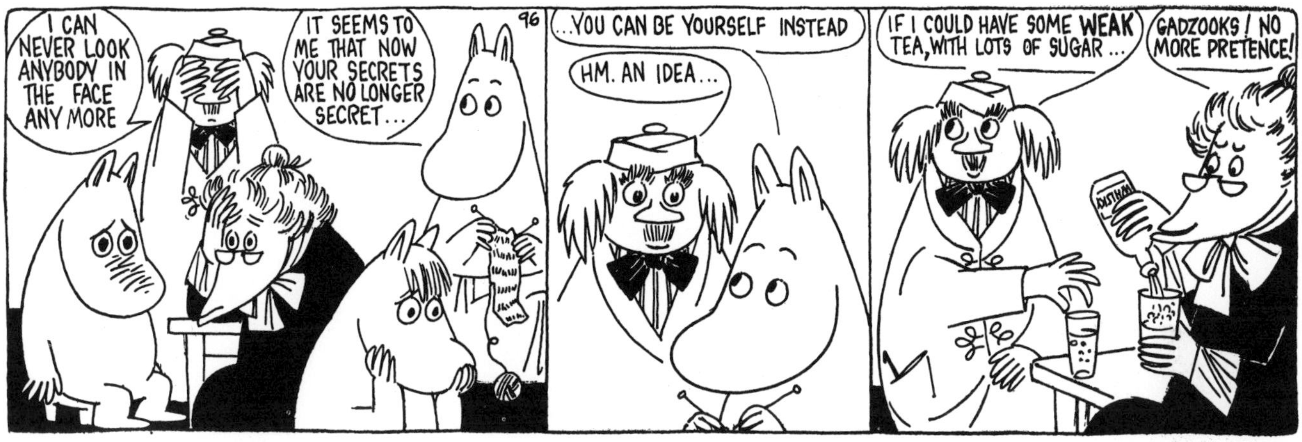
I CAN NEVER LOOK ANYBODY IN THE FACE ANY MORE
IT SEEMS TO ME THAT NOW YOUR SECRETS ARE NO LONGER SECRET...
...YOU CAN BE YOURSELF INSTEAD
HM. AN IDEA...
IF I COULD HAVE SOME **WEAK** TEA, WITH LOTS OF SUGAR...
GADZOOKS! NO MORE PRETENCE!

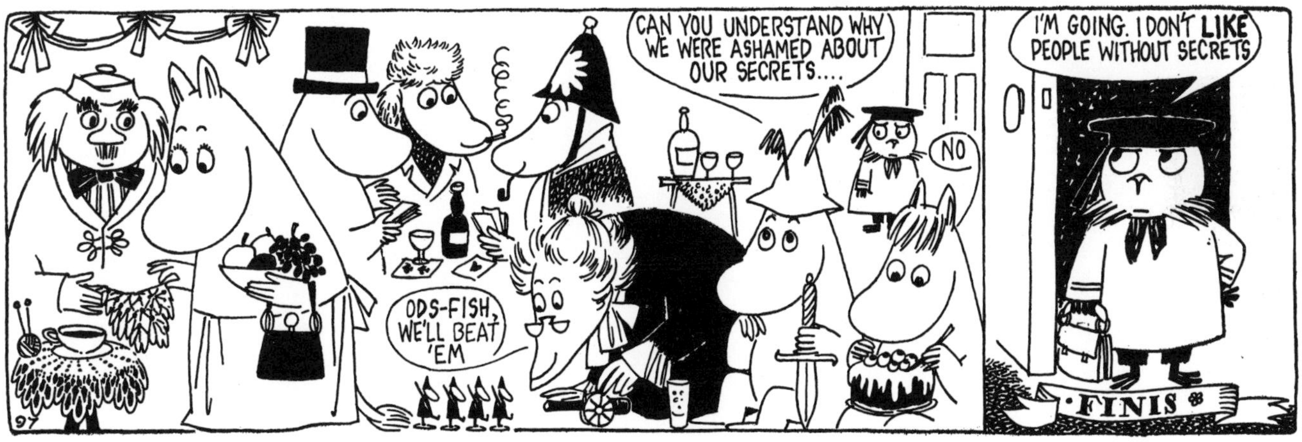
CAN YOU UNDERSTAND WHY WE WERE ASHAMED ABOUT OUR SECRETS....
NO
ODS-FISH, WE'LL BEAT 'EM
I'M GOING. I DON'T **LIKE** PEOPLE WITHOUT SECRETS
FINIS

20. Moomin Under Sail

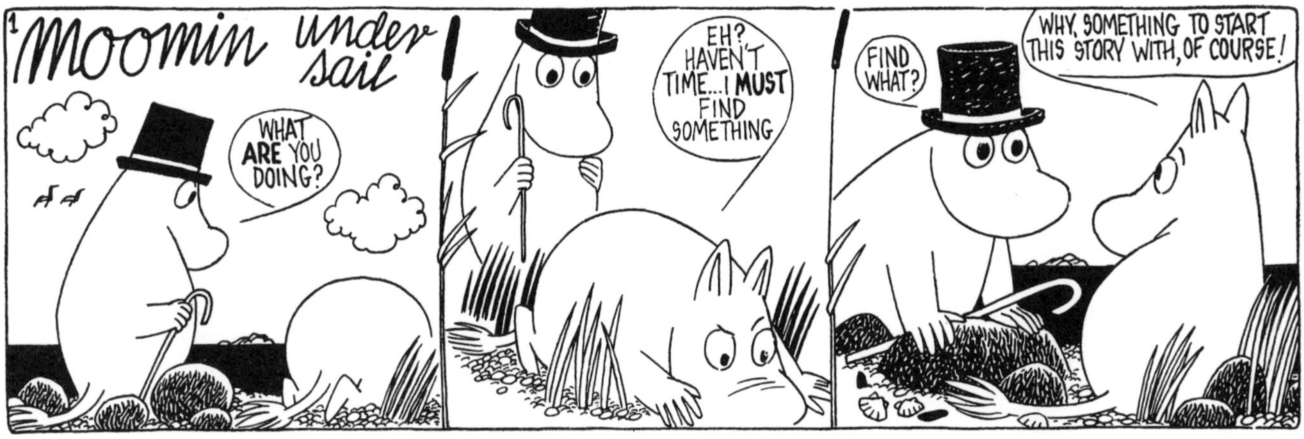
1
Moomin under sail
WHAT ARE YOU DOING?
EH? HAVEN'T TIME...I MUST FIND SOMETHING
FIND WHAT?
WHY, SOMETHING TO START THIS STORY WITH, OF COURSE!

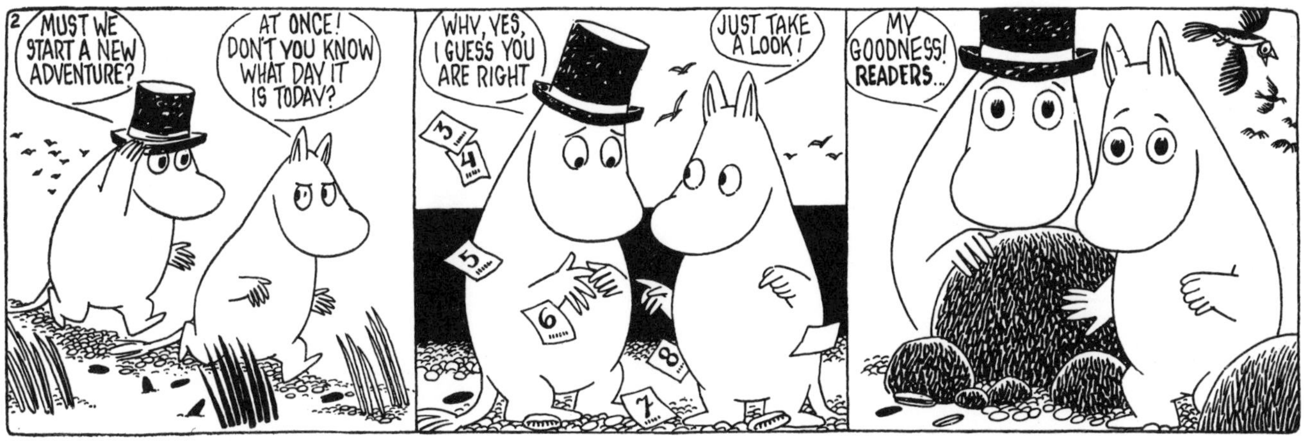
2
MUST WE START A NEW ADVENTURE?
AT ONCE! DON'T YOU KNOW WHAT DAY IT IS TODAY?
WHY, YES, I GUESS YOU ARE RIGHT
JUST TAKE A LOOK!
MY GOODNESS! READERS...

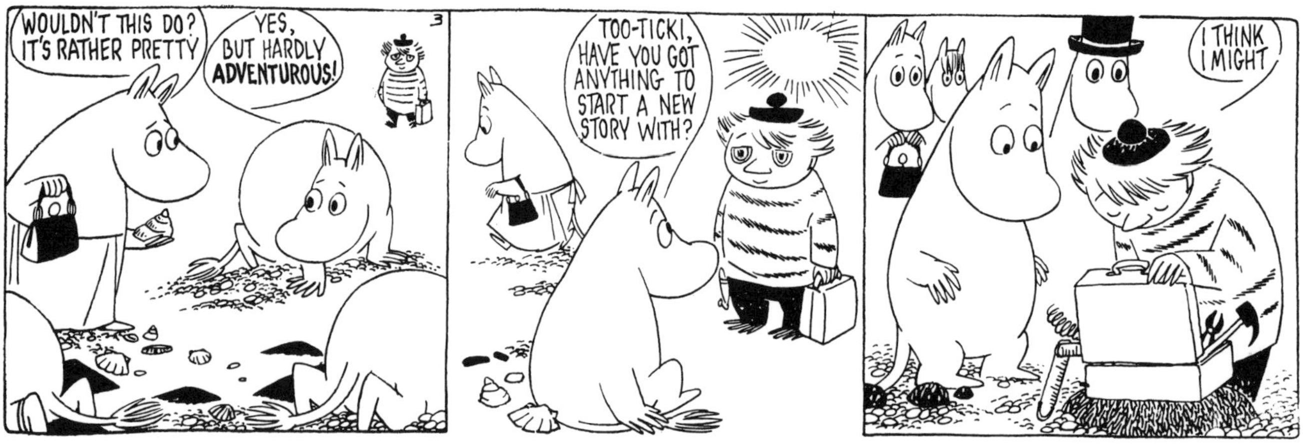
WOULDN'T THIS DO? IT'S RATHER PRETTY
YES, BUT HARDLY **ADVENTUROUS!**
TOO-TICKI, HAVE YOU GOT ANYTHING TO START A NEW STORY WITH?
I THINK I MIGHT

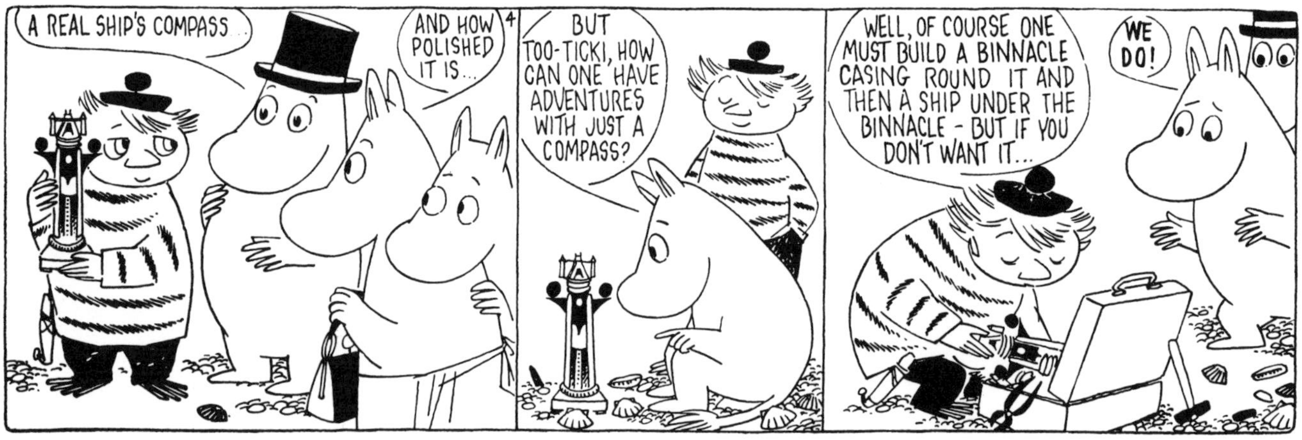
A REAL SHIP'S COMPASS...
AND HOW POLISHED IT IS...
BUT TOO-TICKI, HOW CAN ONE HAVE ADVENTURES WITH JUST A COMPASS?
WELL, OF COURSE ONE MUST BUILD A BINNACLE CASING ROUND IT AND THEN A SHIP UNDER THE BINNACLE - BUT IF YOU DON'T WANT IT...
WE DO!

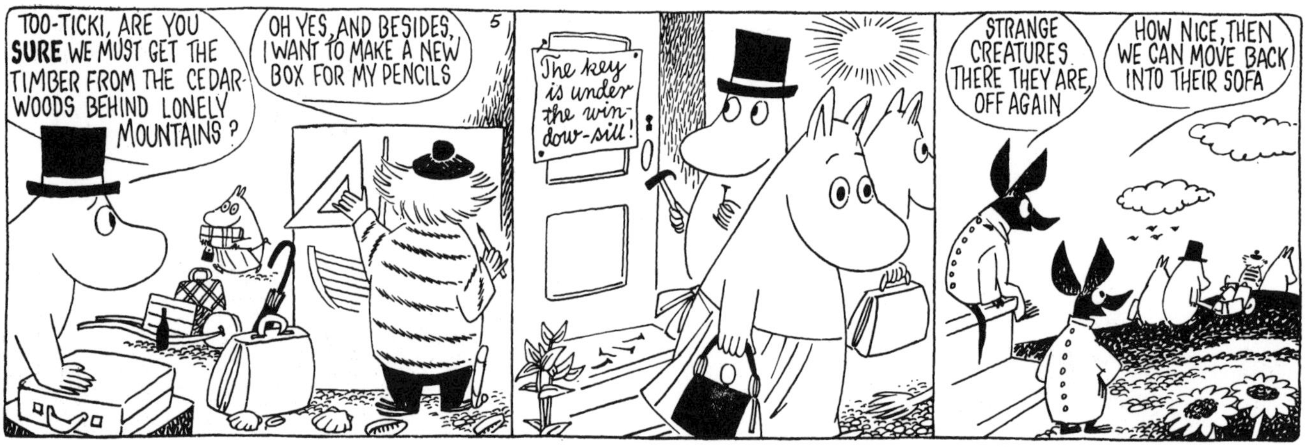
TOO-TICKI, ARE YOU **SURE** WE MUST GET THE TIMBER FROM THE CEDAR-WOODS BEHIND LONELY MOUNTAINS?
OH YES, AND BESIDES, I WANT TO MAKE A NEW BOX FOR MY PENCILS
The key is under the win-dow-sill!
STRANGE CREATURES. THERE THEY ARE, OFF AGAIN
HOW NICE, THEN WE CAN MOVE BACK INTO THEIR SOFA

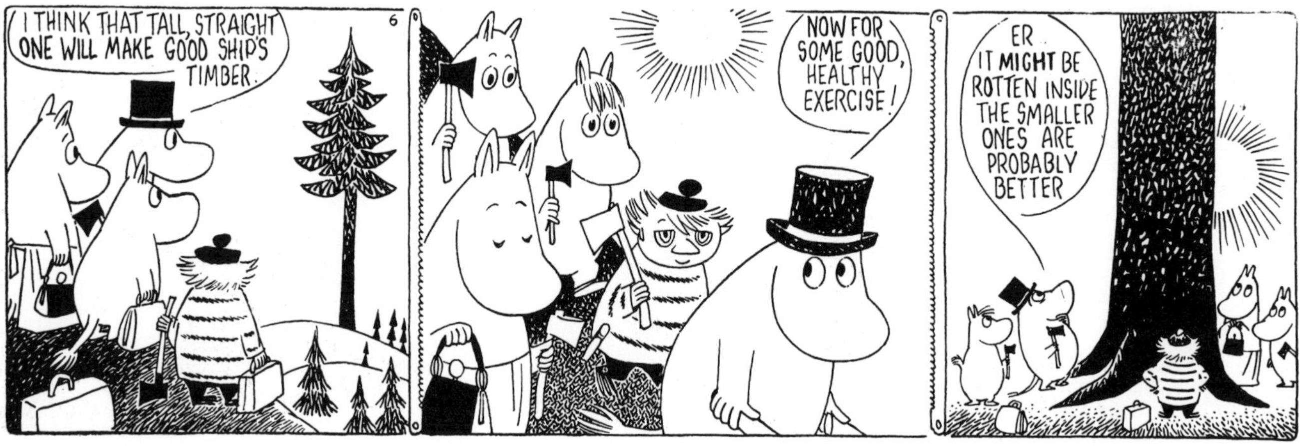
I THINK THAT TALL, STRAIGHT ONE WILL MAKE GOOD SHIP'S TIMBER.
NOW FOR SOME GOOD, HEALTHY EXERCISE!
ER... IT **MIGHT** BE ROTTEN INSIDE. THE SMALLER ONES ARE PROBABLY BETTER

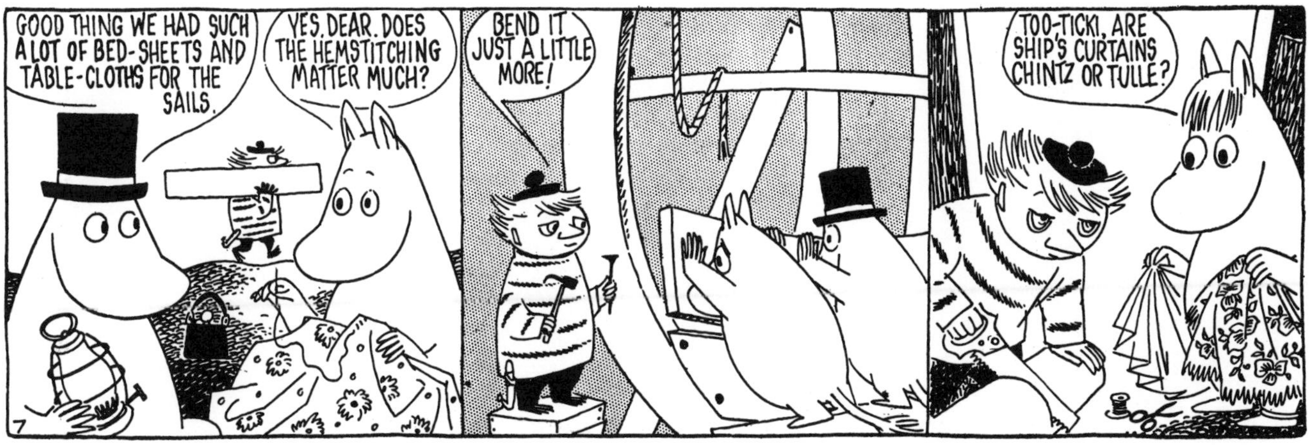
7
GOOD THING WE HAD SUCH A LOT OF BED-SHEETS AND TABLE-CLOTHS FOR THE SAILS.
YES, DEAR. DOES THE HEMSTITCHING MATTER MUCH?
BEND IT JUST A LITTLE MORE!
TOO-TICKI, ARE SHIP'S CURTAINS CHINTZ OR TULLE?

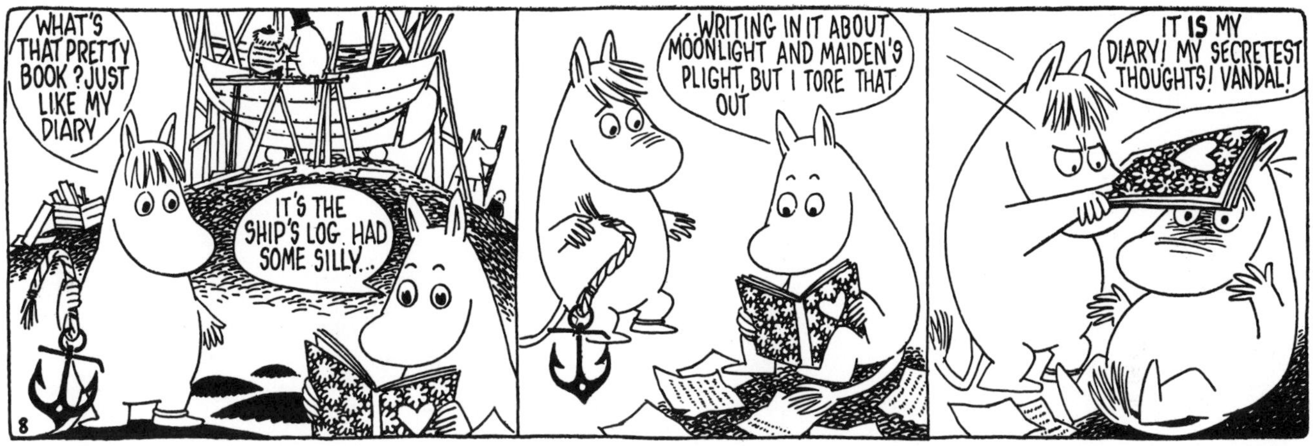
8
WHAT'S THAT PRETTY BOOK? JUST LIKE MY DIARY
IT'S THE SHIP'S LOG. HAD SOME SILLY...
WRITING IN IT ABOUT MOONLIGHT AND MAIDEN'S PLIGHT, BUT I TORE THAT OUT
IT IS MY DIARY! MY SECRETEST THOUGHTS! VANDAL!

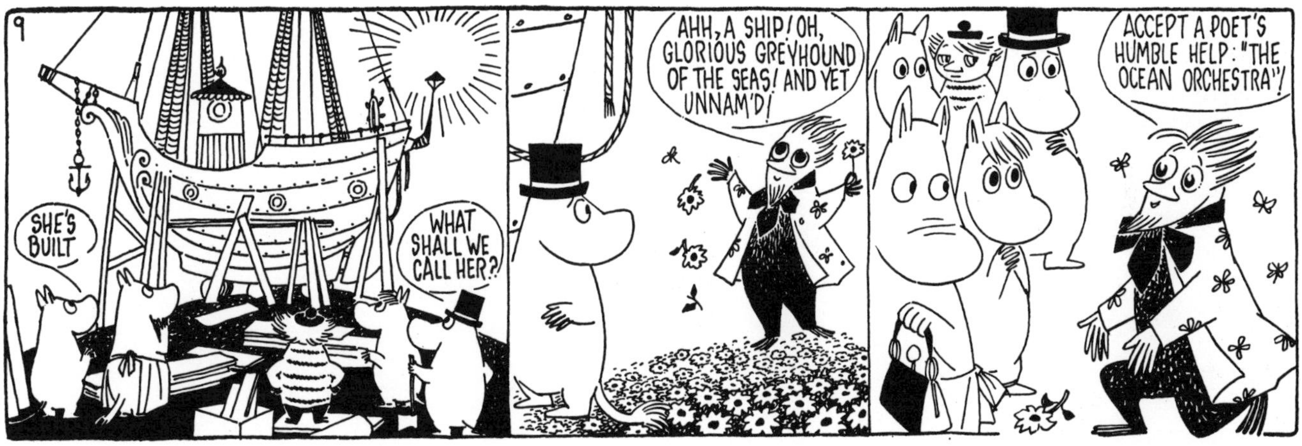
9
SHE'S BUILT
WHAT SHALL WE CALL HER?
AHH, A SHIP! OH, GLORIOUS GREYHOUND OF THE SEAS! AND YET UNNAM'D!
ACCEPT A POET'S HUMBLE HELP: "THE OCEAN ORCHESTRA"!

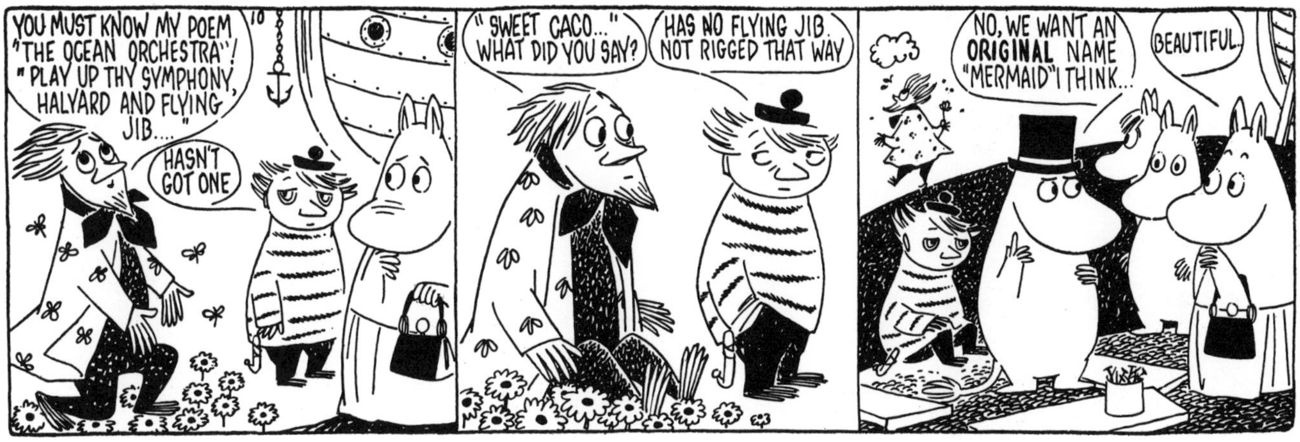
YOU MUST KNOW MY POEM "THE OCEAN ORCHESTRA"! "PLAY UP THY SYMPHONY, HALYARD AND FLYING JIB...."
10
HASN'T GOT ONE
"SWEET CACO..." WHAT DID YOU SAY?
HAS NO FLYING JIB. NOT RIGGED THAT WAY
NO, WE WANT AN ORIGINAL NAME "MERMAID" I THINK...
BEAUTIFUL.

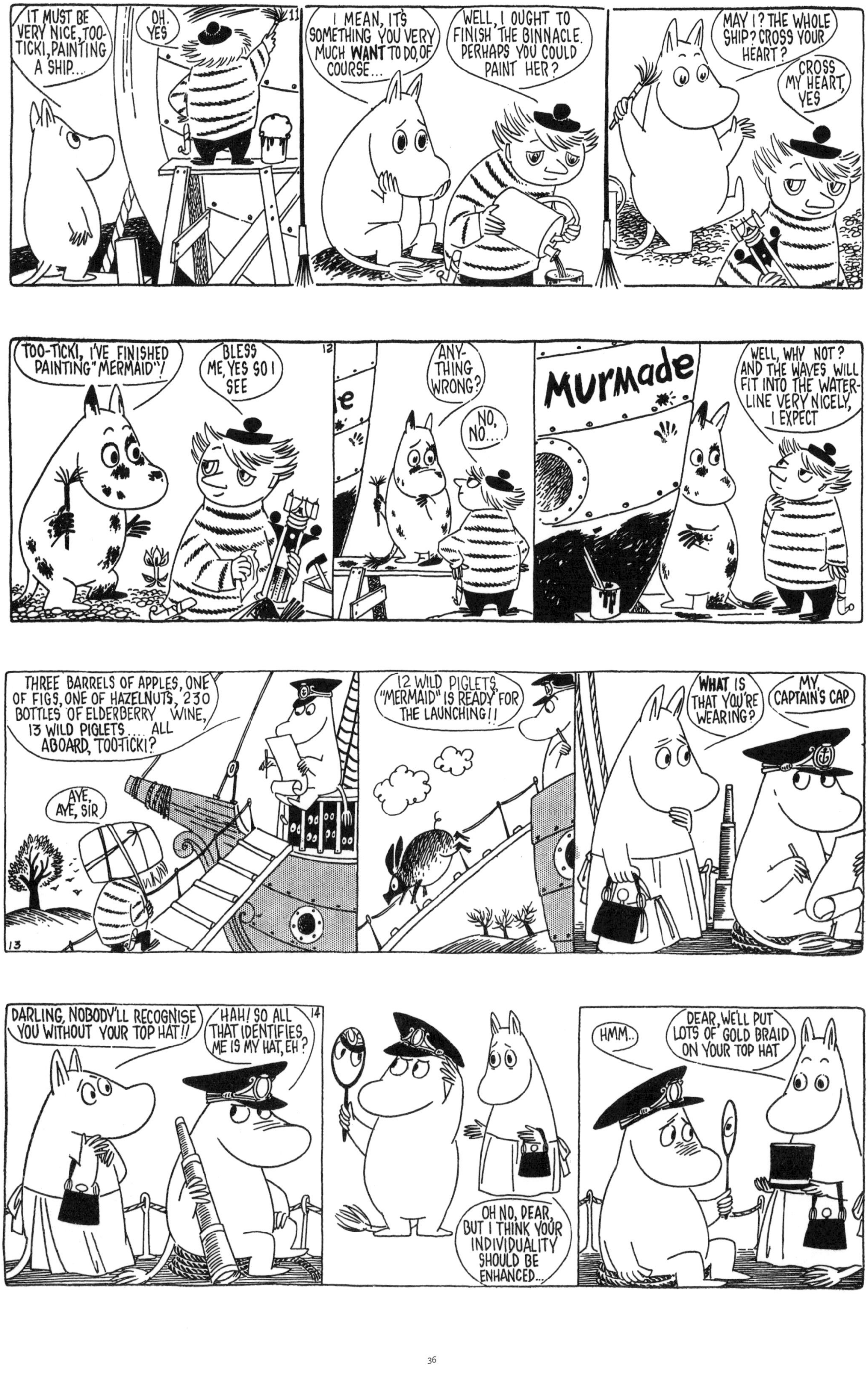
IT MUST BE VERY NICE, TOO-TICKI, PAINTING A SHIP...
OH. YES
11
I MEAN, IT'S SOMETHING YOU VERY MUCH WANT TO DO, OF COURSE...
WELL, I OUGHT TO FINISH THE BINNACLE. PERHAPS YOU COULD PAINT HER?
MAY I? THE WHOLE SHIP? CROSS YOUR HEART?
CROSS MY HEART, YES
TOO-TICKI, I'VE FINISHED PAINTING "MERMAID"!
BLESS ME, YES SO I SEE
12
ANY-THING WRONG?
NO, NO....
Murmade
WELL, WHY NOT? AND THE WAVES WILL FIT INTO THE WATER-LINE VERY NICELY, I EXPECT
THREE BARRELS OF APPLES, ONE OF FIGS, ONE OF HAZELNUTS, 230 BOTTLES OF ELDERBERRY WINE, 13 WILD PIGLETS.... ALL ABOARD, TOO-TICKI?
AYE, AYE, SIR
13
12 WILD PIGLETS, "MERMAID" IS READY FOR THE LAUNCHING!!
WHAT IS THAT YOU'RE WEARING?
MY CAPTAIN'S CAP
DARLING, NOBODY'LL RECOGNISE YOU WITHOUT YOUR TOP HAT!!
HAH! SO ALL THAT IDENTIFIES ME IS MY HAT, EH?
14
OH NO, DEAR, BUT I THINK YOUR INDIVIDUALITY SHOULD BE ENHANCED...
HMM..
DEAR, WE'LL PUT LOTS OF GOLD BRAID ON YOUR TOP HAT

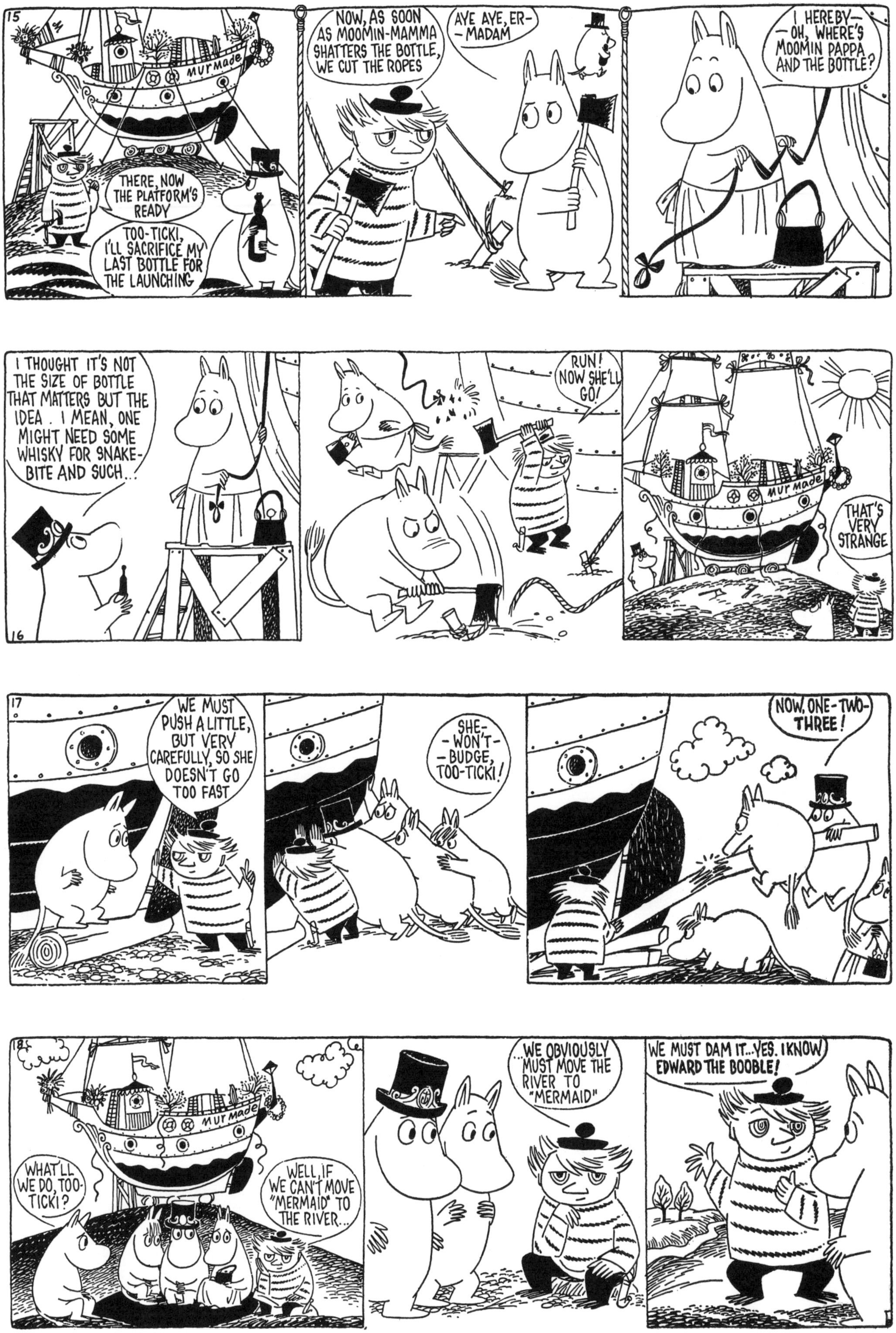
15
MUR MADE
THERE, NOW THE PLATFORM'S READY
TOO-TICKI, I'LL SACRIFICE MY LAST BOTTLE FOR THE LAUNCHING
NOW, AS SOON AS MOOMIN-MAMMA SHATTERS THE BOTTLE, WE CUT THE ROPES
AYE AYE, ER- —MADAM
I HEREBY— —OH, WHERE'S MOOMIN PAPPA AND THE BOTTLE?
I THOUGHT IT'S NOT THE SIZE OF BOTTLE THAT MATTERS BUT THE IDEA . I MEAN, ONE MIGHT NEED SOME WHISKY FOR SNAKE-BITE AND SUCH...
16
RUN! NOW SHE'LL GO!
MUR MADE
THAT'S VERY STRANGE
17
WE MUST PUSH A LITTLE, BUT VERY CAREFULLY, SO SHE DOESN'T GO TOO FAST
SHE- -WON'T- -BUDGE, TOO-TICKI!
NOW, ONE-TWO-THREE!
18
MUR MADE
WHAT'LL WE DO, TOO-TICKI?
WELL, IF WE CAN'T MOVE "MERMAID" TO THE RIVER...
...WE OBVIOUSLY MUST MOVE THE RIVER TO "MERMAID"
WE MUST DAM IT...YES. I KNOW! EDWARD THE BOOBLE!

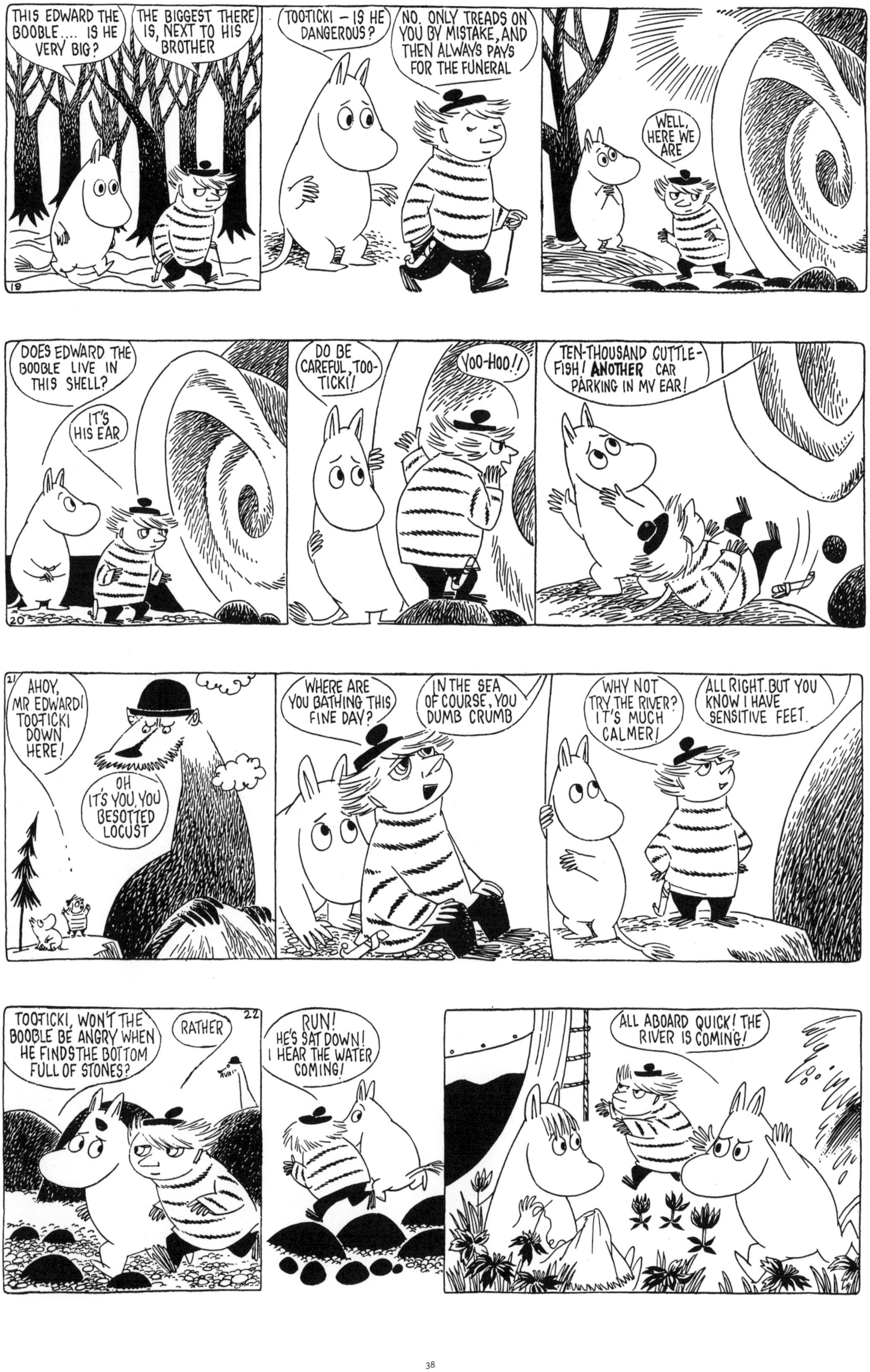
THIS EDWARD THE BOOBLE.... IS HE VERY BIG?
THE BIGGEST THERE IS, NEXT TO HIS BROTHER
19
TOOTICKI – IS HE DANGEROUS?
NO. ONLY TREADS ON YOU BY MISTAKE, AND THEN ALWAYS PAYS FOR THE FUNERAL
WELL, HERE WE ARE
DOES EDWARD THE BOOBLE LIVE IN THIS SHELL?
IT'S HIS EAR
20
DO BE CAREFUL, TOOTICKI!
YOO-HOO!!
TEN-THOUSAND CUTTLE-FISH! **ANOTHER** CAR PARKING IN MY EAR!
21
AHOY, MR EDWARD! TOOTICKI DOWN HERE!
OH IT'S YOU, YOU BESOTTED LOCUST
WHERE ARE YOU BATHING THIS FINE DAY?
IN THE SEA OF COURSE, YOU DUMB CRUMB
WHY NOT TRY THE RIVER? IT'S MUCH CALMER!
ALL RIGHT. BUT YOU KNOW I HAVE SENSITIVE FEET.
TOOTICKI, WON'T THE BOOBLE BE ANGRY WHEN HE FINDS THE BOTTOM FULL OF STONES?
RATHER
22
RUN! HE'S SAT DOWN! I HEAR THE WATER COMING!
ALL ABOARD QUICK! THE RIVER IS COMING!

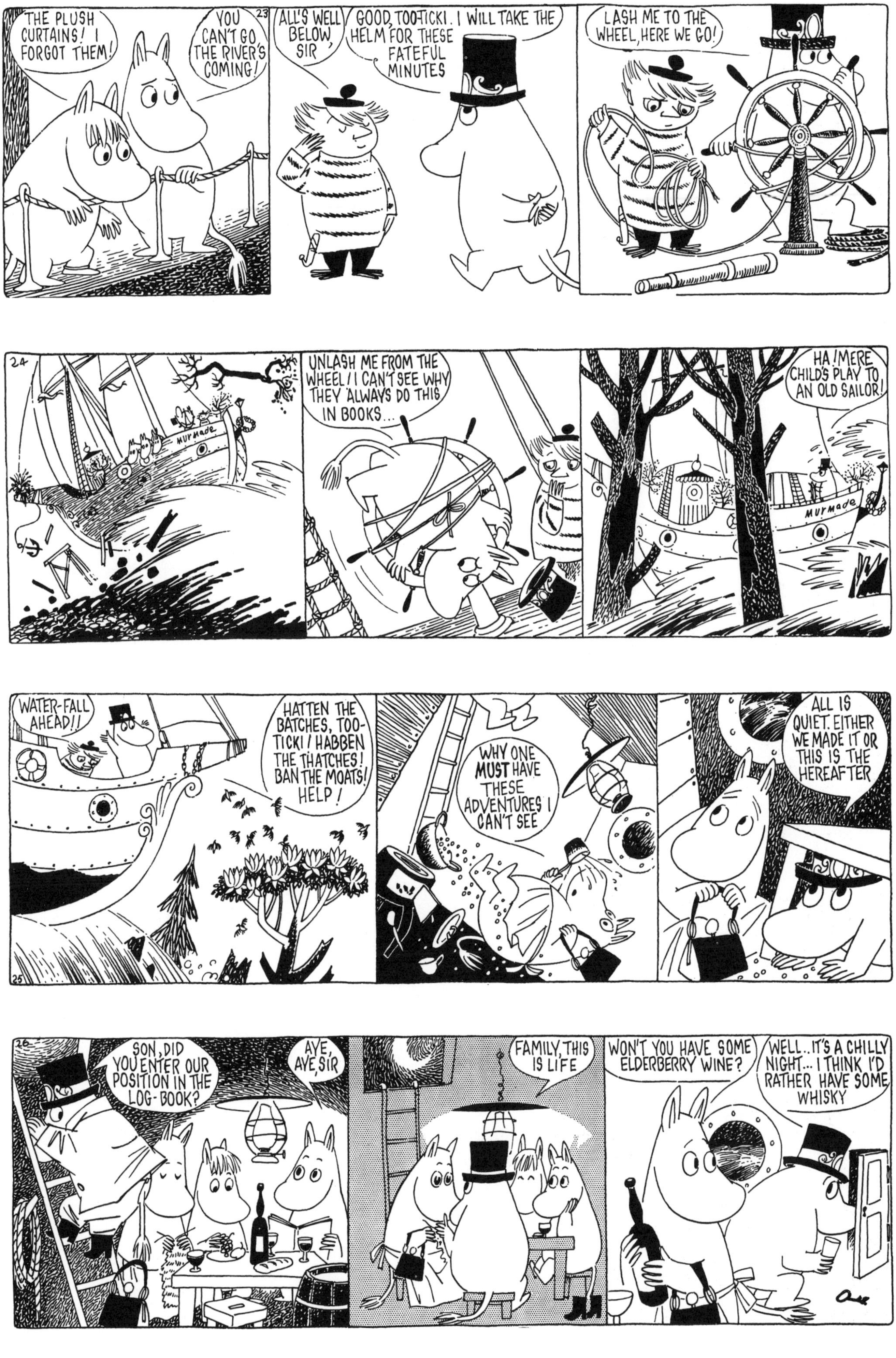
THE PLUSH CURTAINS! I FORGOT THEM!
YOU CAN'T GO THE RIVER'S COMING!
ALL'S WELL BELOW, SIR
GOOD, TOO-TICKI. I WILL TAKE THE HELM FOR THESE FATEFUL MINUTES
LASH ME TO THE WHEEL, HERE WE GO!
Murmade
UNLASH ME FROM THE WHEEL! I CAN'T SEE WHY THEY ALWAYS DO THIS IN BOOKS...
HA! MERE CHILD'S PLAY TO AN OLD SAILOR!
Murmade
WATER-FALL AHEAD!!
HATTEN THE BATCHES, TOO-TICKI! HABBEN THE THATCHES! BAN THE MOATS! HELP!
WHY ONE MUST HAVE THESE ADVENTURES I CAN'T SEE
ALL IS QUIET. EITHER WE MADE IT OR THIS IS THE HEREAFTER
SON, DID YOU ENTER OUR POSITION IN THE LOG-BOOK?
AYE, AYE, SIR
FAMILY, THIS IS LIFE
WON'T YOU HAVE SOME ELDERBERRY WINE?
WELL.. IT'S A CHILLY NIGHT... I THINK I'D RATHER HAVE SOME WHISKY

27
WHY, NOTHING COMES OUT..
IT'S EMPTY! SOMEBODY'S BEEN AT IT!!
NOT I!
I NAME NO NAMES! BUT SOMEBODY HAS DRUNK IT
28
FIRST IT'S THE WHISKY-NOW SOMEBODY'S BEEN AT MY TOBACCO, TOO!
THE CAKE I BAKED YESTERDAY-IT'S GONE!
THERE ARE FOOT-MARKS ON THE NEWLY TARRED POOP!
29
SEARCH THE SHIP WE MUST HAVE A STOWAWAY
WE'D BETTER WALK BACK TO BACK SO HE DOESN'T SNEAK UP ON US FROM BEHIND
MUST WE REALLY WALK LIKE THIS?
30
PSST! THERE'S A CRUNCHING SOUND COMING FROM THE LIFEBOAT....
WHEN I SAY GO, TOO-TICKI, YANK OFF THE TARPAULIN!

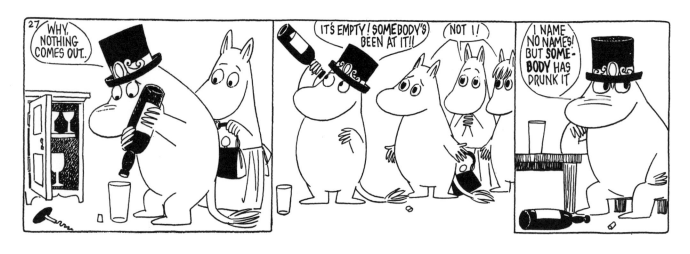

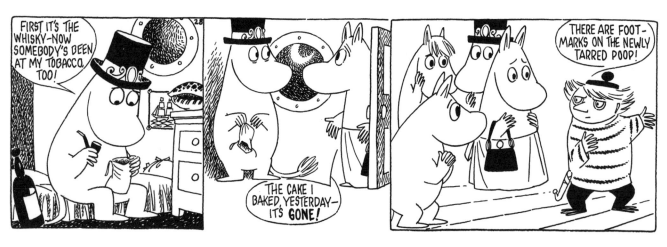

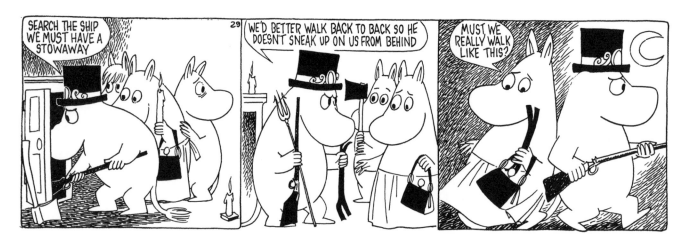

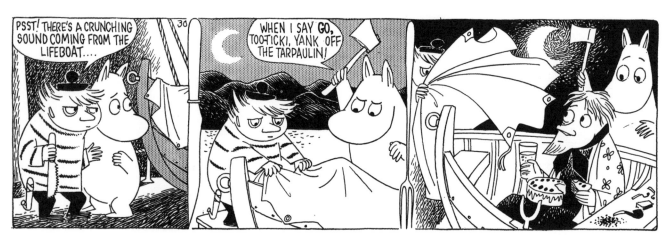

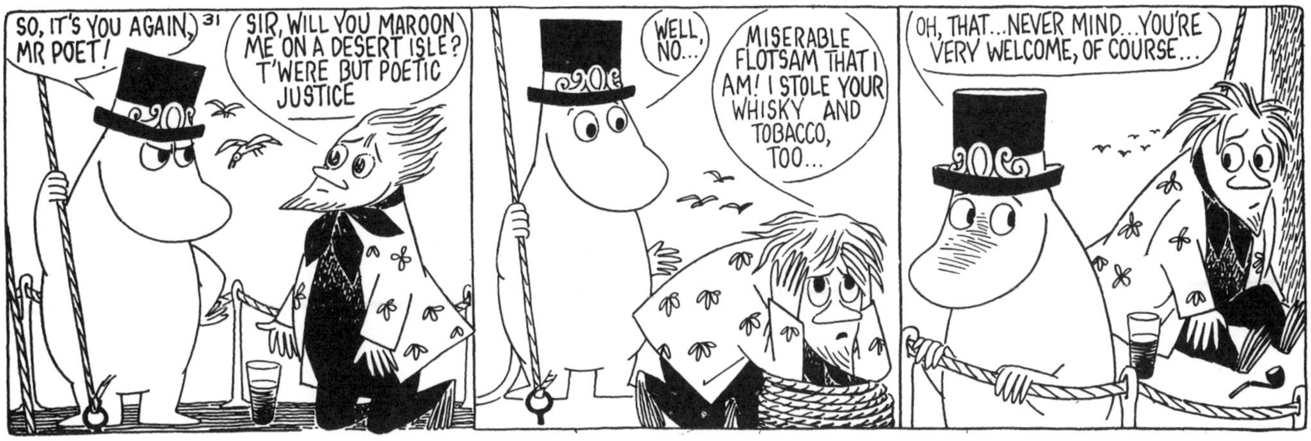
31
SO, IT'S YOU AGAIN, MR POET!
SIR, WILL YOU MAROON ME ON A DESERT ISLE? T'WERE BUT POETIC JUSTICE
WELL, NO...
MISERABLE FLOTSAM THAT I AM! I STOLE YOUR WHISKY AND TOBACCO, TOO...
OH, THAT...NEVER MIND...YOU'RE VERY WELCOME, OF COURSE...

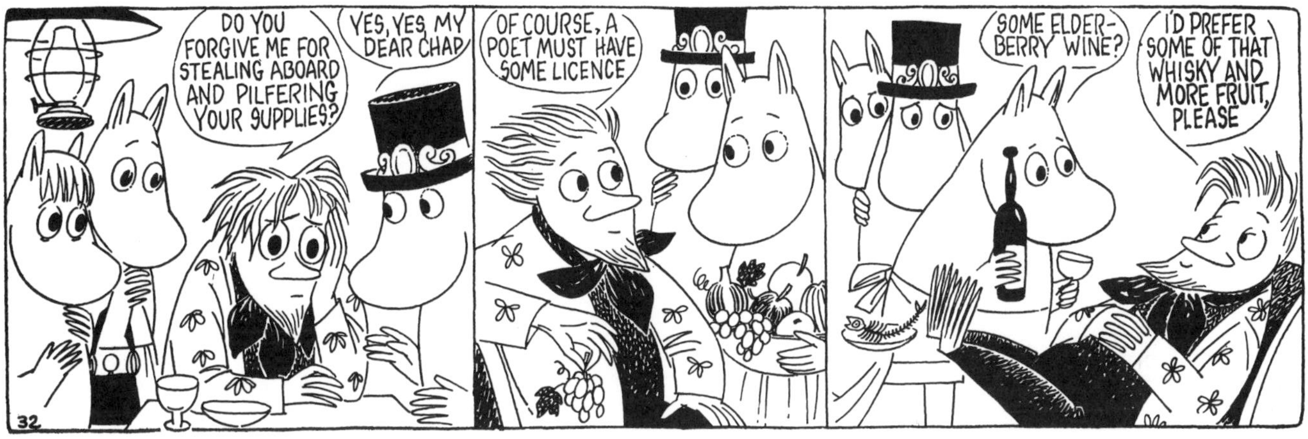
32
DO YOU FORGIVE ME FOR STEALING ABOARD AND PILFERING YOUR SUPPLIES?
YES, YES, MY DEAR CHAP
OF COURSE, A POET MUST HAVE SOME LICENCE
SOME ELDER-BERRY WINE?
I'D PREFER SOME OF THAT WHISKY AND MORE FRUIT, PLEASE

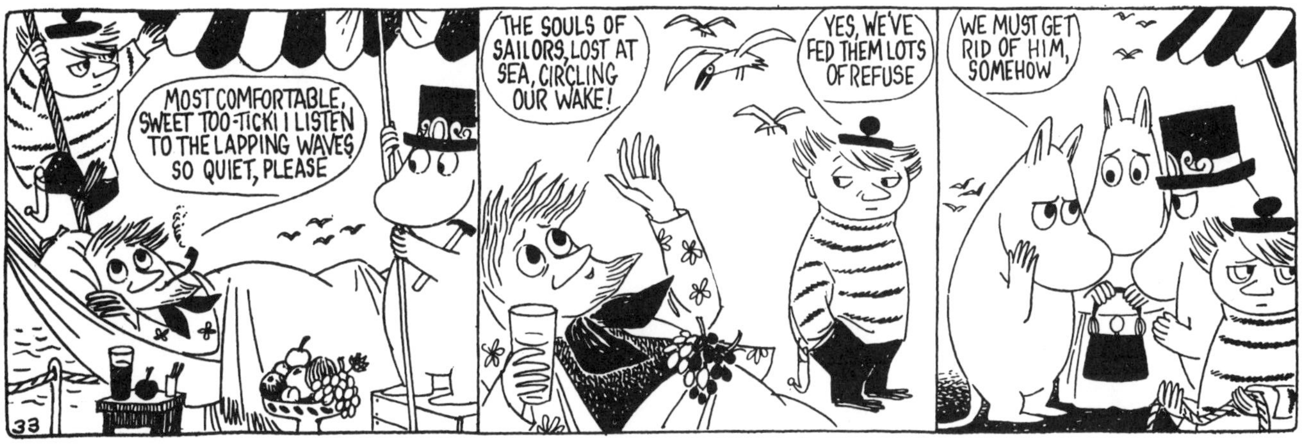
33
MOST COMFORTABLE, SWEET TOO-TICKI I LISTEN TO THE LAPPING WAVES SO QUIET, PLEASE
THE SOULS OF SAILORS, LOST AT SEA, CIRCLING OUR WAKE!
YES, WE'VE FED THEM LOTS OF REFUSE
WE MUST GET RID OF HIM, SOMEHOW

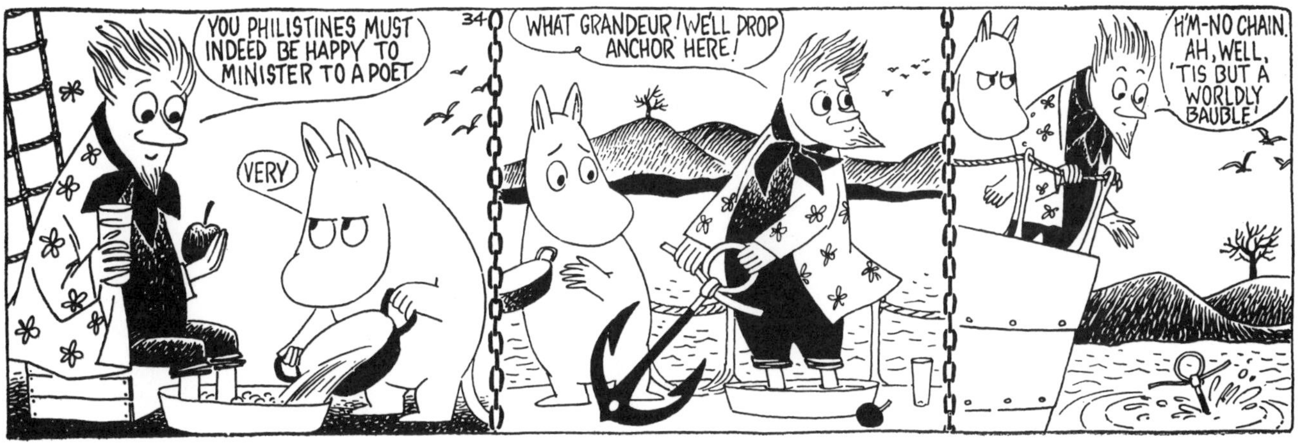
34
YOU PHILISTINES MUST INDEED BE HAPPY TO MINISTER TO A POET
VERY
WHAT GRANDEUR! WE'LL DROP ANCHOR HERE!
H'M-NO CHAIN. AH, WELL, 'TIS BUT A WORLDLY BAUBLE!

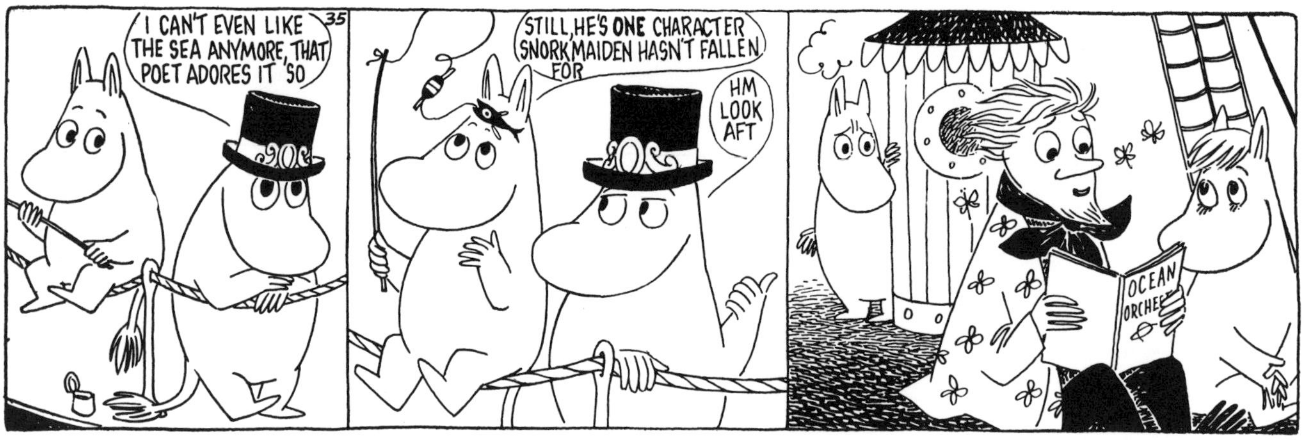
35
I CAN'T EVEN LIKE THE SEA ANYMORE, THAT POET ADORES IT SO
STILL, HE'S ONE CHARACTER SNORKMAIDEN HASN'T FALLEN FOR
HM LOOK AFT
OCEAN ORCHE

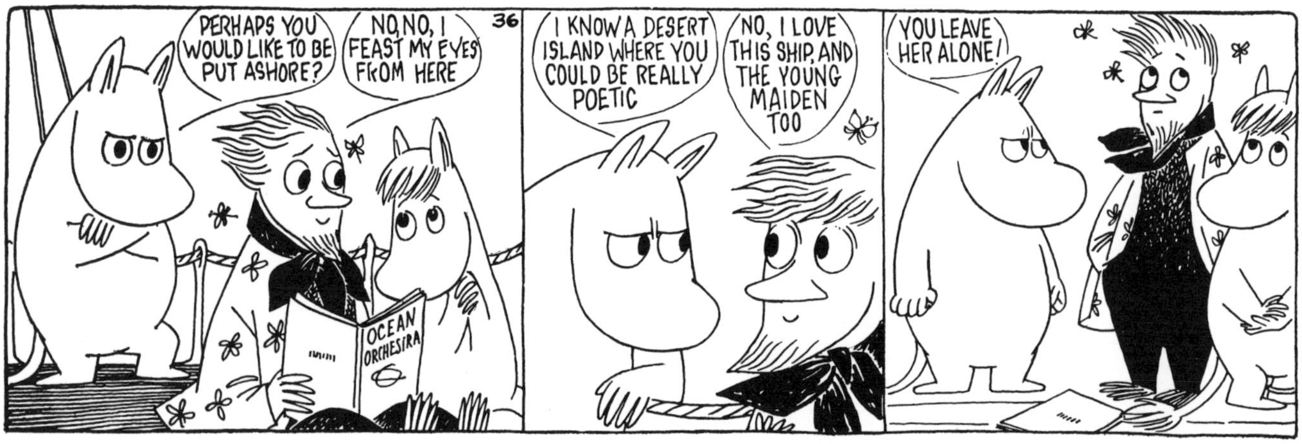
36
PERHAPS YOU WOULD LIKE TO BE PUT ASHORE?
NO, NO, I FEAST MY EYES FROM HERE
OCEAN ORCHESTRA
I KNOW A DESERT ISLAND WHERE YOU COULD BE REALLY POETIC
NO, I LOVE THIS SHIP, AND THE YOUNG MAIDEN TOO
YOU LEAVE HER ALONE!

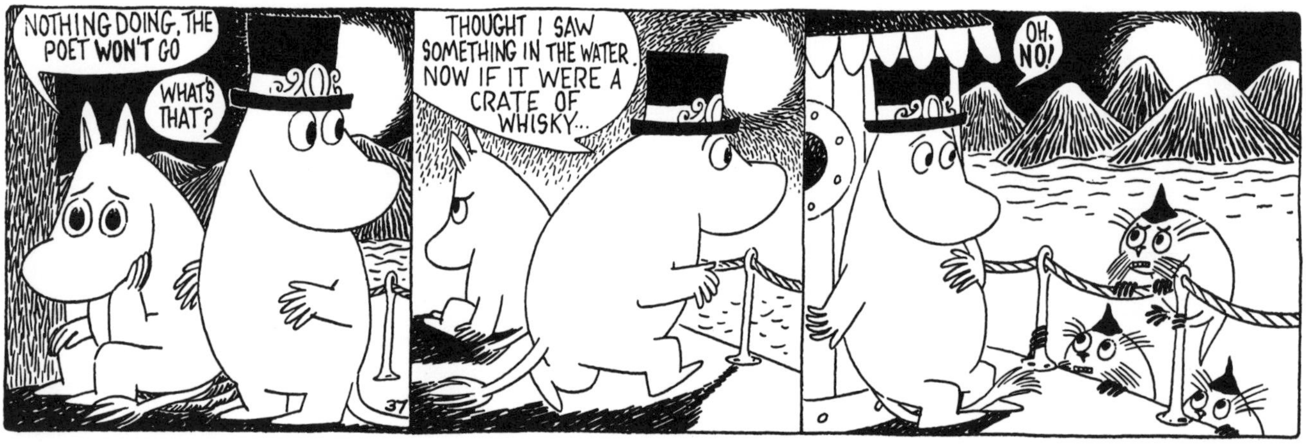
NOTHING DOING, THE POET WON'T GO
WHAT'S THAT?
37
THOUGHT I SAW SOMETHING IN THE WATER. NOW IF IT WERE A CRATE OF WHISKY...
OH, NO!

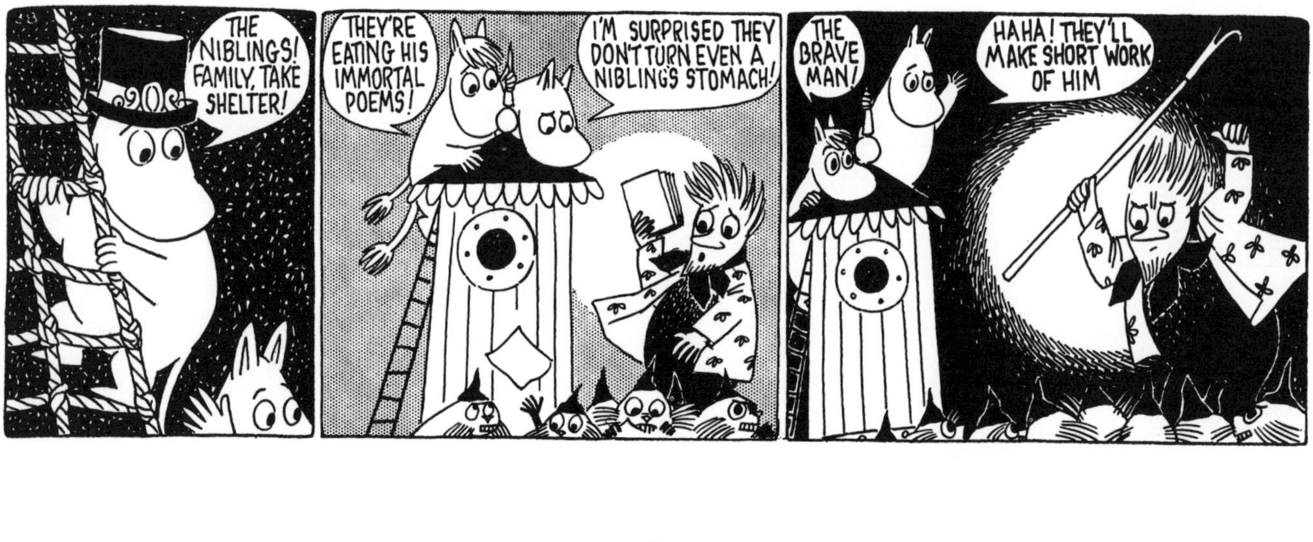
38
THE NIBLINGS! FAMILY, TAKE SHELTER!
THEY'RE EATING HIS IMMORTAL POEMS!
I'M SURPRISED THEY DON'T TURN EVEN A NIBLING'S STOMACH!
THE BRAVE MAN!
HAHA! THEY'LL MAKE SHORT WORK OF HIM

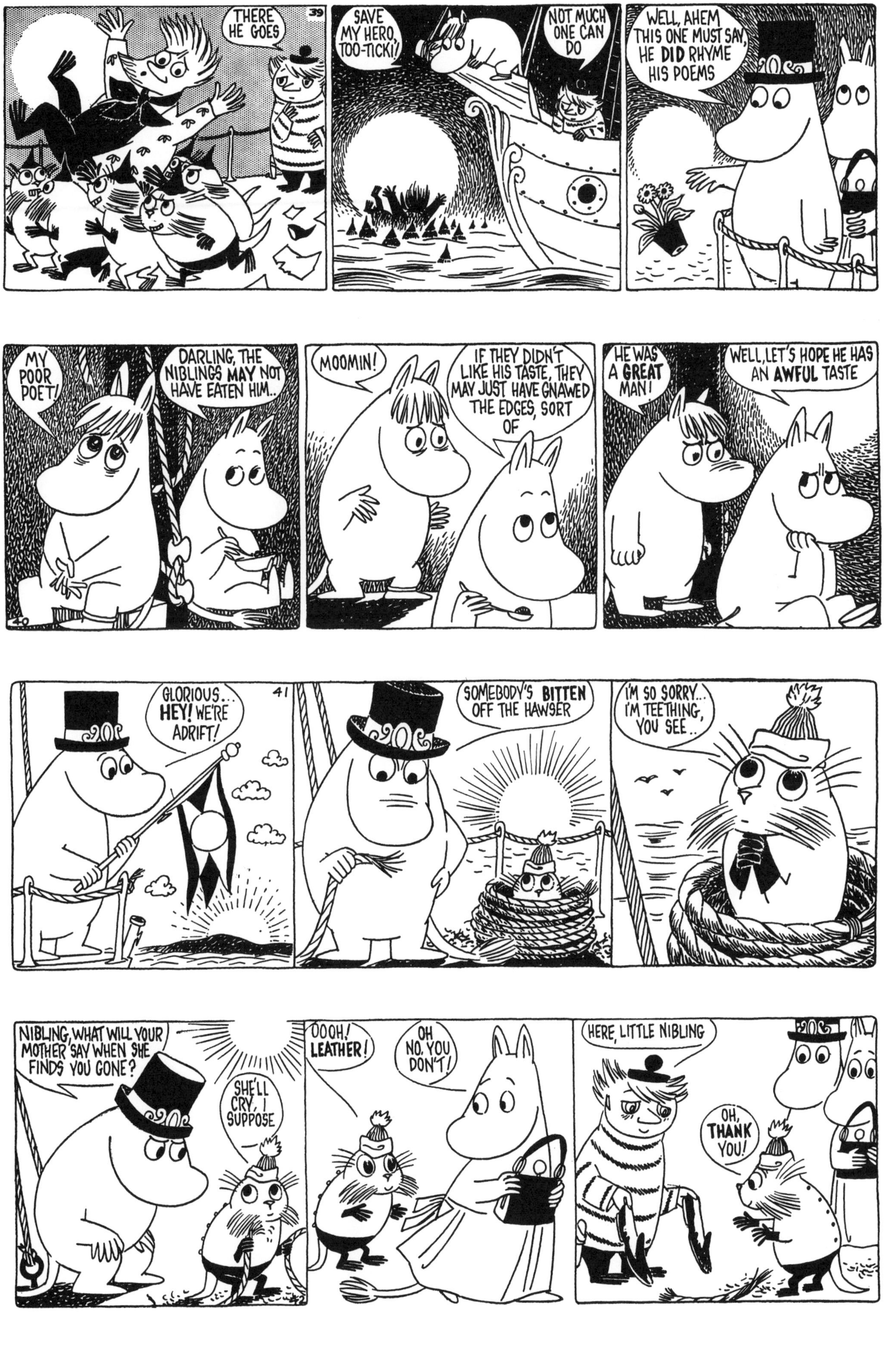
THERE HE GOES
SAVE MY HERO, TOO-TICKI!
NOT MUCH ONE CAN DO
WELL, AHEM THIS ONE MUST SAY, HE **DID** RHYME HIS POEMS
MY POOR POET!
DARLING, THE NIBLINGS **MAY** NOT HAVE EATEN HIM..
MOOMIN!
IF THEY DIDN'T LIKE HIS TASTE, THEY MAY JUST HAVE GNAWED THE EDGES, SORT OF
HE WAS A **GREAT** MAN!
WELL, LET'S HOPE HE HAS AN **AWFUL** TASTE
GLORIOUS... **HEY!** WE'RE ADRIFT!
SOMEBODY'S **BITTEN** OFF THE HAWSER
I'M SO SORRY... I'M TEETHING, YOU SEE..
NIBLING, WHAT WILL YOUR MOTHER SAY WHEN SHE FINDS YOU GONE?
SHE'LL CRY, I SUPPOSE
OOOH! **LEATHER**!
OH NO, YOU DON'T!
HERE, LITTLE NIBLING
OH, **THANK** YOU!

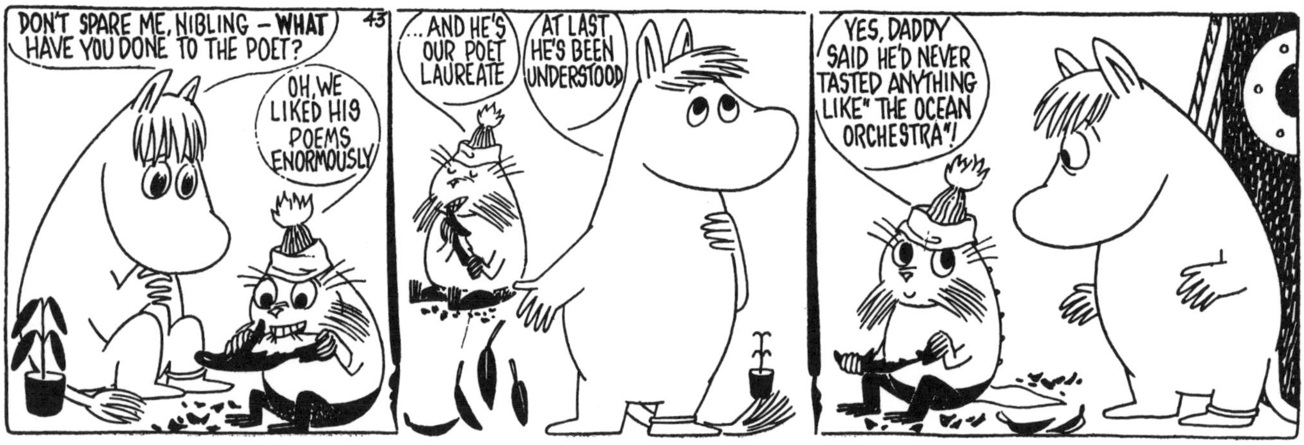
DON'T SPARE ME, NIBLING – **WHAT** HAVE YOU DONE TO THE POET?
43
OH, WE LIKED HIS POEMS ENORMOUSLY
...AND HE'S OUR POET LAUREATE
AT LAST HE'S BEEN UNDERSTOOD
YES, DADDY SAID HE'D NEVER TASTED ANYTHING LIKE "THE OCEAN ORCHESTRA"!

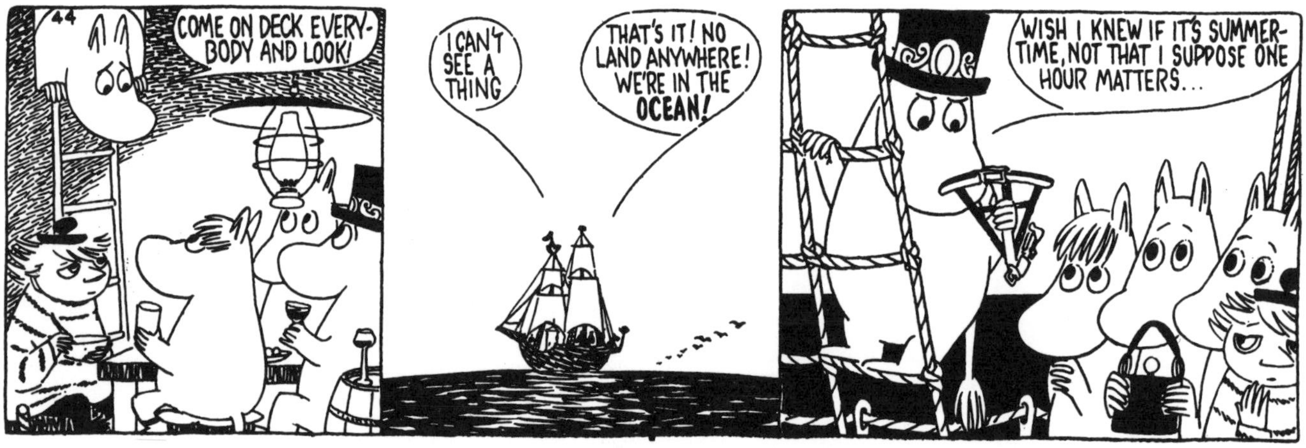
44
COME ON DECK EVERYBODY AND LOOK!
I CAN'T SEE A THING
THAT'S IT! NO LAND ANYWHERE! WE'RE IN THE **OCEAN!**
WISH I KNEW IF IT'S SUMMERTIME, NOT THAT I SUPPOSE ONE HOUR MATTERS...

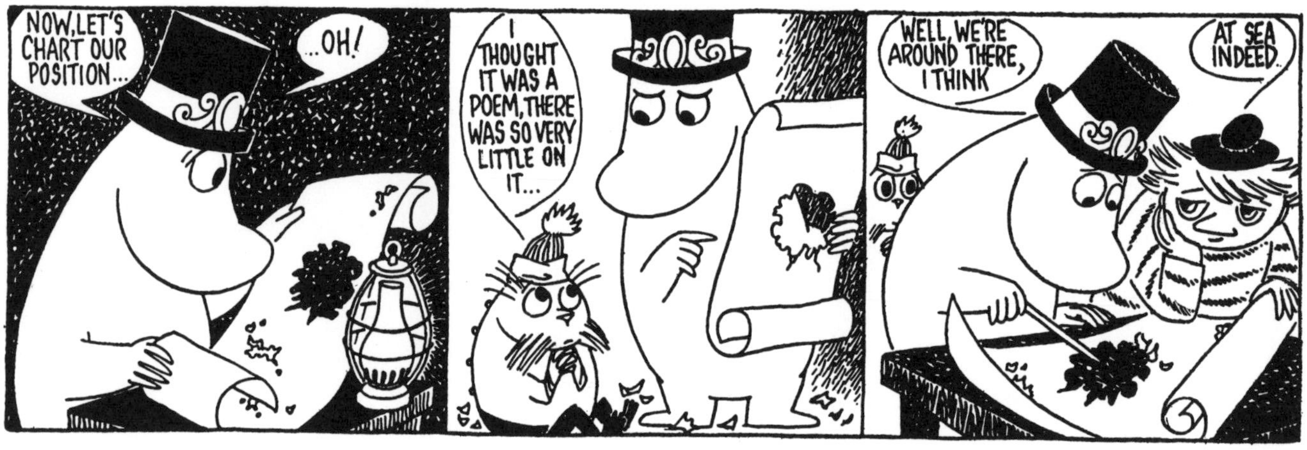
NOW, LET'S CHART OUR POSITION...
...OH!
I THOUGHT IT WAS A POEM, THERE WAS SO VERY LITTLE ON IT...
WELL, WE'RE AROUND THERE, I THINK
AT SEA INDEED.

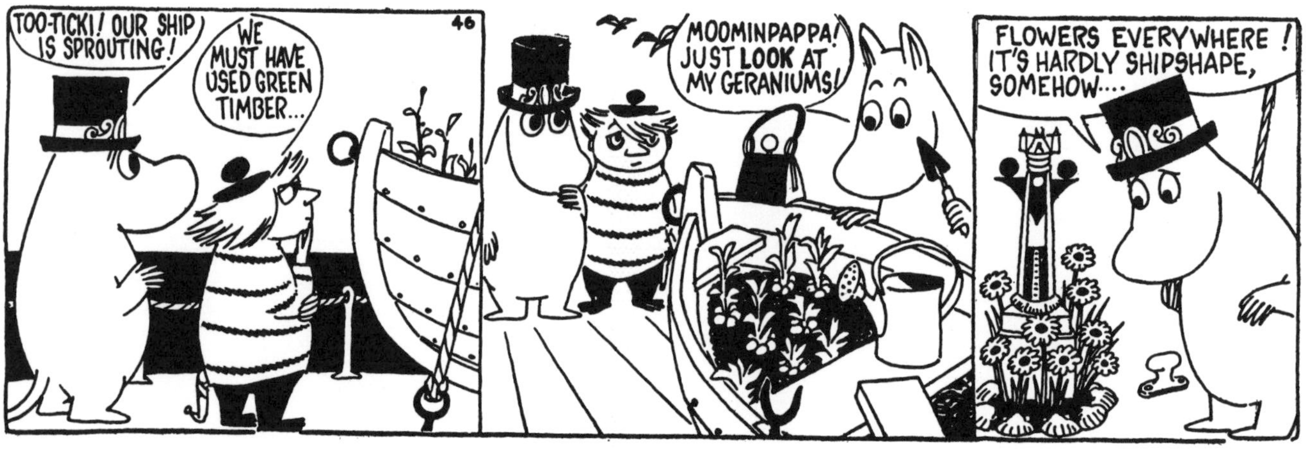
TOO-TICKI! OUR SHIP IS SPROUTING!
WE MUST HAVE USED GREEN TIMBER...
46
MOOMINPAPPA! JUST **LOOK** AT MY GERANIUMS!
FLOWERS EVERYWHERE! IT'S HARDLY SHIPSHAPE, SOMEHOW....

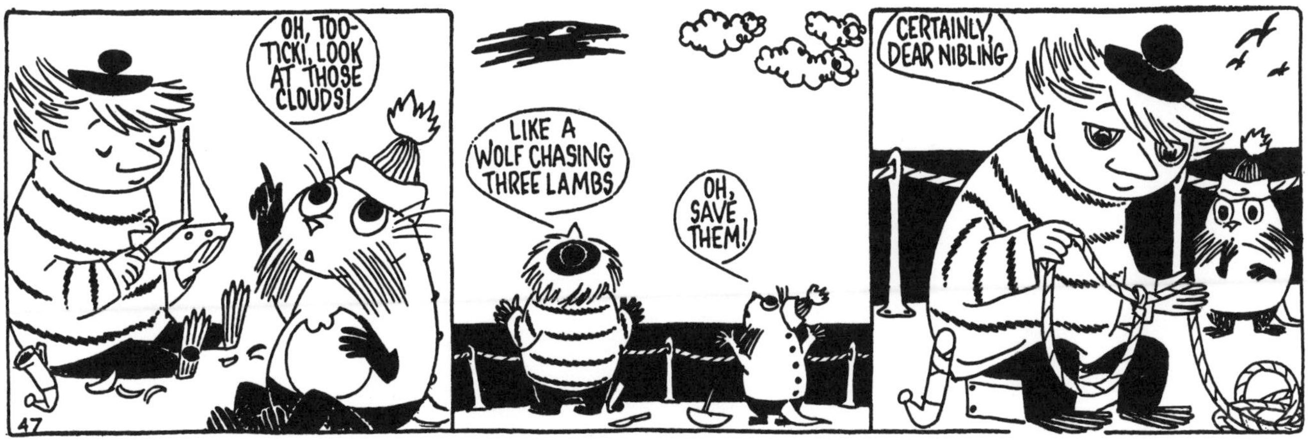
47
OH, TOO-TICKI, LOOK AT THOSE CLOUDS!
LIKE A WOLF CHASING THREE LAMBS
OH, SAVE THEM!
CERTAINLY, DEAR NIBLING

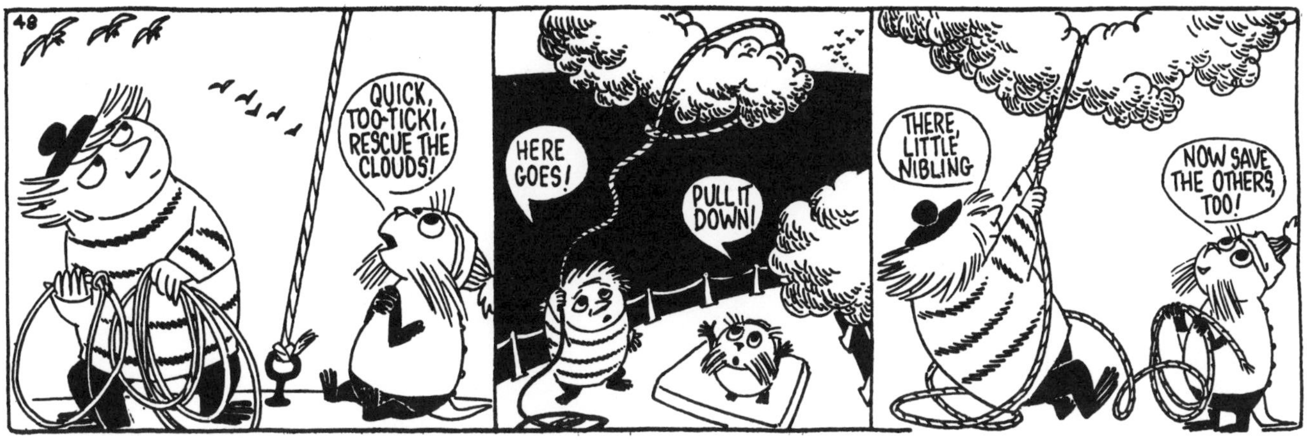
48
QUICK, TOO-TICKI, RESCUE THE CLOUDS!
HERE GOES!
PULL IT DOWN!
THERE, LITTLE NIBLING
NOW SAVE THE OTHERS, TOO!

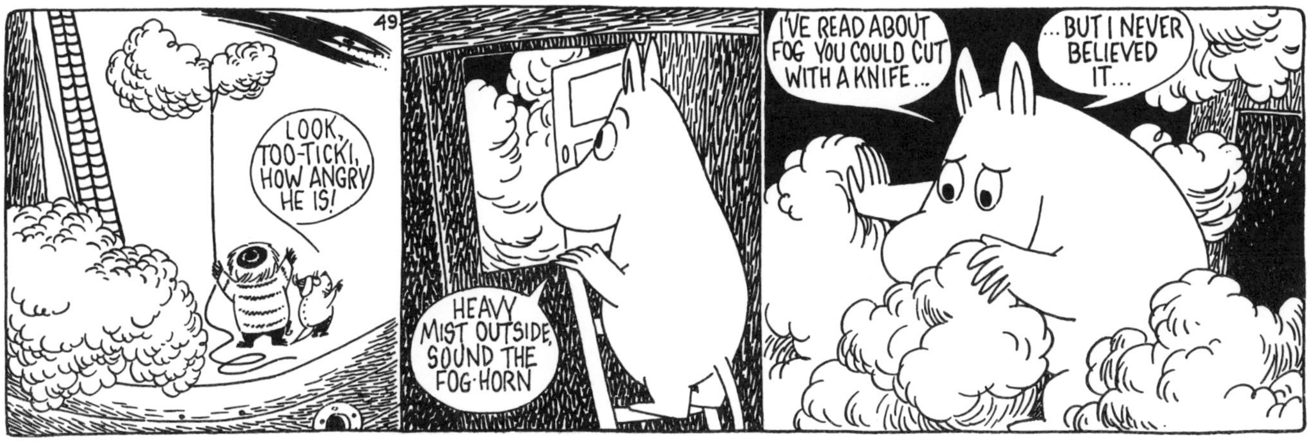
49
LOOK, TOO-TICKI, HOW ANGRY HE IS!
HEAVY MIST OUTSIDE, SOUND THE FOG-HORN
I'VE READ ABOUT FOG YOU COULD CUT WITH A KNIFE...
...BUT I NEVER BELIEVED IT...

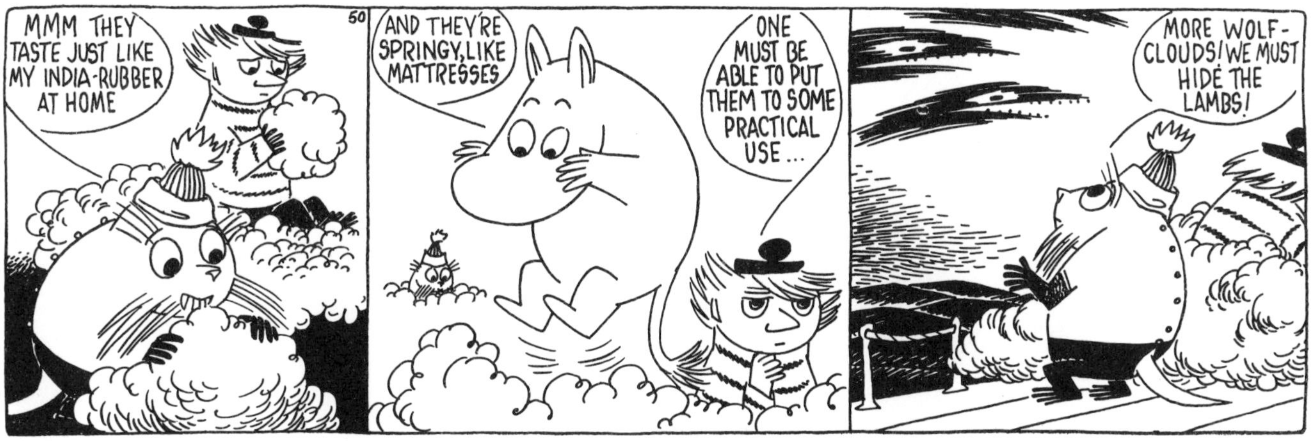
50
MMM THEY TASTE JUST LIKE MY INDIA-RUBBER AT HOME
AND THEY'RE SPRINGY, LIKE MATTRESSES
ONE MUST BE ABLE TO PUT THEM TO SOME PRACTICAL USE...
MORE WOLF-CLOUDS! WE MUST HIDE THE LAMBS!

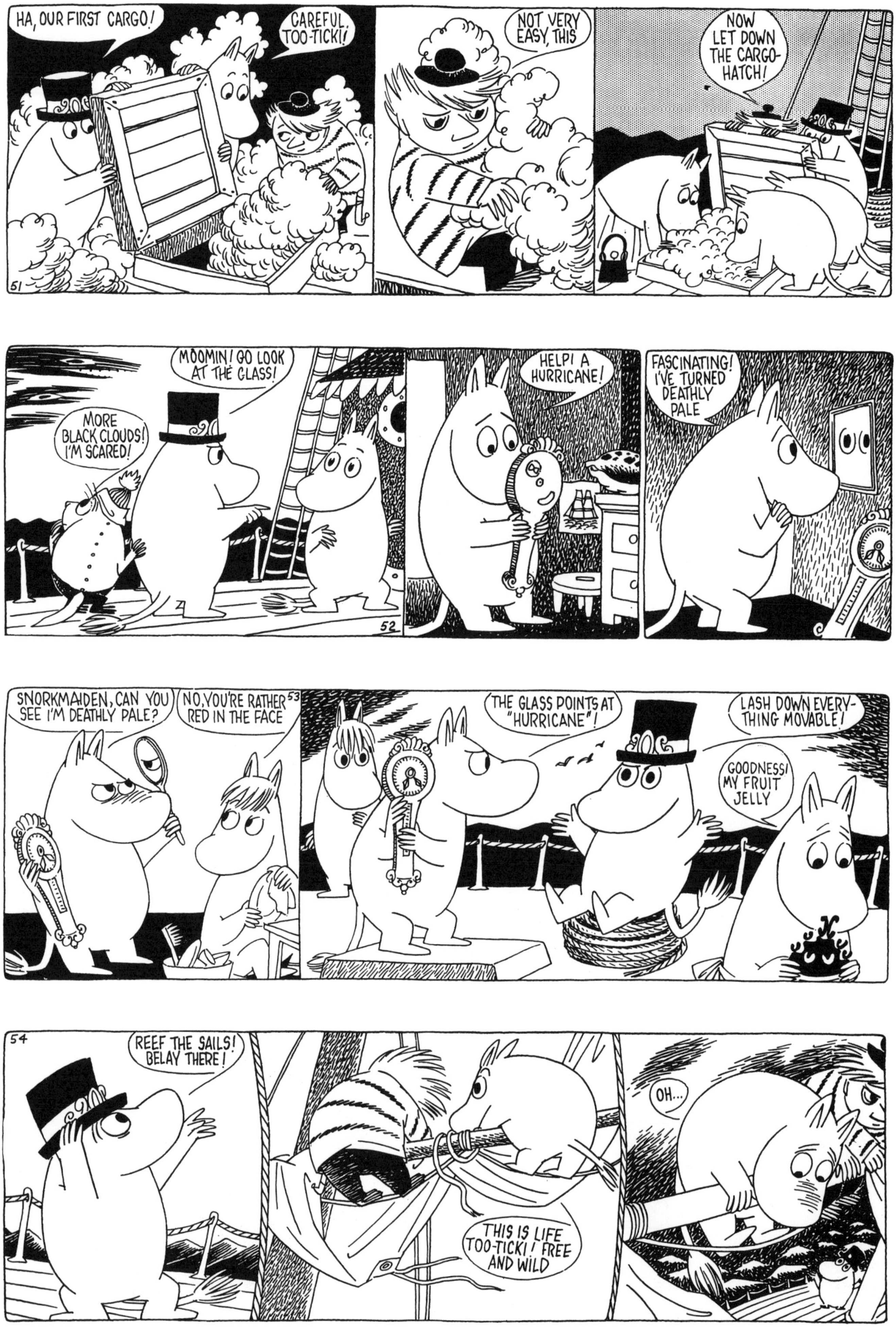
51
HA, OUR FIRST CARGO!
CAREFUL, TOO-TICKI!
NOT VERY EASY, THIS
NOW LET DOWN THE CARGO-HATCH!
MOOMIN! GO LOOK AT THE GLASS!
MORE BLACK CLOUDS! I'M SCARED!
52
HELP! A HURRICANE!
FASCINATING! I'VE TURNED DEATHLY PALE
SNORKMAIDEN, CAN YOU SEE I'M DEATHLY PALE?
NO, YOU'RE RATHER RED IN THE FACE
53
THE GLASS POINTS AT "HURRICANE"!
LASH DOWN EVERYTHING MOVABLE!
GOODNESS! MY FRUIT JELLY
54
REEF THE SAILS! BELAY THERE!
THIS IS LIFE TOO-TICKI! FREE AND WILD
OH...

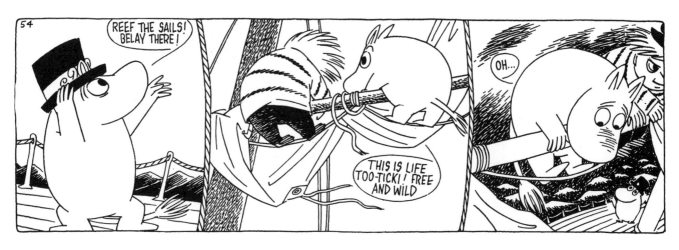

55
HERE COMES THE WIND
HELP— TOO-TICKI!
NEVER MIND THE SAILS!
WE DON'T
WE'RE IN A HURRICANE, TOO-TICKI!
LOOKS LIKE IT... HERE IT COMES
56
HEY! HELP!
57
I CAN'T UNDERSTAND...
58
CHECK THE WIND FORCE, TOO-TICKI! I MUST HAVE THE DETAILS WHEN I DESCRIBE THIS STORM
THE GAUGE HAS BURST
WELL, THEY WONT BELIEVE ME ANYWAY...
THERE GO OUR SAILS!

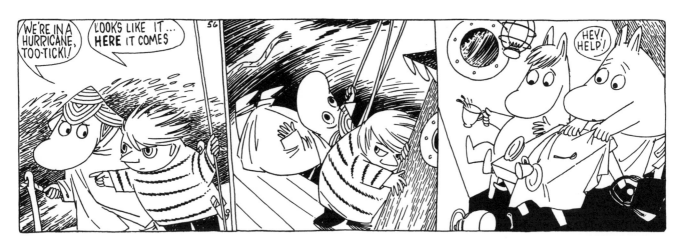

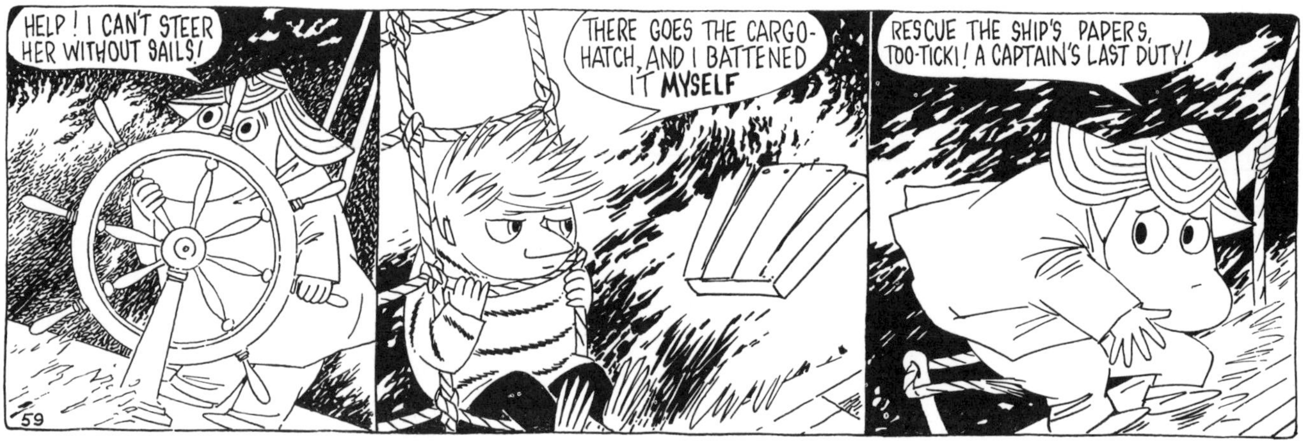
HELP! I CAN'T STEER HER WITHOUT SAILS!
THERE GOES THE CARGO-HATCH, AND I BATTENED IT **MYSELF**
RESCUE THE SHIP'S PAPERS, TOO-TICKI! A CAPTAIN'S LAST DUTY!
59

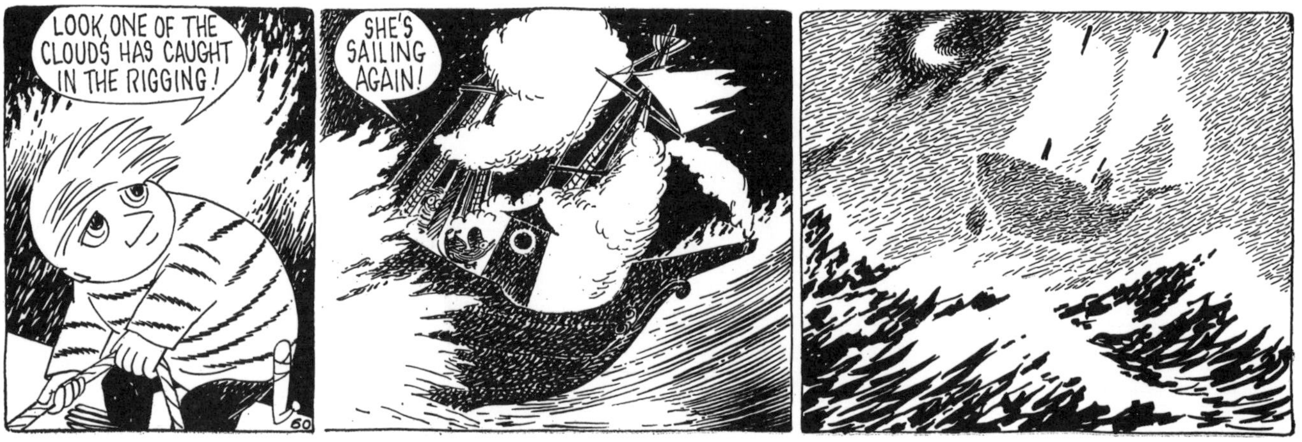
LOOK, ONE OF THE CLOUDS HAS CAUGHT IN THE RIGGING!
60
SHE'S SAILING AGAIN!

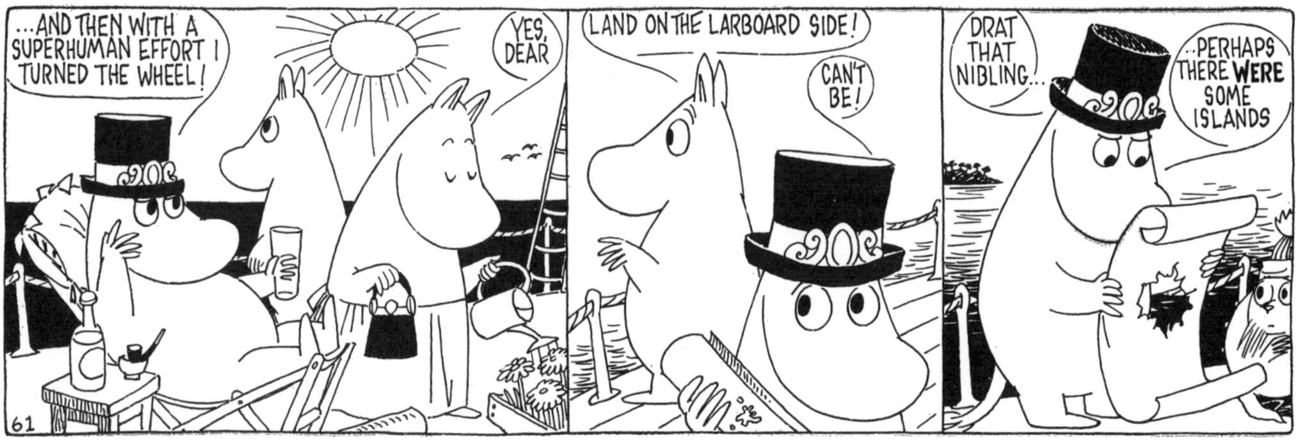
...AND THEN WITH A SUPERHUMAN EFFORT I TURNED THE WHEEL!
YES, DEAR
61
LAND ON THE LARBOARD SIDE!
CAN'T BE!
DRAT THAT NIBLING...
...PERHAPS THERE **WERE** SOME ISLANDS

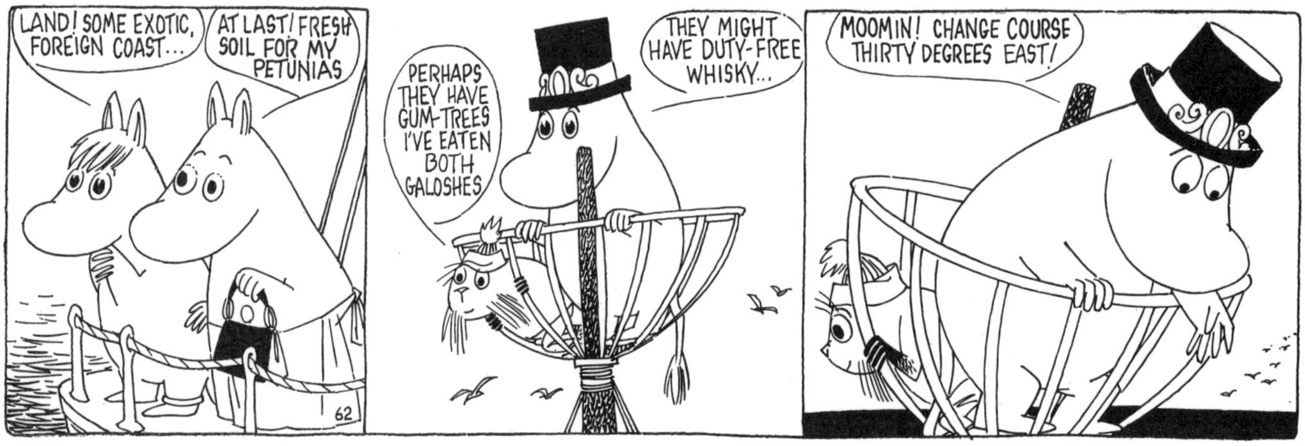
LAND! SOME EXOTIC, FOREIGN COAST...
AT LAST! FRESH SOIL FOR MY PETUNIAS
62
PERHAPS THEY HAVE GUM-TREES I'VE EATEN BOTH GALOSHES
THEY MIGHT HAVE DUTY-FREE WHISKY...
MOOMIN! CHANGE COURSE THIRTY DEGREES EAST!

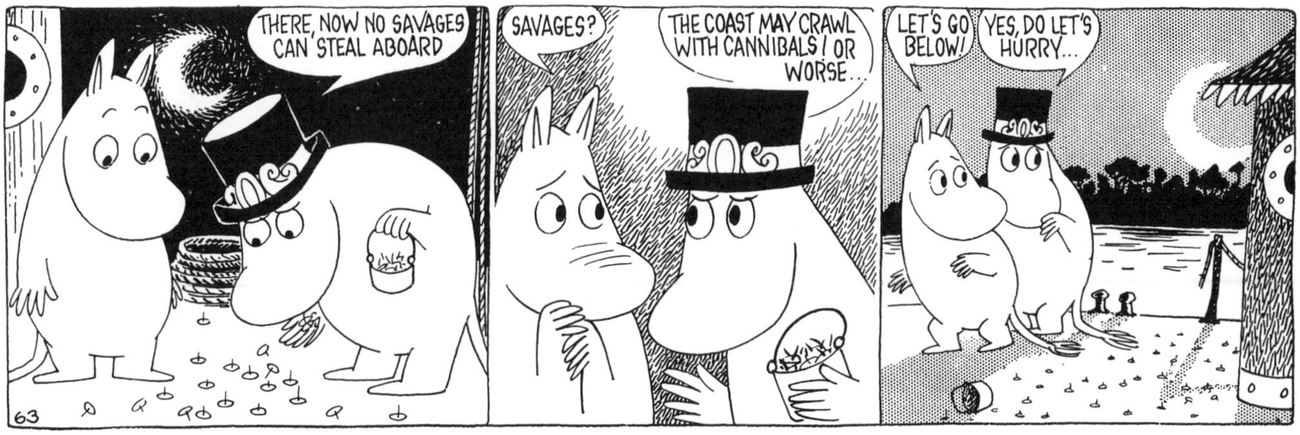
THERE, NOW NO SAVAGES CAN STEAL ABOARD
63
SAVAGES?
THE COAST MAY CRAWL WITH CANNIBALS! OR WORSE...
LET'S GO BELOW!
YES, DO LET'S HURRY...

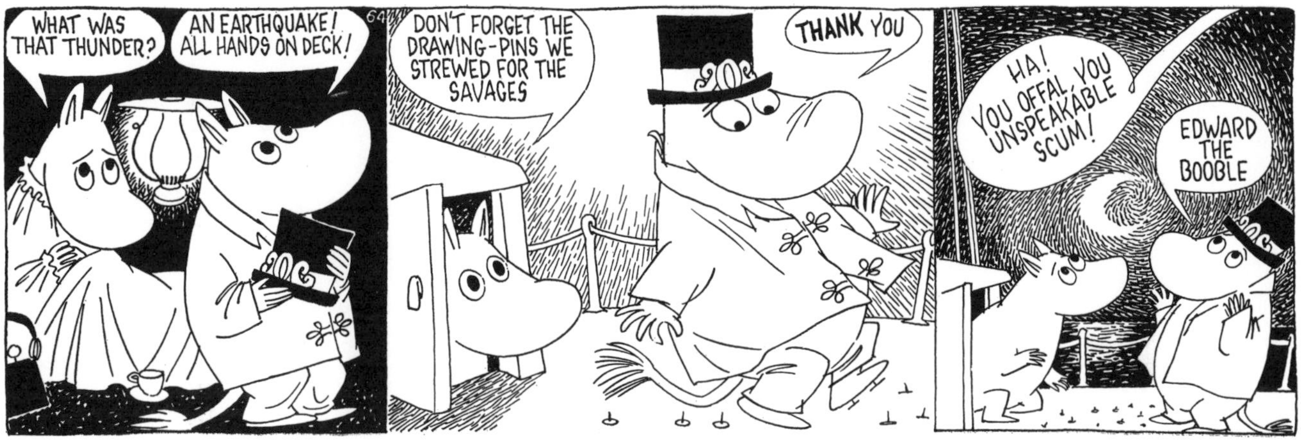
WHAT WAS THAT THUNDER?
AN EARTHQUAKE! ALL HANDS ON DECK!
64
DON'T FORGET THE DRAWING-PINS WE STREWED FOR THE SAVAGES
THANK YOU
HA! YOU OFFAL YOU UNSPEAKABLE SCUM!
EDWARD THE BOOBLE

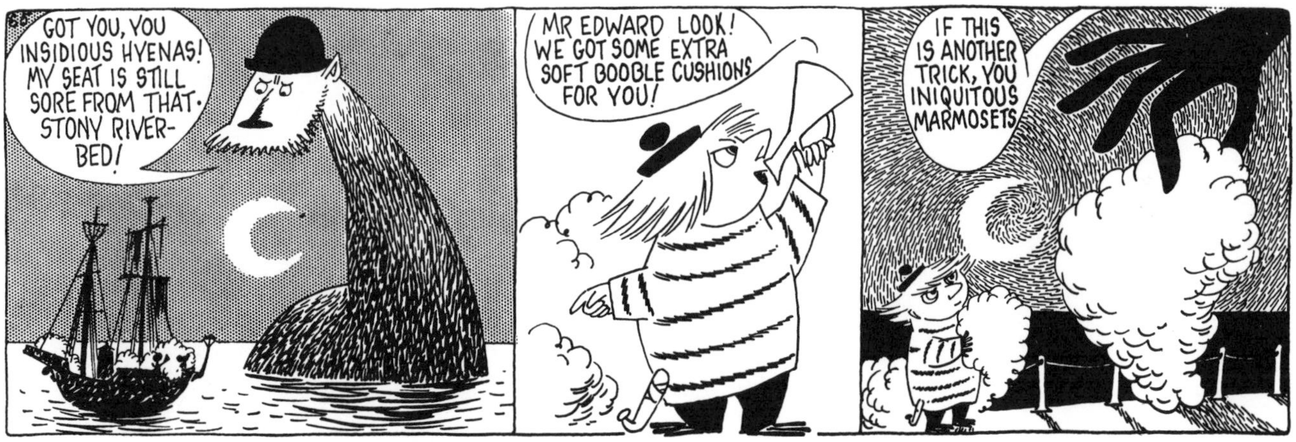
GOT YOU, YOU INSIDIOUS HYENAS! MY SEAT IS STILL SORE FROM THAT STONY RIVER-BED!
MR EDWARD LOOK! WE GOT SOME EXTRA SOFT BOOBLE CUSHIONS FOR YOU!
IF THIS IS ANOTHER TRICK, YOU INIQUITOUS MARMOSETS

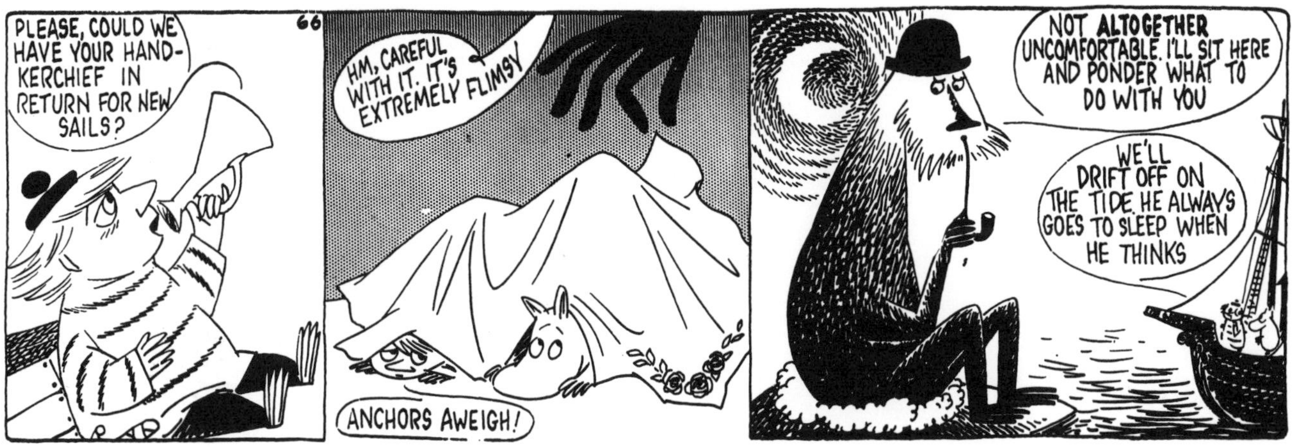
PLEASE, COULD WE HAVE YOUR HAND-KERCHIEF IN RETURN FOR NEW SAILS?
66
HM, CAREFUL WITH IT. IT'S EXTREMELY FLIMSY
ANCHORS AWEIGH!
NOT ALTOGETHER UNCOMFORTABLE. I'LL SIT HERE AND PONDER WHAT TO DO WITH YOU
WE'LL DRIFT OFF ON THE TIDE. HE ALWAYS GOES TO SLEEP WHEN HE THINKS

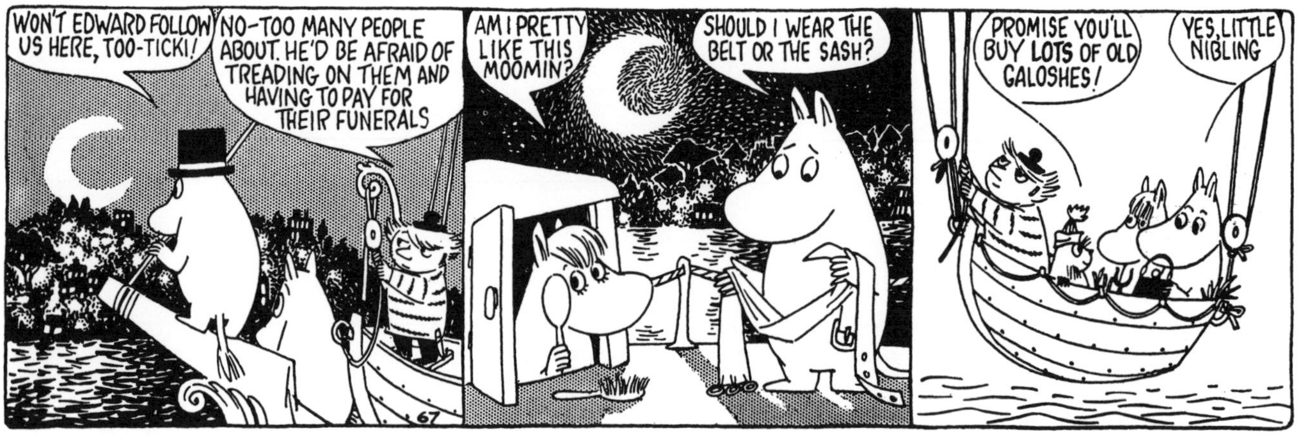
WON'T EDWARD FOLLOW US HERE, TOO-TICKI!
NO–TOO MANY PEOPLE ABOUT. HE'D BE AFRAID OF TREADING ON THEM AND HAVING TO PAY FOR THEIR FUNERALS
67
AM I PRETTY LIKE THIS MOOMIN?
SHOULD I WEAR THE BELT OR THE SASH?
PROMISE YOU'LL BUY LOTS OF OLD GALOSHES!
YES, LITTLE NIBLING

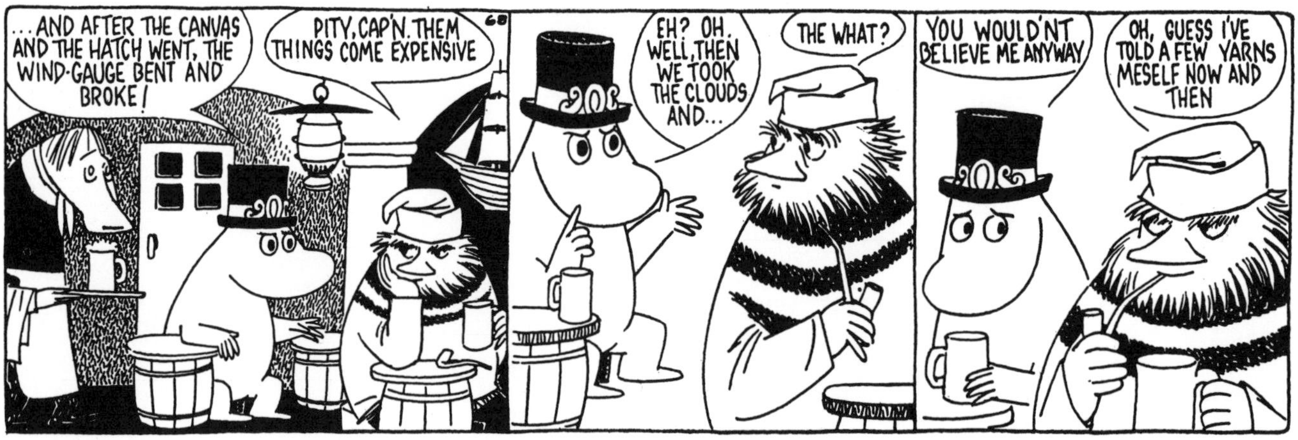
...AND AFTER THE CANVAS AND THE HATCH WENT, THE WIND-GAUGE BENT AND BROKE!
PITY, CAP'N. THEM THINGS COME EXPENSIVE
68
EH? OH. WELL, THEN WE TOOK THE CLOUDS AND...
THE WHAT?
YOU WOULD'NT BELIEVE ME ANYWAY
OH, GUESS I'VE TOLD A FEW YARNS MESELF NOW AND THEN

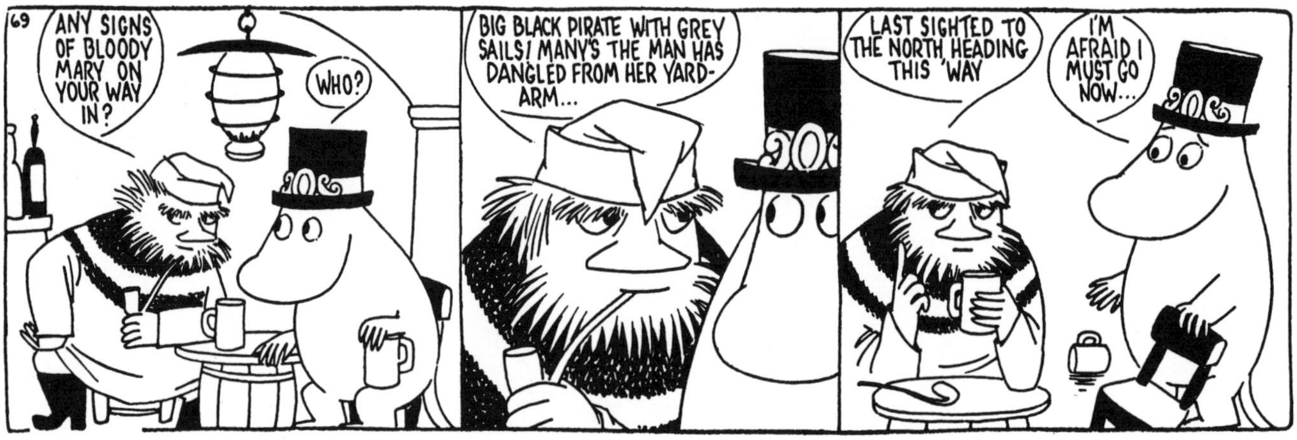
69
ANY SIGNS OF BLOODY MARY ON YOUR WAY IN?
WHO?
BIG BLACK PIRATE WITH GREY SAILS! MANY'S THE MAN HAS DANGLED FROM HER YARD-ARM...
LAST SIGHTED TO THE NORTH HEADING THIS 'WAY
I'M AFRAID I MUST GO NOW...

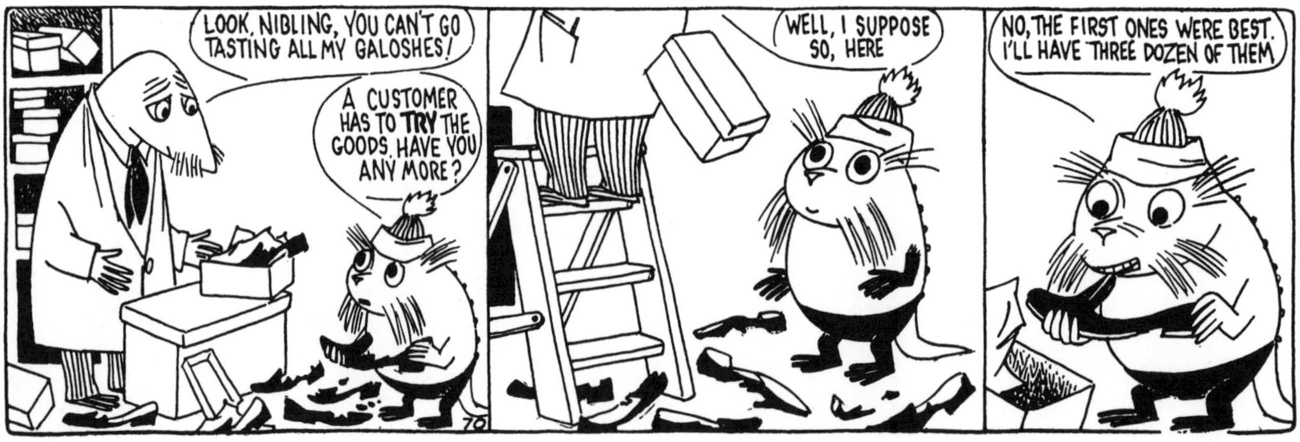
LOOK, NIBLING, YOU CAN'T GO TASTING ALL MY GALOSHES!
A CUSTOMER HAS TO TRY THE GOODS. HAVE YOU ANY MORE?
70
WELL, I SUPPOSE SO, HERE
NO, THE FIRST ONES WERE BEST. I'LL HAVE THREE DOZEN OF THEM

MY PETUNIAS WILL LOVE THIS
Soil
71
GOOD, SOLID GROUND AND NO WATER ANY WHERE!
A REAL SHIP IN A BOTTLE..
OCCAS
FAMILY-Y-Y!
MOOMIN-PAPPA...
72
NOW WE'VE GOT ALL OUR NECESSITIES WE MUST SAIL AT ONCE! THERE ARE PIRATES HEADED THIS WAY!
RUM
GALOSHES
TERRIBLE FOR A NIBLING, THIS MIST. SOON I'LL HAVE TO WEAR MY GALOSHES
73
WE CAN'T ESCAPE THE PIRATES WITHOUT ANY WIND!
NO DEAR. BUT THEY CAN'T PURSUE US, EITHER
THERE SHE IS! BRING ME MY RIFLE!
NO, THAT ISN'T THE PIRATE. SHE HAS WHITE SAILS
STRANGE. NO LOOK-OUT, NO ONE AT THE HELM
WE MUST INVESTIGATE
PREPARE YOURSELVES FOR TRAGEDY!

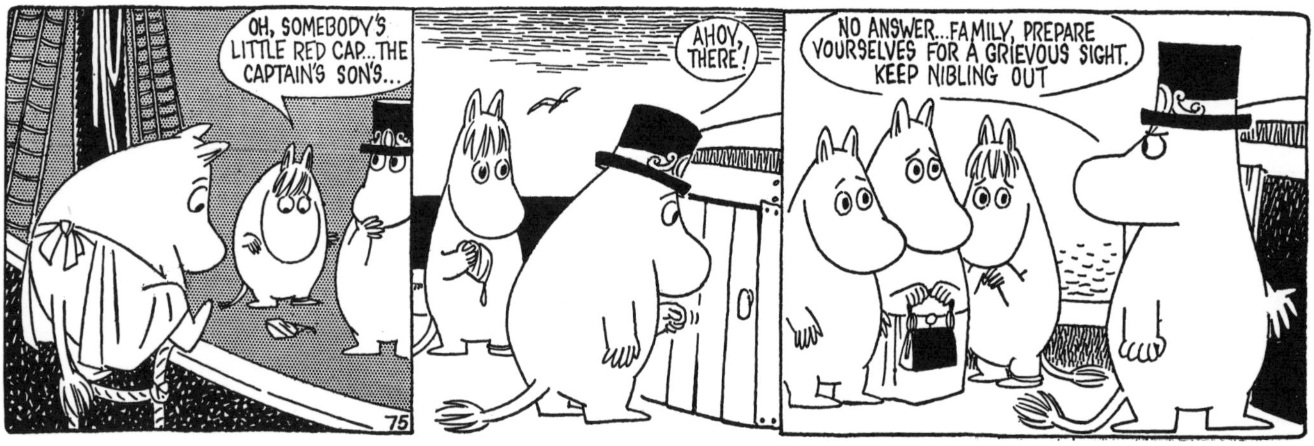
OH, SOMEBODY'S LITTLE RED CAP... THE CAPTAIN'S SON'S...
75
AHOY, THERE!
NO ANSWER... FAMILY, PREPARE YOURSELVES FOR A GRIEVOUS SIGHT. KEEP NIBLING OUT

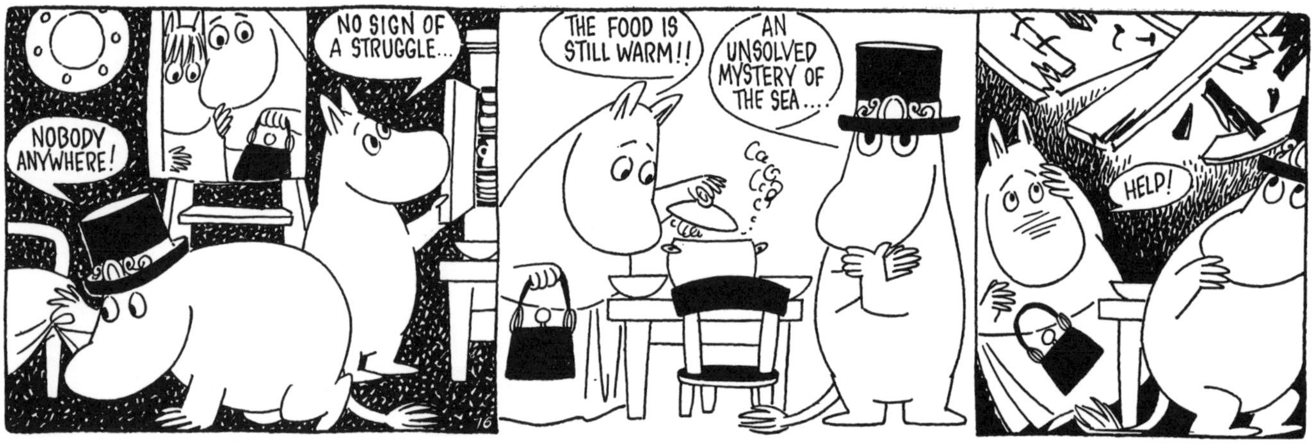
NOBODY ANYWHERE!
NO SIGN OF A STRUGGLE...
76
THE FOOD IS STILL WARM!!
AN UNSOLVED MYSTERY OF THE SEA...
HELP!

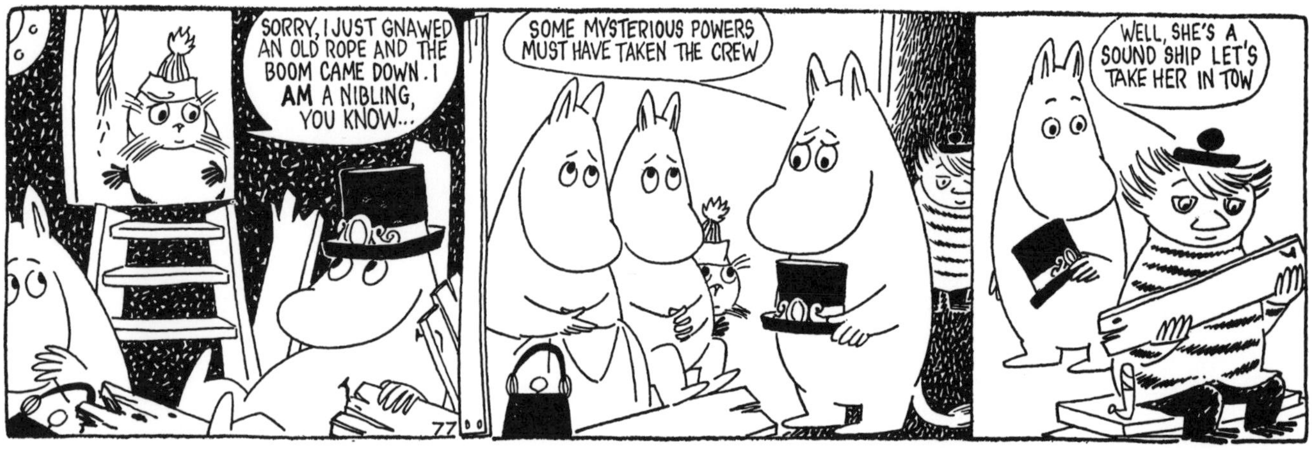
SORRY, I JUST GNAWED AN OLD ROPE AND THE BOOM CAME DOWN. I **AM** A NIBLING, YOU KNOW...
77
SOME MYSTERIOUS POWERS MUST HAVE TAKEN THE CREW
WELL, SHE'S A SOUND SHIP LET'S TAKE HER IN TOW

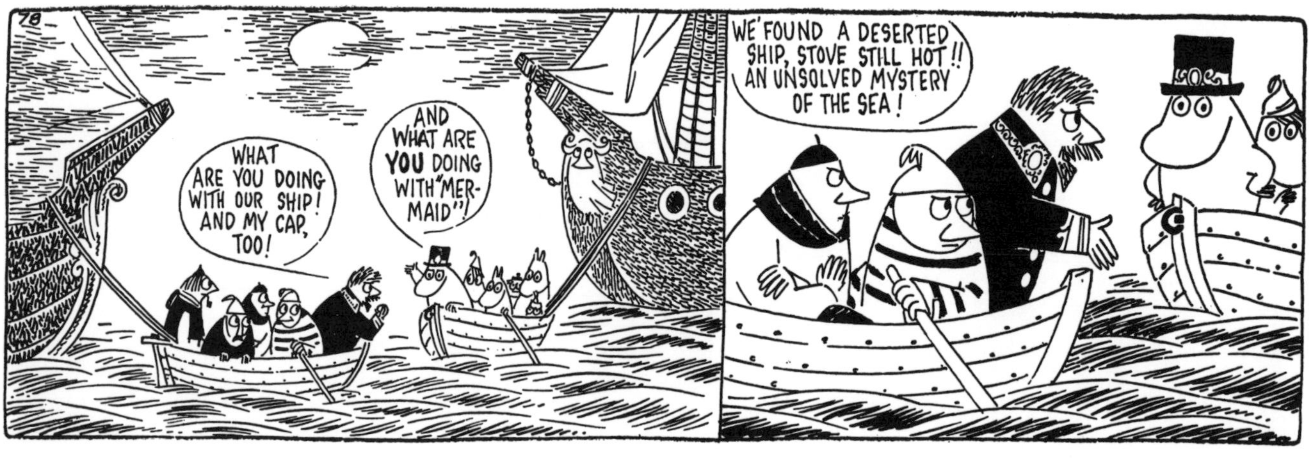
78
WHAT ARE YOU DOING WITH OUR SHIP! AND MY CAP, TOO!
AND WHAT ARE **YOU** DOING WITH "MER-MAID"!
WE'FOUND A DESERTED SHIP, STOVE STILL HOT!! AN UNSOLVED MYSTERY OF THE SEA!

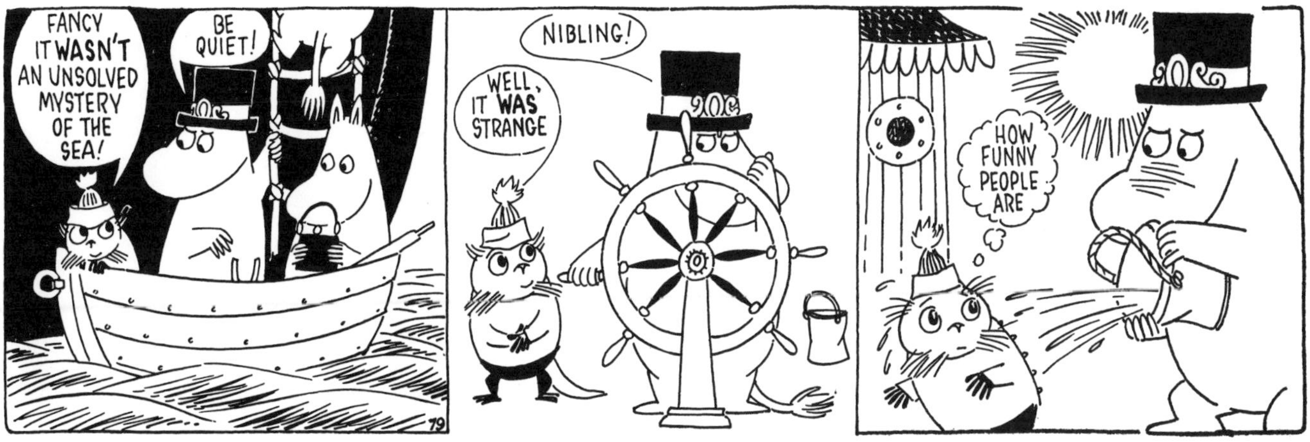
FANCY IT WASN'T AN UNSOLVED MYSTERY OF THE SEA!
BE QUIET!
79
NIBLING!
WELL, IT WAS STRANGE
HOW FUNNY PEOPLE ARE

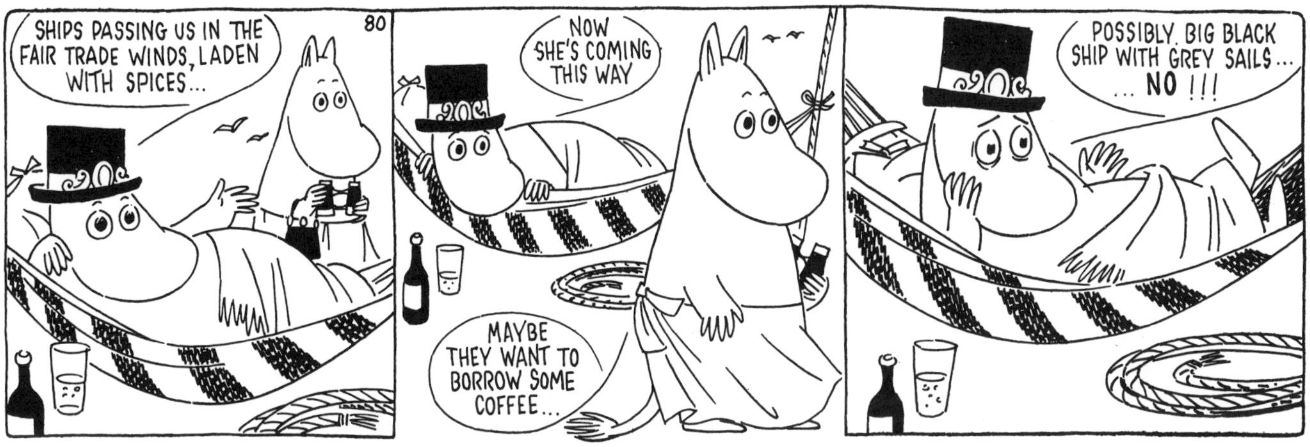
80
SHIPS PASSING US IN THE FAIR TRADE WINDS, LADEN WITH SPICES...
NOW SHE'S COMING THIS WAY
MAYBE THEY WANT TO BORROW SOME COFFEE...
POSSIBLY. BIG BLACK SHIP WITH GREY SAILS... ... NO !!!

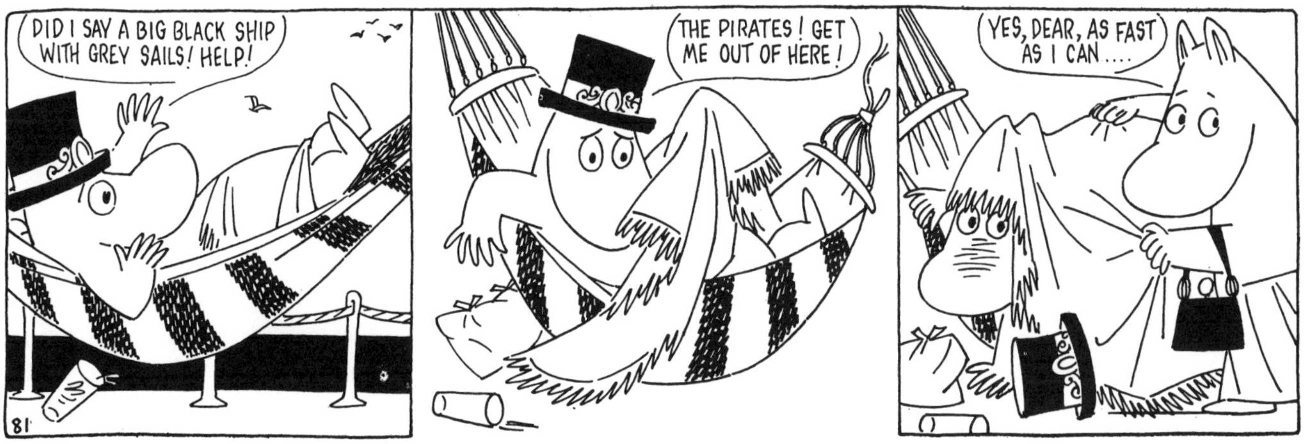
DID I SAY A BIG BLACK SHIP WITH GREY SAILS! HELP!
81
THE PIRATES! GET ME OUT OF HERE!
YES, DEAR, AS FAST AS I CAN....

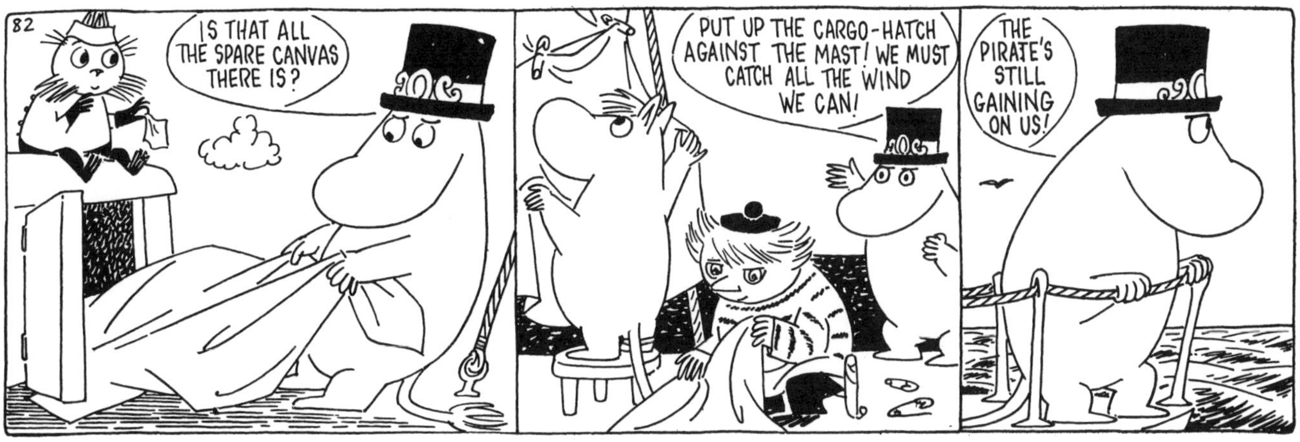
82
IS THAT ALL THE SPARE CANVAS THERE IS?
PUT UP THE CARGO-HATCH AGAINST THE MAST! WE MUST CATCH ALL THE WIND WE CAN!
THE PIRATE'S STILL GAINING ON US!

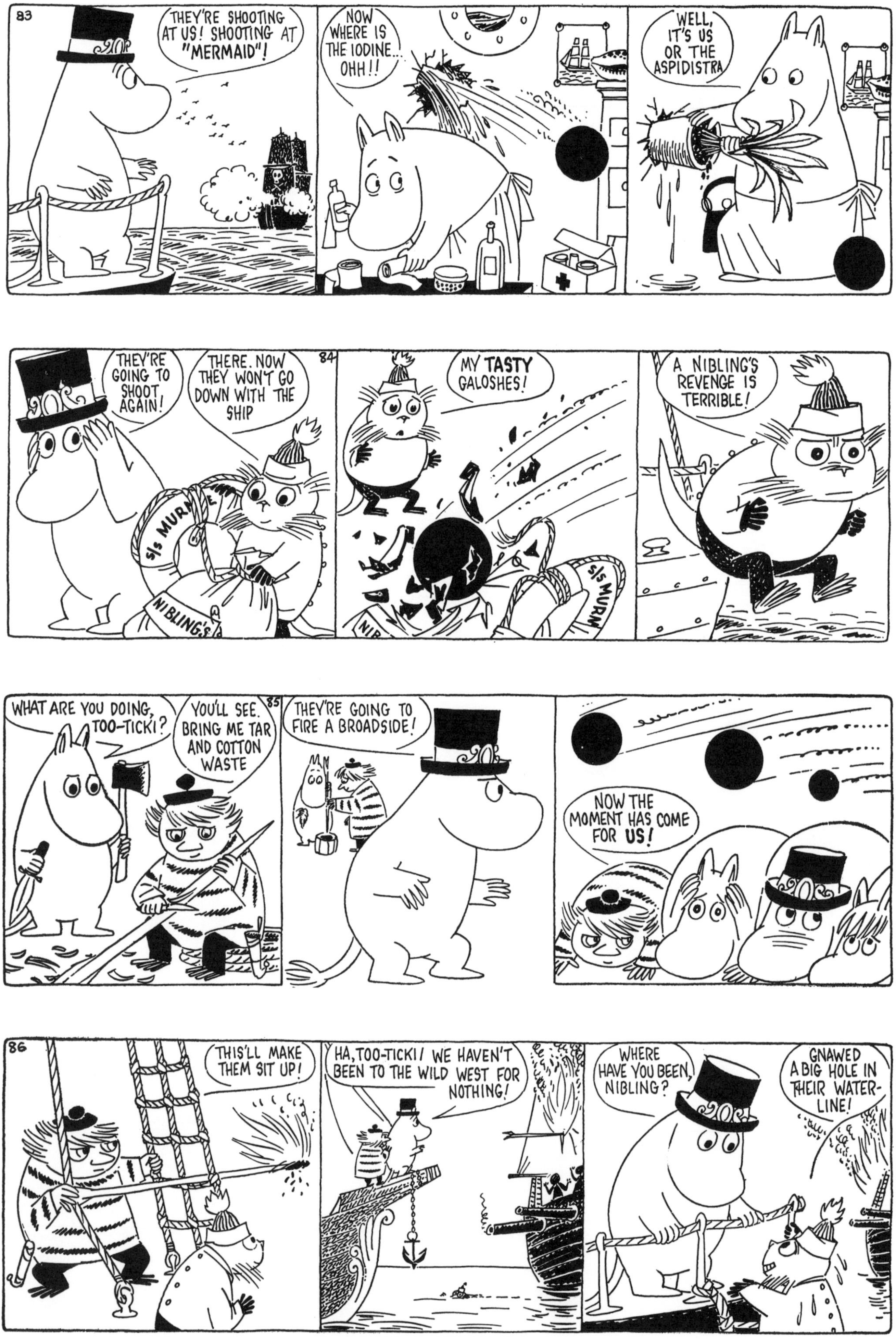
83
THEY'RE SHOOTING AT US! SHOOTING AT "MERMAID"!
NOW WHERE IS THE IODINE... OHH!!
WELL, IT'S US OR THE ASPIDISTRA
THEY'RE GOING TO SHOOT AGAIN!
THERE. NOW THEY WON'T GO DOWN WITH THE SHIP
NIBLING'S
84
MY TASTY GALOSHES!
A NIBLING'S REVENGE IS TERRIBLE!
WHAT ARE YOU DOING, TOO-TICKI?
YOU'LL SEE. BRING ME TAR AND COTTON WASTE
85
THEY'RE GOING TO FIRE A BROADSIDE!
NOW THE MOMENT HAS COME FOR US!
86
THIS'LL MAKE THEM SIT UP!
HA, TOO-TICKI! WE HAVEN'T BEEN TO THE WILD WEST FOR NOTHING!
WHERE HAVE YOU BEEN, NIBLING?
GNAWED A BIG HOLE IN THEIR WATER-LINE!

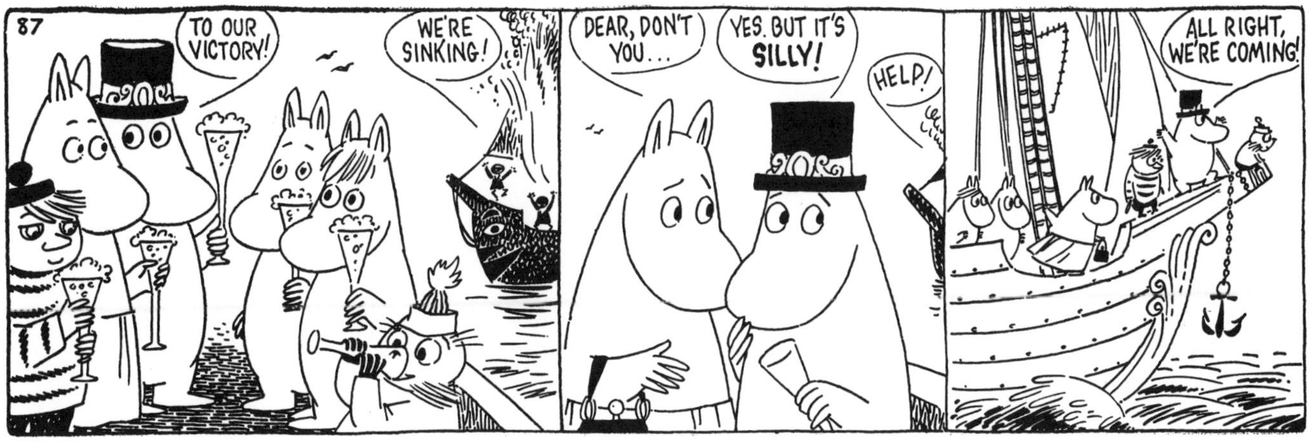
87
TO OUR VICTORY!
WE'RE SINKING!
DEAR, DON'T YOU...
YES. BUT IT'S **SILLY!**
HELP!
ALL RIGHT, WE'RE COMING!

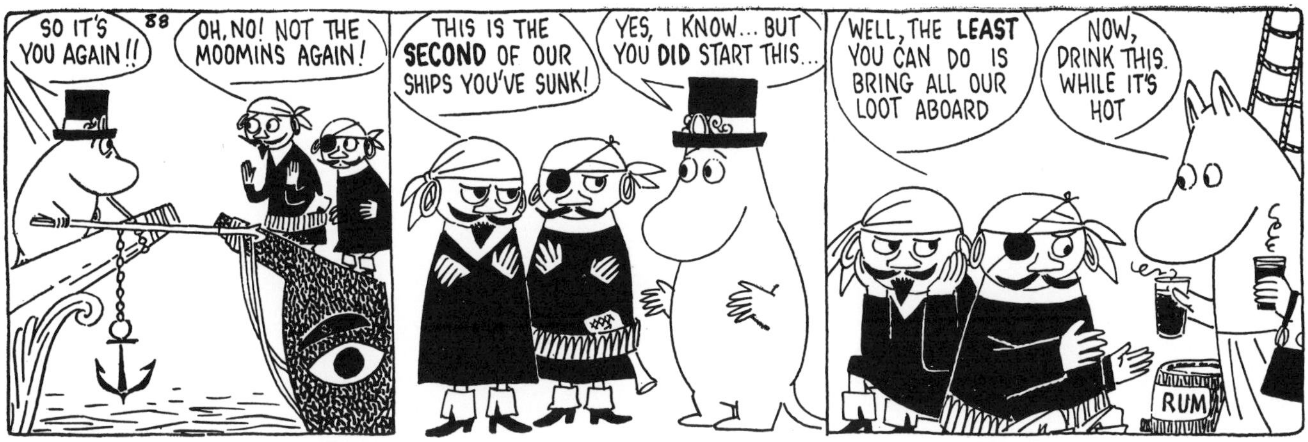
SO IT'S YOU AGAIN!!
88
OH, NO! NOT THE MOOMINS AGAIN!
THIS IS THE **SECOND** OF OUR SHIPS YOU'VE SUNK!
YES, I KNOW... BUT YOU **DID** START THIS...
WELL, THE **LEAST** YOU CAN DO IS BRING ALL OUR LOOT ABOARD
NOW, DRINK THIS. WHILE IT'S HOT
RUM

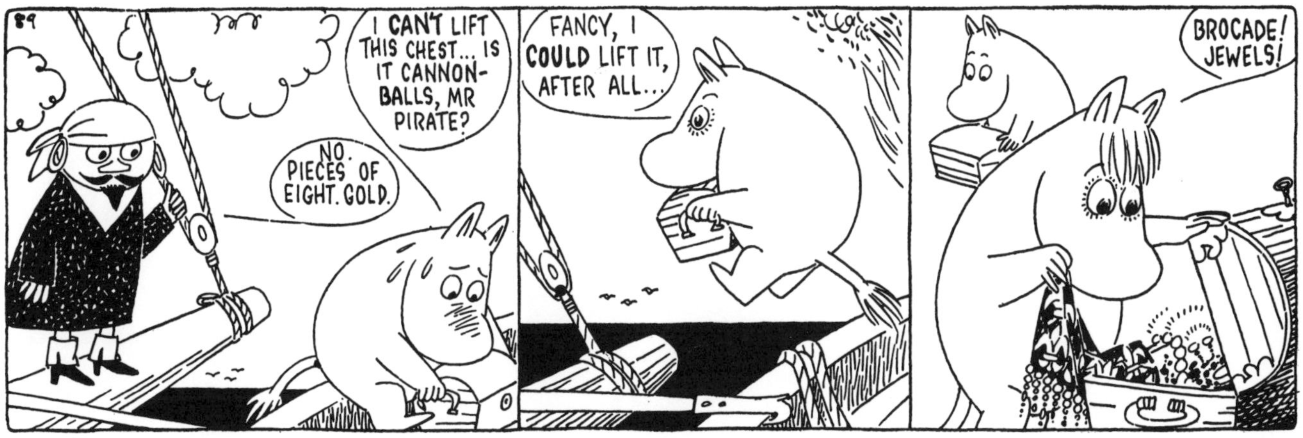
89
I **CAN'T** LIFT THIS CHEST... IS IT CANNON-BALLS, MR PIRATE?
NO. PIECES OF EIGHT. GOLD.
FANCY, I **COULD** LIFT IT, AFTER ALL...
BROCADE! JEWELS!

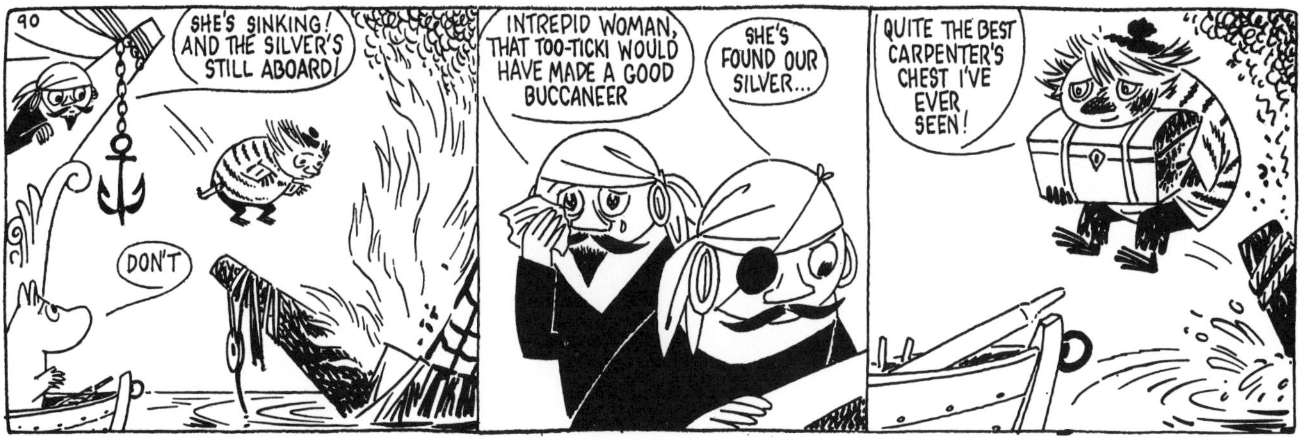
90
SHE'S SINKING! AND THE SILVER'S STILL ABOARD!
DON'T
INTREPID WOMAN, THAT TOO-TICKI WOULD HAVE MADE A GOOD BUCCANEER
SHE'S FOUND OUR SILVER...
QUITE THE BEST CARPENTER'S CHEST I'VE EVER SEEN!

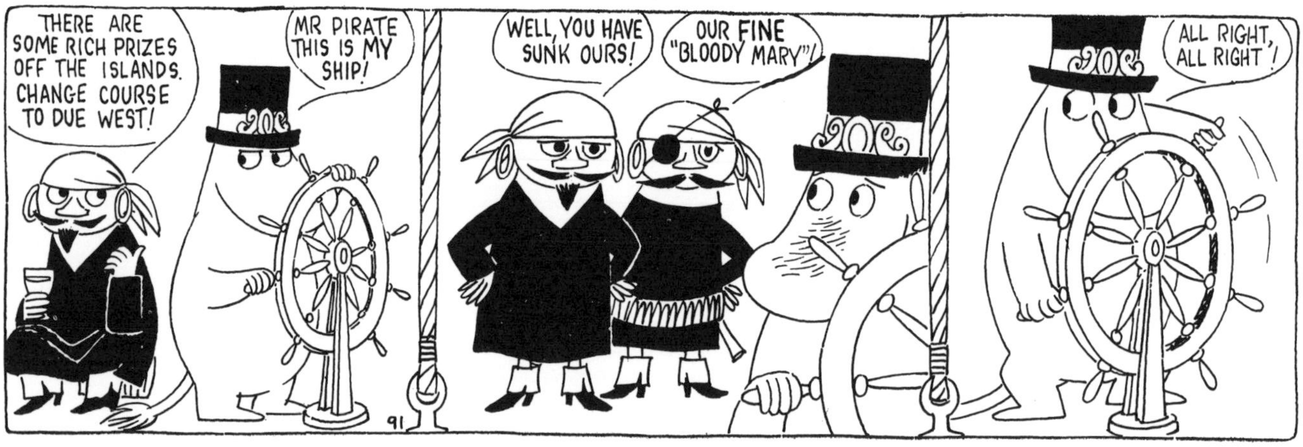
THERE ARE SOME RICH PRIZES OFF THE ISLANDS. CHANGE COURSE TO DUE WEST!
MR PIRATE THIS IS MY SHIP!
WELL, YOU HAVE SUNK OURS!
OUR FINE "BLOODY MARY"!
ALL RIGHT, ALL RIGHT!
91

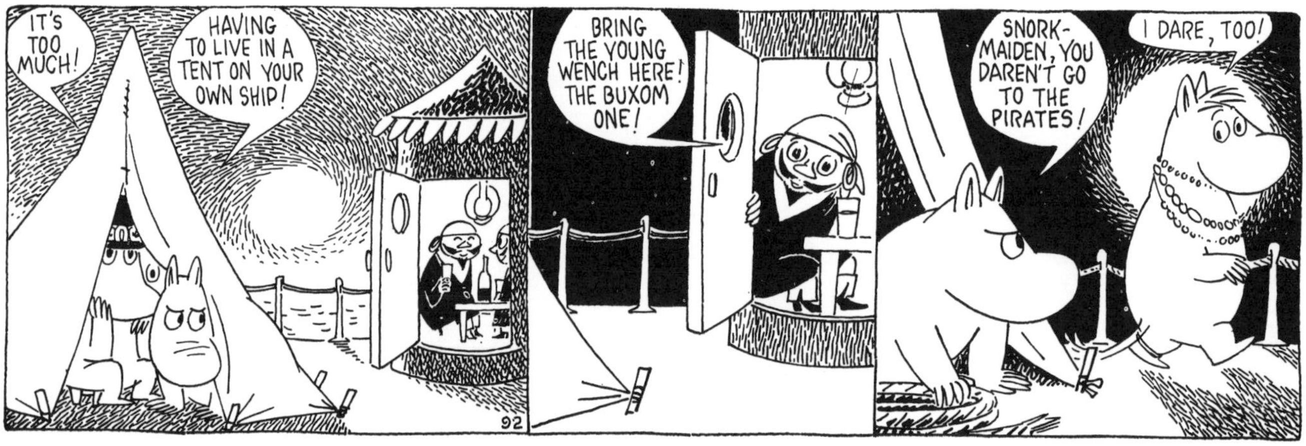
IT'S TOO MUCH!
HAVING TO LIVE IN A TENT ON YOUR OWN SHIP!
BRING THE YOUNG WENCH HERE! THE BUXOM ONE!
SNORK-MAIDEN, YOU DAREN'T GO TO THE PIRATES!
I DARE, TOO!
92

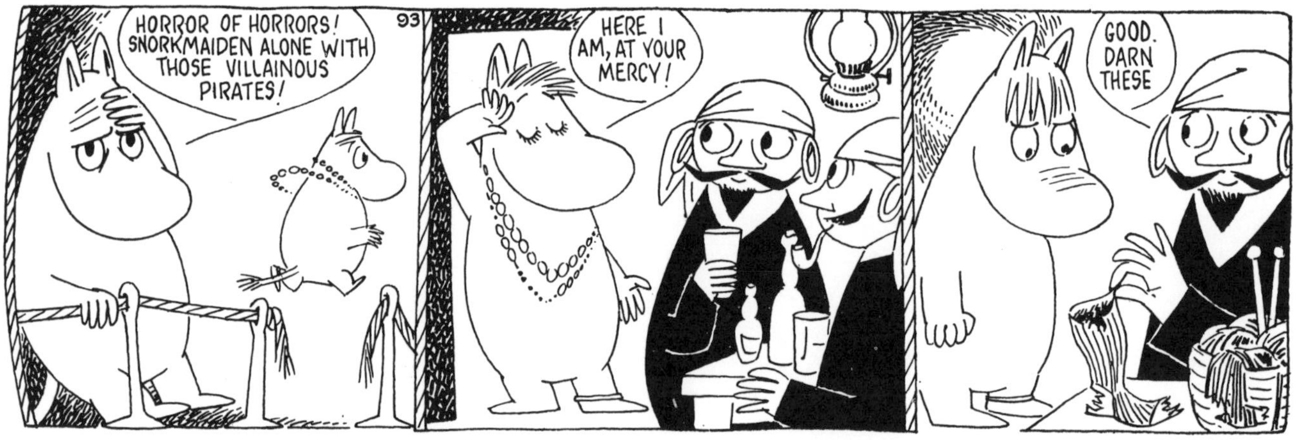
HORROR OF HORRORS! SNORKMAIDEN ALONE WITH THOSE VILLAINOUS PIRATES!
93
HERE I AM, AT YOUR MERCY!
GOOD. DARN THESE

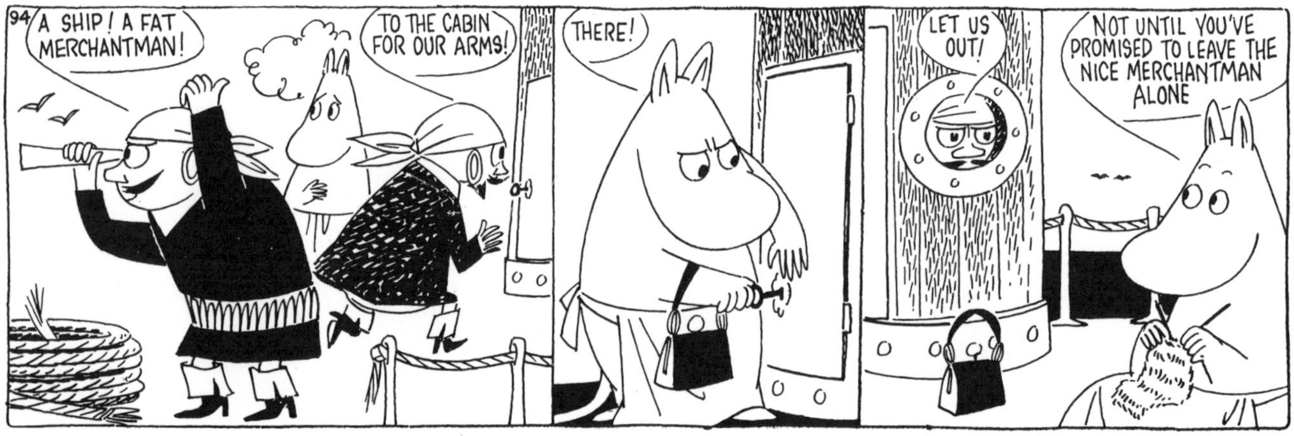
94
A SHIP! A FAT MERCHANTMAN!
TO THE CABIN FOR OUR ARMS!
THERE!
LET US OUT!
NOT UNTIL YOU'VE PROMISED TO LEAVE THE NICE MERCHANTMAN ALONE

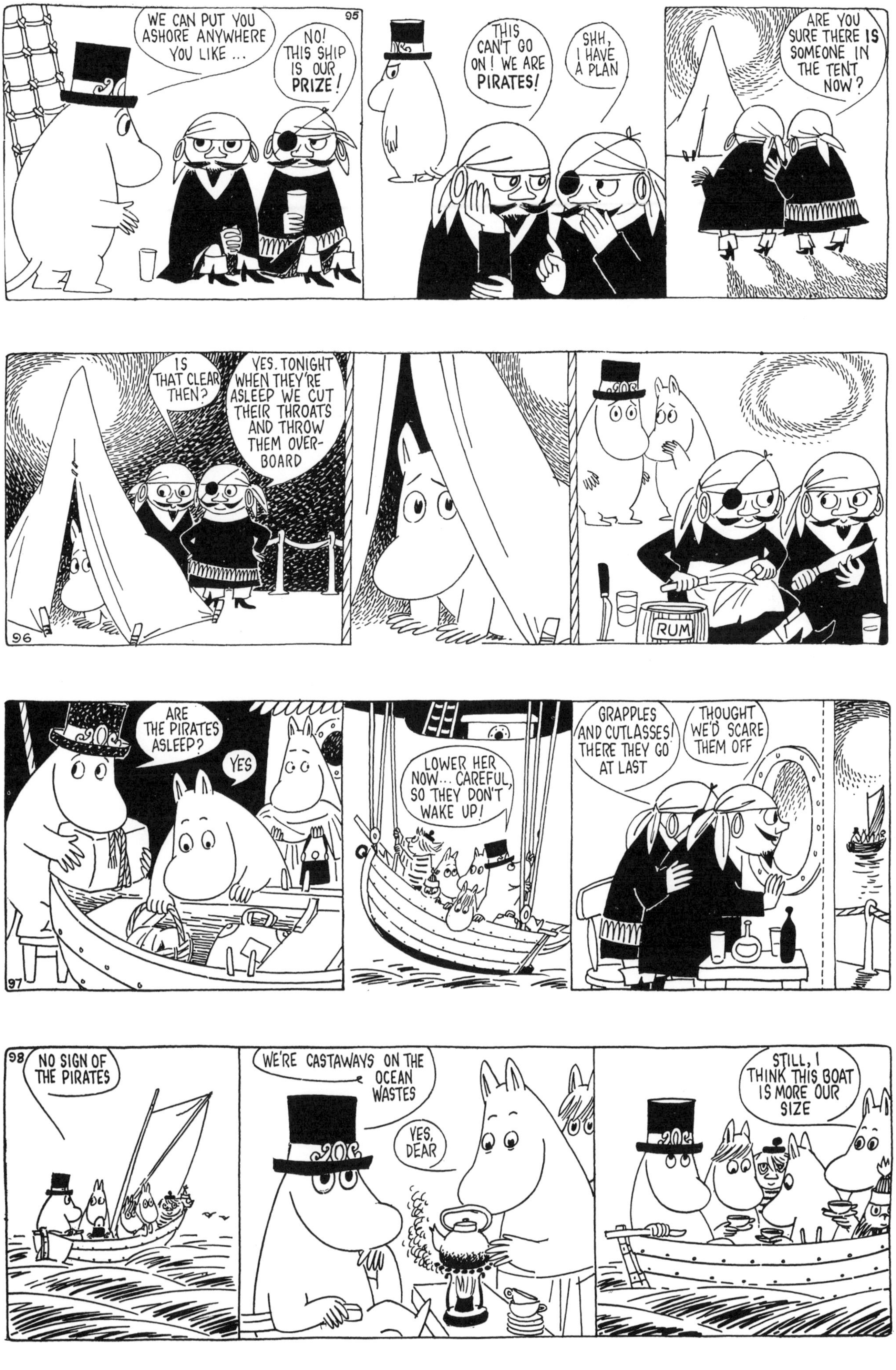
95
WE CAN PUT YOU ASHORE ANYWHERE YOU LIKE ...
NO! THIS SHIP IS OUR **PRIZE**!
THIS CAN'T GO ON! WE ARE **PIRATES**!
SHH, I HAVE A PLAN
ARE YOU SURE THERE **IS** SOMEONE IN THE TENT NOW?
96
IS THAT CLEAR THEN?
YES. TONIGHT WHEN THEY'RE ASLEEP WE CUT THEIR THROATS AND THROW THEM OVER-BOARD
RUM
97
ARE THE PIRATES ASLEEP?
YES
LOWER HER NOW... CAREFUL, SO THEY DON'T WAKE UP!
GRAPPLES AND CUTLASSES! THERE THEY GO AT LAST
THOUGHT WE'D SCARE THEM OFF
98
NO SIGN OF THE PIRATES
WE'RE CASTAWAYS ON THE OCEAN WASTES
YES, DEAR
STILL, I THINK THIS BOAT IS MORE OUR SIZE

99
NOW WE MUST MAKE AN INVENTORY AND RATION OUR FOOD
WHAT'S THIS?
THE PIRATES HAVE FORGOTTEN THEIR PIECES OF EIGHT!
NOW, I WONDER ....
100
ALL OUR COFFEE'S GONE
AND THE APPLES
NOT TO SPEAK OF THE GALOSHES
LAND AHOY!!
101
A DARK, WILD COAST.... AFRICA? TORTUGA? THE OUTER HEBRIDES...?
WHAT IS IT!
WORDS FAIL ME. TAKE THE GLASS
Moominhouse!!!
102
The key is under the win dow sill'
THEY'RE COMING BACK!
BUT HOW SMALL THEIR SHIP HAS BECOME!
OH, WOOD ALWAYS SHRINKS IN THE SUN
PITY, LEAVING THIS SOFA
OH, THEY'LL GO AWAY FOR NEW ADVENTURES SOON!
FINIS

21. Fuddler's Courtship

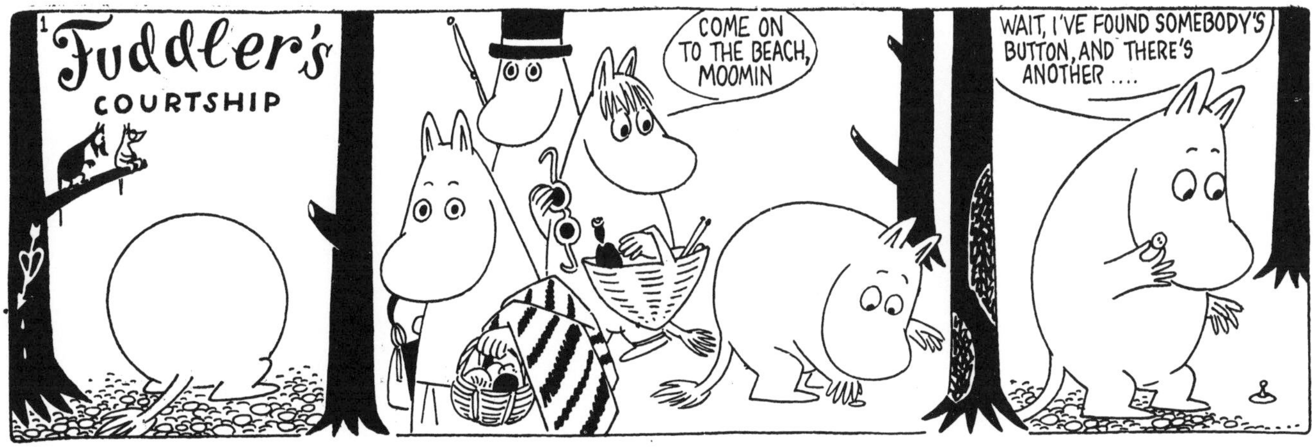
Fuddler's
COURTSHIP
COME ON TO THE BEACH, MOOMIN
WAIT, I'VE FOUND SOMEBODY'S BUTTON, AND THERE'S ANOTHER ....

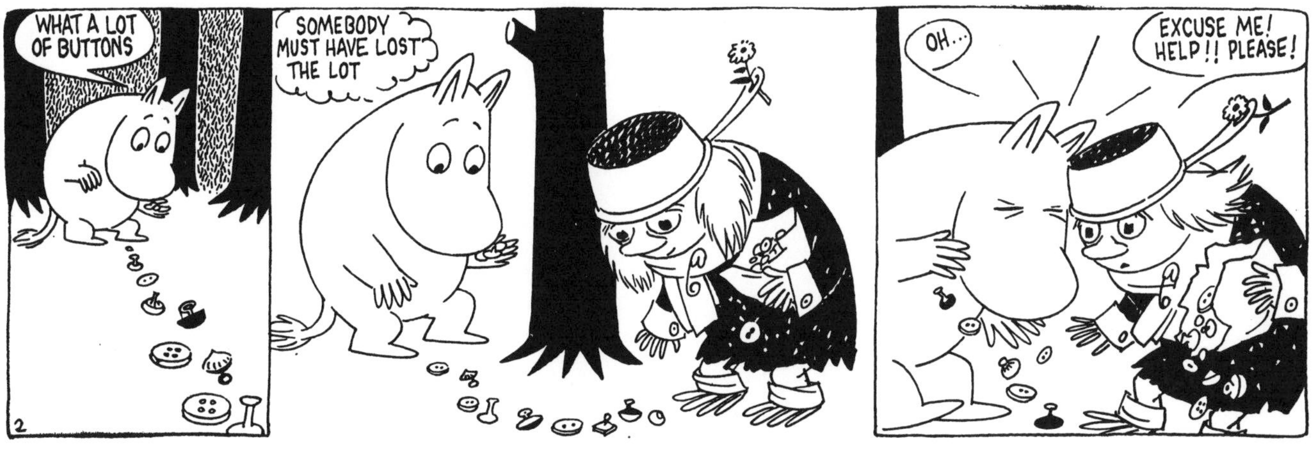
WHAT A LOT OF BUTTONS
SOMEBODY MUST HAVE LOST THE LOT
OH...
EXCUSE ME! HELP!! PLEASE!

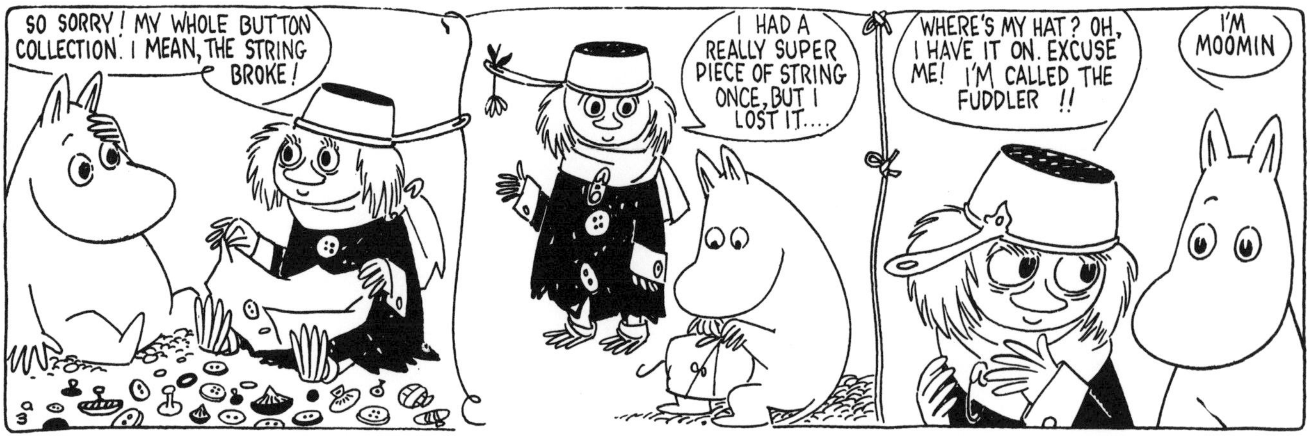
SO SORRY! MY WHOLE BUTTON COLLECTION. I MEAN, THE STRING BROKE!
3
I HAD A REALLY SUPER PIECE OF STRING ONCE, BUT I LOST IT....
WHERE'S MY HAT? OH, I HAVE IT ON. EXCUSE ME! I'M CALLED THE FUDDLER !!
I'M MOOMIN

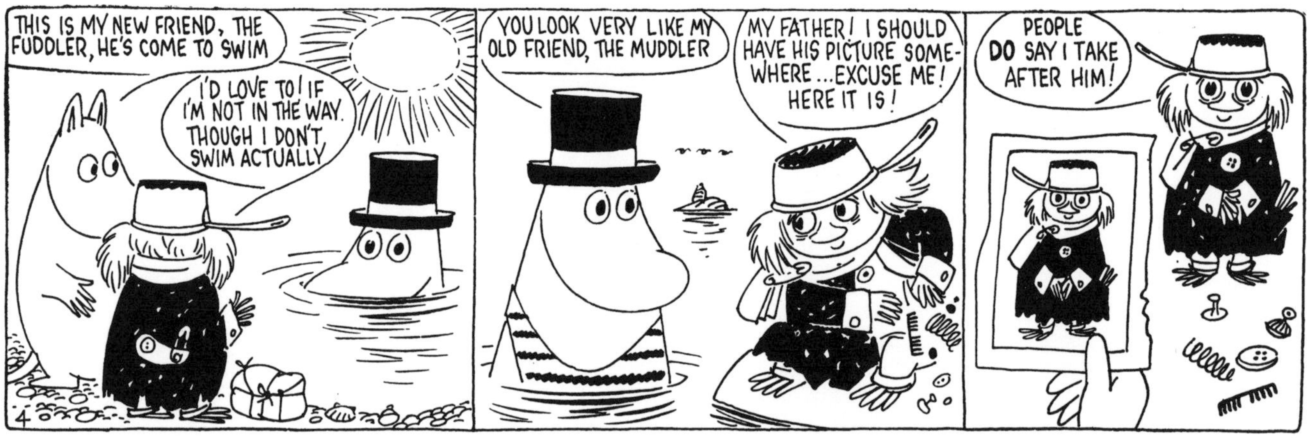
THIS IS MY NEW FRIEND, THE FUDDLER, HE'S COME TO SWIM
I'D LOVE TO! IF I'M NOT IN THE WAY. THOUGH I DON'T SWIM ACTUALLY
4
YOU LOOK VERY LIKE MY OLD FRIEND, THE MUDDLER
MY FATHER! I SHOULD HAVE HIS PICTURE SOMEWHERE...EXCUSE ME! HERE IT IS!
PEOPLE DO SAY I TAKE AFTER HIM!

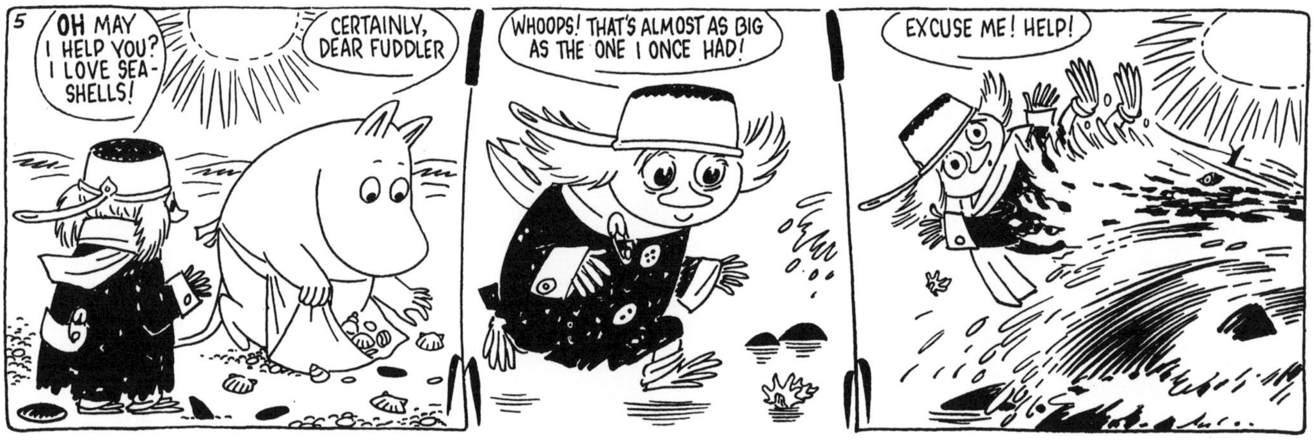
5
OH MAY I HELP YOU? I LOVE SEA-SHELLS!
CERTAINLY, DEAR FUDDLER
WHOOPS! THAT'S ALMOST AS BIG AS THE ONE I ONCE HAD!
EXCUSE ME! HELP!

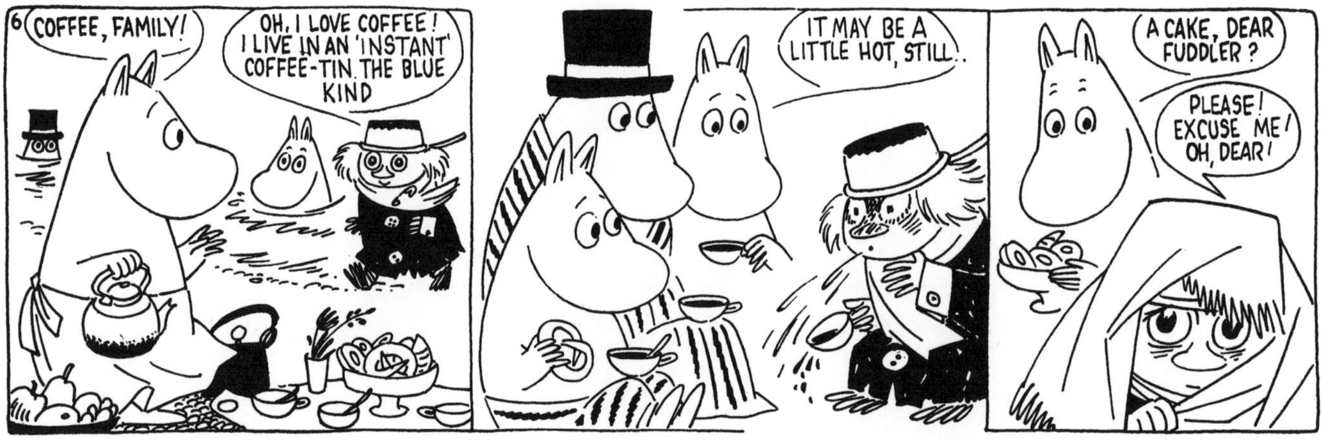
6
COFFEE, FAMILY!
OH, I LOVE COFFEE! I LIVE IN AN 'INSTANT' COFFEE-TIN. THE BLUE KIND
IT MAY BE A LITTLE HOT, STILL..
A CAKE, DEAR FUDDLER?
PLEASE! EXCUSE ME! OH, DEAR!

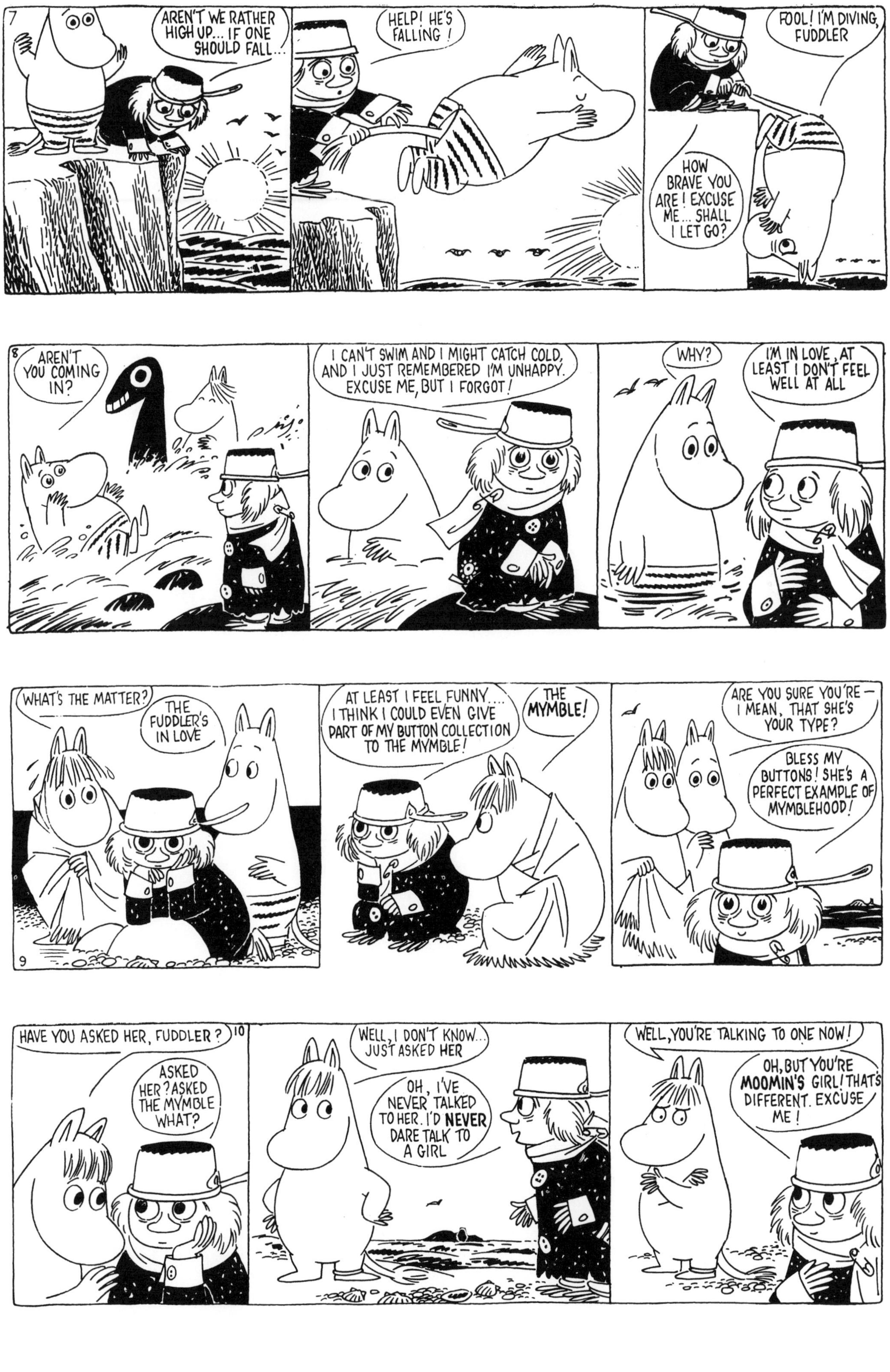
7
AREN'T WE RATHER HIGH UP... IF ONE SHOULD FALL...
HELP! HE'S FALLING!
FOOL! I'M DIVING, FUDDLER
HOW BRAVE YOU ARE! EXCUSE ME... SHALL I LET GO?
8
AREN'T YOU COMING IN?
I CAN'T SWIM AND I MIGHT CATCH COLD, AND I JUST REMEMBERED I'M UNHAPPY. EXCUSE ME, BUT I FORGOT!
WHY?
I'M IN LOVE, AT LEAST I DON'T FEEL WELL AT ALL
9
WHAT'S THE MATTER?
THE FUDDLER'S IN LOVE
AT LEAST I FEEL FUNNY.... I THINK I COULD EVEN GIVE PART OF MY BUTTON COLLECTION TO THE MYMBLE!
THE **MYMBLE**!
ARE YOU SURE YOU'RE — I MEAN, THAT SHE'S YOUR TYPE?
BLESS MY BUTTONS! SHE'S A PERFECT EXAMPLE OF MYMBLEHOOD!
10
HAVE YOU ASKED HER, FUDDLER?
ASKED HER? ASKED THE MYMBLE WHAT?
WELL, I DON'T KNOW... JUST ASKED **HER**
OH, I'VE NEVER TALKED TO HER. I'D **NEVER** DARE TALK TO A GIRL
WELL, YOU'RE TALKING TO ONE NOW!
OH, BUT YOU'RE **MOOMIN'S** GIRL! THAT'S DIFFERENT. EXCUSE ME!

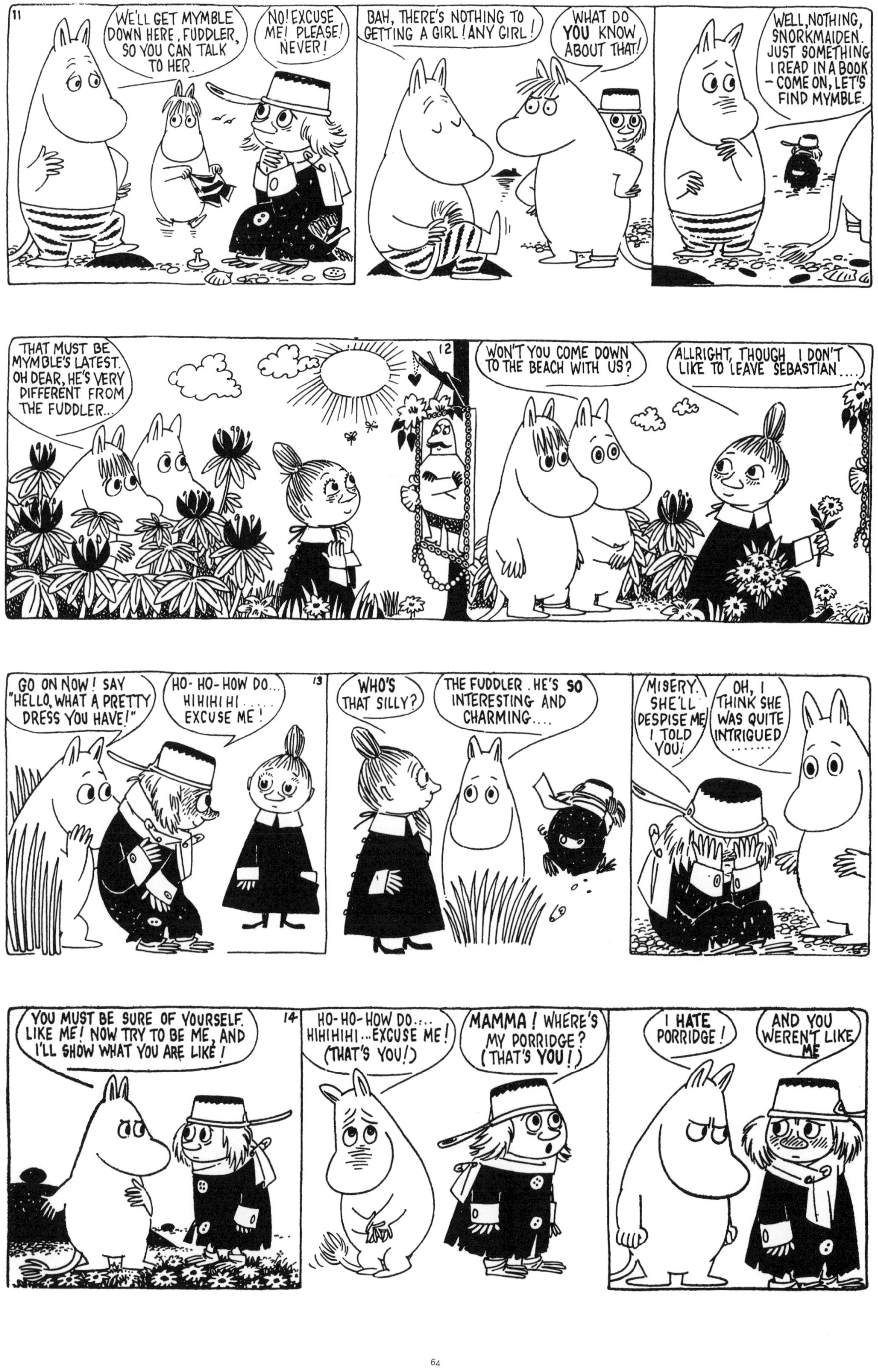
11
WE'LL GET MYMBLE DOWN HERE, FUDDLER, SO YOU CAN TALK TO HER.
NO! EXCUSE ME! PLEASE! NEVER!
BAH, THERE'S NOTHING TO GETTING A GIRL! ANY GIRL!
WHAT DO YOU KNOW ABOUT THAT!
WELL, NOTHING, SNORKMAIDEN. JUST SOMETHING I READ IN A BOOK – COME ON, LET'S FIND MYMBLE.
THAT MUST BE MYMBLE'S LATEST. OH DEAR, HE'S VERY DIFFERENT FROM THE FUDDLER...
12
WON'T YOU COME DOWN TO THE BEACH WITH US?
ALLRIGHT, THOUGH I DON'T LIKE TO LEAVE SEBASTIAN....
GO ON NOW! SAY "HELLO, WHAT A PRETTY DRESS YOU HAVE!"
HO-HO-HOW DO... HIHIHIHI..... EXCUSE ME!
13
WHO'S THAT SILLY?
THE FUDDLER. HE'S SO INTERESTING AND CHARMING....
MISERY. SHE'LL DESPISE ME. I TOLD YOU!
OH, I THINK SHE WAS QUITE INTRIGUED ....
YOU MUST BE SURE OF YOURSELF. LIKE ME! NOW TRY TO BE ME, AND I'LL SHOW WHAT YOU ARE LIKE!
14
HO-HO-HOW DO.... HIHIHIHI...EXCUSE ME! (THAT'S YOU!)
MAMMA! WHERE'S MY PORRIDGE? (THAT'S YOU!)
I HATE PORRIDGE!
AND YOU WEREN'T LIKE ME

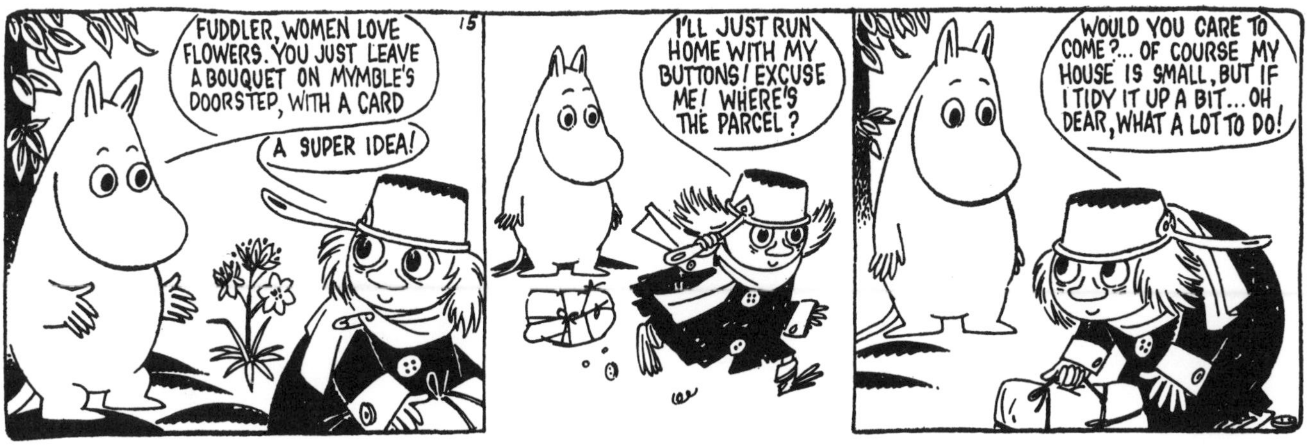
FUDDLER, WOMEN LOVE FLOWERS. YOU JUST LEAVE A BOUQUET ON MYMBLE'S DOORSTEP, WITH A CARD
A SUPER IDEA!
15
I'LL JUST RUN HOME WITH MY BUTTONS! EXCUSE ME! WHERE'S THE PARCEL?
WOULD YOU CARE TO COME?... OF COURSE MY HOUSE IS SMALL, BUT IF I TIDY IT UP A BIT... OH DEAR, WHAT A LOT TO DO!

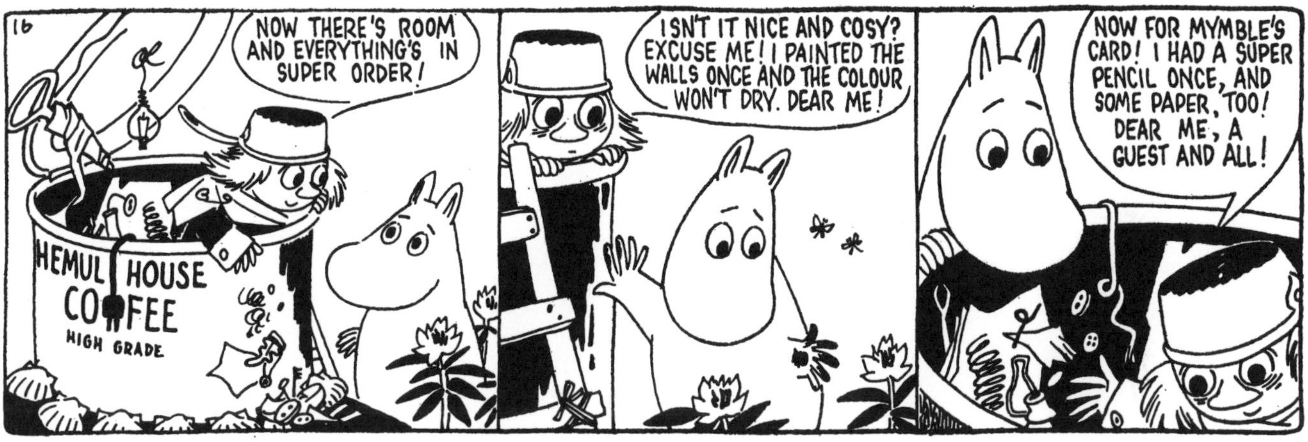
16
NOW THERE'S ROOM AND EVERYTHING'S IN SUPER ORDER!
HEMUL HOUSE COFFEE HIGH GRADE
ISN'T IT NICE AND COSY? EXCUSE ME! I PAINTED THE WALLS ONCE AND THE COLOUR WON'T DRY. DEAR ME!
NOW FOR MYMBLE'S CARD! I HAD A SUPER PENCIL ONCE, AND SOME PAPER, TOO! DEAR ME, A GUEST AND ALL!

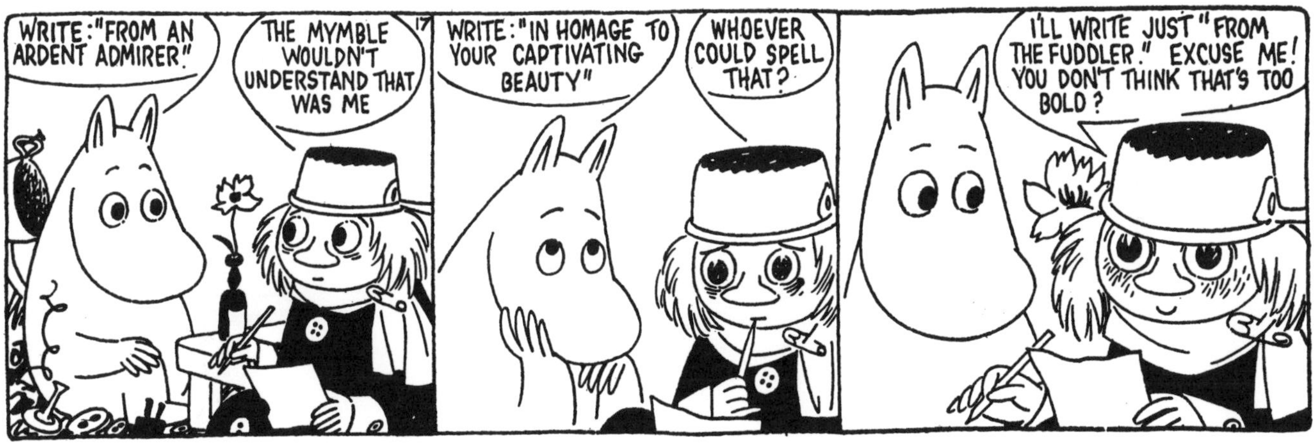
WRITE: "FROM AN ARDENT ADMIRER."
THE MYMBLE WOULDN'T UNDERSTAND THAT WAS ME
17
WRITE: "IN HOMAGE TO YOUR CAPTIVATING BEAUTY"
WHOEVER COULD SPELL THAT?
I'LL WRITE JUST "FROM THE FUDDLER." EXCUSE ME! YOU DON'T THINK THAT'S TOO BOLD?

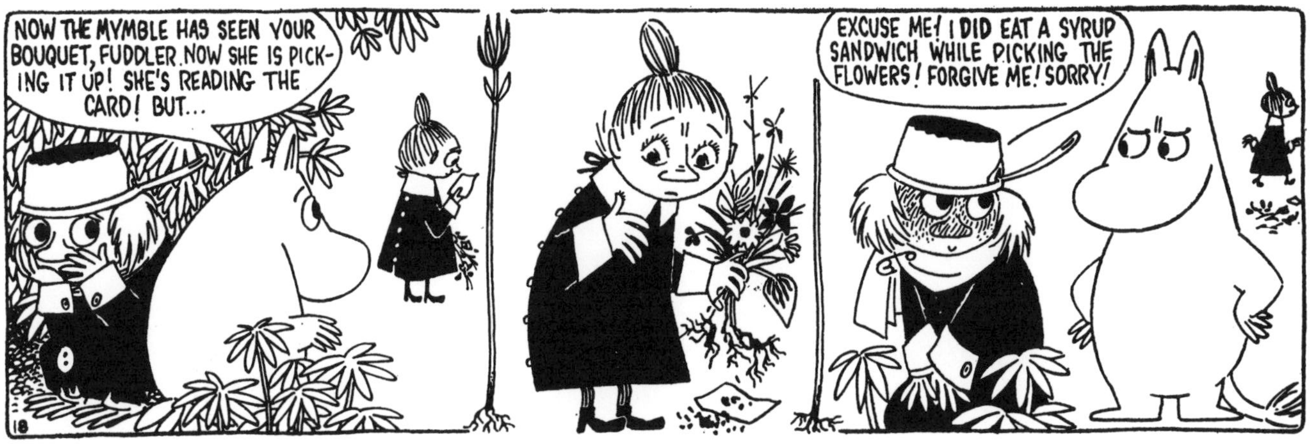
NOW THE MYMBLE HAS SEEN YOUR BOUQUET, FUDDLER. NOW SHE IS PICKING IT UP! SHE'S READING THE CARD! BUT...
18
EXCUSE ME! I DID EAT A SYRUP SANDWICH WHILE PICKING THE FLOWERS! FORGIVE ME! SORRY!

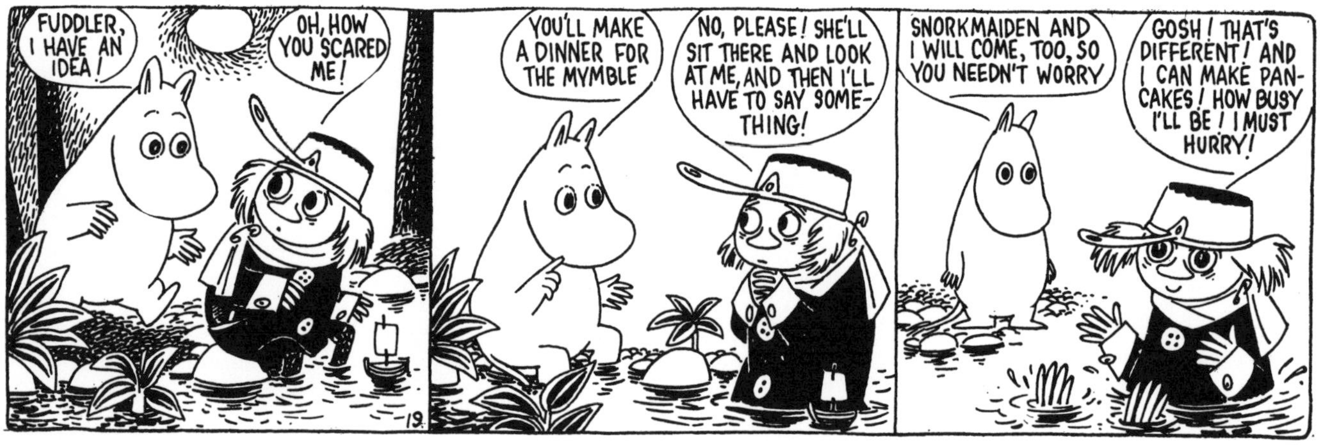
FUDDLER, I HAVE AN IDEA!
OH, HOW YOU SCARED ME!
YOU'LL MAKE A DINNER FOR THE MYMBLE
NO, PLEASE! SHE'LL SIT THERE AND LOOK AT ME, AND THEN I'LL HAVE TO SAY SOMETHING!
SNORKMAIDEN AND I WILL COME, TOO, SO YOU NEEDN'T WORRY
GOSH! THAT'S DIFFERENT! AND I CAN MAKE PANCAKES! HOW BUSY I'LL BE! I MUST HURRY!

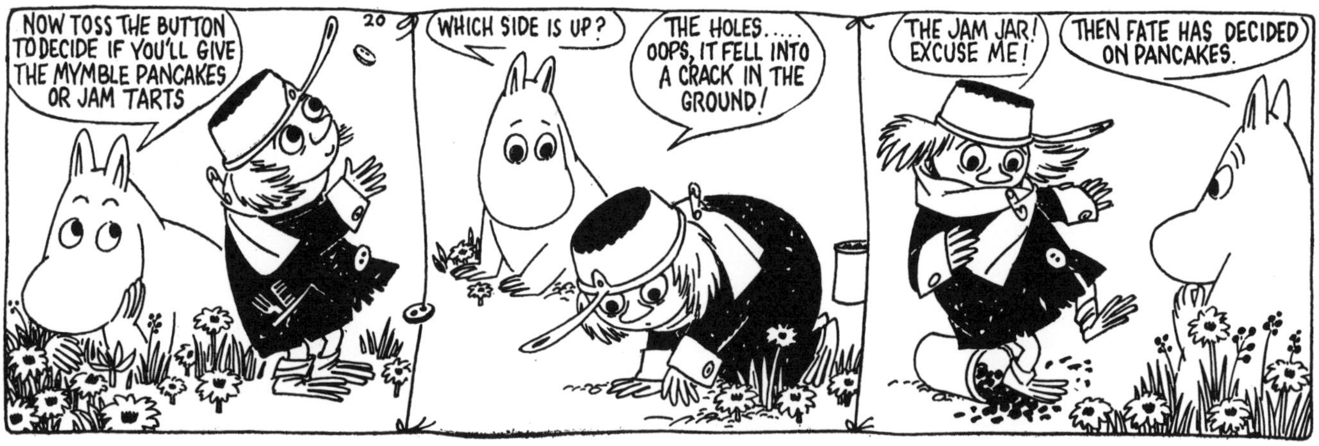
NOW TOSS THE BUTTON TO DECIDE IF YOU'LL GIVE THE MYMBLE PANCAKES OR JAM TARTS
WHICH SIDE IS UP?
THE HOLES..... OOPS, IT FELL INTO A CRACK IN THE GROUND!
THE JAM JAR! EXCUSE ME!
THEN FATE HAS DECIDED ON PANCAKES.

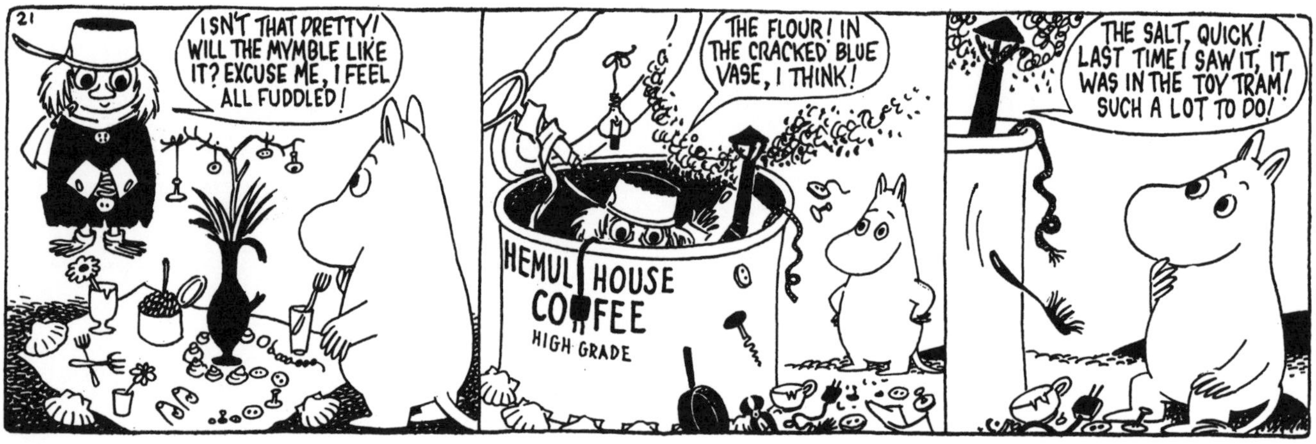
ISN'T THAT PRETTY! WILL THE MYMBLE LIKE IT? EXCUSE ME, I FEEL ALL FUDDLED!
THE FLOUR! IN THE CRACKED BLUE VASE, I THINK!
HEMUL HOUSE
COFFEE
HIGH GRADE
THE SALT, QUICK! LAST TIME I SAW IT, IT WAS IN THE TOY TRAM! SUCH A LOT TO DO!

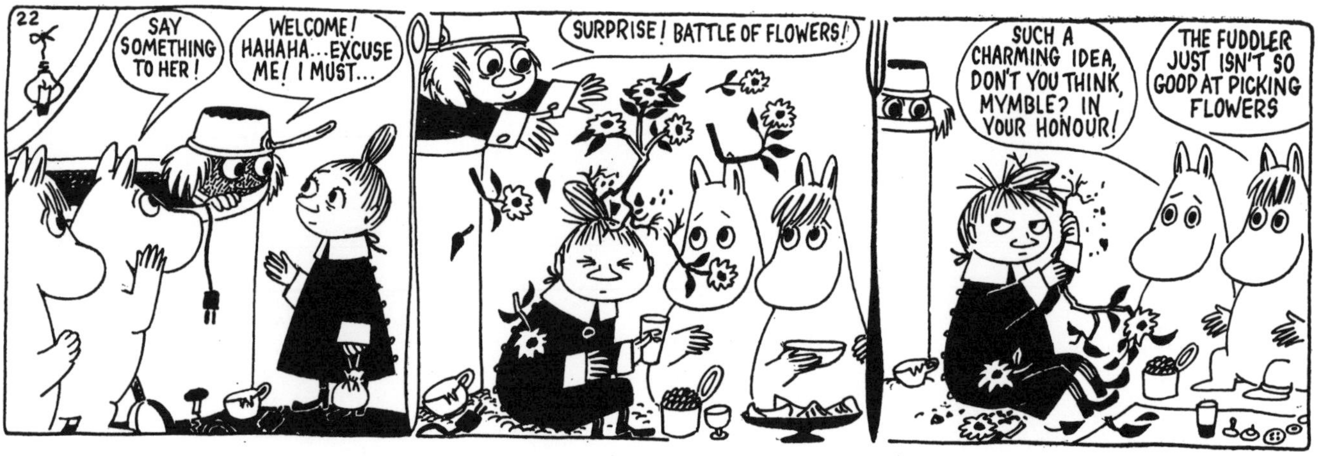
SAY SOMETHING TO HER!
WELCOME! HAHAHA... EXCUSE ME! I MUST...
SURPRISE! BATTLE OF FLOWERS!
SUCH A CHARMING IDEA, DON'T YOU THINK, MYMBLE? IN YOUR HONOUR!
THE FUDDLER JUST ISN'T SO GOOD AT PICKING FLOWERS

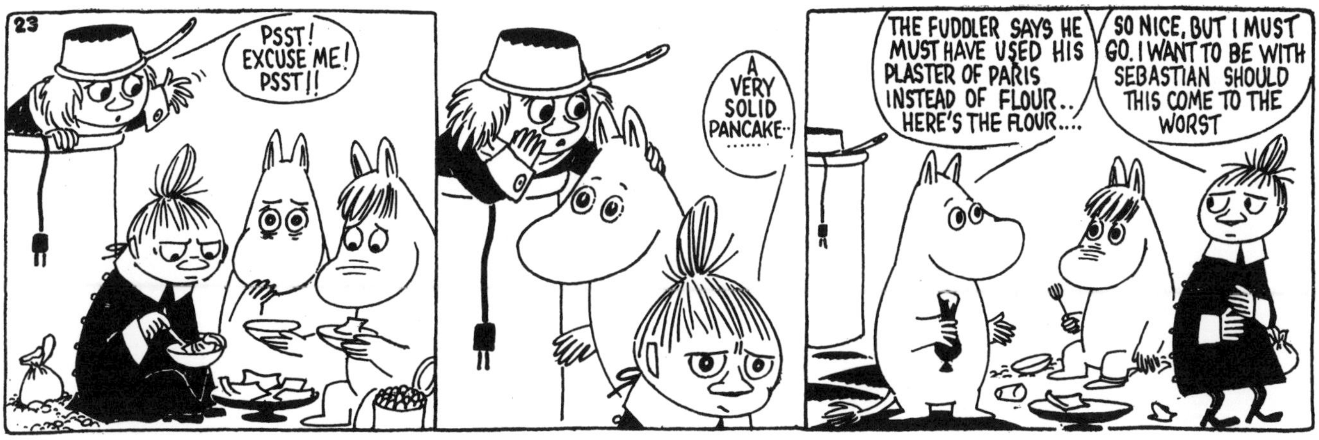
23
PSST! EXCUSE ME! PSST!!
A VERY SOLID PANCAKE......
THE FUDDLER SAYS HE MUST HAVE USED HIS PLASTER OF PARIS INSTEAD OF FLOUR.. HERE'S THE FLOUR....
SO NICE, BUT I MUST GO. I WANT TO BE WITH SEBASTIAN SHOULD THIS COME TO THE WORST

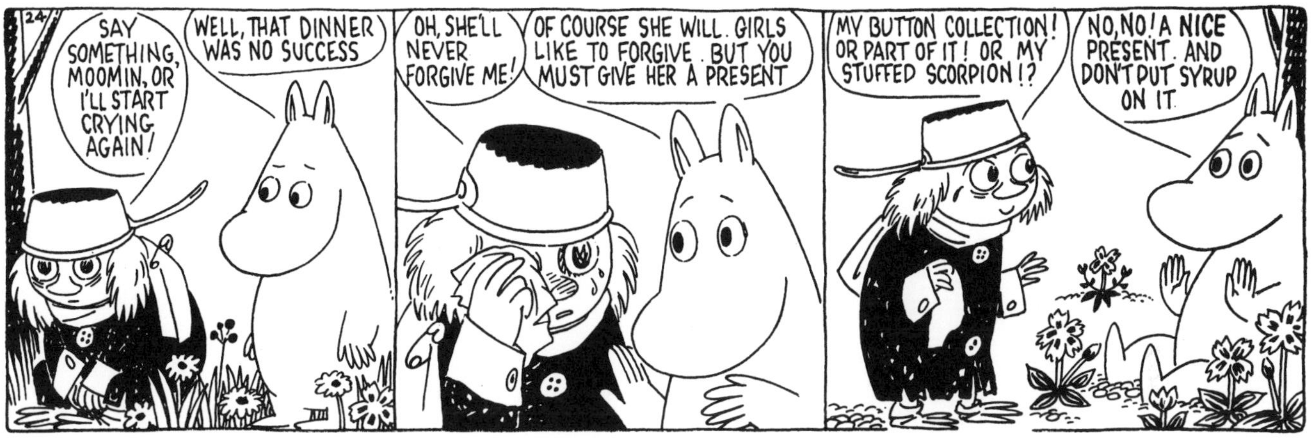
24
SAY SOMETHING, MOOMIN, OR I'LL START CRYING AGAIN!
WELL, THAT DINNER WAS NO SUCCESS
OH, SHE'LL NEVER FORGIVE ME!
OF COURSE SHE WILL. GIRLS LIKE TO FORGIVE. BUT YOU MUST GIVE HER A PRESENT
MY BUTTON COLLECTION! OR PART OF IT! OR MY STUFFED SCORPION!?
NO, NO! A NICE PRESENT. AND DON'T PUT SYRUP ON IT.

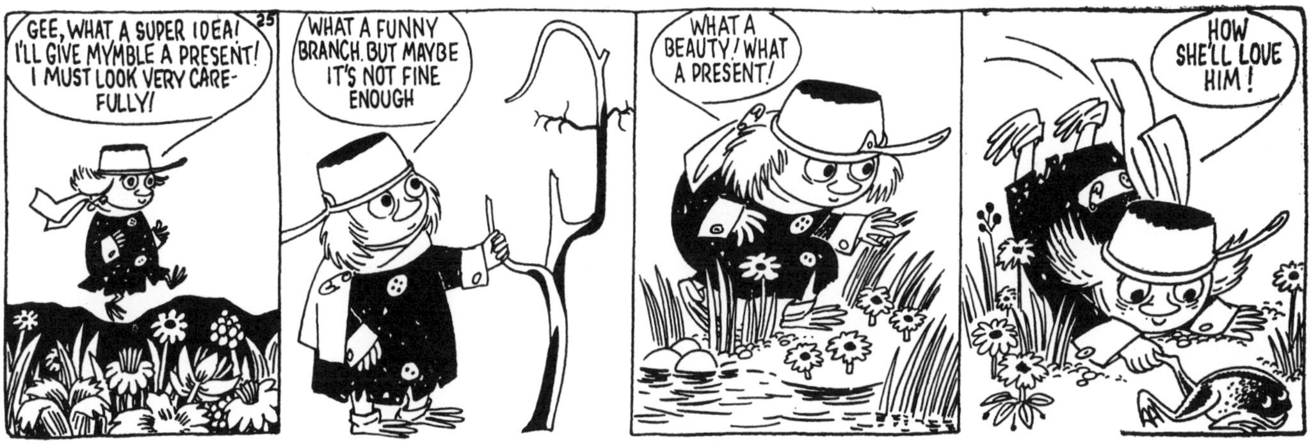
25
GEE, WHAT A SUPER IDEA! I'LL GIVE MYMBLE A PRESENT! I MUST LOOK VERY CARE-FULLY!
WHAT A FUNNY BRANCH. BUT MAYBE IT'S NOT FINE ENOUGH
WHAT A BEAUTY! WHAT A PRESENT!
HOW SHE'LL LOVE HIM!

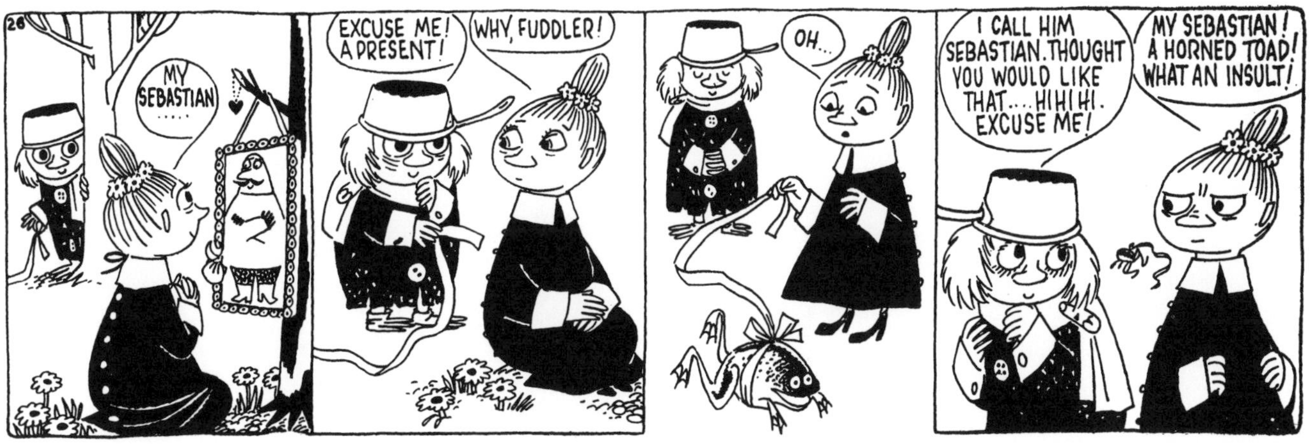
26
MY SEBASTIAN .....
EXCUSE ME! A PRESENT!
WHY, FUDDLER!
OH...
I CALL HIM SEBASTIAN. THOUGHT YOU WOULD LIKE THAT.... HIHIHI. EXCUSE ME!
MY SEBASTIAN! A HORNED TOAD! WHAT AN INSULT!

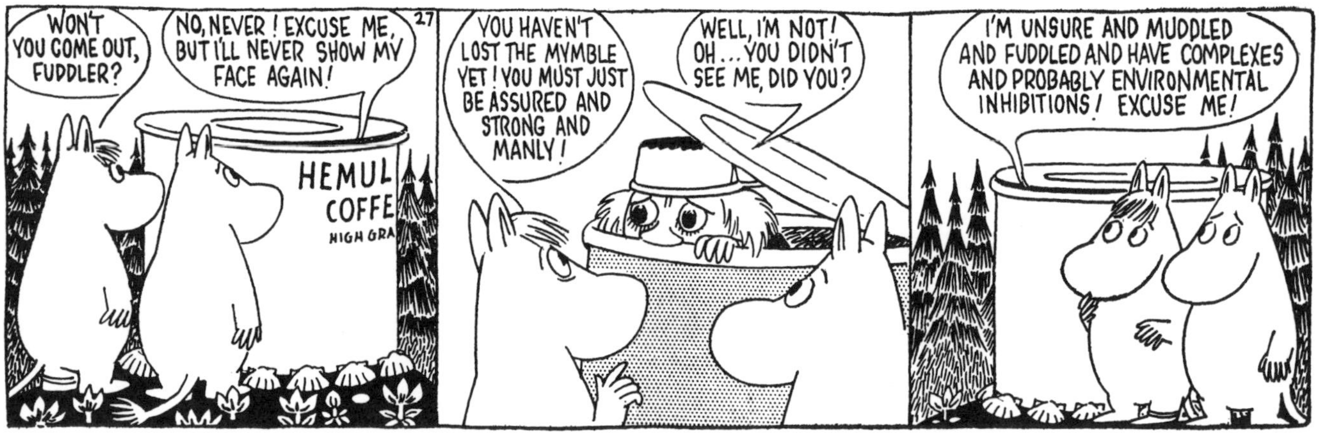
27
WON'T YOU COME OUT, FUDDLER?
NO, NEVER! EXCUSE ME, BUT I'LL NEVER SHOW MY FACE AGAIN!
HEMUL COFFE HIGH GRA
YOU HAVEN'T LOST THE MYMBLE YET! YOU MUST JUST BE ASSURED AND STRONG AND MANLY!
WELL, I'M NOT! OH... YOU DIDN'T SEE ME, DID YOU?
I'M UNSURE AND MUDDLED AND FUDDLED AND HAVE COMPLEXES AND PROBABLY ENVIRONMENTAL INHIBITIONS! EXCUSE ME!

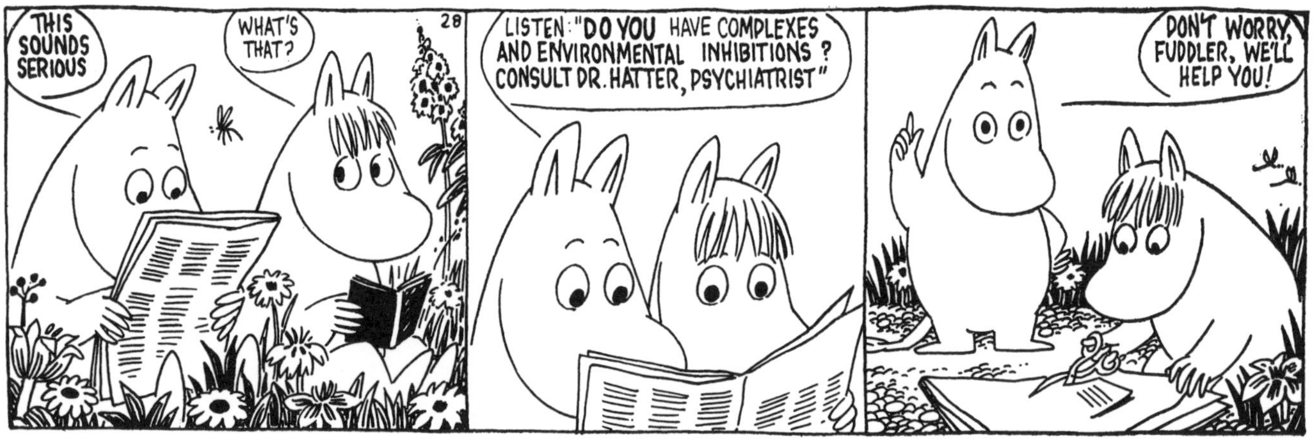
28
THIS SOUNDS SERIOUS
WHAT'S THAT?
LISTEN: "DO YOU HAVE COMPLEXES AND ENVIRONMENTAL INHIBITIONS? CONSULT DR. HATTER, PSYCHIATRIST"
DON'T WORRY, FUDDLER, WE'LL HELP YOU!

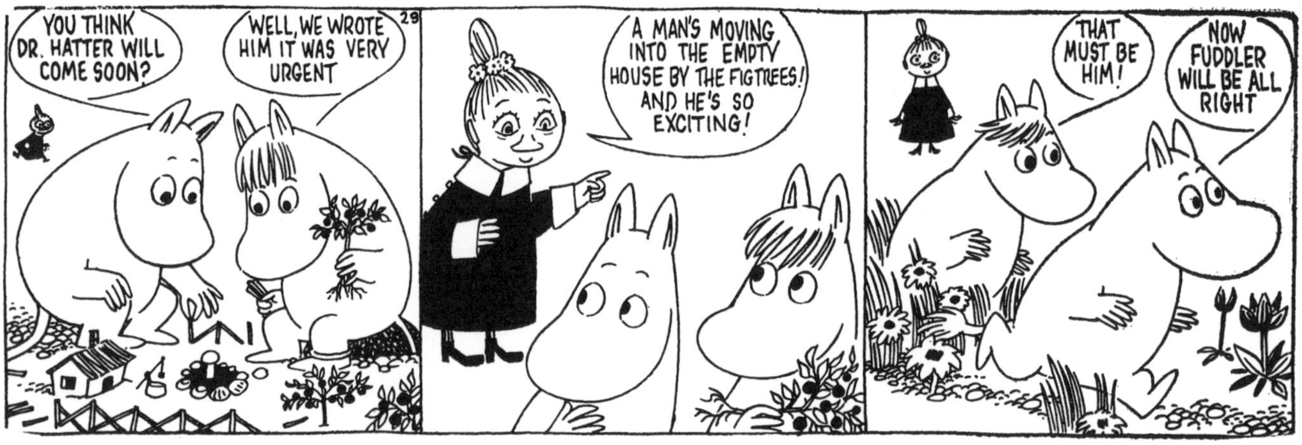
29
YOU THINK DR. HATTER WILL COME SOON?
WELL, WE WROTE HIM IT WAS VERY URGENT
A MAN'S MOVING INTO THE EMPTY HOUSE BY THE FIGTREES! AND HE'S SO EXCITING!
THAT MUST BE HIM!
NOW FUDDLER WILL BE ALL RIGHT

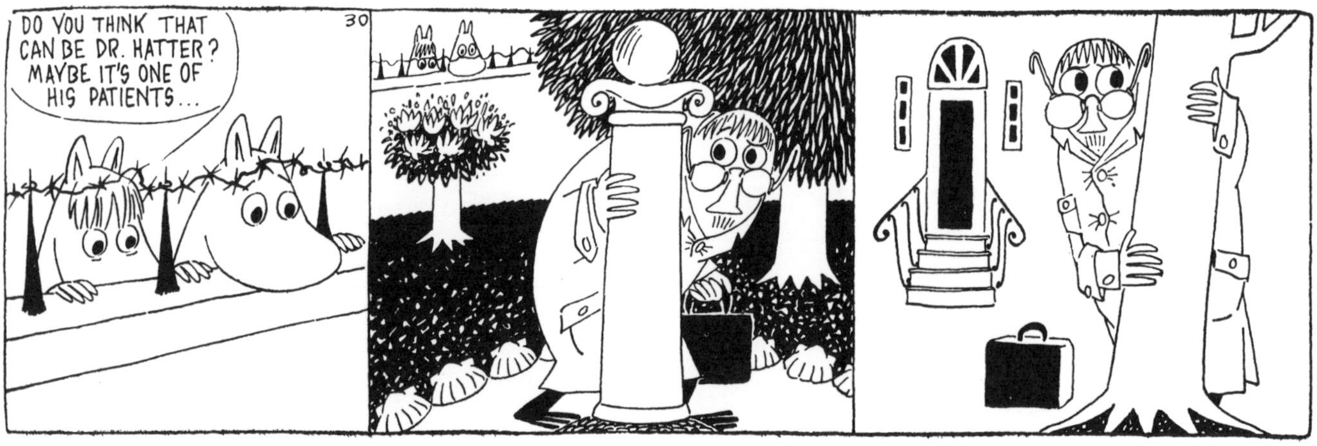
30
DO YOU THINK THAT CAN BE DR. HATTER? MAYBE IT'S ONE OF HIS PATIENTS...

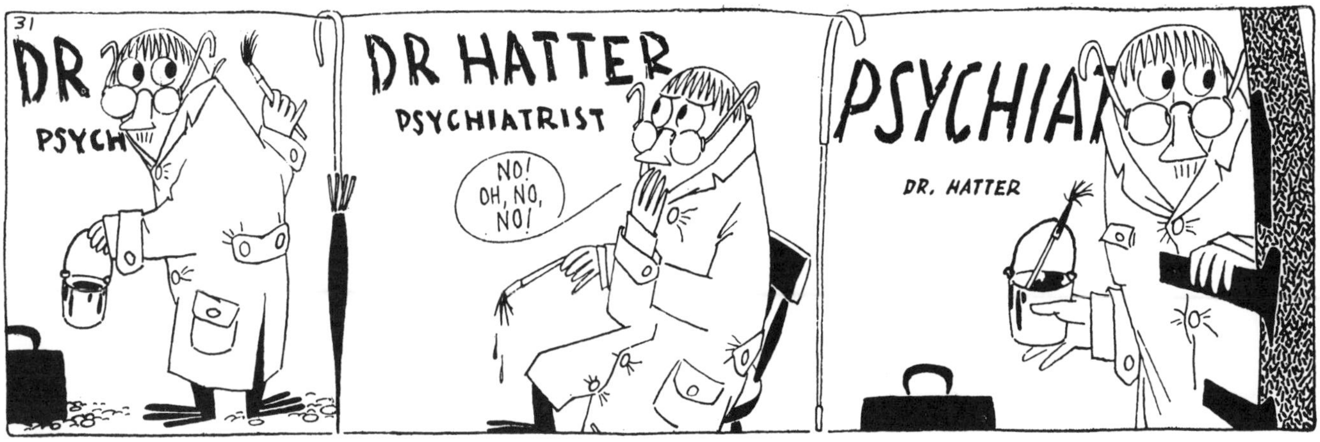
31
DR
PSYCH
DR HATTER
PSYCHIATRIST
NO! OH, NO, NO!
PSYCHIA
DR. HATTER

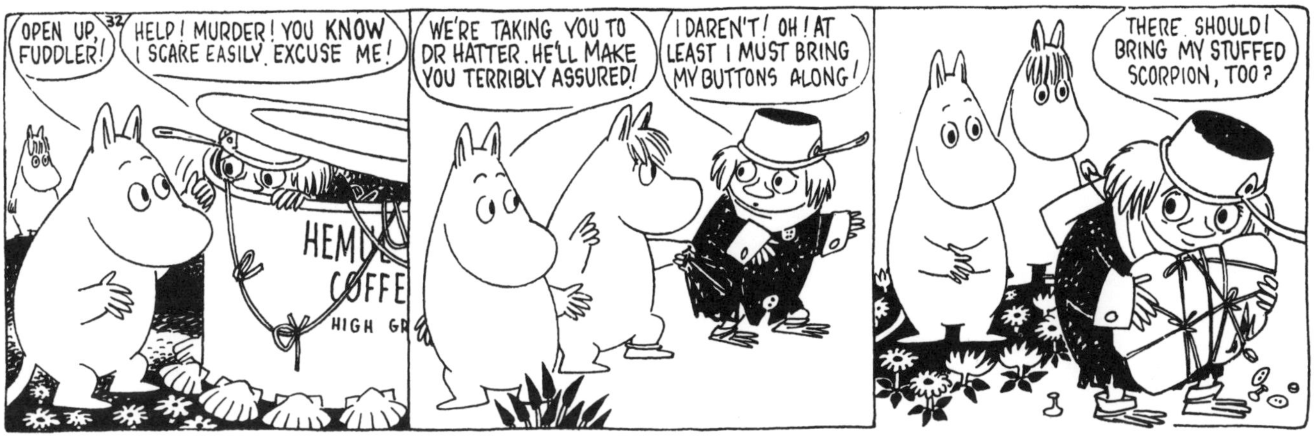
OPEN UP, FUDDLER!
32
HELP! MURDER! YOU KNOW I SCARE EASILY. EXCUSE ME!
HEMU
COFFE
HIGH GR
WE'RE TAKING YOU TO DR HATTER. HE'LL MAKE YOU TERRIBLY ASSURED!
I DAREN'T! OH! AT LEAST I MUST BRING MY BUTTONS ALONG!
THERE. SHOULD I BRING MY STUFFED SCORPION, TOO?

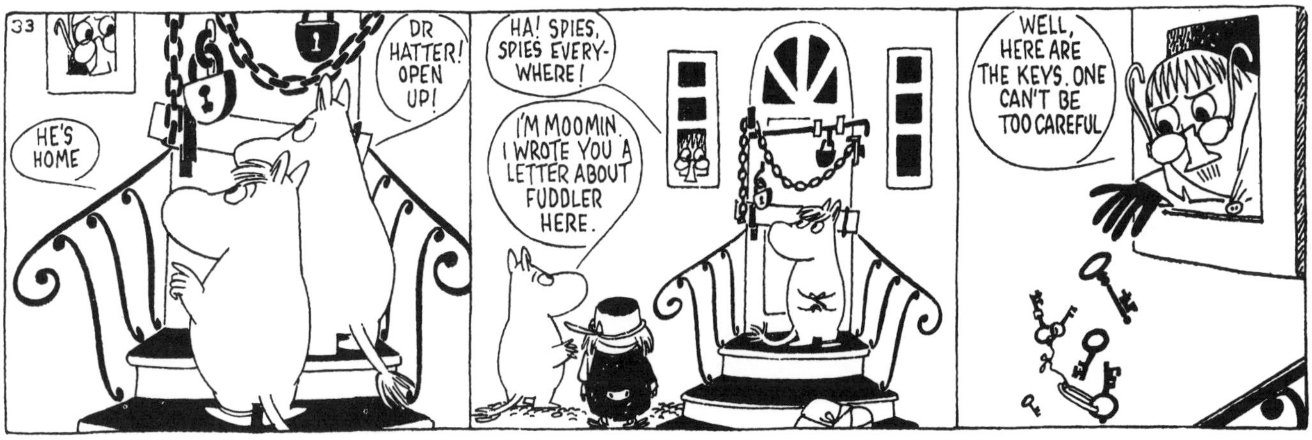
33
HE'S HOME
DR HATTER! OPEN UP!
HA! SPIES, SPIES EVERYWHERE!
I'M MOOMIN. I WROTE YOU A LETTER ABOUT FUDDLER HERE.
WELL, HERE ARE THE KEYS. ONE CAN'T BE TOO CAREFUL

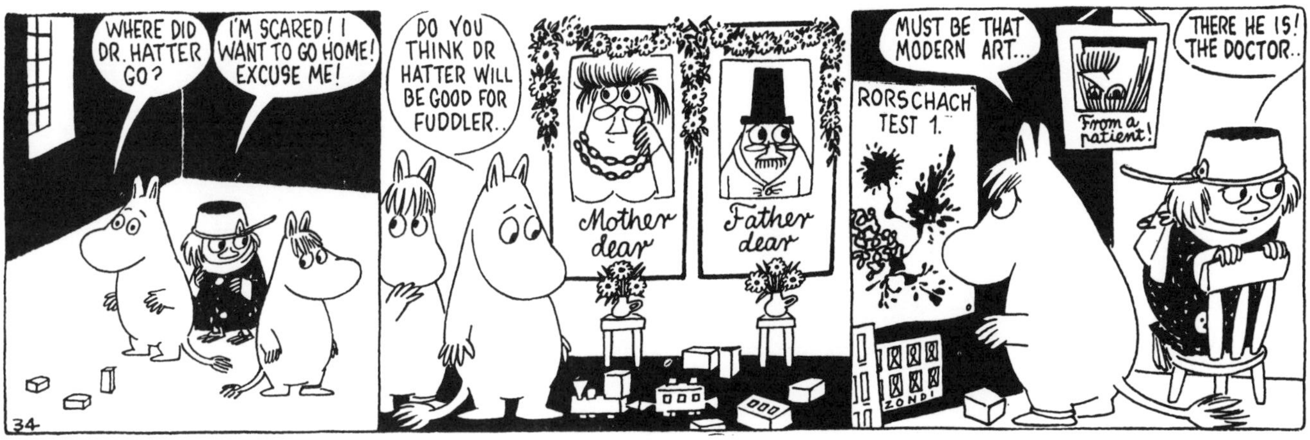
WHERE DID DR. HATTER GO?
I'M SCARED! I WANT TO GO HOME! EXCUSE ME!
34
DO YOU THINK DR HATTER WILL BE GOOD FOR FUDDLER..
Mother dear
Father dear
MUST BE THAT MODERN ART...
RORSCHACH TEST 1.
From a patient!
THERE HE IS! THE DOCTOR..

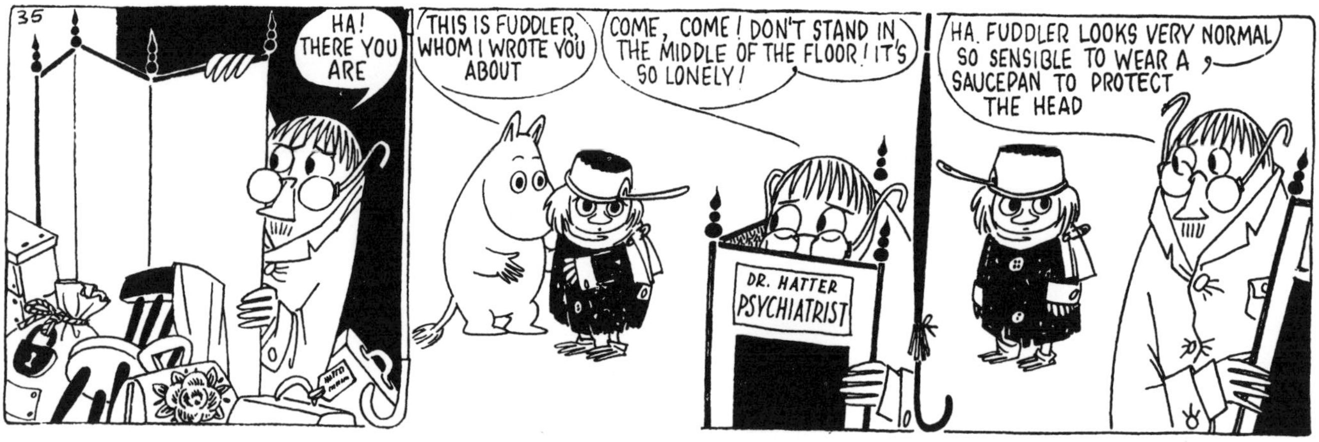
35
HA! THERE YOU ARE
THIS IS FUDDLER, WHOM I WROTE YOU ABOUT
COME, COME! DON'T STAND IN THE MIDDLE OF THE FLOOR! IT'S SO LONELY!
DR. HATTER PSYCHIATRIST
HA. FUDDLER LOOKS VERY NORMAL, SO SENSIBLE TO WEAR A SAUCEPAN TO PROTECT THE HEAD

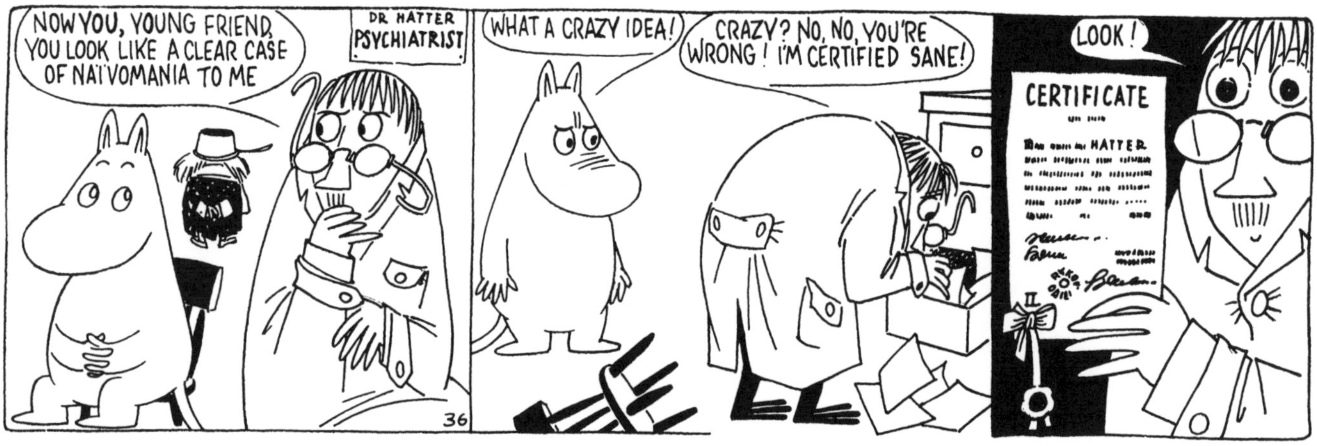
NOW YOU, YOUNG FRIEND, YOU LOOK LIKE A CLEAR CASE OF NAÏVOMANIA TO ME
DR HATTER PSYCHIATRIST
36
WHAT A CRAZY IDEA!
CRAZY? NO, NO, YOU'RE WRONG! I'M CERTIFIED SANE!
LOOK!
CERTIFICATE
HATTER

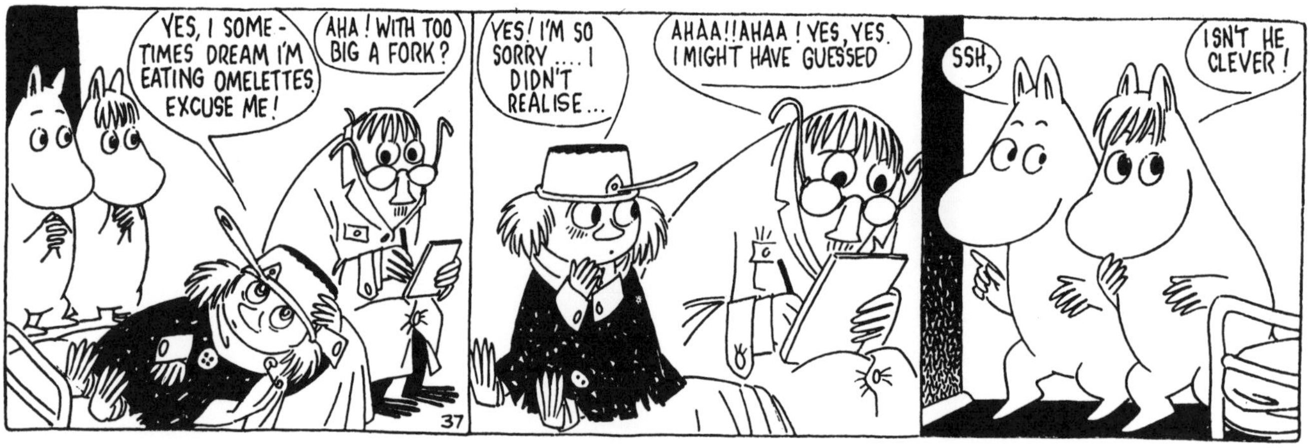
YES, I SOMETIMES DREAM I'M EATING OMELETTES. EXCUSE ME!
AHA! WITH TOO BIG A FORK?
37
YES! I'M SO SORRY.... I DIDN'T REALISE...
AHAA!! AHAA! YES, YES. I MIGHT HAVE GUESSED
SSH,
ISN'T HE CLEVER!

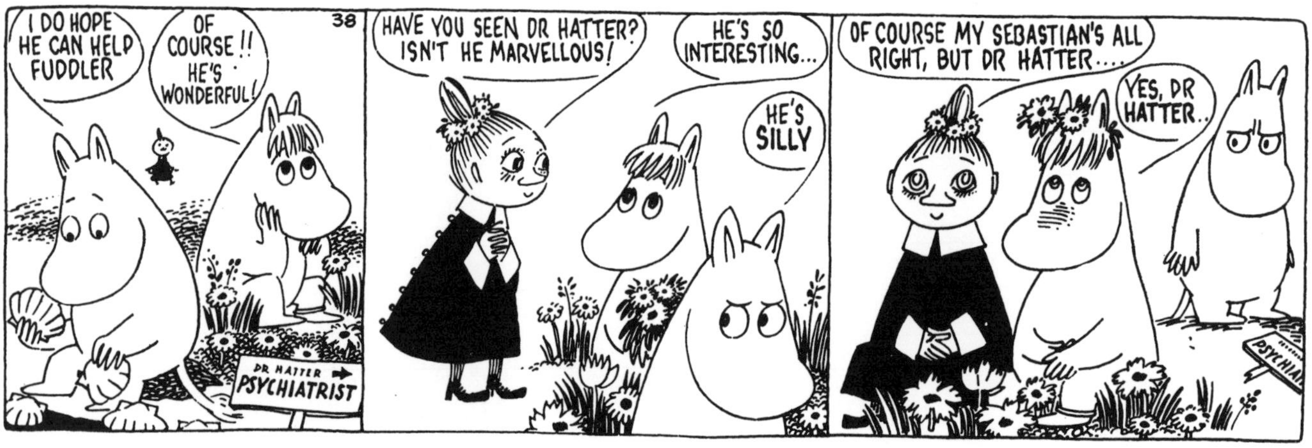
I DO HOPE HE CAN HELP FUDDLER
OF COURSE!! HE'S WONDERFUL!
38
DR HATTER PSYCHIATRIST
HAVE YOU SEEN DR HATTER? ISN'T HE MARVELLOUS!
HE'S SO INTERESTING...
HE'S SILLY
OF COURSE MY SEBASTIAN'S ALL RIGHT, BUT DR HATTER....
YES, DR HATTER..
PSYCHIA

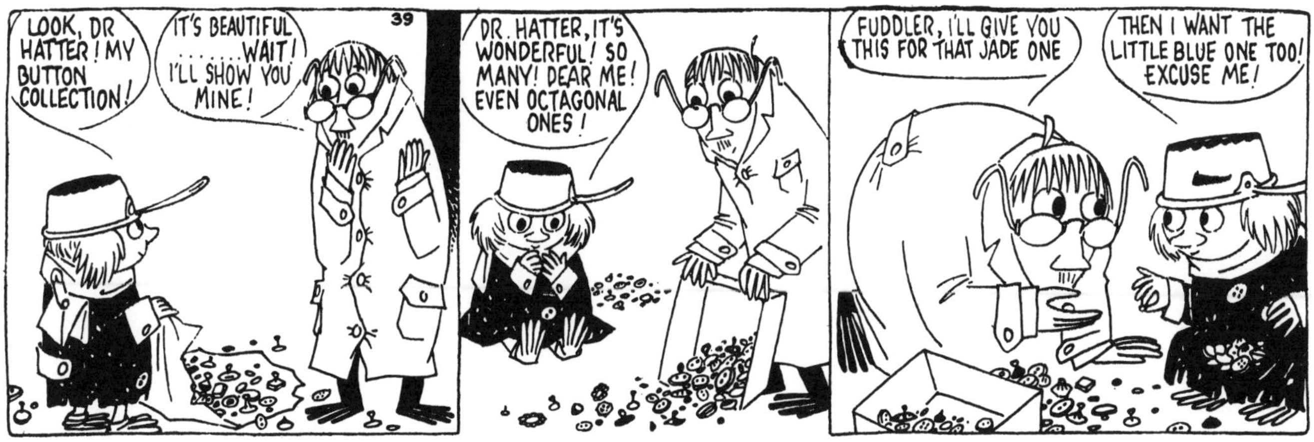
39
LOOK, DR HATTER! MY BUTTON COLLECTION!
IT'S BEAUTIFUL . . . . . . .WAIT! I'LL SHOW YOU MINE!
DR. HATTER, IT'S WONDERFUL! SO MANY! DEAR ME! EVEN OCTAGONAL ONES!
FUDDLER, I'LL GIVE YOU THIS FOR THAT JADE ONE
THEN I WANT THE LITTLE BLUE ONE TOO! EXCUSE ME!

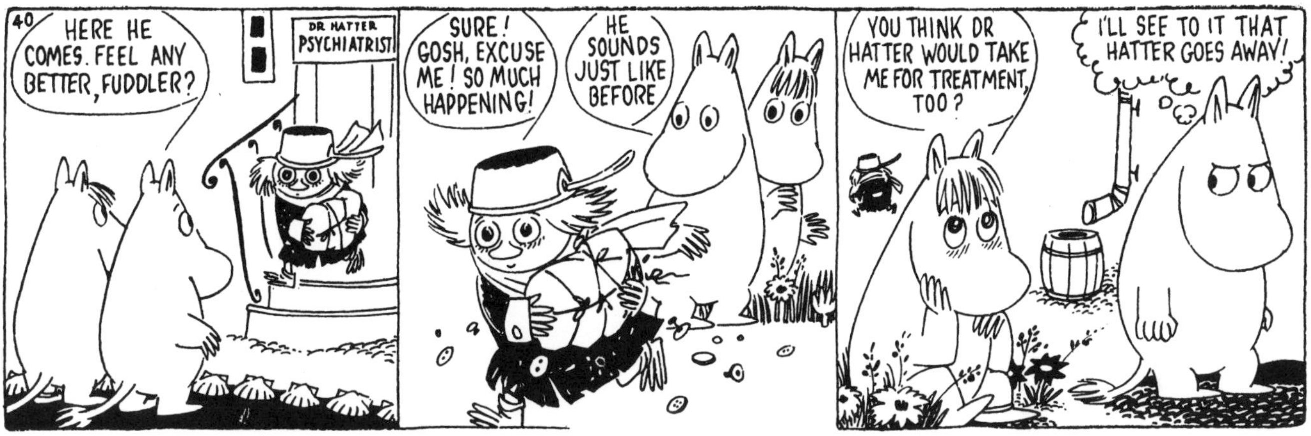
40
HERE HE COMES. FEEL ANY BETTER, FUDDLER?
DR HATTER PSYCHIATRIST
SURE! GOSH, EXCUSE ME! SO MUCH HAPPENING!
HE SOUNDS JUST LIKE BEFORE
YOU THINK DR HATTER WOULD TAKE ME FOR TREATMENT, TOO?
I'LL SEE TO IT THAT HATTER GOES AWAY!

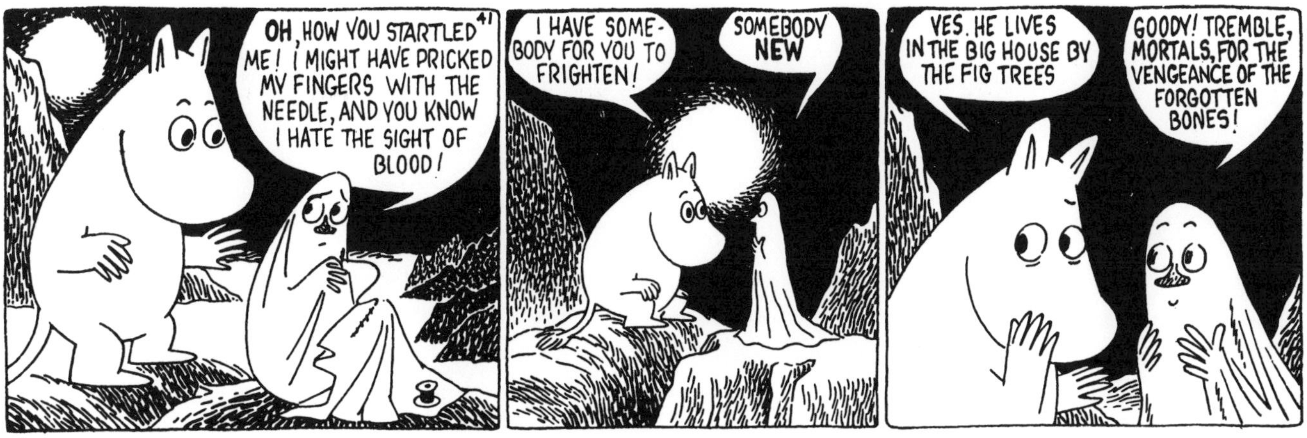
41
OH, HOW YOU STARTLED ME! I MIGHT HAVE PRICKED MY FINGERS WITH THE NEEDLE, AND YOU KNOW I HATE THE SIGHT OF BLOOD!
I HAVE SOMEBODY FOR YOU TO FRIGHTEN!
SOMEBODY NEW
YES. HE LIVES IN THE BIG HOUSE BY THE FIG TREES
GOODY! TREMBLE, MORTALS, FOR THE VENGEANCE OF THE FORGOTTEN BONES!

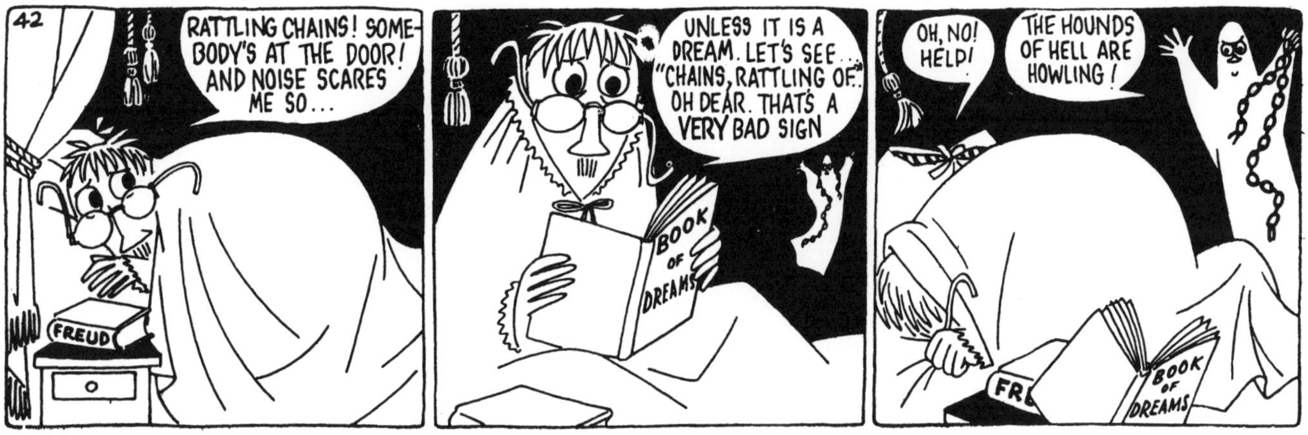
42
RATTLING CHAINS! SOMEBODY'S AT THE DOOR! AND NOISE SCARES ME SO...
FREUD
UNLESS IT IS A DREAM. LET'S SEE... "CHAINS, RATTLING OF." OH DEAR. THAT'S A VERY BAD SIGN
BOOK OF DREAMS
OH, NO! HELP!
THE HOUNDS OF HELL ARE HOWLING!
FR
BOOK OF DREAMS

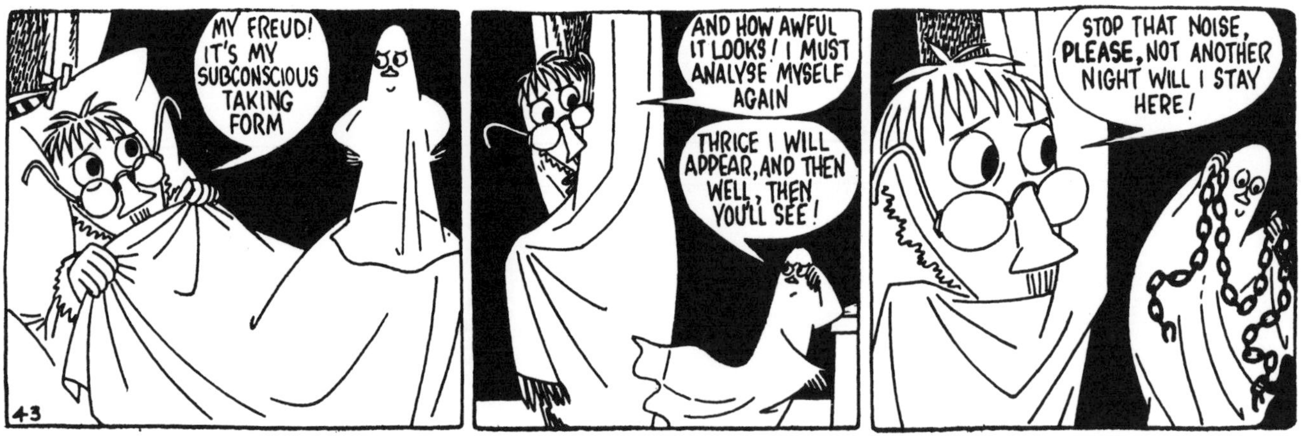
43
MY FREUD! IT'S MY SUBCONSCIOUS TAKING FORM
AND HOW AWFUL IT LOOKS! I MUST ANALYSE MYSELF AGAIN
THRICE I WILL APPEAR, AND THEN WELL, THEN YOU'LL SEE!
STOP THAT NOISE, PLEASE, NOT ANOTHER NIGHT WILL I STAY HERE!

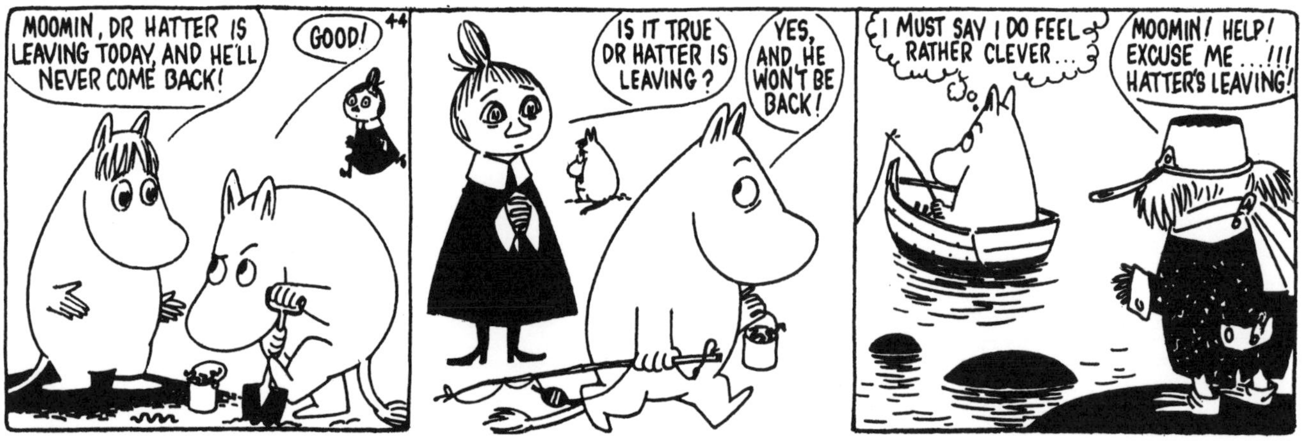
44
MOOMIN, DR HATTER IS LEAVING TODAY, AND HE'LL NEVER COME BACK!
GOOD!
IS IT TRUE DR HATTER IS LEAVING?
YES, AND HE WON'T BE BACK!
I MUST SAY I DO FEEL RATHER CLEVER...
MOOMIN! HELP! EXCUSE ME...!!! HATTER'S LEAVING!

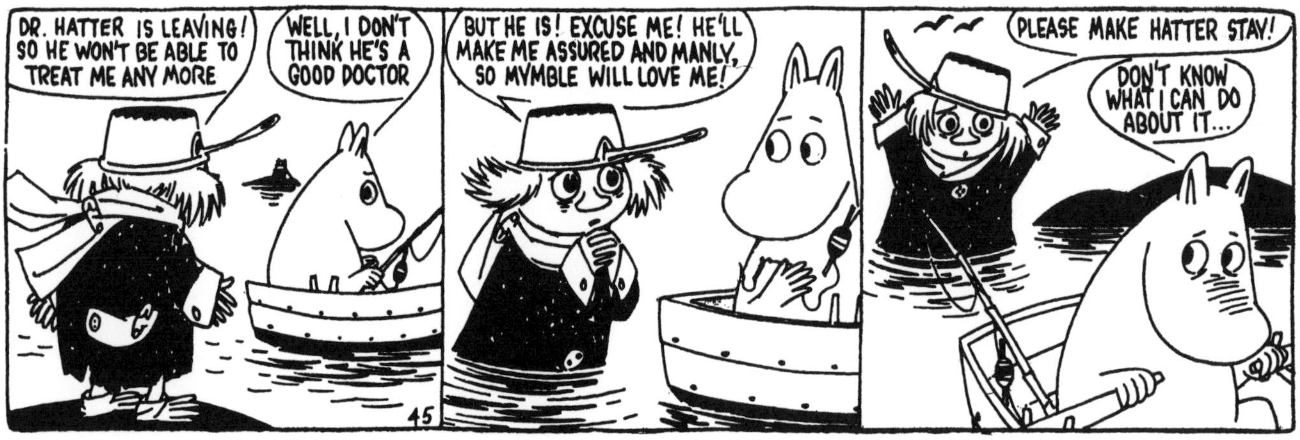
DR. HATTER IS LEAVING! SO HE WON'T BE ABLE TO TREAT ME ANY MORE
WELL, I DON'T THINK HE'S A GOOD DOCTOR
BUT HE IS! EXCUSE ME! HE'LL MAKE ME ASSURED AND MANLY, SO MYMBLE WILL LOVE ME!
45
PLEASE MAKE HATTER STAY!
DON'T KNOW WHAT I CAN DO ABOUT IT...

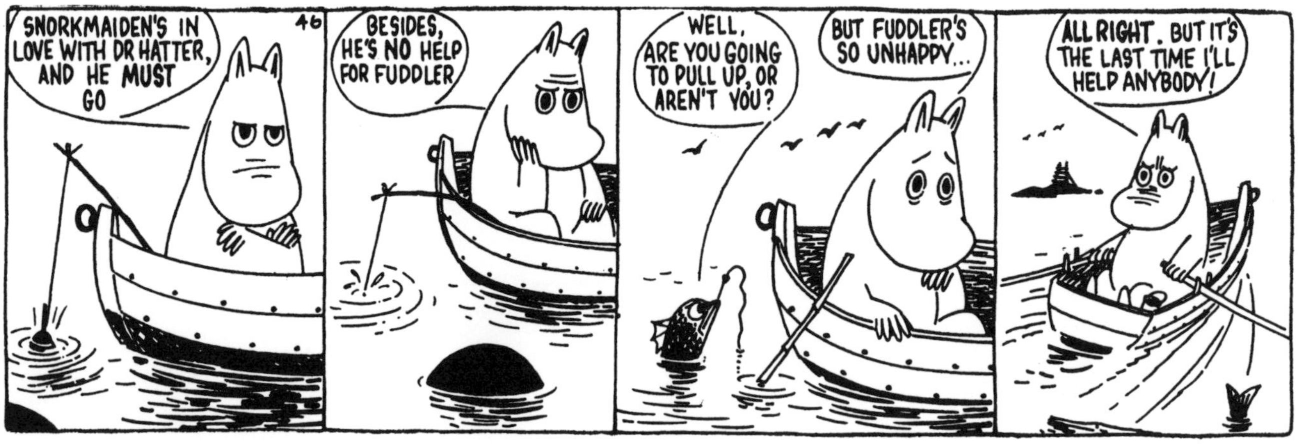
46
SNORKMAIDEN'S IN LOVE WITH DR HATTER, AND HE MUST GO
BESIDES, HE'S NO HELP FOR FUDDLER
WELL, ARE YOU GOING TO PULL UP, OR AREN'T YOU?
BUT FUDDLER'S SO UNHAPPY...
ALL RIGHT. BUT IT'S THE LAST TIME I'LL HELP ANYBODY!

BUT YOU CAN'T LEAVE, DR HATTER!
I MUST! THIS TERRIBLE HOUSE WAKES MY SUBCONSCIOUS!
BUT WE NEED YOU! WE'LL GET YOU LOTS OF PATIENTS!
YOU HAVE MENTAL CASES? EVERYBODY SEEMS SO NORMAL...
Mother dear
WE'RE AWFULLY MENTAL! LIKE THIS!
OH, DEAR...
IT WON'T BE EASY, GETTING PATIENTS FOR DR HATTER. WE DO SEEM RATHER NORMAL...
EXCUSE ME, BUT DO YOU NEED SOME PSYCHOLOGICAL TREATMENT? I KNOW A...
I DON'T THINK THAT'S THE RIGHT APPROACH
HAVE YOU BEEN TO THE NEW PSYCHIATRIST YET, MRS FILLYJONK?
NO! WHY SHOULD I, YOUNG MAN?
WHY, EVERY BODY GOES THERE
REALLY?
WELL, HE CAN ONLY TAKE ONE OR TWO MORE, ANYWAY. SNORK-MAIDEN'S GOING TOMORROW...
OH...
NOW WE'VE GOT A PSYCHIATRIST I SUPPOSE CRIME WILL GO DOWN
YES. ONLY IT'S NEVER BEEN UP...
BUT AS HE HAS NO PATIENTS HE'S LEAVING, SO I THINK IT'S OUR CIVIC DUTY TO CONSULT HIM
YOU DO?
DO YOU THINK HE'LL FIND OUT EVERY THING ABOUT ONE?

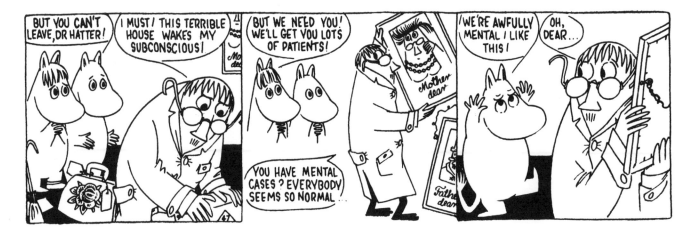

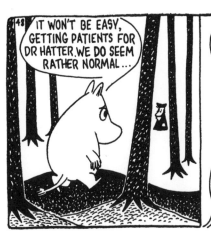

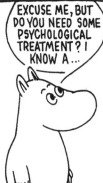

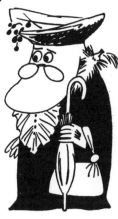

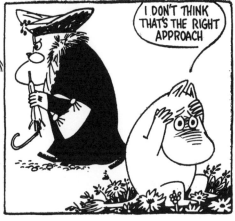

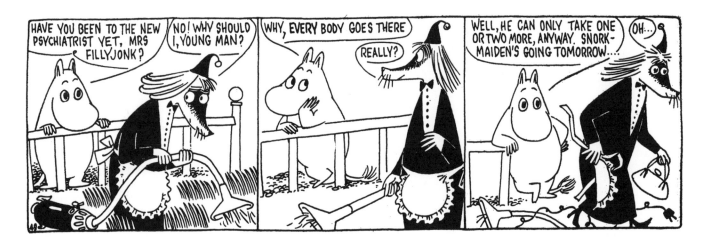

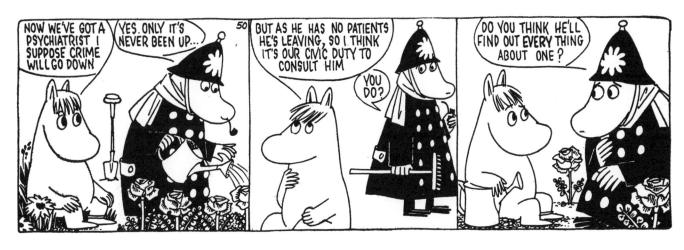

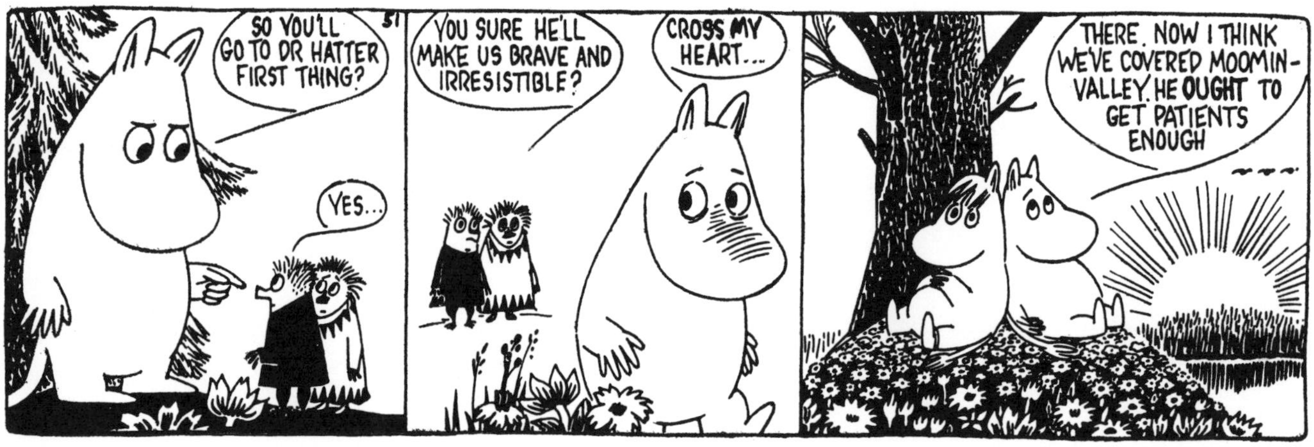
51
SO YOU'LL GO TO DR HATTER FIRST THING?
YES...
YOU SURE HE'LL MAKE US BRAVE AND IRRESISTIBLE?
CROSS MY HEART...
THERE. NOW I THINK WE'VE COVERED MOOMIN-VALLEY. HE OUGHT TO GET PATIENTS ENOUGH

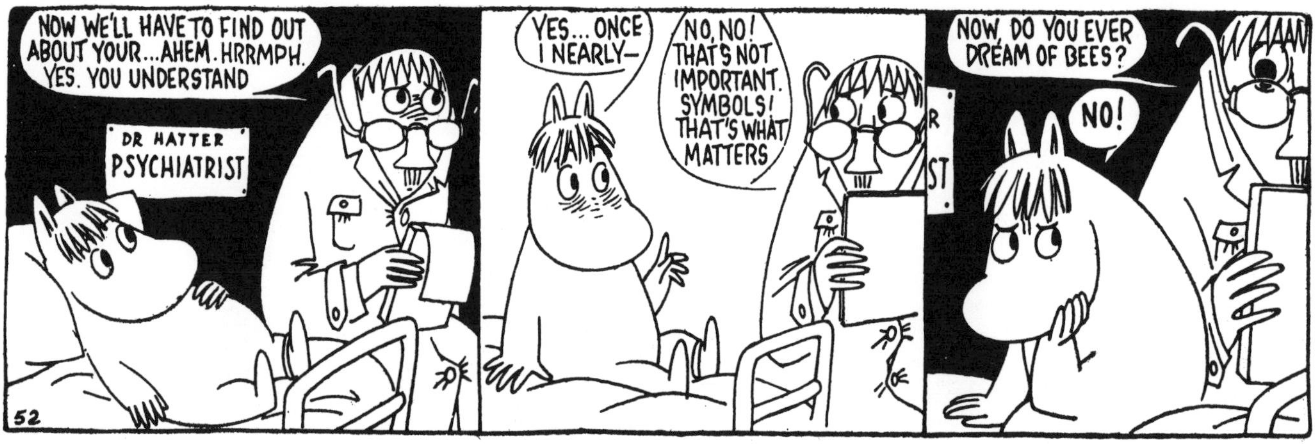
NOW WE'LL HAVE TO FIND OUT ABOUT YOUR...AHEM. HRRMPH. YES. YOU UNDERSTAND
DR HATTER
PSYCHIATRIST
52
YES... ONCE I NEARLY—
NO, NO! THAT'S NOT IMPORTANT. SYMBOLS! THAT'S WHAT MATTERS
NOW, DO YOU EVER DREAM OF BEES?
NO!

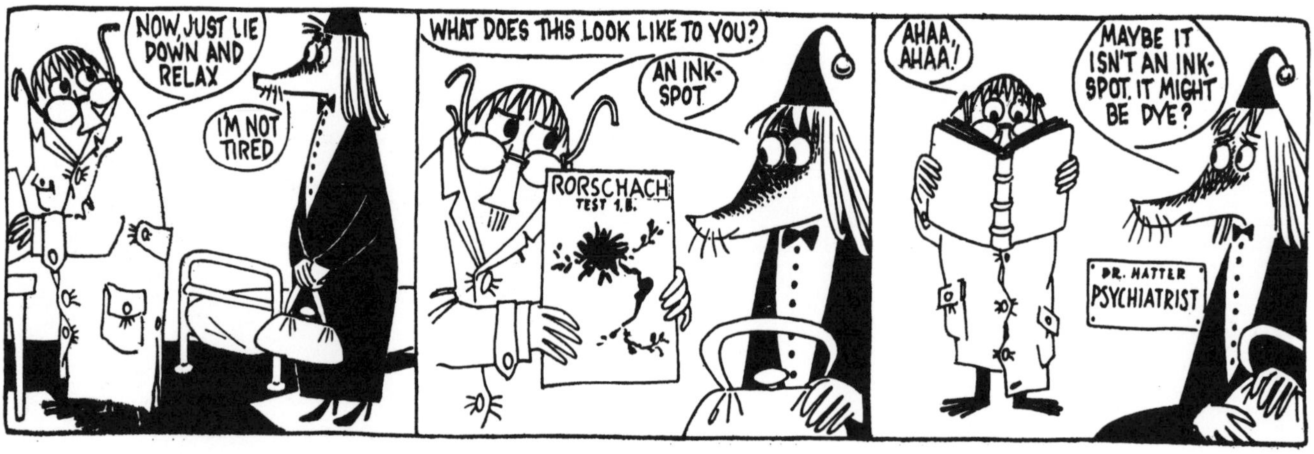
NOW, JUST LIE DOWN AND RELAX
I'M NOT TIRED
WHAT DOES THIS LOOK LIKE TO YOU?
AN INK-SPOT
RORSCHACH
TEST 1.B.
AHAA, AHAA!
MAYBE IT ISN'T AN INK-SPOT. IT MIGHT BE DYE?
DR. HATTER
PSYCHIATRIST

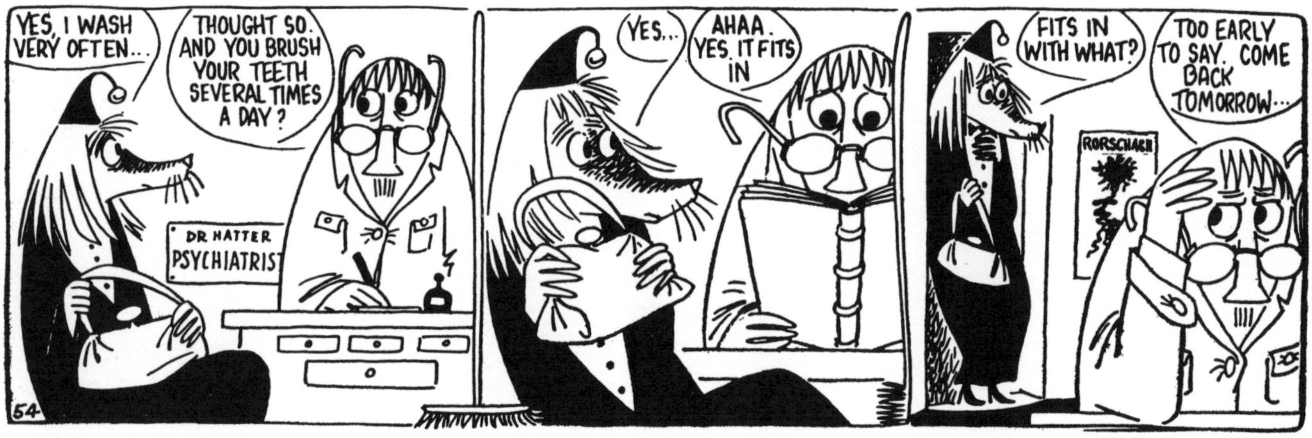
YES, I WASH VERY OFTEN...
THOUGHT SO. AND YOU BRUSH YOUR TEETH SEVERAL TIMES A DAY?
DR HATTER
PSYCHIATRIST
54
YES...
AHAA. YES, IT FITS IN
FITS IN WITH WHAT?
TOO EARLY TO SAY. COME BACK TOMORROW...
RORSCHACH

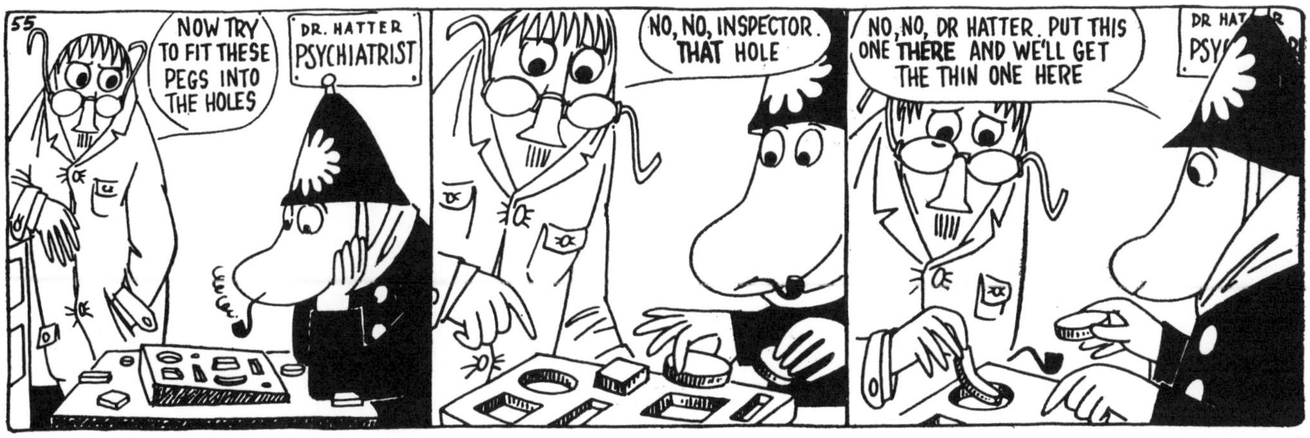
55
NOW TRY TO FIT THESE PEGS INTO THE HOLES
DR. HATTER PSYCHIATRIST
NO, NO, INSPECTOR. THAT HOLE
NO, NO, DR HATTER. PUT THIS ONE THERE AND WE'LL GET THE THIN ONE HERE

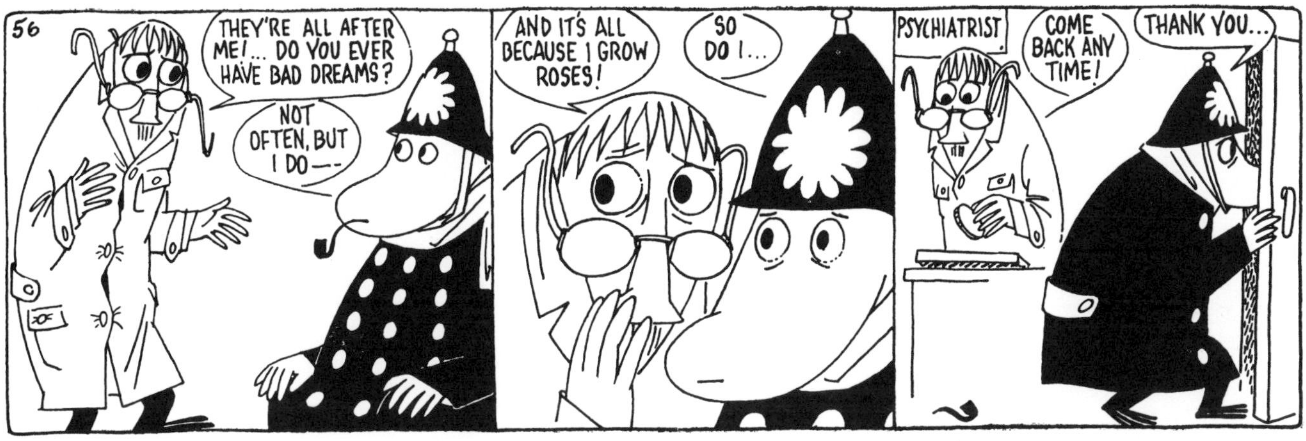
56
THEY'RE ALL AFTER ME! ... DO YOU EVER HAVE BAD DREAMS?
NOT OFTEN, BUT I DO---
AND IT'S ALL BECAUSE I GROW ROSES!
SO DO I...
PSYCHIATRIST
COME BACK ANY TIME!
THANK YOU...

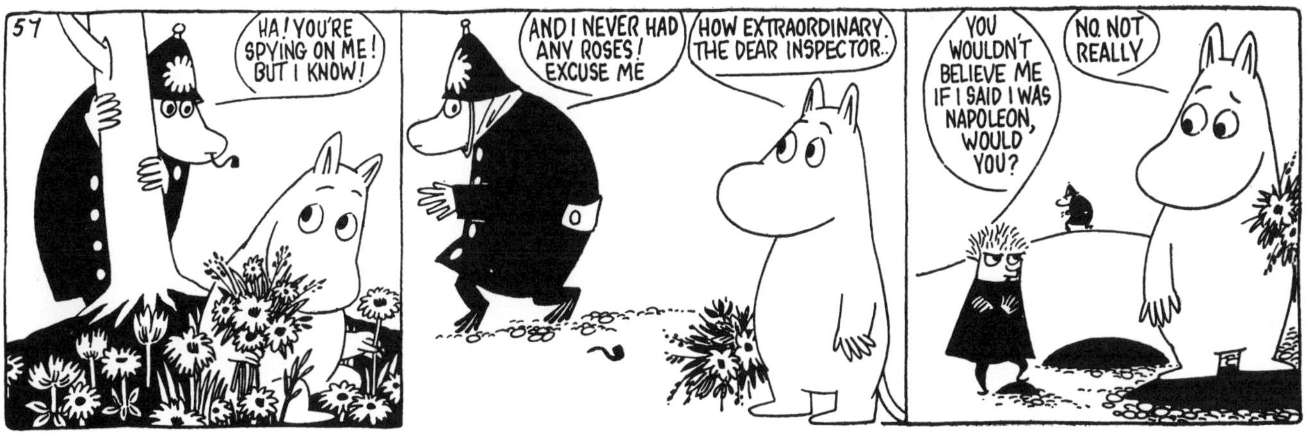
57
HA! YOU'RE SPYING ON ME! BUT I KNOW!
AND I NEVER HAD ANY ROSES! EXCUSE ME
HOW EXTRAORDINARY. THE DEAR INSPECTOR..
YOU WOULDN'T BELIEVE ME IF I SAID I WAS NAPOLEON, WOULD YOU?
NO. NOT REALLY

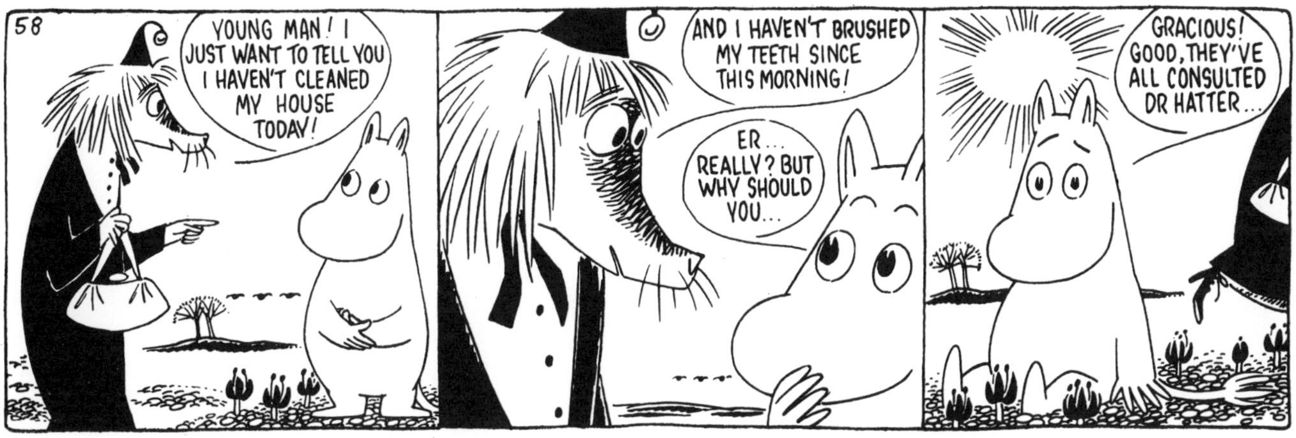
58
YOUNG MAN! I JUST WANT TO TELL YOU I HAVEN'T CLEANED MY HOUSE TODAY!
AND I HAVEN'T BRUSHED MY TEETH SINCE THIS MORNING!
ER... REALLY? BUT WHY SHOULD YOU...
GRACIOUS! GOOD, THEY'VE ALL CONSULTED DR HATTER...

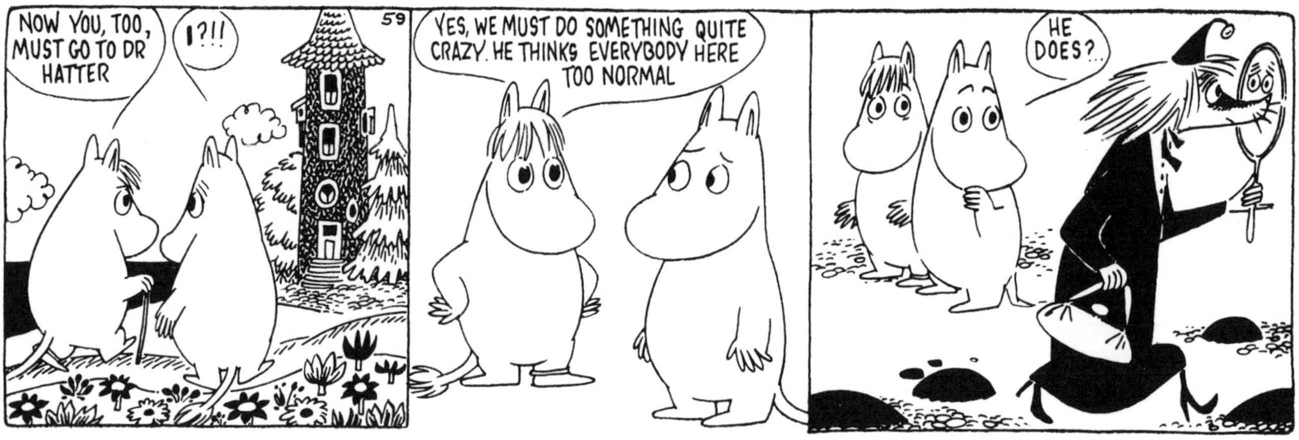
NOW YOU, TOO, MUST GO TO DR HATTER
!?!!
59
YES, WE MUST DO SOMETHING QUITE CRAZY. HE THINKS EVERYBODY HERE TOO NORMAL
HE DOES?..

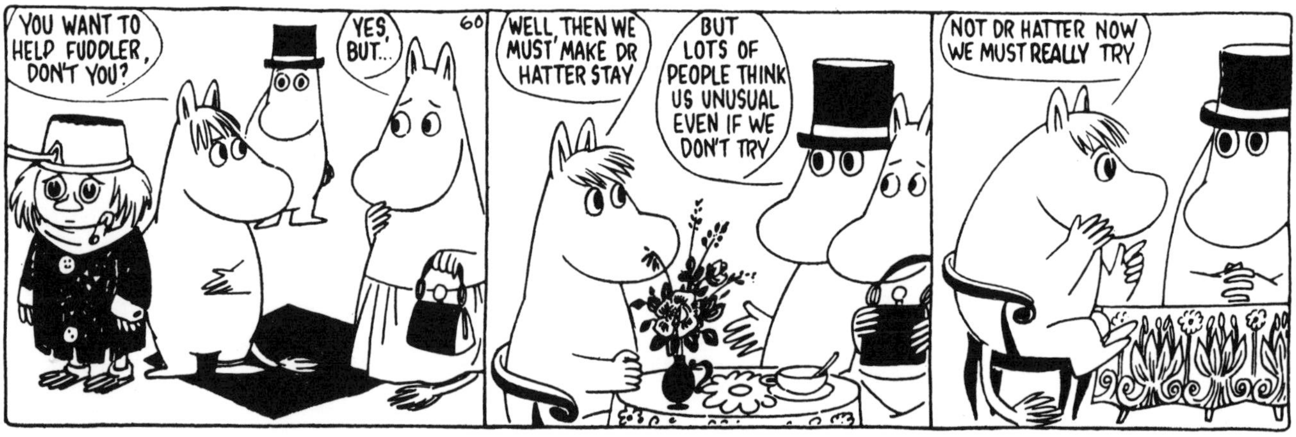
YOU WANT TO HELP FUDDLER, DON'T YOU?
YES, BUT...
60
WELL, THEN WE MUST MAKE DR HATTER STAY
BUT LOTS OF PEOPLE THINK US UNUSUAL EVEN IF WE DON'T TRY
NOT DR HATTER NOW WE MUST REALLY TRY

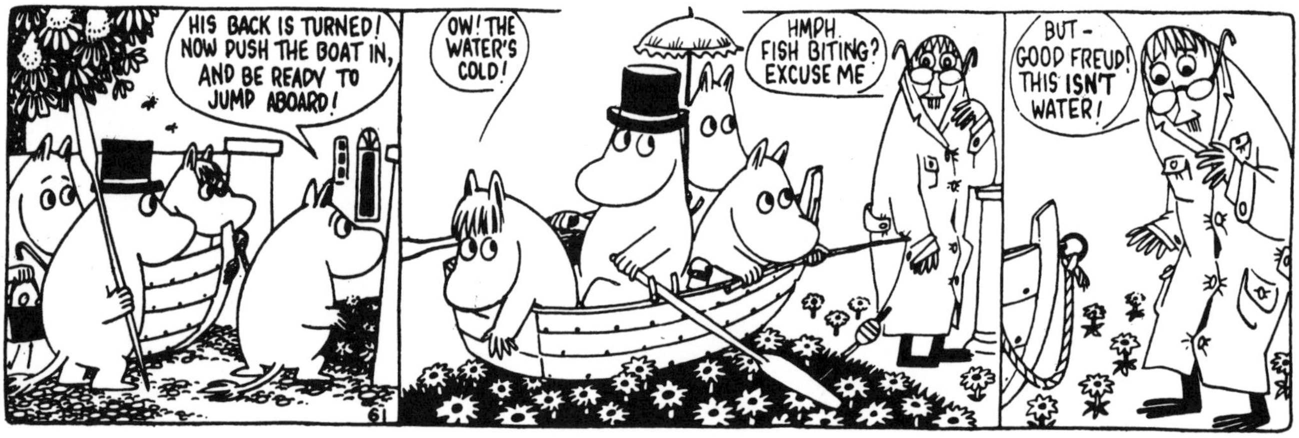
HIS BACK IS TURNED! NOW PUSH THE BOAT IN, AND BE READY TO JUMP ABOARD!
61
OW! THE WATER'S COLD!
HMPH. FISH BITING? EXCUSE ME
BUT - GOOD FREUD! THIS ISN'T WATER!

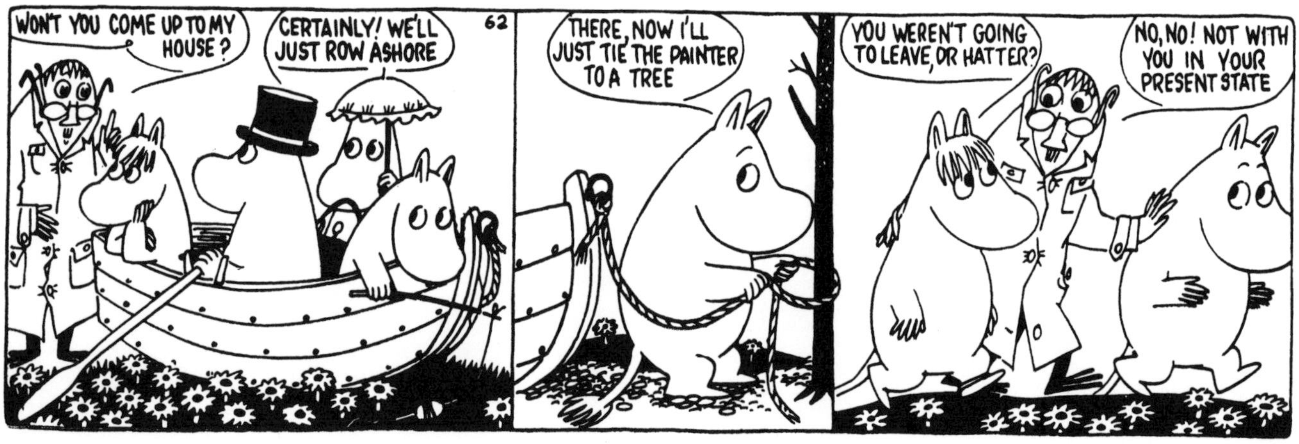
WON'T YOU COME UP TO MY HOUSE?
CERTAINLY! WE'LL JUST ROW ASHORE
62
THERE, NOW I'LL JUST TIE THE PAINTER TO A TREE
YOU WEREN'T GOING TO LEAVE, DR HATTER?
NO, NO! NOT WITH YOU IN YOUR PRESENT STATE

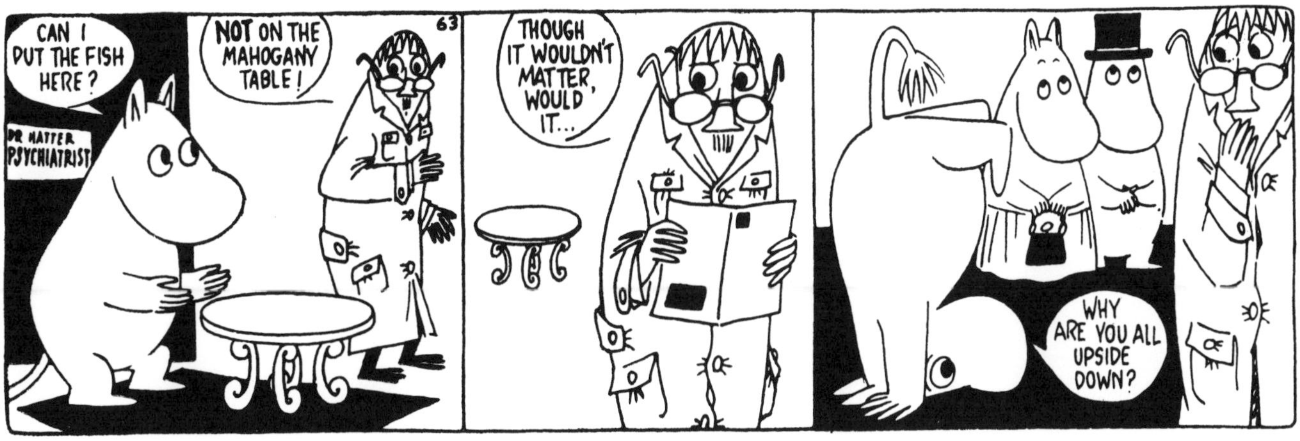
CAN I PUT THE FISH HERE?
DR HATTER PSYCHIATRIST
NOT ON THE MAHOGANY TABLE!
63
THOUGH IT WOULDN'T MATTER, WOULD IT...
WHY ARE YOU ALL UPSIDE DOWN?

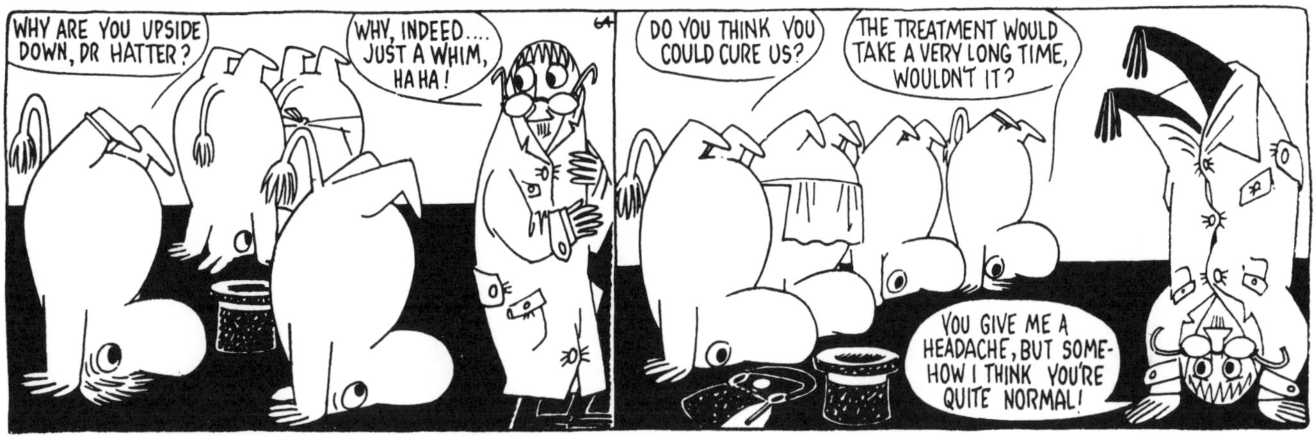
WHY ARE YOU UPSIDE DOWN, DR HATTER?
WHY, INDEED.... JUST A WHIM, HA HA!
64
DO YOU THINK YOU COULD CURE US?
THE TREATMENT WOULD TAKE A VERY LONG TIME, WOULDN'T IT?
YOU GIVE ME A HEADACHE, BUT SOMEHOW I THINK YOU'RE QUITE NORMAL!

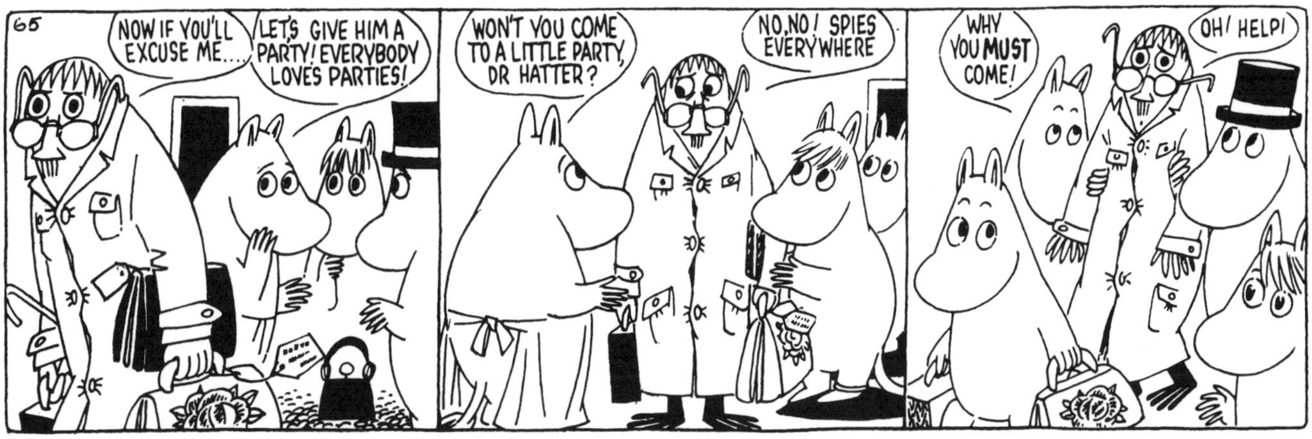
65
NOW IF YOU'LL EXCUSE ME....
LET'S GIVE HIM A PARTY! EVERYBODY LOVES PARTIES!
WON'T YOU COME TO A LITTLE PARTY, DR HATTER?
NO, NO! SPIES EVERYWHERE
WHY YOU MUST COME!
OH! HELP!

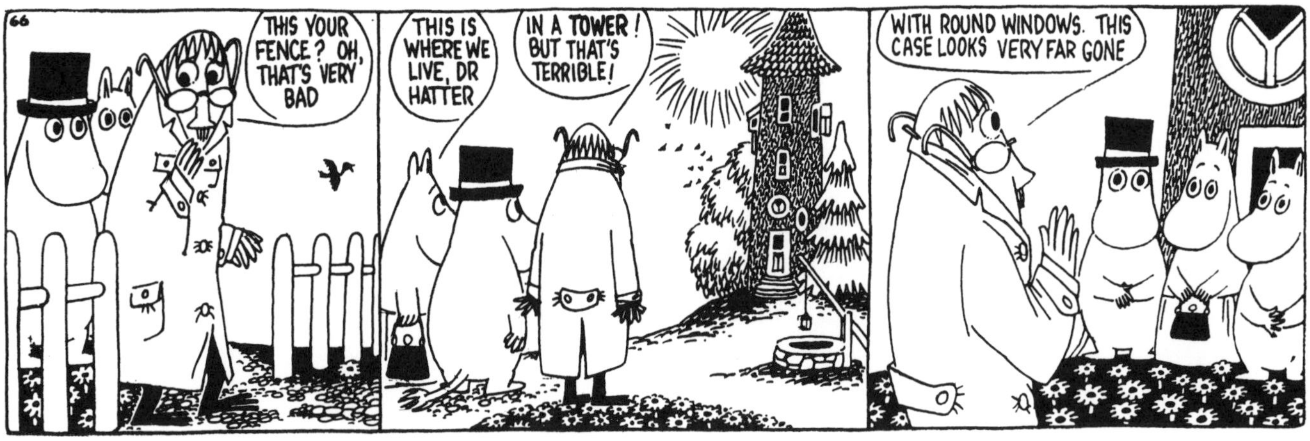
66
THIS YOUR FENCE? OH, THAT'S VERY BAD
THIS IS WHERE WE LIVE, DR HATTER
IN A TOWER! BUT THAT'S TERRIBLE!
WITH ROUND WINDOWS. THIS CASE LOOKS VERY FAR GONE

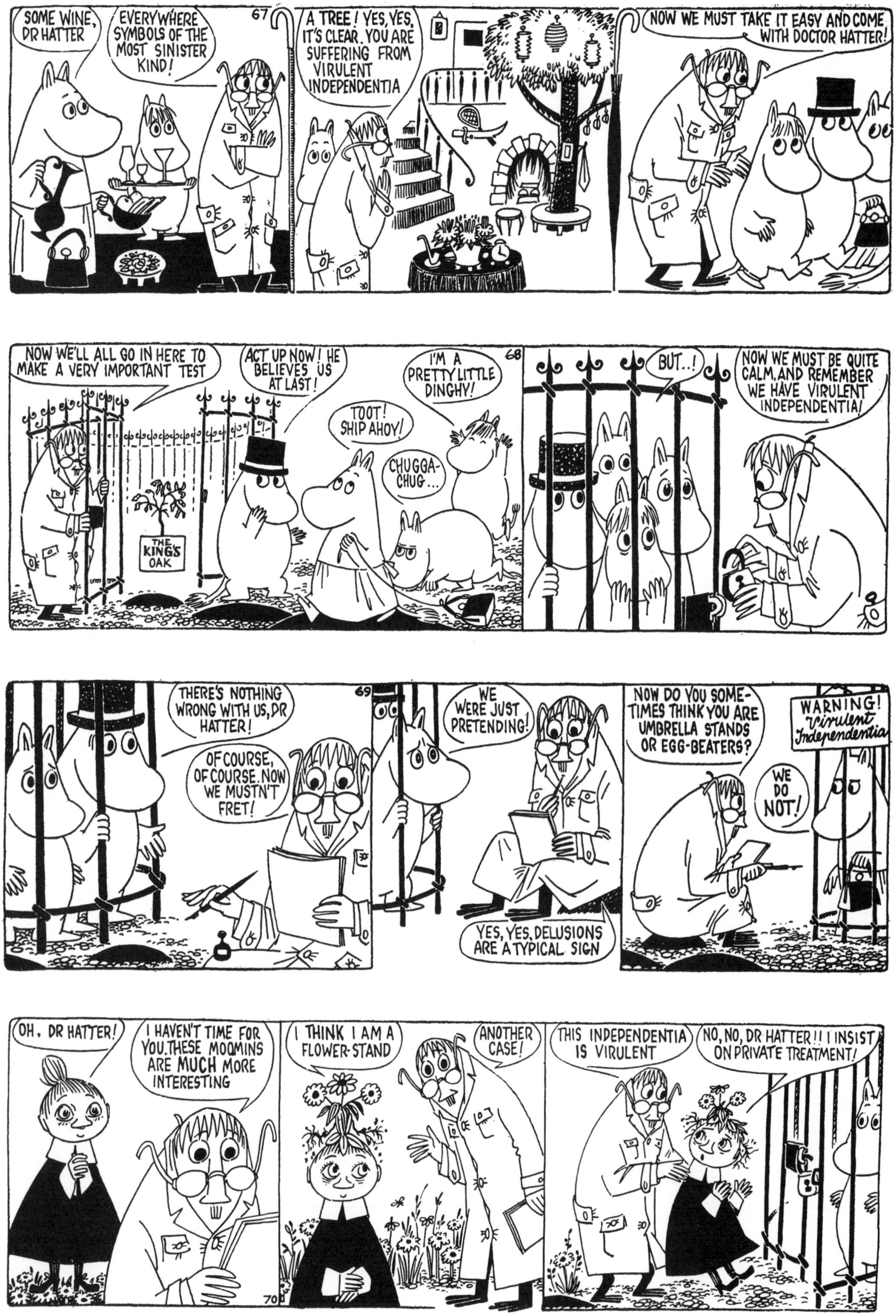
SOME WINE, DR HATTER
EVERYWHERE SYMBOLS OF THE MOST SINISTER KIND!
A TREE! YES, YES, IT'S CLEAR. YOU ARE SUFFERING FROM VIRULENT INDEPENDENTIA
NOW WE MUST TAKE IT EASY AND COME WITH DOCTOR HATTER!
NOW WE'LL ALL GO IN HERE TO MAKE A VERY IMPORTANT TEST
THE KING'S OAK
ACT UP NOW! HE BELIEVES US AT LAST!
I'M A PRETTY LITTLE DINGHY!
TOOT! SHIP AHOY!
CHUGGA-CHUG...
BUT..!
NOW WE MUST BE QUITE CALM. AND REMEMBER WE HAVE VIRULENT INDEPENDENTIA!
THERE'S NOTHING WRONG WITH US, DR HATTER!
OF COURSE, OF COURSE. NOW WE MUSTN'T FRET!
WE WERE JUST PRETENDING!
YES, YES, DELUSIONS ARE A TYPICAL SIGN
NOW DO YOU SOMETIMES THINK YOU ARE UMBRELLA STANDS OR EGG-BEATERS?
WE DO NOT!
WARNING! Virulent Independentia
OH, DR HATTER!
I HAVEN'T TIME FOR YOU. THESE MOOMINS ARE MUCH MORE INTERESTING
I THINK I AM A FLOWER-STAND
ANOTHER CASE!
THIS INDEPENDENTIA IS VIRULENT
NO, NO, DR HATTER!! I INSIST ON PRIVATE TREATMENT!

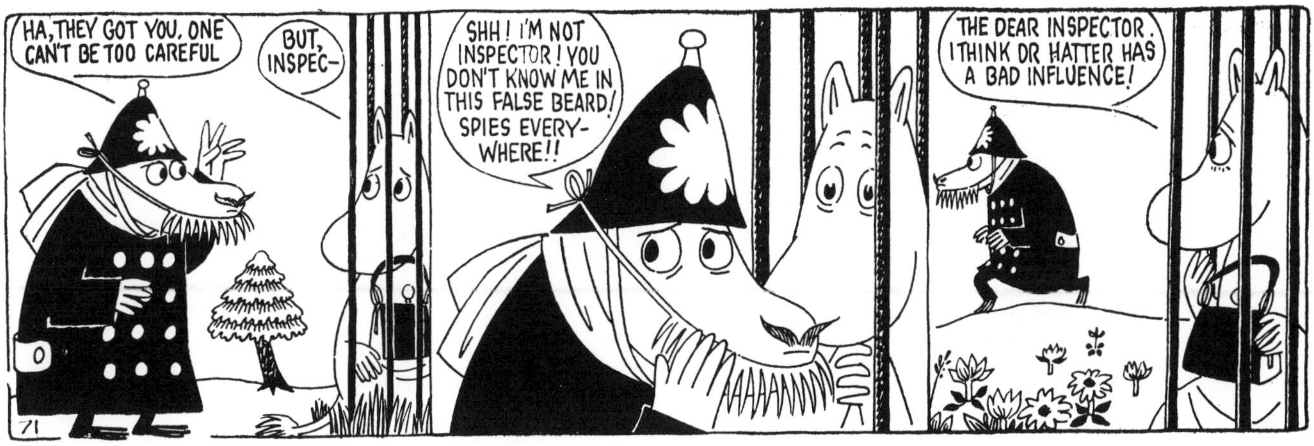
HA, THEY GOT YOU. ONE CAN'T BE TOO CAREFUL
BUT, INSPEC–
71
SHH! I'M NOT INSPECTOR! YOU DON'T KNOW ME IN THIS FALSE BEARD! SPIES EVERY-WHERE!!
THE DEAR INSPECTOR. I THINK DR HATTER HAS A BAD INFLUENCE!

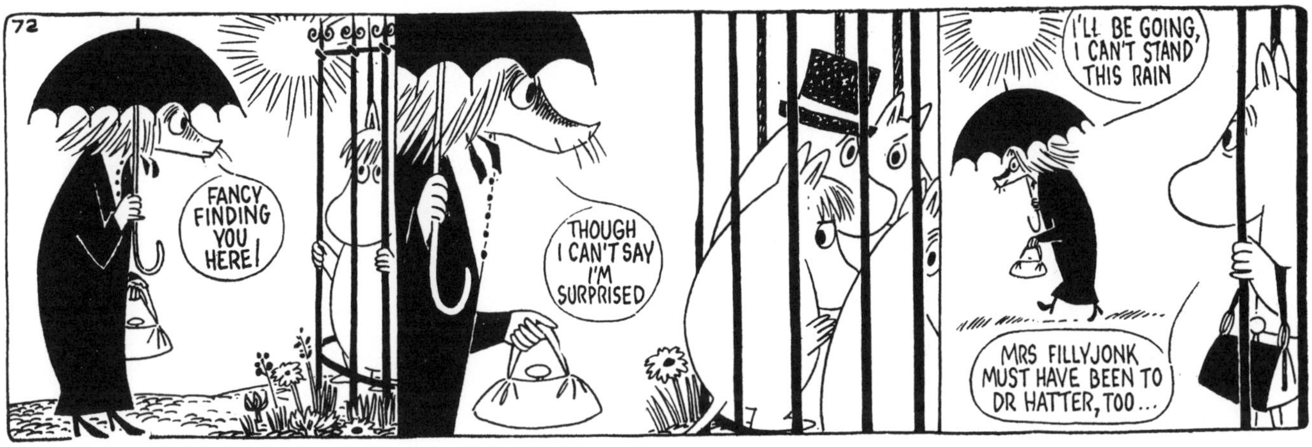
72
FANCY FINDING YOU HERE!
THOUGH I CAN'T SAY I'M SURPRISED
I'LL BE GOING, I CAN'T STAND THIS RAIN
MRS FILLYJONK MUST HAVE BEEN TO DR HATTER, TOO...

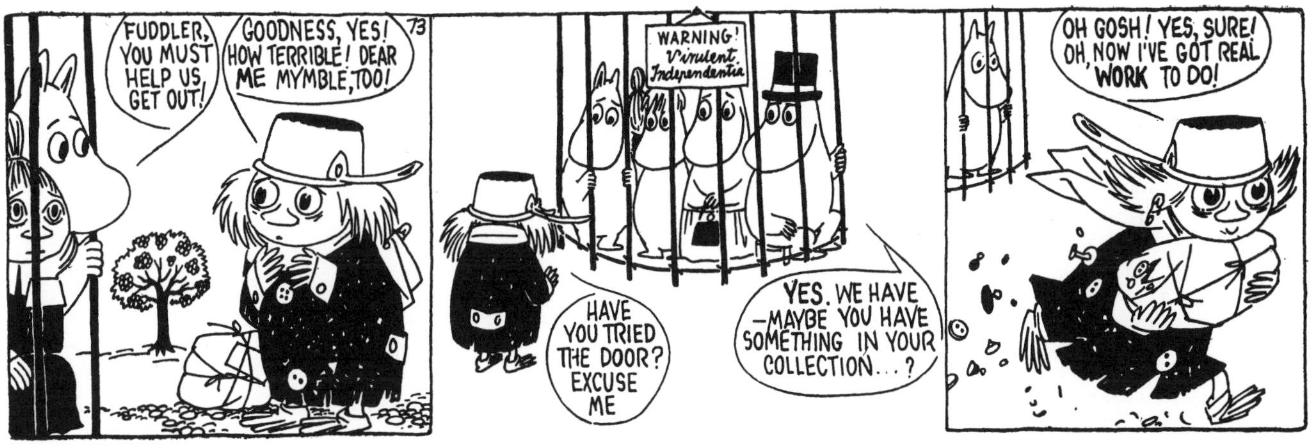
FUDDLER, YOU MUST HELP US GET OUT!
GOODNESS, YES! HOW TERRIBLE! DEAR ME MYMBLE, TOO!
73
WARNING! Virulent Independentia
HAVE YOU TRIED THE DOOR? EXCUSE ME
YES. WE HAVE —MAYBE YOU HAVE SOMETHING IN YOUR COLLECTION...?
OH GOSH! YES, SURE! OH, NOW I'VE GOT REAL WORK TO DO!

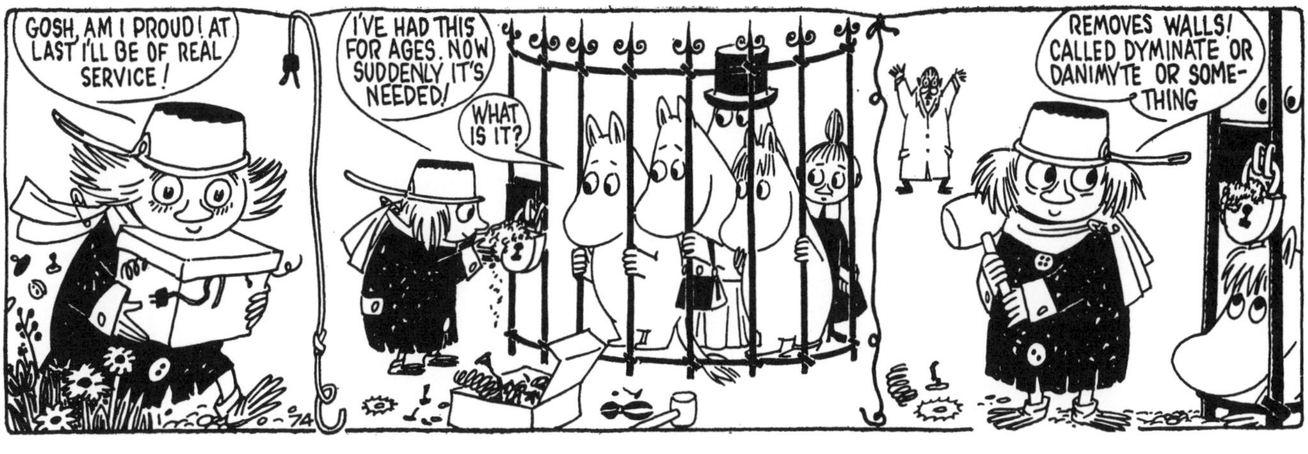
GOSH, AM I PROUD! AT LAST I'LL BE OF REAL SERVICE!
74
I'VE HAD THIS FOR AGES. NOW SUDDENLY IT'S NEEDED!
WHAT IS IT?
REMOVES WALLS! CALLED DYMINATE OR DANIMYTE OR SOME-THING

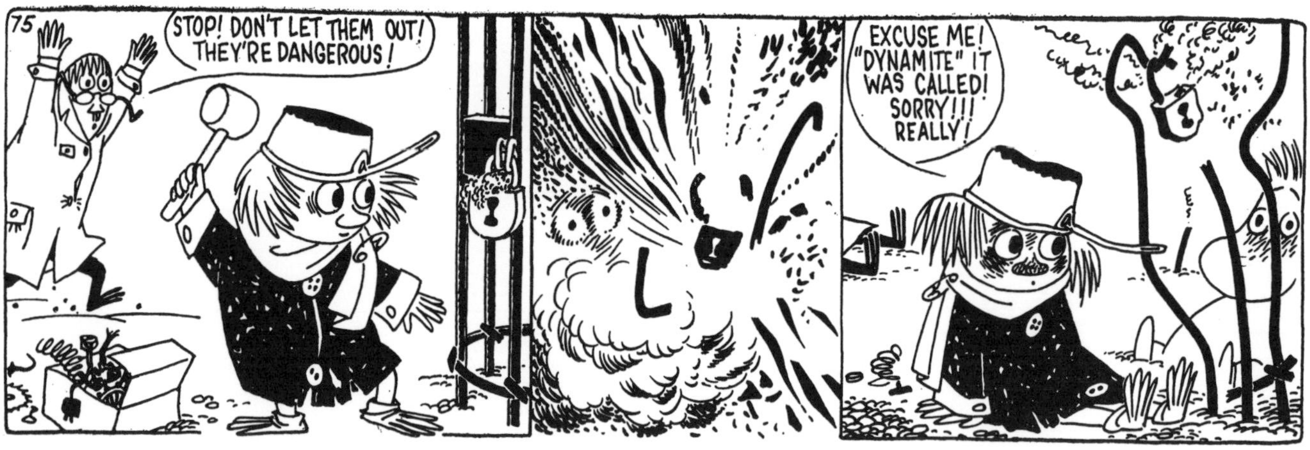
75
STOP! DON'T LET THEM OUT! THEY'RE DANGEROUS!
EXCUSE ME! "DYNAMITE" IT WAS CALLED! SORRY!!! REALLY!

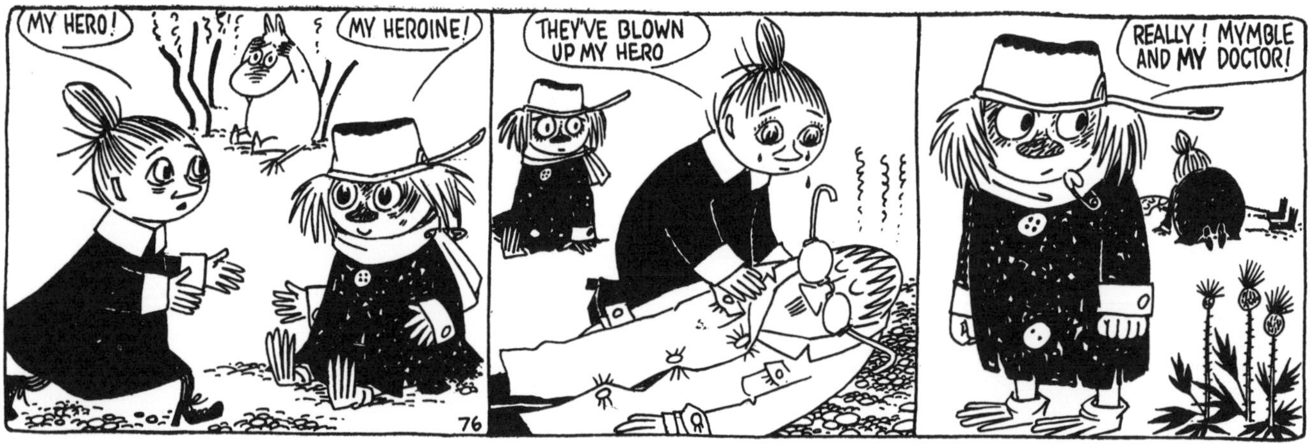
MY HERO!
MY HEROINE!
THEY'VE BLOWN UP MY HERO
76
REALLY! MYMBLE AND MY DOCTOR!

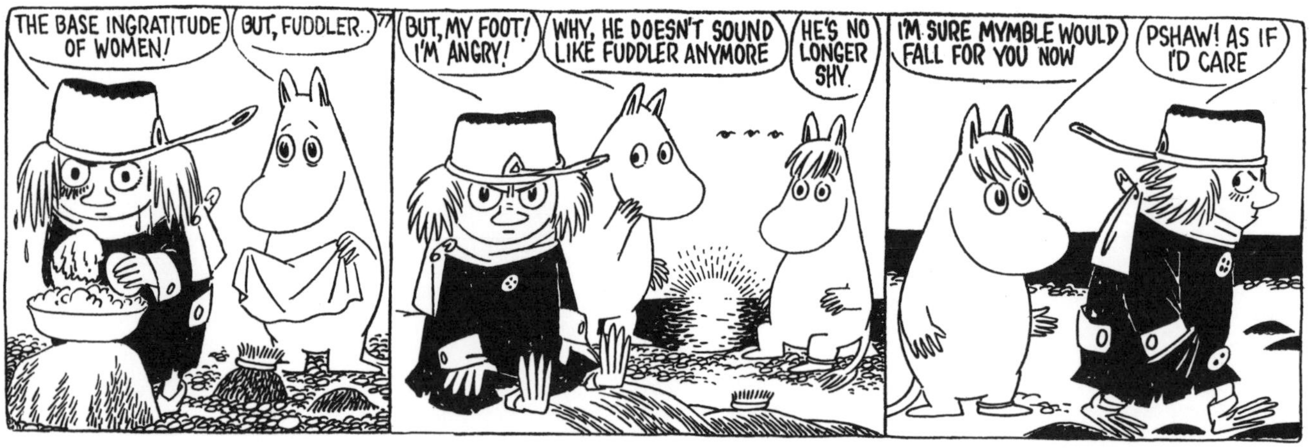
THE BASE INGRATITUDE OF WOMEN!
BUT, FUDDLER..
77
BUT, MY FOOT! I'M ANGRY!
WHY, HE DOESN'T SOUND LIKE FUDDLER ANYMORE
HE'S NO LONGER SHY.
I'M SURE MYMBLE WOULD FALL FOR YOU NOW
PSHAW! AS IF I'D CARE

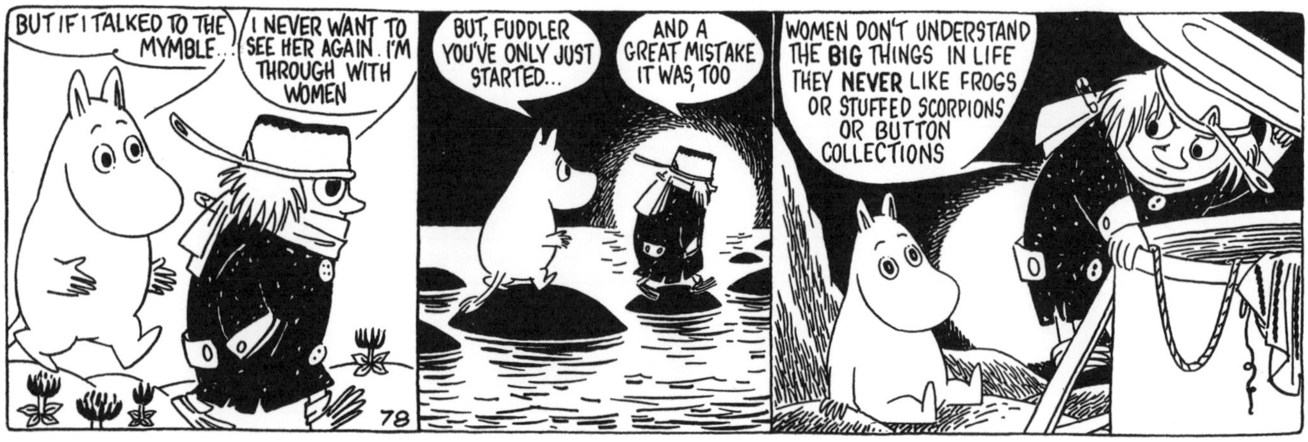
BUT IF I TALKED TO THE MYMBLE...
I NEVER WANT TO SEE HER AGAIN. I'M THROUGH WITH WOMEN
78
BUT, FUDDLER YOU'VE ONLY JUST STARTED...
AND A GREAT MISTAKE IT WAS, TOO
WOMEN DON'T UNDERSTAND THE BIG THINGS IN LIFE THEY NEVER LIKE FROGS OR STUFFED SCORPIONS OR BUTTON COLLECTIONS

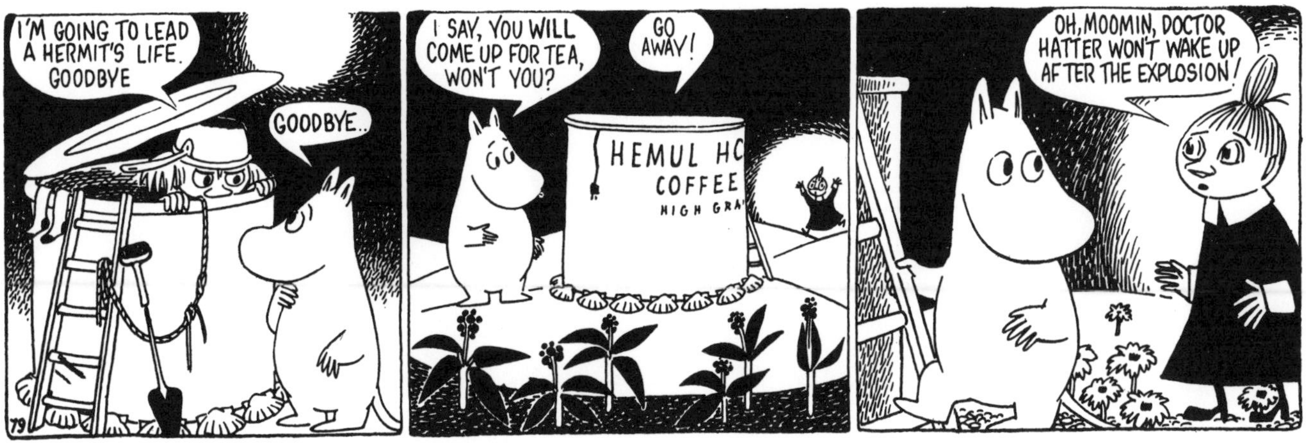
I'M GOING TO LEAD A HERMIT'S LIFE. GOODBYE
GOODBYE...
79
I SAY, YOU WILL COME UP FOR TEA, WON'T YOU?
GO AWAY!
HEMUL HO
COFFEE
HIGH GRA
OH, MOOMIN, DOCTOR HATTER WON'T WAKE UP AFTER THE EXPLOSION!

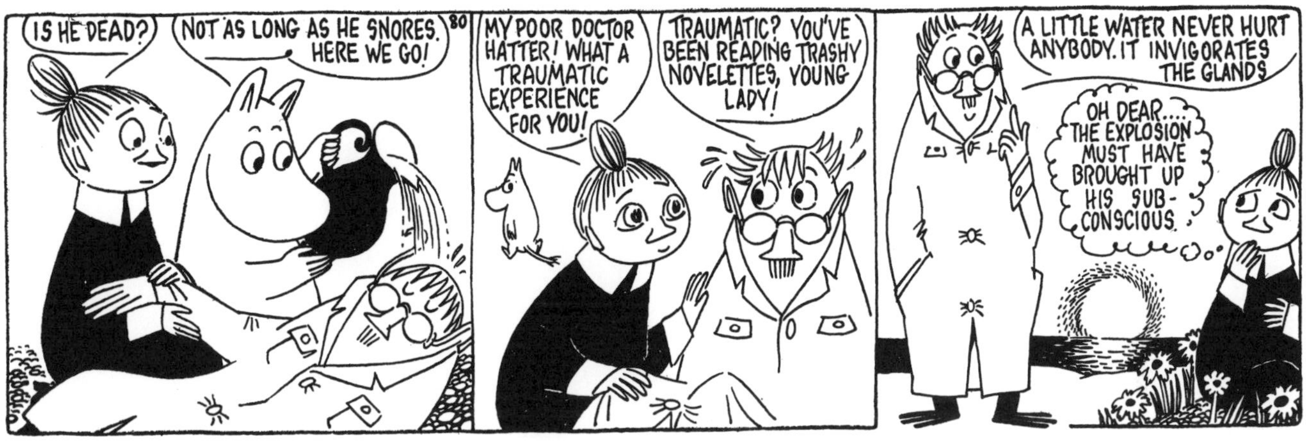
IS HE DEAD?
NOT AS LONG AS HE SNORES. HERE WE GO!
80
MY POOR DOCTOR HATTER! WHAT A TRAUMATIC EXPERIENCE FOR YOU!
TRAUMATIC? YOU'VE BEEN READING TRASHY NOVELETTES, YOUNG LADY!
A LITTLE WATER NEVER HURT ANYBODY. IT INVIGORATES THE GLANDS
OH DEAR.... THE EXPLOSION MUST HAVE BROUGHT UP HIS SUB-CONSCIOUS.

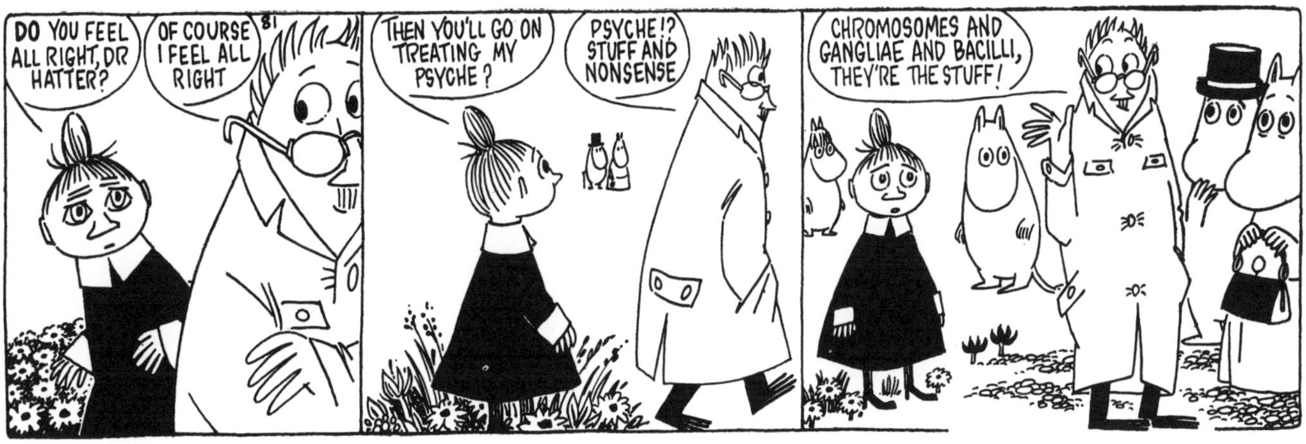
DO YOU FEEL ALL RIGHT, DR HATTER?
OF COURSE I FEEL ALL RIGHT
81
THEN YOU'LL GO ON TREATING MY PSYCHE?
PSYCHE!? STUFF AND NONSENSE
CHROMOSOMES AND GANGLIAE AND BACILLI, THEY'RE THE STUFF!

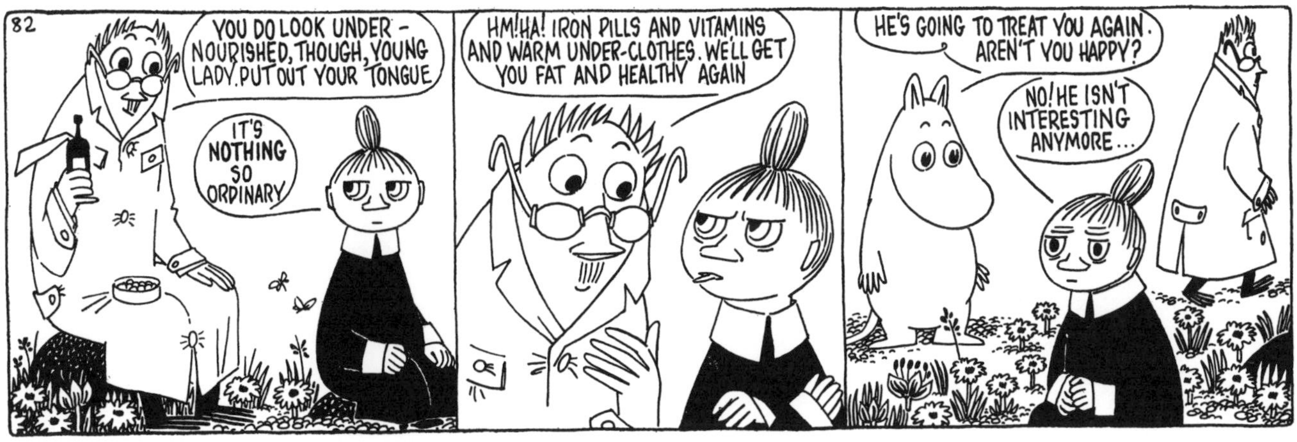
82
YOU DO LOOK UNDER-NOURISHED, THOUGH, YOUNG LADY. PUT OUT YOUR TONGUE
IT'S NOTHING SO ORDINARY
HM! HA! IRON PILLS AND VITAMINS AND WARM UNDER-CLOTHES. WE'LL GET YOU FAT AND HEALTHY AGAIN
HE'S GOING TO TREAT YOU AGAIN. AREN'T YOU HAPPY?
NO! HE ISN'T INTERESTING ANYMORE...

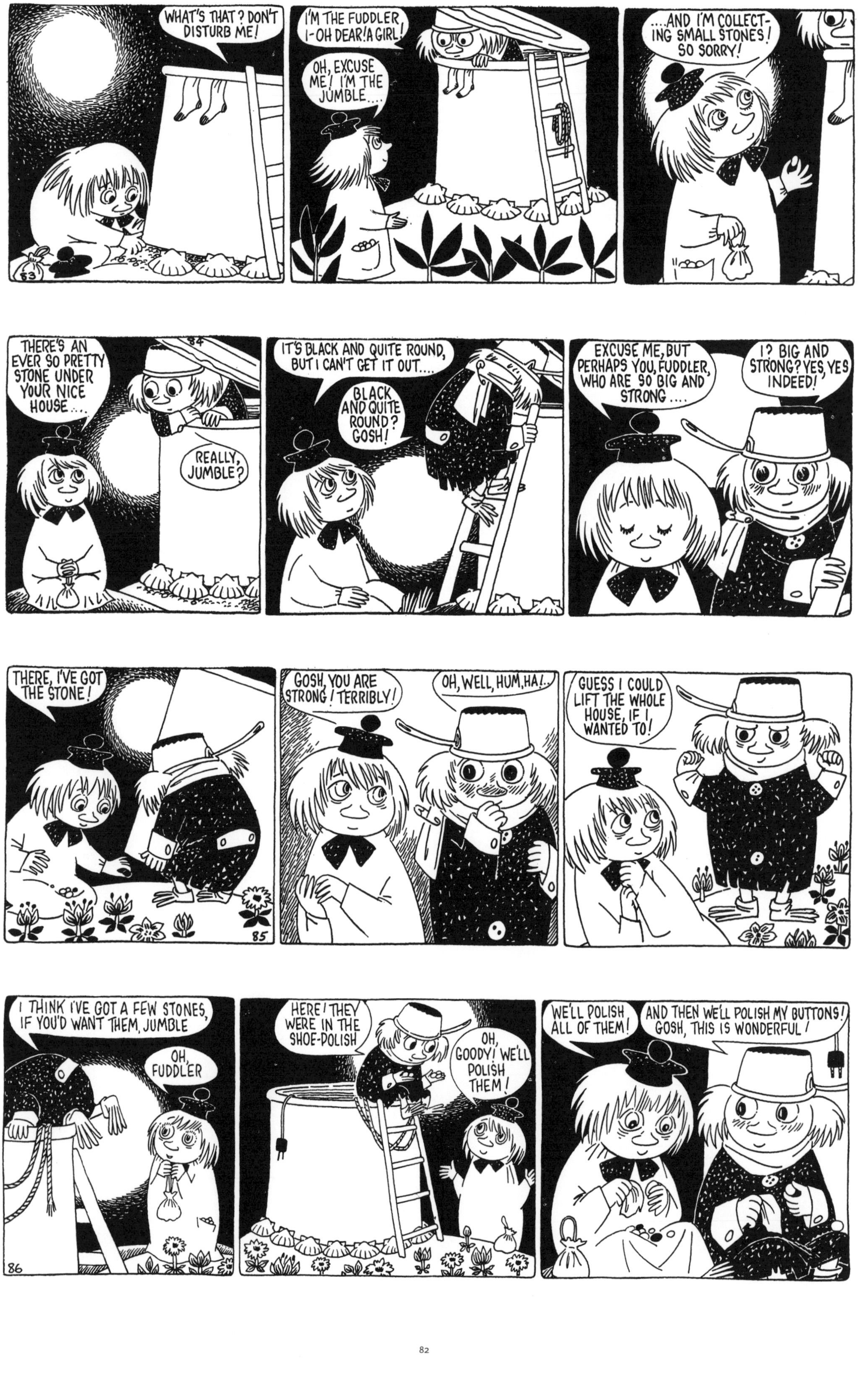
WHAT'S THAT? DON'T DISTURB ME!
83
I'M THE FUDDLER I-OH DEAR! A GIRL!
OH, EXCUSE ME! I'M THE JUMBLE....
....AND I'M COLLECTING SMALL STONES! SO SORRY!
84
THERE'S AN EVER SO PRETTY STONE UNDER YOUR NICE HOUSE....
REALLY, JUMBLE?
IT'S BLACK AND QUITE ROUND, BUT I CAN'T GET IT OUT....
BLACK AND QUITE ROUND? GOSH!
EXCUSE ME, BUT PERHAPS YOU, FUDDLER, WHO ARE SO BIG AND STRONG....
I? BIG AND STRONG? YES, YES INDEED!
THERE, I'VE GOT THE STONE!
85
GOSH, YOU ARE STRONG! TERRIBLY!
OH, WELL, HUM, HA!..
GUESS I COULD LIFT THE WHOLE HOUSE, IF I WANTED TO!
I THINK I'VE GOT A FEW STONES, IF YOU'D WANT THEM, JUMBLE
OH, FUDDLER
86
HERE! THEY WERE IN THE SHOE-POLISH
OH, GOODY! WE'LL POLISH THEM!
WE'LL POLISH ALL OF THEM!
AND THEN WE'LL POLISH MY BUTTONS! GOSH, THIS IS WONDERFUL!

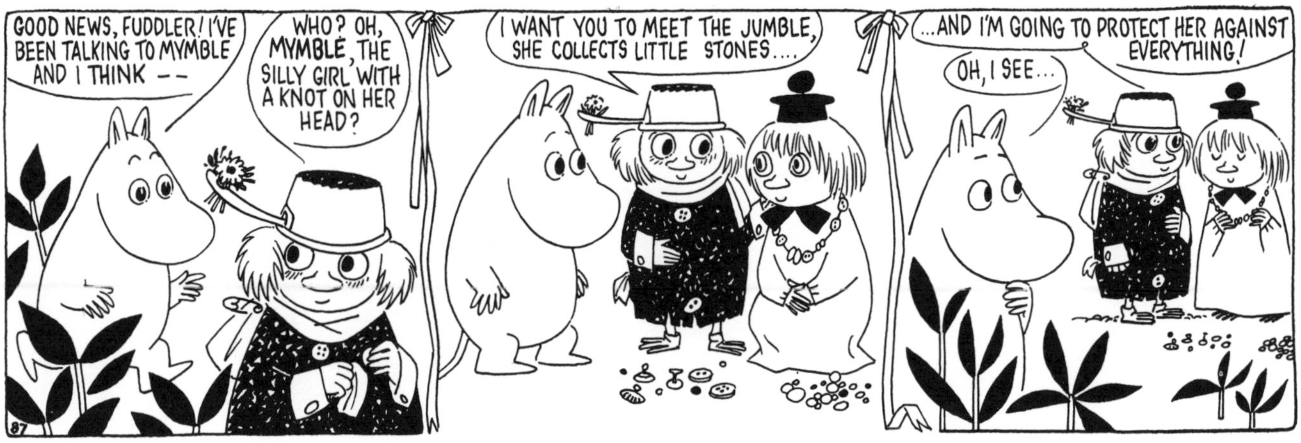
87
GOOD NEWS, FUDDLER! I'VE BEEN TALKING TO MYMBLE AND I THINK --
WHO? OH, MYMBLE, THE SILLY GIRL WITH A KNOT ON HER HEAD?
I WANT YOU TO MEET THE JUMBLE, SHE COLLECTS LITTLE STONES....
...AND I'M GOING TO PROTECT HER AGAINST EVERYTHING!
OH, I SEE...

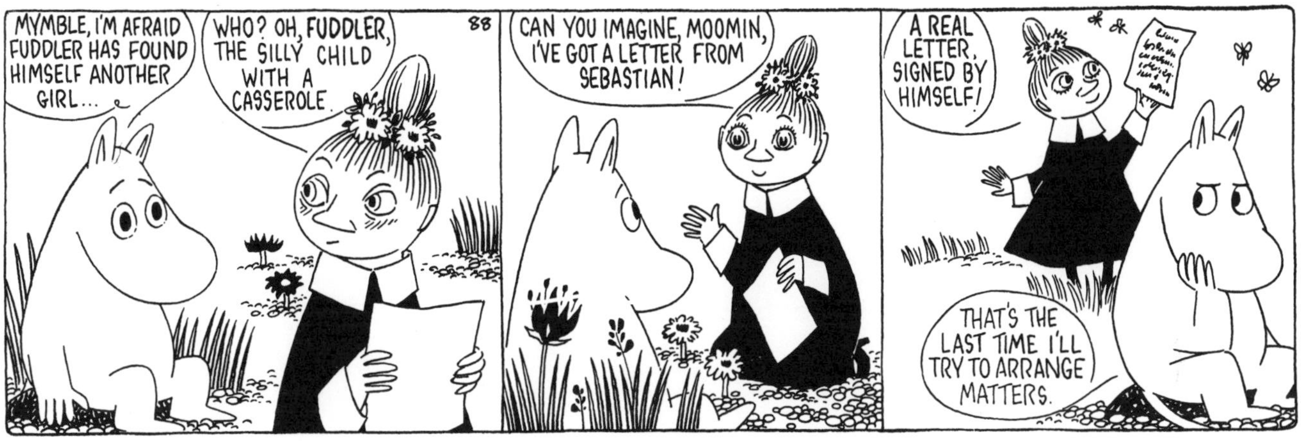
MYMBLE, I'M AFRAID FUDDLER HAS FOUND HIMSELF ANOTHER GIRL...
WHO? OH, FUDDLER, THE SILLY CHILD WITH A CASSEROLE.
88
CAN YOU IMAGINE, MOOMIN, I'VE GOT A LETTER FROM SEBASTIAN!
A REAL LETTER, SIGNED BY HIMSELF!
THAT'S THE LAST TIME I'LL TRY TO ARRANGE MATTERS.

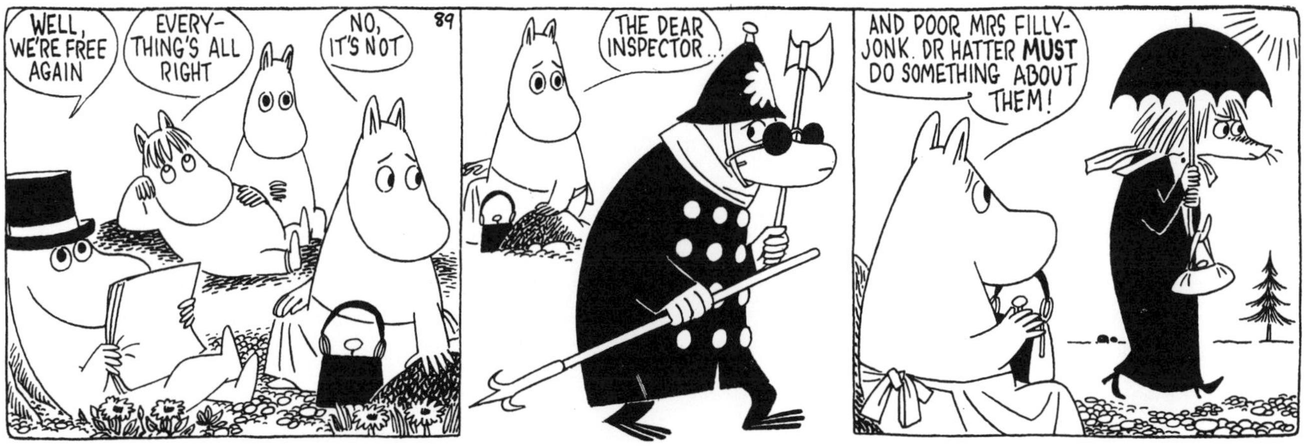
WELL, WE'RE FREE AGAIN
EVERY-THING'S ALL RIGHT
NO, IT'S NOT
89
THE DEAR INSPECTOR...
AND POOR MRS FILLY-JONK. DR HATTER MUST DO SOMETHING ABOUT THEM!

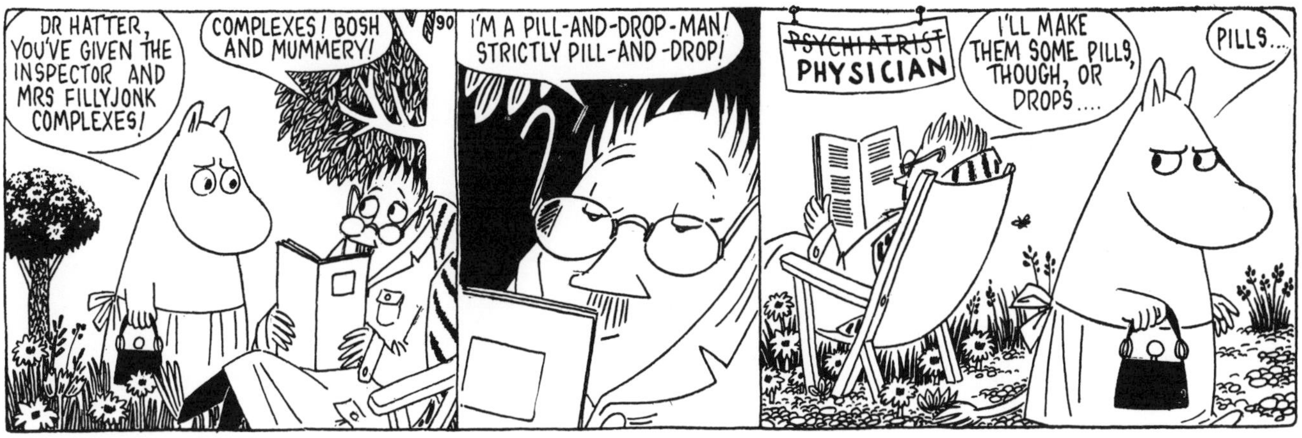
DR HATTER, YOU'VE GIVEN THE INSPECTOR AND MRS FILLYJONK COMPLEXES!
COMPLEXES! BOSH AND MUMMERY!
90
I'M A PILL-AND-DROP-MAN! STRICTLY PILL-AND-DROP!
PSYCHIATRIST
PHYSICIAN
I'LL MAKE THEM SOME PILLS, THOUGH, OR DROPS....
PILLS...

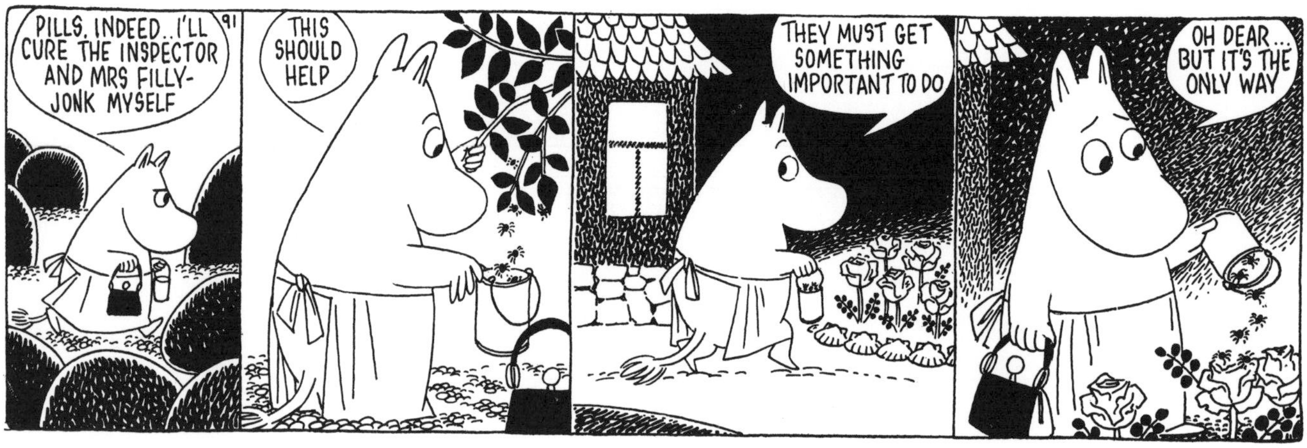
91
PILLS, INDEED...I'LL CURE THE INSPECTOR AND MRS FILLY-JONK MYSELF
THIS SHOULD HELP
THEY MUST GET SOMETHING IMPORTANT TO DO
OH DEAR... BUT IT'S THE ONLY WAY

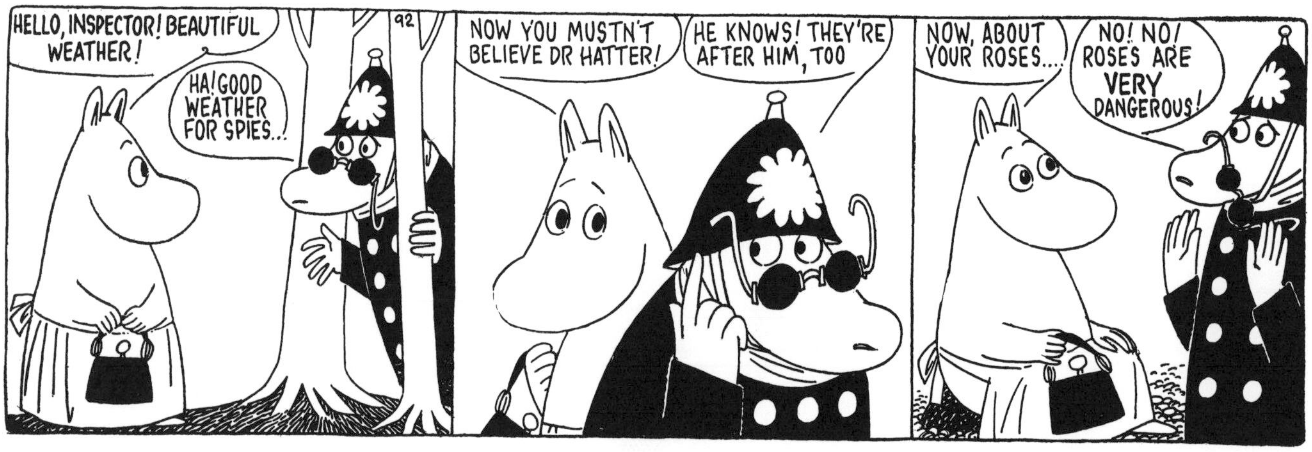
92
HELLO, INSPECTOR! BEAUTIFUL WEATHER!
HA! GOOD WEATHER FOR SPIES...
NOW YOU MUSTN'T BELIEVE DR HATTER!
HE KNOWS! THEY'RE AFTER HIM, TOO
NOW, ABOUT YOUR ROSES....
NO! NO! ROSES ARE VERY DANGEROUS!

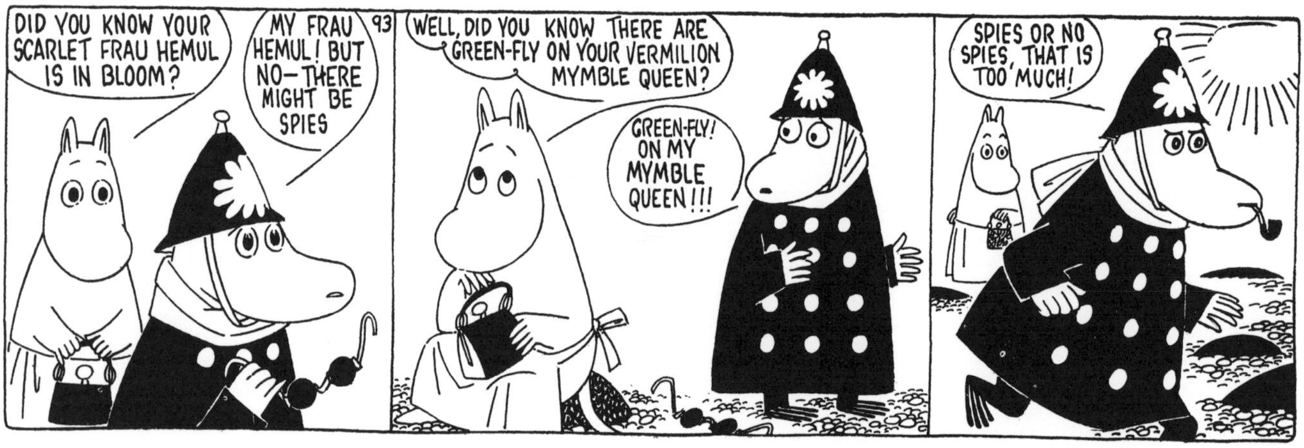
93
DID YOU KNOW YOUR SCARLET FRAU HEMUL IS IN BLOOM?
MY FRAU HEMUL! BUT NO—THERE MIGHT BE SPIES
WELL, DID YOU KNOW THERE ARE GREEN-FLY ON YOUR VERMILION MYMBLE QUEEN?
GREEN-FLY! ON MY MYMBLE QUEEN!!!
SPIES OR NO SPIES, THAT IS TOO MUCH!

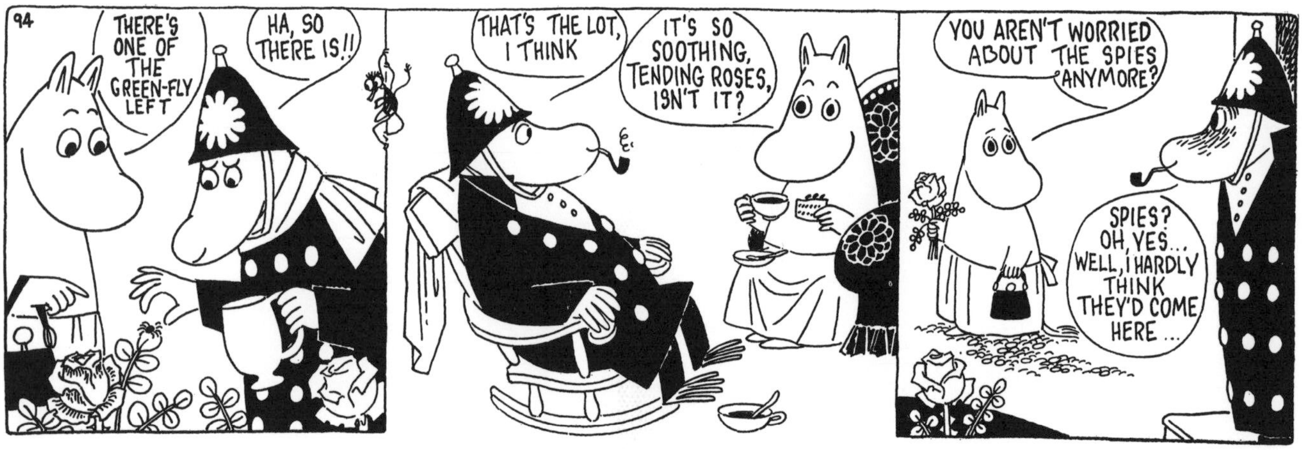
94
THERE'S ONE OF THE GREEN-FLY LEFT
HA, SO THERE IS!!
THAT'S THE LOT, I THINK
IT'S SO SOOTHING, TENDING ROSES, ISN'T IT?
YOU AREN'T WORRIED ABOUT THE SPIES ANYMORE?
SPIES? OH, YES... WELL, I HARDLY THINK THEY'D COME HERE ...

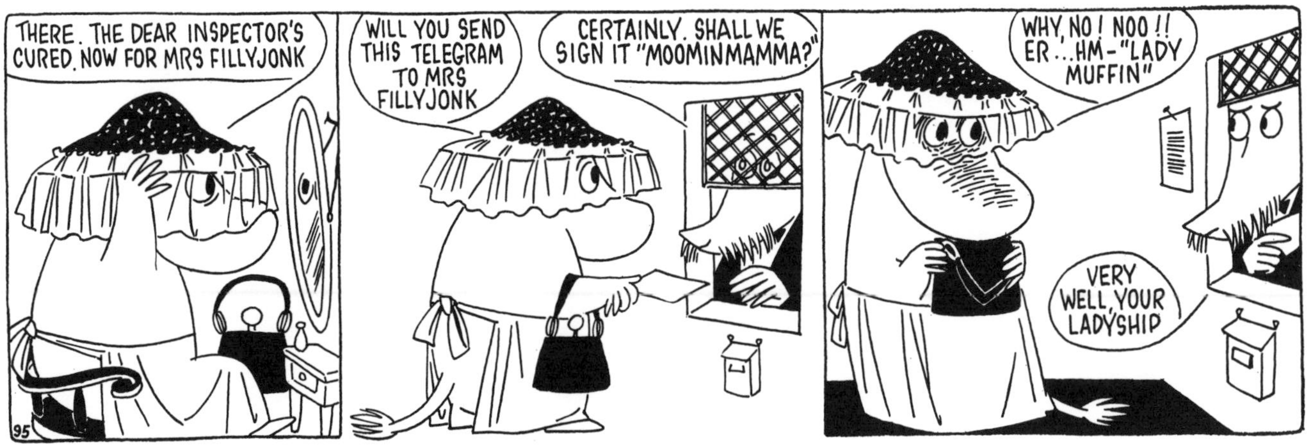
95
THERE. THE DEAR INSPECTOR'S CURED. NOW FOR MRS FILLYJONK
WILL YOU SEND THIS TELEGRAM TO MRS FILLYJONK
CERTAINLY. SHALL WE SIGN IT "MOOMINMAMMA?"
WHY, NO! NOO!! ER...HM-"LADY MUFFIN"
VERY WELL, YOUR LADYSHIP

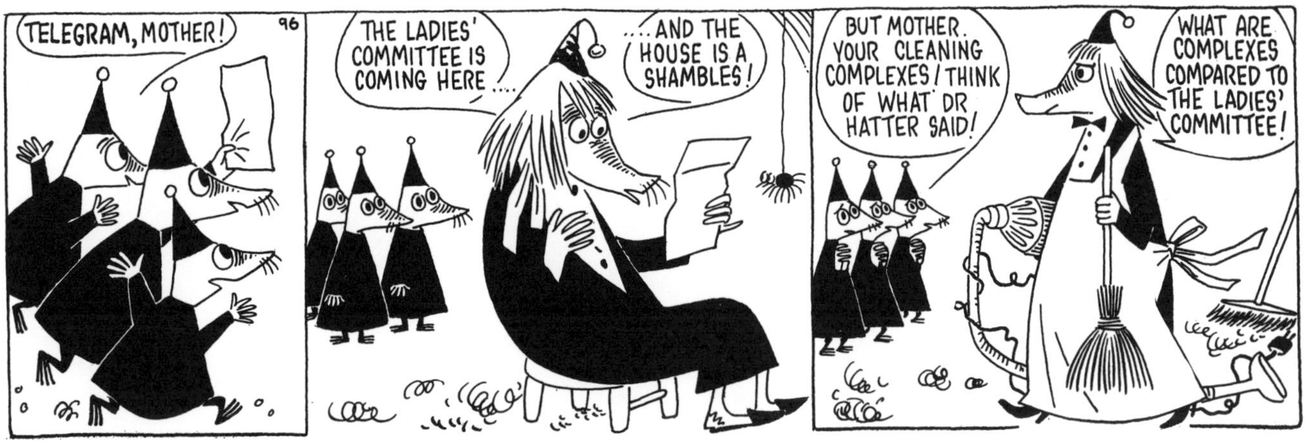
96
TELEGRAM, MOTHER!
THE LADIES' COMMITTEE IS COMING HERE....
....AND THE HOUSE IS A SHAMBLES!
BUT MOTHER. YOUR CLEANING COMPLEXES / THINK OF WHAT DR HATTER SAID!
WHAT ARE COMPLEXES COMPARED TO THE LADIES' COMMITTEE!

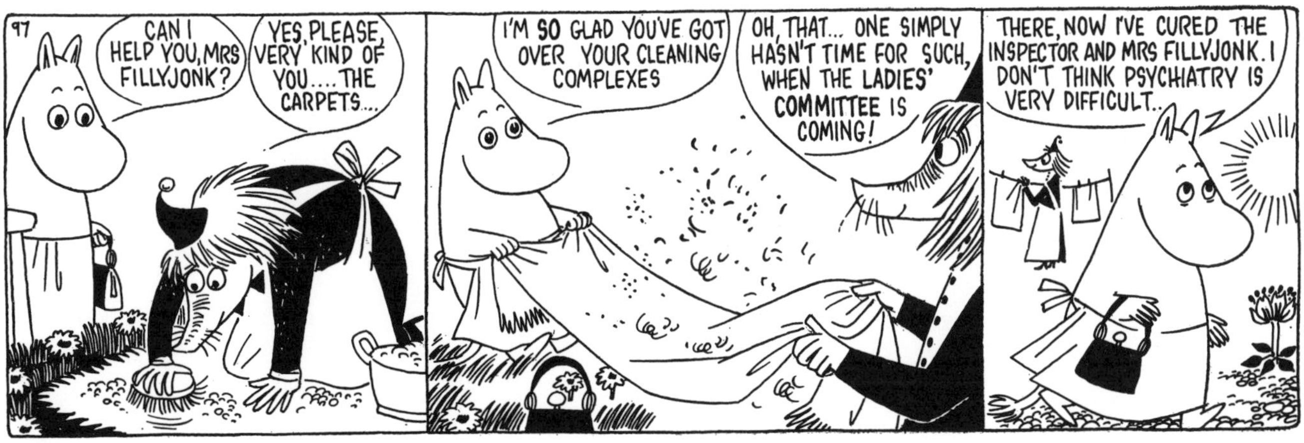
97
CAN I HELP YOU, MRS FILLYJONK?
YES, PLEASE, VERY KIND OF YOU.... THE CARPETS....
I'M SO GLAD YOU'VE GOT OVER YOUR CLEANING COMPLEXES
OH, THAT... ONE SIMPLY HASN'T TIME FOR SUCH, WHEN THE LADIES' COMMITTEE IS COMING!
THERE, NOW I'VE CURED THE INSPECTOR AND MRS FILLYJONK. I DON'T THINK PSYCHIATRY IS VERY DIFFICULT..

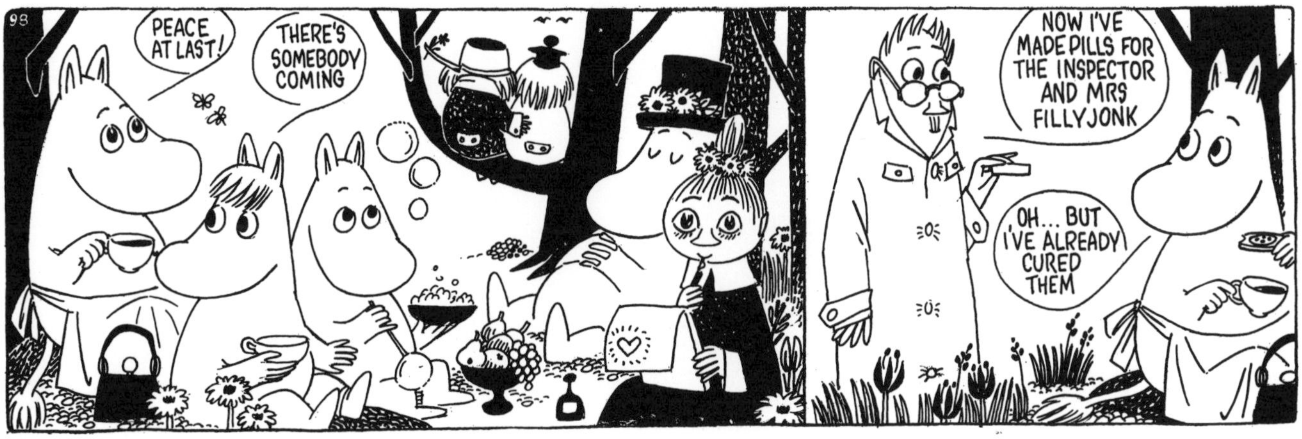
98
PEACE AT LAST!
THERE'S SOMEBODY COMING
NOW I'VE MADE PILLS FOR THE INSPECTOR AND MRS FILLYJONK
OH... BUT I'VE ALREADY CURED THEM

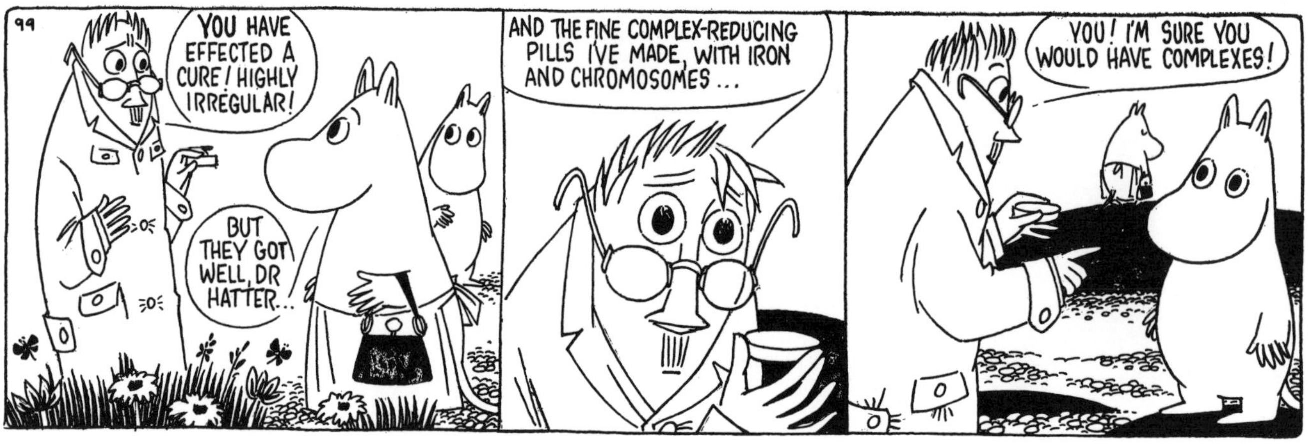
99
YOU HAVE EFFECTED A CURE! HIGHLY IRREGULAR!
BUT THEY GOT WELL, DR HATTER...
AND THE FINE COMPLEX-REDUCING PILLS I'VE MADE, WITH IRON AND CHROMOSOMES ...
YOU! I'M SURE YOU WOULD HAVE COMPLEXES!

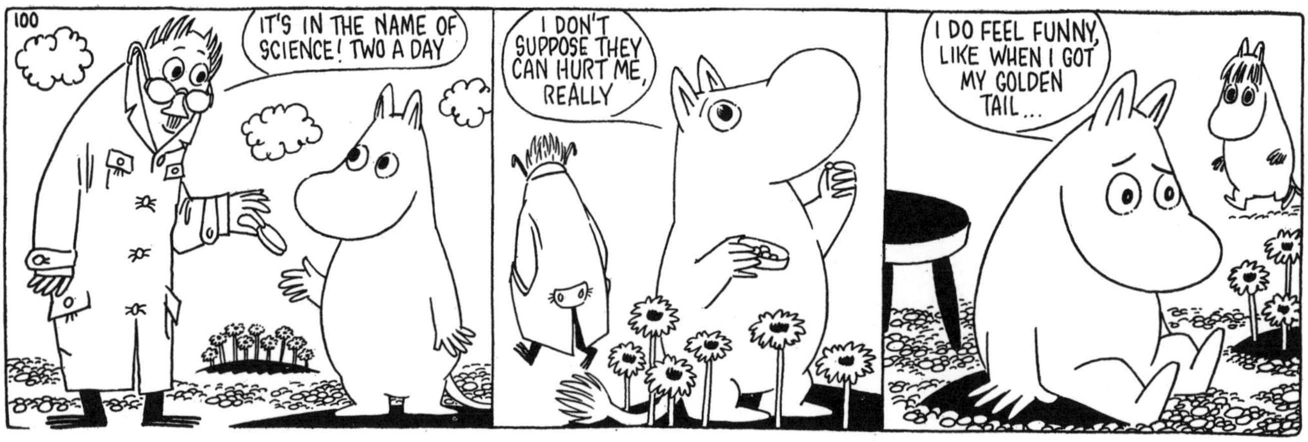
100
IT'S IN THE NAME OF SCIENCE! TWO A DAY
I DON'T SUPPOSE THEY CAN HURT ME, REALLY
I DO FEEL FUNNY, LIKE WHEN I GOT MY GOLDEN TAIL...

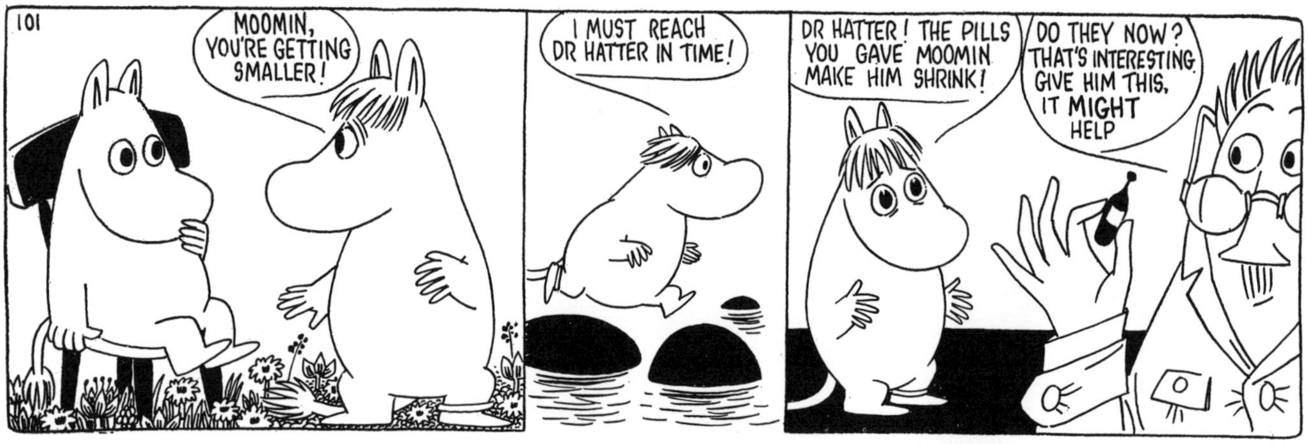
101
MOOMIN, YOU'RE GETTING SMALLER!
I MUST REACH DR HATTER IN TIME!
DR HATTER! THE PILLS YOU GAVE MOOMIN MAKE HIM SHRINK!
DO THEY NOW? THAT'S INTERESTING GIVE HIM THIS, IT MIGHT HELP

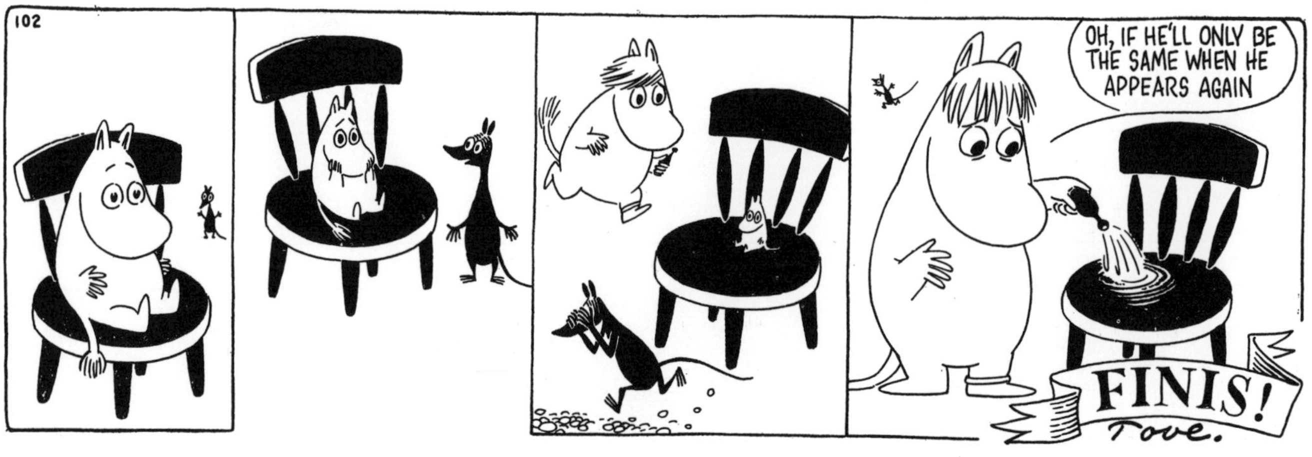
102
OH, IF HE'LL ONLY BE THE SAME WHEN HE APPEARS AGAIN
FINIS!
Tove.